T0245693

Praise for *The Medoran Chronicles*
by Lynette Noni

"Lynette Noni is a marvellous and inventive storyteller, whose books are absolutely impossible to put down. I can't wait to see what she comes up with next!" — **Sarah J. Maas**, #1 *New York Times* and *USA Today* bestselling author of the *Throne of Glass* and *A Court of Thorns and Roses* series

"Let me say right up front that Lynette Noni is a very talented writer. Her books tell stories that draw you in and refuse to let go. Her characters are memorable and quick to surprise. I cannot wait to see what she will do next." — **Terry Brooks**, #1 *New York Times* bestselling author of *The Shannara Chronicles*

"Lynette Noni is a masterful storyteller. Her characters steal into your heart and won't let go!" — **Maria V. Snyder**, *New York Times* bestselling author of the *Poison Study* series

"When Lynette Noni opens the door to another world, don't hesitate: jump in and enjoy." — **Trudi Canavan**, internationally bestselling author of *The Black Magician* trilogy

"Noni crafts a vividly textured narrative landscape with an irresistible cast of lovable and love-to-hate characters. The perfect balance of humour, heart and high stakes makes *The Medoran Chronicles* a reader's delight." — **Rachael Craw**, award-winning author of the *Spark* trilogy and *The Rift*

"Lynette Noni's compelling stories keep readers turning pages to the very end." —**Juliet Marillier**, multi-award winning author of the *Sevenwaters* series

"Lynette Noni is a creative powerhouse. Her books leave fans wanting more every time." — **Gabrielle Tozer**, award-winning author of *Remind Me How This Ends* and *The Intern*

"Lynette Noni is an absolute powerhouse of Australian YA fantasy: young readers are in Harry-Potter-level fervour about the *Medoran* series, and she engages with her community with such warmth and genuine enthusiasm. She's who I want to be when I grow up." — **Steph Bowe**, author of *Girl Saves Boy* and *Night Swimming*

"Lynette Noni creates vivid characters who jump off the page and demand we care for (or hate) them. She also paints a vibrant Medora that is as real as it is fantastic. Lynette entwines both of these writing skills to create a fantasy series up there with *Harry Potter*, *Nevermoor* and *Narnia*." —**James Lindsay**, author of the *Plato Wyngard* series

DRAEKORA

BY LYNETTE NONI

The Whisper Series

Whisper

Weapon

The Medoran Chronicles

Akarnae

Raelia

Draekora

Graevale

Vardaesia

The Medoran Chronicles Novellas

We Three Heroes

DRAEKORA

THE MEDORAN CHRONICLES

BOOK THREE

LYNETTE NONI

PANTERA
PRESS

PANTERA
PRESS

First published in 2017 by Pantera Press Pty Limited
www.PanteraPress.com

This edition published in 2022

Please send all permission queries to:
Pantera Press, P.O. Box 1989, Neutral Bay, NSW, Australia 2089 or
info@PanteraPress.com

ISBN 978-0-6487951-5-5 (Paperback)
ISBN 978-1-921997-69-3 (eBook)

Cover and Internal Design: Xou Creative www.xou.com.au
Editor: James Read
Proofreader: Lucy Bell
Typesetting: Kirby Jones
Author Photo: Lucy Bell

For those overwhelmed by fear of the future.
Live in the moment.

One

"This is officially the worst idea I've ever had."

It was true. Alex may have made some questionable decisions in the past, but the dilemma she and her friends now faced was off the charts, comparatively.

"We can still pull this off," Bear whispered from somewhere to her left.

It was too dark for Alex to see anything other than his silhouette blacking out what little light shone through the crack in the door. But she knew both he and D.C. were right there alongside her, as always. What she *didn't* know was who else was nearby—namely, just how many guards were patrolling the high-security ChemTech facility they were trying to break into. And how dangerous their weapons were.

Alex was fully aware they were being reckless. But after losing their best friend, Jordan Sparker, to a fate of being a mindless pawn in Aven Dalmarta's blood-bonded, brainwashed army, Alex and her friends were more than motivated. They were desperate.

"We need to move," D.C. said. "It won't take long for them to find us here."

A light flashed in the darkness when Bear activated his ComTCD, casting a bluish glow over his face. His pupils were wide and beads of sweat dotted his forehead despite the cool temperature. "The codes Johnny gave us only work for another hour," he said, flicking through the data stored in his Device. "We need to be in and out in that time, or we'll be stuck here."

"Right," Alex said. "So, it's a 'damned if you do, damned if you don't' situation. We can work with this."

"Wouldn't be the first time," D.C. said with a half-hearted grin. Had Jordan still been with them, her smile would have been more genuine, but Alex knew to take what she could get from her friend. "We trust you."

Alex wondered, not for the first time, if their trust was sorely misguided. After all, it was her fault they were stuck in some dingy janitor's closet to begin with. Sure, her motives were honourable, but that didn't mean she hadn't brought her closest friends on a fool's errand.

It had all begun just over a week ago, when the three of them had left Raelia and returned to Bear's home in Woodhaven for the Kaldoras holidays. The loss of Jordan had caused such a hollow ache in each of them that it had been impossible to enjoy their holiday break. So instead, they'd begun planning.

All they'd known was their endgame: freeing Jordan from Aven's clutches. Their friend might have been 'irreversibly' Claimed, but they still had hope, knowing Alex had once freed herself from Aven's grasp. But even if that didn't turn out to be possible, their back-up plan was to isolate and protect Jordan from the immortal Meyarin, using any means necessary, even imprisonment.

Their task was made infinitely more complicated by the fact that Aven had promised Jordan something important to him—the deliverance of his previously-believed-deceased-but-now-apparently-alive-and-only-missing brother. Luka had supposedly killed himself six years ago, but Aven had shown the brainwashed Jordan surveillance footage of Luka breaking into a ChemTech lab just last month.

So that was where Alex and her friends had decided to start. Their plan was to verify whether or not the footage existed, and if they found evidence showing Luka to be alive, then they would just have to find him before Aven could use him as leverage against their friend.

Easy, right?

The good news was that Johnny, Bear's eldest brother, was a Techno—basically a technology genius—and as a ChemTech employee he had insider knowledge of its facilities. It hadn't taken much coercing from Alex, Bear and D.C. to convince him to join Team Saving Jordan, and he'd been forthcoming with as much intel as they'd needed. While he'd never been to the exact lab in Mardenia where Luka had been sighted, Johnny had managed to hack into the highly classified TCD server to download an entire data file containing the layout of the facility, complete with security codes and a detailed map of the building.

With access to so much information, Alex had originally thought her plan infallible. They would arrive just outside the building's security ward via Bubbledoor, sneak through the entrance using Johnny's codes, hike up the eleven floors to the surveillance room and search through the database until they found the footage of Luka.

Sure, there were a few holes in the plan, but it should have been a breeze.

What they *hadn't* counted on were the unforeseen complications—complications like the decidedly human guards.

"How close are we?" Alex asked, looking over Bear's shoulder as he used the touch-screen of his TCD to project a holographic map of the facility into the air between them.

"We're here," he said, pointing to their location. He then expanded the map and swivelled it around, indicating to another room three floors up on the other side of the building. "We need to get there."

"Not impossible," D.C. said. "We've managed to get this far; what's a few more stairs?"

Alex bit back her retort and just hoped she wasn't about to get the crown princess of Medora arrested—or shot. They'd already had one close call with a security guard who'd thankfully been looking the other way when they nearly walked into him—an encounter that clued them in to the fact that they weren't alone in the building. And Alex had clearly seen the Stabiliser holstered to the man's belt. She wasn't sure if he'd carried other weapons, but that alone was cause for concern—one shot would lead to ten minutes of unconsciousness and a second shot instant death.

Not a pleasant thought.

"I don't suppose you guys would be willing to stay here and keep watch?" Alex asked. "Lessen the chances of us all getting caught?"

Firm headshakes met her question, not that she'd expected anything less.

"We've talked about this," Bear said, his tone unyielding. "We're going to help save Jordan, no matter the consequences."

"No way are we staying behind," D.C. confirmed, her arms folded and an expression of distaste on her face. "Don't even try to stop us."

Alex raised her hands in a placating manner. "Fine, fine, but you can't blame me for trying." She attempted a conciliatory smile, but she knew it fell flat. Straightening her shoulders, she told them, "Stay close, then. And don't make a sound."

Bear shoved his ComTCD back into his pocket, extinguishing their light source. As soon as Alex's eyes adjusted to the nearly black room again, she pushed the door open, silently leading the way out into the corridor beyond. She had to blink her vision clear when the hallway's brighter, halogen-like lights seared through her retinas, all the while keeping a lookout for the slightest indication of guards nearby.

Frustratingly, the facility didn't have one central staircase that led to different floors. Instead, the staircases were designed in an architectural nightmare of ups, downs and all arounds. As if it were a Snakes and Ladders game, each set of stairs ended in a different location, but never directly where Alex and her friends needed to go.

Their staircase dilemma could have been avoided if they'd simply used the elevator, but the access codes Johnny had hacked to activate the lift were for an emergency only, since any elevator usage was monitored closely and their presence would undoubtedly be detected. For obvious reasons, they wanted to avoid that.

After what felt like an unending journey of twisting staircases—including one that went straight up to the twelfth floor, one that sent them back down to the third and one leading back up to the ninth—Alex began to question their decision to avoid the elevator. Her thighs were burning from all the repeated climbing despite her Combat and PE-honed level of fitness, and the panting noises from Bear and D.C. put her on edge, reminding her it had been a while since they had heard any of the guards patrolling close by.

Turning questioning eyes to Bear, Alex gestured for his ComTCD. Reactivating the holographic map, she saw they only had one final staircase to go until they reached the eleventh floor, before traversing the entire length of the building to arrive at their destination. This would be made more challenging by the glass-walled skywalk in the centre, since the facility diverged into two separate towers from the eighth floor up.

Handing back the Device, Alex hurried forward again, ignoring her protesting muscles when she hit the next staircase. They had only forty minutes left to use Johnny's codes and she was feeling the pressure.

Finally on the eleventh floor, Alex guided them through zigzagging corridors, pausing at every corner to peek around and make sure the next section was clear. It was time-consuming but proved necessary, since an automatic door clicked open nearby and Alex was forced to pull Bear and D.C. back behind the bend in the hallway.

Carefully peering around the corner, Alex confirmed there was another security guard, a woman this time. Like the first, she was dressed in a gunmetal-grey jumpsuit and had a Stabiliser holstered to her belt. She also sported a sword strapped across her back, the hilt of which poked menacingly above her shoulders. Worse still, her purposeful strides meant she was quickly eating up the distance between them.

Realising their side of the corridor was too long and narrow to avoid being spotted, Alex hurried her friends to the closest door, intending to hide in whatever room lay beyond until the coast was clear. But since the eleventh floor was dedicated to Research and Development—or so Johnny had said—the door wouldn't open without clearance.

Noticing the touch-screen access panel mounted on the wall, Alex gestured to Bear and waited anxiously while he tapped on his TCD screen. A life-sized holographic hand quickly floated out of the Device and encased his skin like a shimmery glove, which he moved closer to the access panel. After the forged handprint was scanned and accepted, he hit a few more buttons until another image came to life—an eyeball, to Alex's disgust.

As soon as the retinal scan cleared, the door clicked open, allowing Alex, Bear and D.C. to tumble into the room and escape the *click-click-click* of the guard's boots nearing them.

The moment the door sealed them inside, there was a violent hiss of air depressurising, the only warning Alex had before she rose from the ground. She heard both Bear and D.C. curse as they too were lifted weightlessly upwards until the three of them were suspended in the air as if floating in water.

"It must be some kind of anti-gravity field," Bear said, waving his hands around, his movements appearing as if in slow motion.

"Um," Alex said, feeling like an uncoordinated turtle as she bobbed mid-air. "How are we supposed to—uh—" She trailed off with a distressed sound when her torso tipped forward too far and she was left to somersault her way back around until she was close to the right way up again.

"This is so unnatural!" D.C. exclaimed, looking like she was trying to use swimming strokes to move, but to little effect.

"Hold on a second, guys," Bear said. "We won't get anywhere with you fighting gravity like that. We need a plan."

You don't say? Alex thought. But she reined in her inner sarcasm and did her best to stay as still as her current state of floating would allow. While Bear was deciding their exit strategy, she took the chance to look around the room. With cream-coloured padded walls, floor and ceiling, it was empty of furniture or anything else. It was clearly a room intended for one purpose—messing with gravity.

Alex heard a beeping sound and she arched her neck until she could see Bear again, his ComTCD in hand. A holographic body came into view above it.

"Yo, little brother. I take it things aren't going so well?" Johnny said, and Alex could hear the humour in his voice. She wondered how much of their current predicament was showing through his Device and figured it was enough to give him a good laugh at their expense.

"You could say that," Bear answered. "We wouldn't be stuck in here if you'd given us a warning about the guards."

"Guards?" Johnny repeated. Alex managed to float close enough to see his quizzical expression. "There aren't supposed to be any guards there. Not on site, at least."

"We've seen two already," Bear said. Johnny looked genuinely concerned. "We had to break into this room to avoid one of them, but now we're caught in an anti-gravity field. Can you help us out?"

Johnny gave a quick nod. "Give me a sec." He disappeared for a moment and soon reappeared with a larger, tablet-style Device. "I take it you're on the eleventh floor? Anti-gravity is R&D for sure. But if I'm right, you're still on the wrong side of the facility."

"We haven't crossed the skywalk yet," D.C. said. Having given up on her breaststroke, she was now attempting to freestyle her way across the room, looking even more ridiculous than before and still getting nowhere.

"You guys better get a move on," Johnny muttered, distracted by whatever he was doing with the tablet. "You're pushing it for time."

"Yeah, well, if we'd known about the—" Bear started, but his brother interrupted.

"Got it!"

With Johnny's exclamation, the air-hissing sound came again and Alex dropped like a rock to the floor.

Grateful for the padding that saved her from a very bruised backside, she jumped to her feet and walked over to where Bear was rising. "Thanks, Johnny. We owe you one."

"Listen, guys," he said, squinting at the other Device he held. "I don't know what's with the guards, but heat sensors indicate there's one patrolling every floor. That's fifteen in total. You're lucky you've only come across two, but if you trip any alarms, they'll all come running."

Alex closed her eyes, wondering again what she'd been thinking leading her friends here.

"One of those guards is wandering up and down the hallway outside your room. There's no way for you to get out without being seen. But you're only a few rooms away from the skywalk, and once you make it over, you'll be in the clear. I think I can guide you there without you having to step foot in the corridor. But you'll have to trust me."

The trio looked at one another before turning back to Johnny. "We're listening."

There were three other doors leading from the padded room, and using Johnny's remote access to open the furthest one, they followed his direction into the long, dark chamber before them.

It was only once the door sealed behind them that he absentmindedly said, "Heads up, you're about to get wet."

"Wha—"

Alex's question was cut off when a billowing mass of cloud materialised above them just seconds before a torrential downpour of water fell straight onto their heads.

"Run!" Bear cried, his voice garbled by the lashing rain. He grabbed both Alex and D.C.'s arms and yanked them along. Not that they needed the motivation, since they were just as desperate to escape the unnatural weather phenomenon.

"No, Bear, stop! Alex! Dix! Stop! *Stop!*"

It took a few shouts before Alex was able to hear Johnny's yelling over the sound of the deluge, but she came to a sudden halt as soon as his words processed. It was only then that she began to feel the rain vaporise around her and a glow of artificial sunlight kiss her skin. She looked up and marvelled at the sight high above them.

Glancing backward, Alex could still see the rain bucketing down from miserable-looking clouds by the entrance. But looking around her now…

"Is this some kind of weather room?" she asked.

The large chamber appeared to be sectioned into different climate categories. Where Alex and her friends currently stood was a clear blue sky, fluffy white cumulus clouds and, perhaps strangest of all, a synthetic sun. Looking further across the room, she could see all kinds of weather scenarios playing out within bordered segments of the room. Clearly the ChemTech R&D department was earning their keep.

"Yes, Alex, and don't move another step!" Johnny ordered, his features pinched and his tone laced with anxiety. "I thought I could deactivate the room remotely but the coding is more complex than I anticipated. I can do it, but it will take a few minutes and you don't have the time to spare. You'll have to make a run for it."

"Then why'd you tell us to stop?" Bear sounded belligerent as he squeezed water from his shirt.

D.C. gave a frowning nod of agreement as she too wrung out her sodden clothes and twisted her soaked hair, leaving a puddle of water on the marble tiles.

With a troubling feeling that they weren't out of the worst of it yet, Alex didn't bother attempting to dry off.

"Because I need to warn you," Johnny said, "that some of the weather is… reactive."

D.C. stopped wringing out her hair. "Reactive?"

Johnny chose not to explain. Instead he gave them an impishly apologetic look and said, "Keep moving and you should be fine. The last section will be the most dangerous, but I'll have your exit door open by the time you get there, so just sprint straight through. Okay?"

"No, not okay!" D.C. cried. "Do you want to give us some more details?"

Johnny turned his attention to his second Device and muttered, "I have a door to unlock. You'd better start running."

Before D.C. could open her mouth to protest, Alex grabbed her arm and pulled her along. "Come on, Dix. The sooner we get moving, the sooner we'll be out of here."

Two

Leading the way at a fast pace, Alex felt the air turn clammy as the sunshine dissolved behind them. Visibility was near to nothing as they entered the next weather zone and a fog-like mist arose from beneath their feet, swiftly obscuring everything in sight. It was disorienting, but Alex pressed on, running forward until she crossed into the next climate. Almost immediately her feet slipped out from underneath her and she fell onto the hard, ice-covered floor.

Dazed from the fall, she managed to yell, "Watch your step!"

But it was too late for D.C., who hit the slippery ground and slid along until she came to a jarring stop in a tangle of limbs at Alex's feet.

Bringing up the rear, Bear at least heard the warning in time, and was able to get away with a slight skating of his feet without losing his footing.

"Eugh," D.C. grunted, pushing up to stand. She made a whimpering sound, causing Alex to glance at her with alarm.

"Are you hurt?"

Holding her left hand tenderly, D.C. bit her lip. "I landed pretty hard on my wrist."

"Here, let me look," Bear said as Alex stood and slid her way over to them.

He gently rolled D.C.'s wrist back and forth, pressing carefully against the bones.

"Your movement is good," Bear said. "I think it's just sprained."

D.C.'s face was tight with pain. "I'll be fine. Let's keep moving."

"Dix—"

"Alex, I'm fine. Really. Let's go."

Taking in the determined look on her friend's face, Alex slowly nodded. But before she led the way onwards, she unwound the scarf from her neck and used it to tie her ComTCD to D.C.'s wrist as an improvised splint.

"Try to keep it as still as possible," Alex said. "The more you move it, the worse you'll make it."

"You've spent way too much time in the Med Ward," D.C. observed, studying Alex's rudimentary attempt at first aid. "But thanks. It already feels a bit better."

"Thank Fletcher," Alex said. "He's patched me up so many times, I was bound to learn a thing or two."

On that wry note, Alex edged her way forward again, carefully this time. Her feet slid along the icy floor, and more than once she had to catch herself before taking another header onto the ground. Their slow progress was made more frustrating when greenish clouds rolled in and began to spit small hailstones at them. They weren't large enough to cause worrying injuries, but Alex certainly obtained her fair share of stinging bruises. It was a relief, therefore, when they crossed into the next weather section, even if it sent them directly into a blustery snowstorm.

"This place is *mental*!" Alex cried over the howling wind as they trudged their way through the knee-deep snow. A mass of flurries blew straight into her mouth just from emitting those few words, so she refrained from yelling anything else to her friends until they reached the next section.

Soaked and shivering from the piercing chill of the blizzard, they were grateful to cross the boundary into a section that was both silent and still. But just when Alex thought they were in the clear, the back of her neck began to prickle with warning and a peculiar tingly feeling overcame her.

"Run!" came Johnny's urgent voice from Bear's ComTCD. "Run, run, *run*!"

Alex didn't need to be told twice. She remembered what he'd said about the last section being the most dangerous, and when a ferocious rumble was followed closely by a blinding light and an ear-splitting *CRACK*, she understood exactly why he hadn't given them more details.

They were right in the middle of an electrical storm. And judging by the amount of static charge Alex felt and the strong smell of ozone in the air, it was a nasty one, at that.

With Bear and D.C. right behind her, Alex took off at a sprint through the low-hanging dark clouds, heading for the open door that was still an alarming distance away. Another thunderous roar had Alex slapping her hands over her ears, and she couldn't suppress a shriek when a spike of lightning struck the floor so close that she felt the power of the bolt surge along her skin.

Alex picked up her speed, but as they reached the halfway mark of the storm-section, the lightning and thunder increased to the point that the three of them had to zigzag their way in short, sharp lunges to avoid being struck. It was only then that Alex remembered Johnny saying that some of the weather was reactive—the storm was actively *tracking* them, targeting their movements as they hurried through the room.

With that insight, Alex struggled against her rising panic. Instead, she focused on getting out of there alive, blinking furiously to combat the blinding explosions of light. Just a few feet away from the door, she heard the loudest *CRACK* yet and knew they had but a few seconds before their luck would run out and they would be burnt to a crisp.

"Hurry!" she yelled, taking a running leap directly through the doorway, noting with relief that Bear and D.C. were right on her heels.

She came to a sudden, messy stop when she soared straight into a mud-filled pond. Bear and D.C. managed to avoid the pile of dirty sludge, but Alex was elbow deep in the muck and covered from head to toe from the splash of her landing.

"Eww, gross," she said, pushing up and wiping a hand across her face, only smearing the mess further.

She heard a muffled snort and whipped her head around to see a wild-haired D.C. with her uninjured hand over her mouth, her eyes sparkling with humour. It was the liveliest Alex had seen her since Jordan's Claiming—even if it was at the expense of Alex's own dignity.

As for Bear, his hair was standing on end, and half his face was streaked with what looked like charcoal—the effect of a close call with the lightning—but he, too, appeared to be struggling to hold back laughter as he took in Alex's muddy predicament.

"Not a word," she said with a warning glare.

D.C. and Bear were shaking with silent hysterics, but they swallowed back their hilarity with pressed lips and quick nods.

"Johnny, please tell me we're close?" Alex called, deliberately ignoring his muffled chuckle when he noted her appearance through the ComTCD.

"Just get through this last room and you'll hit the skywalk," he said, eyes dancing with mirth. "There's a guard still patrolling your side of the tower, so you'll have a straight path along the corridor from there."

Finally, some good news, Alex thought.

"What are we dealing with in here?" Bear asked his brother.

Glancing around, Alex noted that it appeared to be some kind of plant-filled greenhouse.

"The schematics say it's a terrarium," Johnny answered. "You shouldn't have anything to worry about. Just follow the path and take a right at the fork. You'll hit the next door soon after. I'll have it ready for you."

Walking through the quiet of the plant-strewn terrarium would have been almost peaceful, but Alex was too preoccupied with swatting away the swarms of insects wanting to feast on her flesh. All too soon she was covered in itchy welts and desperate to escape the incessant creatures.

While slapping at the bugs, Alex, Bear and D.C. managed to avoid three more large mud ponds before arriving at one that was bordered by a forest so dense they had to squelch their way through the grunge to get to the other side. Alex was already covered in the filth so she didn't care so much, but neither Bear nor D.C. were thrilled about suctioning their way through the knee-high mud.

They took a right at the fork as directed and continued on until the door came into view.

"That wasn't so bad, comparatively," D.C. said, scratching her bites as they approached the exit.

When Johnny gave the go-ahead, they stepped out of the room and into another identical hallway.

Alex could clearly see the boundary of their side of the building, since the walls came to an abrupt end, yet the hallway continued through a glass-enclosed tunnel joining the two towers of the facility.

"Hope you guys aren't afraid of heights," Alex said, approaching the skywalk.

D.C. swallowed. "I'm not a huge fan of them."

"Nothing is as bad as the Meyarin's *Valispath*, right?" Bear said, reminding them of the invisible rollercoaster that was the Eternal Path. "You managed okay with that."

D.C. sent him a disbelieving look. "I didn't have much choice at the time, if memory serves."

"Unless you want to get friendly with the guard, you don't have much of a choice now, either," Alex interjected. She nudged D.C. and offered her a quick, teasing grin. "Suck it up, princess."

Laughing inwardly at the face D.C. pulled, Alex stepped out onto the skywalk, closely followed by her friends.

Bear was right; it was nothing compared to the sheer terror of riding the *Valispath*. But they *were* quite high, and Alex had to make a concentrated effort not to look down. She only just managed to bite back a smile when she heard D.C. whispering to herself something along the lines of, "I'm going to kill Jordan for this."

That's the D.C. I know, Alex thought, happy to see some of her zest and spirit returning, even if the cause of it wasn't exactly ideal.

When they safely reached the other side, Bear informed them that they had less than fifteen minutes to get into the server room and out of the facility before their access codes would be invalid. Alex knew then that it was not only a foolish mission, but it was also an impossible one. But they'd come this far. And there was no turning back now.

Hurrying straight down the thankfully clear corridor, they headed directly towards the surveillance room. Bear opened the doorway by repeating the TCD handprint and retinal scans, and as soon as the three of them flew into the room, he called his brother back onto the screen to ask, "What now?"

"Turn your Device around and show me what you see."

As Bear followed Johnny's command, Alex looked around the bright, circular room. Standing in the centre of the otherwise empty space was a large golden globe that glistened against a pearlescent, nearly glowing floor.

"See the TechSphere?" Johnny said. "Press your hand against it to activate it."

When Bear reached his arm forward to follow Johnny's order, his brother cried out, "No! Not *your* hand—the hand I gave you!"

Alex let out a quiet huff of laughter at the absurdity of their situation—or perhaps more at the nearly identical frustrated expressions on both Bear and Johnny's faces.

After accepting the scanned handprint clearance, the TechSphere lit up, and with it, so did the rest of the room. The previously blank walls were now buzzing with energy as if ready and waiting at attention.

"Now input the codes I gave you," Johnny instructed, and Bear did so using quick finger swipes too complex for Alex and D.C. to follow.

Johnny's complicated guidance began to fly over their heads and blur into gibberish, but thankfully Bear was able to keep up and he cried out a triumphant, "I'm in!" when the system unlocked.

"Awesome," Alex said, moving up beside him to peer at the bunch of letters and numbers within the Sphere, all written in code. "Do you know how to find—"

"Just a sec, Alex," Bear distractedly interrupted. "I think I'm... There! I think I've got it! Johnny, can you confirm?" He pulled the Device close and spun it around, showing the TechSphere's code to his brother.

Johnny's hologram squinted at the sequence of random symbols and he nodded enthusiastically. "That entry was definitely hacked in the not-too-distant past. A dodgy job too, since whoever it was didn't clean the feed or wipe clear their tracks. I'm pretty sure that's what you're after, guys."

Needing no further prompting, Bear input something into the Sphere's server and one wall of the room instantly came to life, like a massive television screen. The footage that began playing was grainy and the poor quality degenerated further as the feed dropped in and out, but Alex could still recognise the same room they were standing in on the screen, with very few differences. The main one being the young man shown in the video.

"Is that…?" D.C. whispered, her eyes wide.

As if he heard her, the man abruptly turned to face the hidden surveillance camera. D.C. let out a strangled sounding noise and even Alex sucked in a breath, recognising his profile. His blond hair was about six years overdue for a cut and his scraggly beard made him look like a caveman, but his bright blue eyes combined with his bone structure and athletic body shape made his resemblance to Jordan unquestionable.

"I don't believe it," Bear said in a quiet, incredulous voice. "Aven… Jordan's parents… They were all telling the truth. Luka's alive."

Alex was able to pull herself together first. If what Jordan had said really was him speaking freely—and outside of Aven's influence—then the footage he'd seen had to have been believable enough to *ask* Aven to Claim him. Though, Alex wasn't sure whether to believe that actually happened or if Aven really did take Jordan against his will.

To her unending frustration, Alex knew nothing was certain.

"Johnny," she called, "are you able to confirm if this footage is legit?"

After some more incomprehensible gibberish, Alex ascertained that Johnny had managed to open a network through Bear's Device to download the footage directly—which was something he hadn't been able to do remotely without having someone on the inside to input the codes manually.

"I'm running it through my scanners as we speak," he said, ending his Techno-babble spiel by answering her question. "I just need a minute."

He took two, but when he came back to them it was with a shuttered, disappointed expression. "It's fake, guys. I'm sorry."

"What?" D.C. exhaled sharply. "But—But he looks just like Jordan!"

"It's an enhanced digital likeness, likely rendered from an image of Jordan himself and aged a decade into the future."

Jordan had been deceived all along, and Alex felt the crushing devastation of what that meant. If they ever found a way to free their friend from Aven, he'd have to come to terms with Luka's death all over again.

"I'm sorry, guys," Johnny filled the hanging silence. "I know that's not the news you were after."

At least we now know the truth, Alex thought, sad as it was.

"If you hurry, I can still get you out before—" Johnny broke off and his face paled when something on his other Device caught his attention. He leaned in closer to it and his eyes widened as he released a string of curse words. "Guys, it looks like you left muddy footprints in the corridor and that guard in the other tower has just flagged them and raised the alarm. She's on her way to you, along with every other guard in the facility. You need to move. *Now*."

Three

An indefinite amount of time later, Alex restlessly paced back and forth in a holding cell that was much cleaner than her current state of hygiene. The white walls surrounding her were immaculate, made more so by the slight glow of energy zinging along them: a seemingly innocuous halo of light that was augmented by a hair-raising electrical hum of warning. Despite the powerful barrier, Alex was tempted to reach out and smear dried mud across the pristine surface just to annoy some underling who clearly had OCD tendencies when it came to bleach—or whatever the Medoran cleaning equivalent was.

Suffice it to say, she and her friends *hadn't* made it out of the ChemTech facility without being caught. They'd barely had time to cut the feed to the surveillance footage and disconnect their ComTCD link with Johnny before the door to the server room had flown open. Hoping that Bear's brother was busy using his hacking skills to hide his digital footprint and the illegal download of the footage to his offsite Device, Alex and her friends had been left throwing their hands up in surrender when the guards stormed the room.

They'd quickly discovered that the ChemTech security team didn't play around and were the 'shoot first, ask questions later' variety of guards. Alex, Bear and D.C. had, therefore, experienced their first taste of what it felt like to be intimately acquainted with a blast from a Stabiliser.

For the record, it hurt like hell.

The weapon had caused a searing burn to spread throughout Alex's body, stinging along her nerve endings fast enough to force her into unconsciousness within a fraction of a second. When she awoke ten minutes later, Alex found herself lying on the unnaturally clean floor of her cell and suffering from a splitting headache; one which was still thumping through her skull after what felt like hours of incarceration.

"What's taking them so long?" D.C. grumbled, sitting on the floor with her head in her hands. "We've been in here for ages without anyone coming by. Why can't they hurry up and tell us how much trouble we're in?"

The only upside to their predicament was that Alex, Bear and D.C. had all been locked up together in the same cell. But since they were each dealing with Stabiliser-induced headaches, none of them had the capacity to offer good company or stimulating conversation.

"Standard practice for interrogations. They're letting us sweat," Bear said, standing with one hand massaging his temple and the other arm cradled protectively against his stomach. He'd been the unfortunate test dummy who had reached out first to touch the glowing walls, discovering that they were, in fact, charged with something akin to live electricity. His hand was covered in blistering welts from contact with the walls, which only added to his discomfort from the earlier insect bites.

Alex was just about to open her mouth and suggest they try to come up with an escape plan when the glowing energy around them deactivated and one of the white walls slid open. D.C. scrambled to her feet and Bear dropped his hands and moved forward until the three of them stood in a line, presenting a united front.

Four people entered the cell. Three of them wore the gunmetal-grey uniforms of the security guards, but the person leading the group wore the familiar black attire of a Warden. His fiery red hair was cropped close to his skull, but it was still thick enough to stand out vividly against his dark clothing and pale skin.

Alex felt D.C. stiffen and relax again just as quickly, apparently not recognising the Warden. This was good, since the last thing any of them needed was for word to get back to D.C.'s parents about their little... expedition.

"I'm Warden Renko," the man in black said as he came to a halt a few steps away. The three security guards stopped beside him, their Stabilisers trained on Alex, Bear and D.C as a silent warning. "You three were caught trespassing on a secure ChemTech facility without authorised clearance. You've since been detained and transported here for questioning. Hands behind your backs, please."

Alex blinked in surprise, not sure what to process first—the fact that they had been transported to an unknown location while unconscious, or the brusque manner of the Warden's efficient command.

When the guards moved forward threateningly, she hastily complied and they roughly bound her arms together. She winced in sympathy at the thought of the pain D.C.'s sprained wrist and Bear's burnt hand must be causing them.

"Follow me," the Warden directed once they were all secured.

"Just a second," Bear said, and Alex raised her eyebrows in question—and alarm. She wasn't keen on repeating her experience with the business end of a Stabiliser if Renko decided not to indulge Bear's interruption.

Fortunately, the Warden seemed curious enough to halt his forward movement and he turned back to her friend.

"We're really sorry to have bothered you," Bear said, "but you need to let us go free now. We don't want any more trouble;

we just want to go home. When you let us out of here, you'll never have to worry about us again."

His words were audacious, and yet Alex had to suppress a grin when the guards and even D.C. all began nodding along while listening to his hypnotic tone. It was fascinating—the last time Bear had used his gift around Alex, her own willpower hadn't been fully activated, and the mesmerising nature of his ability had sucked her right in. But no longer did it affect her, since she was now fully in control of her own gift.

For a moment, Alex thought Bear had come up with the perfect escape plan. But then she realised there was one person, other than herself, who wasn't nodding along with the rest.

"Nice try, kid," Renko said, a hint of a smile curling his lips. "But you're not the only one with a gift around here."

As if his words broke the spell, suddenly the other guards—and D.C.—shook off the glamour of Bear's charm and came back to their senses, frowning slightly in bewilderment.

"Now, let's try this again," Renko said, gesturing pointedly for Alex and her friends to follow him from the cell.

Throwing an 'it was worth a shot' look at Bear, Alex stepped forward and trailed Renko down a series of blindingly white corridors until they passed a guarded checkpoint and walked in single file through some kind of body scanner. It reminded Alex of stepping through airport security, and she wondered what the point of it was, since not even their ComTCDs had been confiscated from them during their imprisonment—though, they *had* somehow been deactivated, meaning no incoming or outgoing calls, despite their desperate attempts to contact Johnny for escape options.

Whether the body scanner was searching for weapons or something else—or perhaps it acted like an EMP field and was now *re*activating their Devices, or so Alex hoped—it let them through without issue, and from there, Alex and her friends were pushed into an elevator. After an ear-popping journey upwards, it opened into a large room bustling with people smartly dressed and wandering about with purpose.

Until that moment, Alex had presumed from Renko's words that they'd been moved to some kind of high-tech, uncommonly clean prison, but now she had no idea where they were. Not until she saw the sign posted directly above the spiral glass staircase they were being led towards. HIGH COURT OF MEDORA was written in large, bold letters, with an engraving of the Wardens' emblem beneath it: two swords crossed together behind a crown.

There was an addition to this picture Alex hadn't seen before, with the emblem positioned in the middle of a shield above the words: Sosaar de ne lenorsa.

"We are many, yet we are one," D.C. recited quietly, answering Alex's unspoken question. "It's meant to be a reminder that our actions affect the lives of those around us every day." Her eyes travelled over the room and she continued in a whisper, "I can't believe we're at the High Court. This is *so* not good, guys." The guard behind her prodded his Stabiliser into her back and she snapped her mouth closed.

The moment their entourage stepped onto the spiralling staircase, Renko tapped something into the railing and it came to life, moving them upwards like an escalator. When they reached what Alex judged to be about four floors up, she was nudged off by a guard to follow the Warden down another long hallway, this one with a glass-walled view that held Alex's attention for the entire length of the walk.

"Mardenia. The city on a hill," Renko said, tracking her gaze as he fell into step beside her.

Feeling as if he expected a response, she squinted out at the view and said, "It's very... clean."

As strange as her description was, it was the only thing Alex could come up with on the fly. Looking at the city sprawled across the side of what was most definitely a hill, Alex marvelled at just how white everything was. Much like the High Court, the buildings running alongside the vibrant blue ocean were bleached of colour. The scenery brought to mind a memory of the time she'd travelled around the Greek Islands with her parents when they'd been working on a dig outside of Athens. They'd taken a four-day vacation from their work and hired a boat, cruising around the Aegean Sea and setting foot on as many islands as time allowed.

Before Alex could properly indulge in her nostalgia, they came to the end of the windowed walkway and Renko ordered them to sit in a small waiting room.

"Your trial will begin in five minutes. Wait in here until you're called."

Alex anxiously flicked her eyes to Renko as he and the guards exited the room. "Our trial?"

He turned to her when he reached the door, his face blank. "You illegally infiltrated a top-secret facility. Did you expect to get off with just a warning?"

And with that, he locked them in the small room.

"So what are we looking at here?" Alex asked D.C.

"My guess?" D.C. chewed nervously on her lip. "Nothing good. We were caught red-handed, Alex. As much as it'll suck, we may have to get someone to contact my parents."

"I can see that conversation going well." Alex pitched her voice to mimic D.C., "*Excuse me, Warden Renko, do you mind contacting the king and queen to tell them you've got their daughter locked up in prison? No, really, I promise you, I'm the princess.*" Alex finished her recitation by looking pointedly up and down her friend's lightning-zinged, muddy appearance. "For some reason, I have a feeling he'll have a hard time believing us."

"Fortunately for you, little human, you won't have to wait to find out if that is true."

Alex whirled around only to gape at the sight of the huge Meyarin guard, Zain, leaning casually against the wall.

"I leave you alone for a few days and you end up incarcerated," he said, taking in their messy appearances with a mixture of exasperation and amusement. "You once told me you didn't need a babysitter, but all evidence points to the contrary."

"What are you doing here, Zain?" Alex asked, amazed to see him standing there with them. "How did you even get in here? No, scratch that. How did you know where to find us?" She paused. "Wait, you *are* here for us, right?"

"Always so curious," Zain said, pushing off from the wall and moving with Meyarin grace towards her. "Turn around, Alex."

He didn't give her the option of following his command since his heavy hands came to rest on her shoulders, swivelling her body until her back faced him. She heard a *snick* before her bonds fell to the ground. Massaging the pins and needles from her wrists, Alex watched him liberate D.C. and Bear with a lethal-looking blade. Zain didn't miss their winces when their injured hands were released.

"Step closer, humans, and we'll address your wounds back in Meya."

When Alex opened her mouth to repeat her questions, he sent her a quelling look and said, "Unless of course you want to stay here and end up with criminal records and prison time?"

She snapped her mouth shut and the three of them moved closer to Zain. Almost immediately, the ground tore out from underneath them as the *Valispath* activated, shooting them straight through the walls of the High Court and out into the sunset horizon.

Zain, thankfully, had recently spent quite some time with Alex's human self, so he knew to reach out and fiddle with the settings of the Eternal Path—settings that were invisible to human eyes. He pressed a patterned sequence into the transparent wall, causing the wind chill to disappear instantly. Even though they were soaring over the white buildings of Mardenia at a stomach-churning speed, their ride was smooth and silent. In fact, if Alex closed her eyes, she wouldn't know she was moving at all.

"I think I'm going to be sick," D.C. whispered, staring pale faced at the blurring scenery as the *Valispath* picked up more speed.

Alex had forgotten that only she had experienced the Path at full velocity before. Her friends had been on it with her twice, but only between Meya and Raelia, and at a much more sedate pace.

"Here," Zain said, pulling a crumpled white flower from his cloak and handing it to D.C. "Chew this, it will make you feel better."

Ill as she was, D.C. didn't question him. She put the flower in her mouth, closing her eyes and taking deliberately controlled breaths. Within moments the colour returned to her face and she opened her eyes again, looking stunned. "Wow," she said, still chewing. "This is good stuff."

"*Fraedonweed*," Zain said. "Cures most superficial stomach illnesses." His eyes lit up with mischief and he added, "When ground into a paste, it's a remarkably effective boot polish as well."

D.C.'s rapidly improving face blanched again and she turned to Alex. "Am I eating boot polish?"

Alex hesitated. "Does it taste like boot polish?"

When D.C.'s colour continued draining away, Alex realised that she could have chosen her words more carefully.

"What I meant was, who cares if it's boot polish if it tastes all right?" Alex tried again.

"I suggest we change the topic unless you want Dix to puke all over our feet," Bear said pointedly.

Taking his advice, Alex turned back to Zain. "How did you know we needed rescuing? And where to find us?"

Zain answered with only one word, but it was explanation enough. "Hunter."

Alex closed her eyes slowly. It figured that her Stealth and Subterfuge teacher would know what they'd been up to—and that they'd needed help. Somehow the mysterious man seemed to know *everything*, and not just because he had a supernatural gift of awareness and perception.

"Hunter was following us?" Bear asked, and Alex reopened her eyes to see his surprise.

"He thought it wise," Zain responded. He didn't get a chance to say anything else before the *Valispath* shot them straight into a snow-covered mountain, and for a few seconds, all light disappeared until they broke through to the other side and rejoined the open sky.

Bear let out a quiet groan. "Now I think *I'm* going to be sick."

Zain shook his head and muttered, "Humans."

Alex pressed her lips together to keep from laughing. He'd been with them for less than five minutes and already appeared eager to dump them in the forest below.

"You're sure looking better than the last time I saw you," Alex said, hoping to keep him from acting on his urge to abandon them. "Are you completely healed?"

It had been less than a fortnight, but when she'd last laid eyes on Zain he'd been suffering from a wound poisoned by Hyroa blood—the Meyarin equivalent of kryptonite—and he'd nearly died. Now, however, he appeared healthy and strong, much to Alex's relief.

Noticing Alex's clinical perusal, Zain sent her a warm smile. "As you can see, I'm fully recovered. And ready to assist in your training."

Alex unconsciously scrunched up her face and resolutely decided to ignore his words, choosing instead to visit a happy place in her mind; a place where she never had to consider the worrisome idea of training with the hulk of a Meyarin. Or any others of his kind.

"It won't be so bad," Zain said, nudging her with his elbow. "I'll go easy on you."

Alex very much doubted he would. The reason she had to learn how to fight with the Meyarins was so she could hold her own against Aven. Therefore, she needed to know what she was up against. Being babied, as much as she liked the idea, wouldn't help her—or anyone else.

"You said you're taking us to Meya," D.C. said to Zain. "Is there a reason we're not going straight back to Woodhaven?"

"Prince Roka planned on collecting Alex tomorrow for us to begin working with her," Zain answered, causing Alex's eyebrows to shoot up, "but then Hunter contacted us and said you could use... some assistance..."—his lips twitched at that, but he continued—"so I was sent to retrieve you all today instead. Now Alex will simply be able to begin her training earlier than anticipated."

Oh, goodie, Alex thought. *And I thought this day couldn't get any better.*

Four

Before Alex could ask Zain exactly what her training would entail, the *Valispath* began to slow. She hadn't even noticed them gliding through the Silverwood. The snow-dusted forest was now darkening into hues of bright gold as they moved towards their destination. And sure enough, within seconds, they breached the tree line and soared over the Golden Cliffs, with the Eternal Path spiralling them down through the spray of waterfalls and into the valley below.

The silvery spires of the palace at the centre of the city lit up like a beacon, shining with the light of the setting sun that bounced off the snowy surrounds with an iridescent radiance. Alex could hear Bear and D.C.'s outspoken awe, and she knew that whether seventeen or seventy, there was nothing any of them would see in the rest of their lives that would rival the beauty of the Lost City.

It took hardly any time at all before the Path led them directly into the palace, stopping only when they reached a long corridor intricately decorated with swirls of Myrox and gold. Ordinarily it would have seemed gaudy and ostentatious, but given the rest of the opulence surrounding them, the décor was almost bland in comparison to the city.

"Prince Roka is expecting us," Zain said, moving off the invisible transportation and towards the nearest door. Bear and D.C. followed directly behind him, both somewhat wobbly from their experience on the *Valispath*.

Trailing after them, Alex wondered why Zain kept referring to Roka as 'Prince' when she knew the Meyarin royal preferred to be casual with his title, but then she realised it must be because of D.C. and Bear. The Meyarins trusted Alex, but she knew they didn't have the same confidence in her friends. In fact, not so long ago Roka had pleaded with Alex to remain quiet about the Meyarin qualities she'd inherited from Aven's attempted Claiming, making her promise to keep it a secret from her friends—and anyone else—to lessen the risk of Aven finding out. But after her recent experience with the banished prince, Aven had to now realise something was different about Alex, and since her friends had been caught up in that mess with her, she'd decided they deserved to know the truth. True to form, they'd been nothing but encouraging, with D.C. offering compassion and Bear thinking it was the coolest thing ever. They were also firmly in favour of Alex training with the Meyarins, despite knowing her reluctance. But the fact was, they all knew she would likely come face to face with Aven again, and when that time came, Alex would need to embrace her Meyarin abilities should she have any hope to survive the confrontation.

"Any day now, little human."

Alex glanced up to see Zain waiting for her to follow Bear and D.C. through the very same doorway she had once used on her midnight visit to Meya after crossing paths—and swords— with Aven at Sir Oswald's dinner party. That felt like years ago to Alex, given everything that had happened since.

"Sorry," she said. "I spaced out for a moment. This headache is killing me."

Sliding past him to enter the room beyond, Alex was surprised to see him continue on down the corridor rather than join them. Shrugging mentally, she turned back to the room and found Roka and his betrothed, Kyia, waiting for her. Alex easily returned their smiles, but the expression slid from her face when their eyes widened at her appearance and they burst into laughter.

"And I thought your friends looked bad," Roka said, walking over and placing a welcoming hand on her shoulder. "It's good to see you, Alex, even if it looks like you found a swamp and missed the 'watch your step' sign."

"Ha, ha, you're hilarious," Alex grumbled, crossing her arms. Unfortunately she was too happy to see the Meyarins to feel any real annoyance at their reactions. That, and she was fully aware of how ridiculous she and her friends looked. Bear's hair was still standing on end from their earlier encounter with the lightning, his face streaked with charcoal. D.C. also looked particularly wild, with her red hair frizzing exponentially by the second as it aired out naturally. Dried mud covered both their legs, but even that couldn't compete with Alex's state of crustiness, her body coated from head to toe.

She couldn't blame Roka and Kyia for their laughter—in fact, she was surprised Zain had held back from commenting earlier. Furrowing her brow, Alex looked around, but their bulky escort was still nowhere to be seen. Then, as if on cue, Zain strode back into the room.

"Here," he said, handing a golden chalice to Alex and passing two others to her friends. "Drink."

Alex watched the steam rising out of the goblet and looked down at the silvery liquid with suspicion. "Is it supposed to be glowing like that?"

Zain huffed with impatience. "Just drink it, Alex."

She felt the need to quote from a responsible-drinking advertisement, but she figured it would go straight over their otherworldly heads, so instead of making a fuss, she did as commanded, taking a small sip of the pleasantly sweet liquid.

"Mmm." She smacked her lips together and took another sip, larger this time. "Tastes like vanilla."

And indeed it did taste like vanilla, or perhaps caramel. She couldn't quite decide, almost like it was a mixture of the two rich flavours. Either way, it was delicious, and she made a note to never doubt Zain's drink offerings again, regardless of how psychedelic they looked.

"What's in it?" Alex asked, entranced by the glowing liquid.

"You said you had a headache," Zain answered just as she took another large mouthful. "Meyarin blood is known for its healing properties. Enjoy, little human."

Alex violently spat out her mouthful. The silver liquid sprayed everywhere as she bent at the waist and tried to repress her urge to vomit all over the floor. She was only able to gain control of her gag reflex when she heard the uproarious laughter and realised she'd been played.

Alex stood straight again and scowled at Zain who was laughing the hardest.

"The—look—on—your—face—" he managed to get out between guffaws. "Priceless!"

It took every fibre of her being to resist throwing the remaining contents of her goblet at the hulking Meyarin. Instead, she grit her teeth and waited for them all—D.C. and Bear included—to settle down again.

"That was unkind of us, Alex," Roka said, looking apologetic even if his golden eyes still gleamed with humour. "Of course Zain didn't give you blood to drink. Your chalice contains an infusion of what we call *laendra*. It's a plant native to the Silverwood and has fast-acting healing properties. You should already be feeling its effects."

True enough, the headache Alex had endured since being Stabilised had disappeared the moment she'd begun drinking the *laendra*, and now that she thought about it, she couldn't feel her itchy bites anymore, either. Looking at her friends, she could see the blisters on Bear's forearm were healing before her eyes. D.C., too, was in the process of unwrapping Alex's scarf bandage from her wrist, and when she was free of the makeshift splint, she handed the ComTCD back to Alex, rotating her hand with a look of incredulous wonder.

Swallowing her ire—because Zain *had* gone to retrieve the medicine after hearing her complain about her headache—Alex finished the remains of her goblet and offered a quiet, "Thanks, Zain."

He chuckled quietly in response, still amused by the whole scenario, making it challenging for Alex to maintain her gratitude. She decided her best course of action was to instead turn her attention to the other Meyarins.

"Thanks for sending Zain to come get us," she said to Roka. "His timing was perfect."

"Yes, Hunter mentioned you could use some assistance," the prince said, his lips quirking at the corners. "Tell me, did you find what you were after?"

At his question, Alex turned wide eyes to D.C. and Bear. "Johnny! He's probably freaking out!"

Understanding immediately, Bear pulled out his ComTCD and activated a link to his brother. Just before it connected, he glanced around the opulent room and evidently remembered that even if Johnny knew a lot more about their story than most, they were still technically in a hidden city and it was probably best to keep it that way until someone more important decided to change the 'Lost City' status. Upon making that realisation, Bear swiftly deactivated the holograph feature so that their connection was audio only.

"Bear? You there?" Johnny's voice called.

"We're all here," Bear answered. "We're okay."

Johnny let out an audible sound of relief. "You had me worried, little bro. I watched on the surveillance feed as they blasted you and dragged you through a Bubbledoor—that was intense! It took me a while to find you again at the High Court since that place is wired like you wouldn't believe, but when I finally made it into their system and found a way to get you past their security, you were gone. The guards are still in an uproar—what gives?"

Bear shuffled his feet and mumbled, "Long story. I can't really talk now, but I wanted you to know we're all safe. Do me a favour and distract Mum and Dad until we get home, yeah?"

"Blake's already on that," Johnny answered. "He's been running interference all day."

At that moment, Alex was relieved they'd decided to trust not only Johnny, but also Bear's other brother, Blake, with the truth about Jordan's Claiming. Both brothers had helped to keep the rest of the Ronnigan household—Dorothy, William, Gammy and Evie—oblivious to what was going on.

"They think you've spent the last few hours at On The House with Benny and Sal," Johnny continued. "But I'm not sure how long you've got left before they send one of us down to get you. They probably think you're all in dillyberry-induced comas by now."

Alex shuddered at the thought, knowing all too well the crazy side effects that came from overdosing on the bubbly purple drink.

"Don't worry," Bear said. He looked from Roka, Kyia and Zain and then to Alex before adding, "I have a feeling we'll be home soon."

Johnny was silent for a beat. "Where *are* you?"

"Gotta go," Bear said, avoiding the question. "See you soon."

Just as Bear moved to disconnect their call, Johnny called out, "Wait!" causing Bear to pause.

"What?"

"News of three teenagers escaping the High Court is all over the Warden network and Dad's probably already putting the pieces together, so in case we don't get a chance to talk later, I want you to know I ran the footage I downloaded through another decryption program, just to be sure."

Alex spoke up then, stepping closer to Bear and ignoring the curious looks from the Meyarins. "And?"

"I'm sorry," Johnny said. "There's no doubt about it now— it's definitely fake."

Alex let out a quiet sigh, as did both D.C. and Bear.

"Thanks for checking anyway, Johnny," Alex said. "We appreciate it."

"I only wish I could have given you different news," he returned. "But anyway, I better let you—"

"Johnny? Can you go into town with Blake and find your brother? It's nearly time for dinner and I'm beginning to worry about him and the girls. Also, would you mind—"

Whatever Bear's mother said next was cut off when Johnny disconnected their communication.

D.C. was the first to say what they were all thinking. "We'd better get going before Johnny and Blake turn up empty handed and have to come up with some excuse for why they couldn't find us."

When Bear nodded his agreement along with Alex, Roka stepped forward to say, "Zain will take you two directly back to Woodhaven. The *Valispath* will return you in time for no one to be further concerned by your absence."

Alex wasn't the only one who picked up on Roka's mistaken count.

"The two of us?" Bear repeated as he swallowed the last of his *laendra*, catching sight of his messy reflection in the shiny golden metal as he lowered the empty goblet. Eyes widening, he lifted the collar of his shirt to scrub it across his face, frantically wiping away the charcoal smears to keep his family from seeing evidence of their trespassing adventure. "Don't you mean the three of us?"

Roka shook his head. "I was going to collect Alex at first light tomorrow, but now that she's here, she might as well stay the night so we can discuss our upcoming plans. That, and I'm guessing her muddied appearance more than either of yours may draw unwanted attention."

As apprehensive as Alex was at the idea of staying the night in Meya, let alone *without* her friends, she knew Roka's words were valid. Given that Johnny and Blake were likely on their way to collect them right now, she wouldn't have time to clean herself up before they would all be expected back at the house for dinner. And there was no way she'd be able to sneak past the keen eyes of Dorothy, William and Gammy looking like a walking, talking Swamp Thing. Bear and D.C. were at least clean from their knees up. Other than their muddy legs and eccentric hairstyles, they looked normal, especially since the *laendra* had cured their insect welts and other injuries. They, unlike Alex, could probably get away with some kind of half-baked excuse about trekking in the forest if Bear's family asked about their state of disarray.

"However," Roka said, turning to Alex, "if you're uncomfortable with that idea, we can stick to the original plan."

"No, it's fine," Alex said quickly. "It'll be good to hear what you have planned. I haven't had a decent nightmare in forty-eight hours—I'm overdue for some new creative material."

Her attempt at flippancy didn't quite hide the nervous edge to her voice, or so she figured, judging by Roka and Kyia's knowing smiles and Zain's snort of amusement.

"Come, mortals," Zain said, striding purposefully from the room and beckoning D.C. and Bear to follow. "I won't be long," he called back over his shoulder to Roka.

D.C. skipped over to Alex on her way towards the door and leaned in to whisper, "Are you sure you're going to be all right here?"

"You know they can hear you, right?" Alex said back, not bothering to whisper. "Meyarin hearing."

"Yes, but if I whisper, they can at least be polite and act like they're not listening."

Alex heard Zain snort again from outside the room.

"I'll be fine, Dix," she replied, putting to a stop the conversation about Meyarin courtesy, knowing it was pointless. "I have my ComTCD. If you're worried, call me."

"Same goes for you," Bear said, stepping up beside them while attempting to pat down his hair, to little effect. "And good luck with your training." He shifted a quick glance to Roka and Kyia and said, "Bring her back to us in one piece, yeah?"

Grins were the only response he was given, so Alex rolled her eyes at the Meyarins and moved forward to give him an impulsive hug of gratitude for at least trying. But before she could wrap her arms around him, he hurriedly stumbled back with his hands raised in protest.

"Uh, no offence, Alex, but, well..." He broke off and gestured towards her body, reminding her that she was covered in dried mud.

She offered him an apologetic grin. "Oops."

"Mortals!" Zain barked from around the corner, sounding impatient. "Make haste!"

Alex made a shooing motion to her friends. "You better go before he conveniently forgets to make the *Valispath* human friendly. Believe me when I say you'll freeze your backsides off if he does."

Roka attempted to cover his laugh with a cough, likely remembering the first time Zain collected Alex from Akarnae in the middle of the night and delivered her to the palace as a living icicle. And that was when it *hadn't* been the middle of winter.

"Make sure they get there alive, Zain!" Alex called as she watched her friends hurry out of the room.

"Don't worry, Alex," Roka reassured her. "He'll keep them safe."

Choosing to trust him, Alex turned away from the doorway and asked, "What happens now?"

"Now you're coming with me," Kyia said, stepping forward and gently wrapping her fingers around Alex's arm, guiding her towards the door. "Let's get you cleaned up."

Five

Alex stood in the middle of her bedroom in Meya's majestic palace after having enjoyed the most luxurious bath imaginable. Once clean, she'd been given a dress made of gossamer so fine that she feared the slightest snag would tear it. It was undoubtedly beautiful, but it also made her feel like a Meyarin version of a fairy princess—something she wasn't entirely comfortable with. Given her clothes and her surroundings, Alex half wondered if she had fallen into a dream.

"This place is unreal," she whispered, glancing around the room in all its glory. The bed alone was like something straight out of a painting. Its tree-like posts were decorated with shining Myrox vines, which tangled into a luminescent arch across the top of a sunburst canopy. But even more spectacular was the open-aired balcony that offered a bird's-eye view of the city spread out over the waterfall-bordered valley.

"I hope you find it to your liking," Kyia said, moving to the fireplace and kneeling down in front of it. Moments later, a rainbow light flared in the hearth and Alex peered around the Meyarin to watch multi-coloured flames dancing in the grate.

"Whoa," Alex said, stepping closer and feeling the heat hit her as if it were an ordinary fire. "What *is* that?"

"*Myraes*," Kyia said, standing again and showing Alex the pouch of glittering powder she held in her hand. "It gives off the heat of a normal flame and burns without wood, yet it's harmless to the touch. It doesn't smoke, either."

"Where can I get some?" Alex asked, entranced by the brilliant flames dancing at her feet. Testing Kyia's words, she crouched down and reached out her hand, carefully moving it forward until the fire tickled her fingers. Sure enough, Alex felt only a pleasant warmth envelop her skin, rather than the searing pain of burning flesh.

Kyia laughed. "Unfortunately, there's very little *myraes* available to us these days. It's a rare commodity amongst our race."

Alex let out a dramatically disappointed sigh. "I guess that means I can't steal your powder and take it home with me?"

Grinning, Kyia said, "You can try, but I don't think you'll get very far."

Alex didn't think so either.

"Come," Kyia said, moving away from the fireplace. "Roka has asked that you dine with us tonight."

Following the Meyarin from the room and onto the *Valispath* that whisked them speedily through the palace corridors, Alex felt the swish of her dress brush against her bare ankles.

"Uh, Kyia? Aren't we a little overdressed for dinner?"

While Alex felt like a royal imposter for traversing the palace in a dress that flowed like running water from her shoulders to the floor, her only comfort was that Kyia had traded in her weapon-strapped warrior getup for a similarly elegant gown— hers being a deep forest green that brought out the emerald in her eyes.

"Correct me if I'm wrong," Kyia responded to Alex's query, "but I thought it best if you weren't covered in mud during your first meal with the royal family and some of the ruling council."

Alex's pulse stuttered. "The royal family? As in…?"

Before Kyia could answer, the *Valispath* came to a halt in front of an impressive double-arched doorway that opened inwardly upon their arrival.

The air rushed out of Alex as Kyia boldly led her into the opulent dining hall where seven Meyarins were seated around a large, ornate table.

All eyes were on Alex as she followed the graceful strides of her escort. In comparison to Kyia's effortless movement, Alex was certain her own steps were reminiscent of a drunken giraffe on rollerskates. Beautiful dress or not, there were undeniable differences between her mortal self and the perfection of the Meyarin race.

Not usually one to care about such things, Alex still felt her face heat up at the eyes gliding over her. She had to remind herself that it had been thousands of years since most Meyarins had set eyes on a human; they were merely curious. But she still couldn't help feeling as if she didn't quite live up to their expectations. Regardless, she held her head high and returned the stares directed her way.

Alex was grateful to see Roka and Zain had saved two empty seats between them, and as Kyia ushered her towards them, she noticed another familiar face.

"Your Majesties," Alex greeted respectfully when she and Kyia neared the two Meyarins seated at the head of the group—one male, one female—wearing intricately jewelled Myrox circlets across their foreheads. She offered her most graceful curtsey to the royal couple, silently thanking D.C. for all the practice she had enforced upon her in their spare time back at the academy last year.

"Alexandra Jennings," King Astophe said, rising to his feet and offering a kind smile. The rest of the table stood as well, and Alex felt even more heat flood her face. "It is good to see you again. I trust you are well?"

"I am, thank you," Alex answered, before tacking on a quick, "Your Majesty." Curtseying lessons aside, D.C. had taught Alex very little about the correct manner in which to address royals. Roka had always been an anomaly, being so friendly that Alex had felt completely at ease around him since the first day they'd met.

"Alex," Roka said, reading her anxiety and moving to her side, "you already know my father, King Astophe. But allow me to introduce my mother, Queen Niida."

The queen was the only Meyarin who had remained seated when the king rose, but at Roka's introduction, she slowly moved to her feet and eyed Alex shrewdly. While lovely to behold, the darkly beautiful Queen Niida displayed no outward affection or kindness. Her ruby lips were pinched tight and her golden eyes blazed with repressed emotion, reminding Alex all too well of the way Aven often glared at her. It was remarkable that both sons had inherited the queen's eye colour, yet only Roka's gaze managed to hold any kind of warmth when he looked upon Alex. In fact, the queen's piercing stare was so cold that Alex had to resist taking a step back.

"It is an honour to meet you, young mortal," the queen said, her lyrical voice like a song. The gentle tone she used was at odds with her harsh body language, causing Alex no small amount of confusion.

"And you as well, Queen Niida," Alex said, carefully pronouncing her name just as Roka had. *Nye-duh*. She wasn't sure if she was supposed to curtsey again since she'd already done so once, so she looked away from the queen's frosty gaze and back to Roka for guidance. His lips quirked in response and he gave an amused shake of his head, swivelling her around until she faced the others standing at the table.

"My father's council," Roka said, gesturing towards the three other Meyarins. "Or at least, part of it. *Lasa* Riza, *Loro* Gaiel and *Loro* Roathus."

Alex nodded at them each in turn, first the willowy female, Riza, and then the two males: the strangely feline Gaiel and the wizened old Roathus. The latter was the oldest Meyarin Alex had ever seen, causing her to wonder just how long he must have lived in order for his hair to turn grey and the wrinkles to start lining his skin. The Meyarin race was immortal, Alex knew, but it surely had to have its limits. Roka and Aven were both thousands of years old, yet they only appeared to be in their late twenties—or early thirties at most. Astophe and Niida looked perhaps in their late thirties or early forties, and they were obviously considerably older than their children. Roathus, however, was pushing what would equate to the appearance of a seventy-year-old man. Alex felt overwhelmed just being in the same room as him, fully aware that he likely owned the wisdom of the ages.

"Please be at rest," the king said to the table, prompting them to take their seats again.

Roka led Alex to her place between Zain and Kyia, with the prince taking the chair on the other side of his betrothed.

"You endured that well, little human, especially knowing the council wanted to lock you up not so long ago," Zain said into her ear. "Well done."

He sounded genuine in his praise, so she sent him a smile of gratitude while hiding her shaking hands under the table. She'd actually forgotten that the council had wanted to hold her captive in a desperate attempt to keep her from opening a doorway for Aven to reach Meya. If it hadn't been for the king and Roka's support, she probably would have been imprisoned, just as Zain had said. But given that Aven *had* made his way through a doorway she'd opened—unintentionally or not—Alex wondered if perhaps she *should* have been incarcerated until the threat had passed. And judging by the looks of both Gaiel and Riza, not to mention the queen, she was not alone in such thinking.

Unable to hold their hostile gazes, she looked to the table, noting absentmindedly that it was made of dark wood, but it also had intermittent splashes and whirls of both Myrox and gold along its design. It was almost too fancy to eat off—or so she thought, until a grumble from her stomach offered an audible sound of disagreement.

As if sensing her hunger, a group of Meyarins dressed in pristine white tunics and tights entered the room, each holding an assortment of platters which they placed carefully around the table. When they were done, they bowed to the royal family and promptly left again.

"*Aegis de garsa. Tenorae sana graifos. Les vael tor,*" Astophe said, and Alex jumped slightly when everyone around the table repeated the words after him. It must have been some kind of prayer or blessing, she realised. Though, who exactly an immortal race would pray to, she had no idea.

"It's an offering of gratitude," Kyia whispered, sensing her confusion. "We give thanks to those who provided the meal, those who prepared the meal, and those in whose company we enjoy the meal."

Alex nodded her understanding and looked surreptitiously around the table, watching as the Meyarins reached for various platters and began dishing food onto their plates. As the servings were passed around to her, Alex followed their lead. When she had a sizeable collection in front of her—all of it unrecognisable to her eyes—she turned to Zain.

"Is this like fairy food?" she asked, as quietly as she could. "If I eat it, am I going to be stuck here dancing naked on the table tops for all eternity?"

Zain, having just taken a bite of something that looked like mashed potato except that it was bright green, instantly began choking. He coughed loudly, trying to clear his throat, drawing the attention of the table. After a few hacking breaths, his airways cleared and he held up his hands to communicate he was okay, and the others slowly returned to their food and quiet conversations.

"Would you like to ask that question again in a way that makes even the slightest amount of sense?" he wheezed out, his voice raspy from coughing so hard.

"You know, fairy food," Alex said. "Food of the Fae."

Seeing his blank look, she glanced shiftily around the table, aware that she had to be careful with her next words. "Where I... come from... there are legends warning that if you enter the land of the Fae—the Fair Folk—or elves, depending on which story you hear, you'll remain there forever if you let any food or drink touch your lips. They usually say you'll be dancing until your feet bleed because you literally can't stop, since the Fae are supposedly not very nice and will laugh at you forever." Alex shrugged. "Of course, there are different tales too, but that one stuck in my head as a child. And let's face it, you guys are as close to elves or Fae as I can imagine."

For some reason, Zain, who had been amused throughout her explanation, scowled at her ending.

"The Fae here are an annoying race of hair-pulling, stone-throwing, insult-hurling critters who are no larger than the size of your hand," he said. "Everything else you've heard is an urban myth circulated by the mortals of this world so their children don't wander off alone. They say that if a youngling enters a mushroom circle, the Fae will shrink them down and take them into their tree hollows, never letting them leave. But I can assure you, they have no such power."

Alex felt a pang in her chest at the memory of Skyla's terror when they encountered the mushroom circle surrounding Raelia. In fact, the last words she'd said to Alex before Aven had ordered her death had been, *'Don't let the Fae take me.'* Even though she'd been shape-shifted into Jordan's body at the time, the panic in her words had resulted in Alex awakening from many a nightmare in the last fortnight. Mostly because Skyla's fears had at least somewhat come true, just not at the hand of the beings Zain described.

"We are not related to those troublesome pests in any way, shape or form," Zain said. His offended look remained in place, but he nodded to her plate. "So eat up, little human, and enjoy the delicacies of Meya—and for the love of the stars, keep your clothes on."

He pointedly turned back to his food, clearly done with their conversation. It was then that Alex felt Kyia's shoulders shaking with laughter beside her, and when she glanced over, Roka was also looking down at his plate and fighting a grin.

Well, at least *they* were amused.

Trusting Zain's answer, Alex picked up her cutlery—which was, like most things in the Meyarin palace, made of Myrox— and cut into what looked like a steaming golden pear. *When in Rome*, she told herself, taking a small bite. As soon as the taste hit her, her eyes lit up with pleasure, and she automatically reached for more of the strange fruit.

Trying one thing after another, Alex steadily made her way through her meal, with each dish bringing more and more delight to her senses.

"You guys sure know how to impress a girl," Alex said to Zain, wondering if it would be against royal etiquette to lick her plate clean once she was finished. "This is incredible."

"This is nothing," he replied, gesturing to the table. "You should see the banquets we hold at the turning of each season. Nothing can compare to the food and merriment of those celebrations."

"That sounds wonderful," Alex said. "I'll have to come along and see for myself one day."

A loud clatter diverted her eyes to the head of the table where she was instantly seared by the burning gaze of the queen. Niida looked irate. In fact, Alex half expected the monarch to leap bodily across the table and attack her with a fork.

"Or, um…" Alex cleared her throat. "Not."

She lowered her eyes and ate the rest of her meal in silence, acutely aware of the queen's hateful glare locked onto her the whole time.

"So, Alexandra," Astophe said, drawing Alex's startled gaze from where she was idly playing with what remained of her food, hoping dinner would soon be over so she could finally leave the tense atmosphere. "I hear you'll be undertaking the *varrungard* tomorrow. How do you believe you'll fare?"

Alex flicked her eyes to Roka, wondering what the king was talking about.

"I haven't had a chance to tell Alex about the trial yet, Father," Roka said. "I was planning on doing so after our meal."

The king raised an eyebrow, letting out a hearty chuckle. "Well, she's certainly in for a surprise, isn't she?"

"I give her an hour," Gaiel said in a snide tone, his face set in a sneer. "Two at most."

"I don't know," Riza said, her voice contemplative. "She seems rather durable for a mortal, and she does continue to surprise us. I say half a day."

Alarmed by their words, Alex looked to Roathus, expecting him to offer his own opinion. But all he did was crinkle his eyes and send her an encouraging wink, something she found unexpectedly reassuring.

"I have the utmost faith in Alex's ability to complete the *varrungard*," Roka said, his words strong and confident. "And without any assistance at all."

Gaiel scoffed. "You expect us to believe you won't be monitoring her progress?"

"Monitoring, yes," Zain answered for Roka. "Interfering, no."

"We'll maintain the same restrictions as we would for any who wish to become *Zeltora*," Kyia said. "Meyarin or otherwise."

"No mortal has done what will be required of her if she is to return within the allocated time," Gaiel said.

"Then she will be the first," Roka said, his assertive tone ending the matter.

Alex, meanwhile, wanted to throw her hands up and demand someone explain what they were all talking about.

Gaiel locked eyes with Roka for a tense moment but then he looked back at Alex, his mouth stretching into an unpleasant smirk. "Let the mortal have her fun. *Sendasa fraes del la norae. Selth gratus fin morna.*"

Roka's jaw clenched in response, and Zain half rose out of his seat, his face livid. But before either of them could retaliate, the king spoke.

"Gaiel, enough," Astophe said firmly, his eyes narrowed. "I think it's time we all retire for the evening." His features relaxed again when he looked at Alex. "May the blessings of the stars be with you tomorrow, young mortal. I look forward to hearing of your success upon your return."

Alex sent him a small smile of gratitude and nodded her head in feigned understanding.

The king rose to his feet and those around the table stood with him, Alex included. Together with the queen, Astophe left the room, followed closely by the council members—with Roathus offering Alex a twinkled smile but Gaiel and Riza ignoring her entirely. Alex rolled the tension from her neck, relieved to be in the sole company of her Meyarin friends again.

"You did well, Alex," Roka told her, with Kyia nodding her agreement beside him. "I'm sorry about my mother. She can be... difficult at times."

'Difficult' wasn't quite the word Alex would have used.

Reading the look on her face, he winced with apology and said, "She hasn't always been so trying. In fact, she used to adore mortals. But things… changed. Try not to take it personally."

"Don't worry, Roka. It's all good." And it was. Because it wasn't as if Alex planned on spending quality time with the queen. She was in Meya for one reason—to train with Roka and learn how to fight Aven.

"Does anyone want to tell me about this thing I'm supposed to be doing tomorrow?" she asked, looking between the three of them.

Zain slung a heavy arm across her shoulders and said, "Let's retire to Roka's suite. We'll explain there."

Six

"Let me get this straight," **Alex said,** attempting to calm her skyrocketing nerves while staring at the three Meyarins lounging in Roka's quarters. "You plan on leaving me out in the forest without any supplies or any… *anything*… and expect me to find my way back here on my own? And I have to do this *overnight*?"

At their nods, she shrieked, "Are you mad? It's the middle of winter out there! I'm going to get lost and end up freezing to death!"

"We won't let that happen, Alex," Kyia said soothingly.

"You said you won't be interfering," Alex returned. "Saving my life is interfering."

"I said we'll abide by the rules given to those monitoring any who wish to become *Zeltora*," Kyia corrected. "Rules which state that, while we cannot *help* you reach your goal, if something were to threaten your life, we would step in. You won't see us, but we'll be closely watching your progress."

That at least gave Alex an illusion of safety, even if she still wasn't keen on being dropped off in the middle of a snow-covered forest and left to fend for herself. The last time she found herself stranded in the woods, she'd ended up with her back torn open by a Hyroa and had to watch Aven kill the beast and steal its blood—blood that later almost killed Zain.

"What's this *Zeltora* thing you keep mentioning?" Alex asked, shrugging off images of the snarling beast.

"It's what we call Meya's elite guard," Roka answered. "Zain here is the... what's the word you would use? Captain? General?" The prince nodded to himself. "Yes, Zain is General of the *Zeltora*. He holds the highest rank of all his fellow guards."

Impressed but not surprised, Alex turned to look at Zain. "No wonder you didn't want to be put on babysitting duty. Talk about a demotion."

He didn't deign to respond, but his silence spoke volumes.

"Those who wish to enter into training as *Zeltora* must undergo the trial—the *varrungard*—for testing," Roka explained. "But it isn't as challenging as it sounds, Alex. We wouldn't send our younglings out on their own if we were concerned for their lives. Try not to worry."

"But I don't want to be a part of your *Zeltora*," Alex said. She then turned to Zain and quickly added, "No offence. I'm sure it's a barrel of laughs having you as a general."

Zain pursed his lips, and Alex realised belatedly that she probably shouldn't antagonise one of only three Meyarins who actually liked her—four including the king, but she wasn't exactly buddy-buddy with him, so he didn't count.

"We're not using the *varrungard* for your recruitment into the guard, Alex," Roka said patiently. "Above all else, it's an aptitude test. It will allow us to assess your character and observe what skills you naturally exhibit, such as strength, endurance, agility, critical reasoning, and the ability to think quickly under pressure. It gives us an indication of what we need to work on most with your training, and how best to teach you."

"You have to remember, we've never trained a mortal like you before," Zain said.

At that moment, Alex thought she saw Roka's eyes flicker with unfocused confusion, as if she'd caught him in a daydream, but then she blinked and he was back to looking steadily at her again.

"Having experienced your Combat classes at the academy, I for one know there is much you must learn before you are ready to cross blades with Aven again," Zain continued. "Not the least of which is allowing yourself to yield to your Meyarin instincts. And without hesitation."

Alex only just managed to suppress a shudder at the reminder of just how abnormal she now was thanks to the psychotic, banished prince's blood running through her veins.

Musing out loud, she said, "So, from what I'm understanding, this *varrungard* thing is less like the Running of the Bulls and more like a peaceful stroll in the woods to see how I handle the scenery?"

Roka shared an uncertain glance with Zain and said, "I'm not sure I understand your reference to oxen, but in essence, I believe you are correct. At least for the stage of the *varrungard* that you'll be completing."

"And you promise to step in if my fingers and toes start to fall off from frostbite?"

"You have our word."

Alex sighed deeply. "Fine. Bring on the fun times." She then had a thought and turned to Kyia with hopeful eyes. "I don't suppose I can borrow some of that *myraes* fire stuff to take with me? Just a pinch?"

Kyia's green eyes sparkled. "Sorry, Alex. Even if I had any to spare, rules say you can't take anything but the clothes on your back."

Resigned, Alex said, "Well, let's make sure I have plenty of those and I just might survive the weekend."

Roka offered a hum of agreement and stood to his feet. "Now that's settled, you should get to bed. You have an early morning tomorrow—we leave at dawn."

"Can't wait," Alex said with clear sarcasm.

Failing to hide her smile, Kyia took Alex's arm and escorted her from Roka's chambers and back through the palace to her room. Their journey was made faster when the Meyarin activated the *Valispath* yet again, transporting them through the walls and up, around and down the floors until they reached the hall outside Alex's quarters.

"Sleep well, Alex," Kyia said, leaving her at the door. "I'll see you in the morning."

Left to her own devices, Alex changed into a nightgown that was even more comfortable than the dress, as impossible as that should have been. Shaped perfectly to fit her body, it fell to just above her knees and felt like silk against her skin.

"I could get used to these clothes," she murmured to herself, twirling in place like a little girl.

Knowing she looked ridiculous but also not caring, Alex continued circling until she was dizzy and then sat down in front of the *myraes* flames, allowing the multi-coloured blaze to lull her into a relaxed trance. She pulled out her ComTCD to touch base with her friends only to notice she had a message notification glowing on her screen, so she activated the link and watched as a miniature D.C. appeared.

"Just checking in, Alex," D.C. said, her voice whispering. "Things here are a bit tense—I think William knows it was us who broke into ChemTech today but he hasn't said anything, so Bear and I are laying low and hanging out with Johnny, Blake and Evie tonight. Gammy made apple pie for dessert, which sucks for you because we know how much you love it."

D.C. looked over her shoulder as if making sure no one was there, then turned back to face Alex again, her voice lower than before. "Zain said he doesn't think we'll see you until the day after tomorrow when we're all back at Akarnae for dinner. He didn't say why, just that it was for your training and we shouldn't worry if we don't hear from you. He promised they'd all look after you, but please be careful, Alex. I know you always try to be, but let's face it—"

She was interrupted by a high-pitched giggle and a little girl calling, "Dikthie! Are you playing wiff me? We haff to beat the boyth!"

"Evie, come say goodnight to Alex," D.C. said just as Bear's sister ran into view. She was currently missing her two front baby teeth, making her even more adorable than normal, especially when she tried to speak and all she could do was lisp.

"Lekthie! Are you coming home to play with uth?" Evie asked, her rosy cheeks and bright eyes adding to her irresistible cuteness.

"It's a holomessage, baby girl," D.C. told Evie, drawing her up into her arms. "Alex will have to play with us some other time. But you and I, little missy, are going to go and kick some boy butt. Am I right?"

Evie nodded enthusiastically. "Leth go!" She turned to face front again and waved wildly, saying, "Buh-bye, Lekthie!"

"Remember what I said, Alex," D.C. said solemnly. Then she offered a hint of a smile and finished, "Now go and show those Meyarins what you're made of."

With that, her friend disconnected the communication and Alex's TCD turned dark again.

Shaking her head with amusement, Alex quickly sent off a written message, the Medoran equivalent of an SMS, that simply said:

```
All good here.
See you on Sunday night.
Will try to stay alive until then.
Can't promise anything once back at academy.
Karter + Finn + Hunter = Death.
A. xx
```

Knowing she had an early morning and a huge weekend ahead of her, Alex allowed herself five more minutes in front of the hypnotising fire before she dragged herself to bed. She quickly discovered that it was, like everything in Meya, beyond luxurious.

"I could get used to this, too," she mumbled, closing her eyes and sinking into the softness beneath her.

It was the middle of the night when something pulled Alex from her sleep. One minute she was dead to the world, the next she was lying there wide eyed and impossibly alert. Heart thudding in her chest, she turned her head when she saw movement in the corner of her room, a shadow outlined by the glow of the city from her balcony view.

Alex leapt out of bed, ready to scream bloody murder until the owner of the shadow stepped into the light of the glowing Myrox. Even when recognition hit her, she still wondered if she should scream.

"Queen Niida?" Alex was proud when her voice didn't wobble, especially considering the fear-spiked adrenaline rushing through her system. "Is everything all right?"

"Is everything... *all right?*" Queen Niida repeated in her whispery, musical voice. She let out a quiet laugh, but there was no real joy in it. "With you here, how can *anything* be all right?"

Alex felt the temperature in the room drop and she shivered as nervous goose bumps arose on her skin.

"I'm sorry," Alex tried. "I don't—"

She broke off when the queen started coming towards her. As much as Alex wanted to retreat, there was no place for her to go, wedged as she was beside the bed and the wall.

"Heed my warning, *mortal*," Niida spat, her voice low. "You are nothing. *Nothing.* I cannot fathom why my son tolerates an abomination like you, nor do I know why my husband indulges Roka's desire to keep you here and train you like a pet. But what I *do* know is that I won't endure your presence along with them."

Eyes aflame, Niida stepped closer and continued, "I don't care how you do it, but I expect you to make up some excuse, some reason to not come back here after you return from your *varrungard*. Go back to that school of yours, go back to your insignificant mortal life, and most importantly, stay away from my family."

The queen was already invading Alex's personal space, but she leaned in further to deliver her parting threat, her melodic voice at odds with the hostility of her words. "I've already lost one son because of your race. I won't allow you to take another from me. If you don't do as I have asked, you'll find I'll do it *for* you, with or without your consent."

Speechless, Alex could only watch as the queen speared her with one final glance before she spun on her heel and silently glided from the room.

Alex wasn't sure how long she stood there, staring at the door, her body trembling. It took her a while to pull herself together, but when she did, she realised she wasn't scared—or, she wasn't *only* scared—she was furious.

"Who the hell does she think she is?" Alex whispered, casting angry eyes around her room in search of anything she could throw without causing damage.

It wasn't as if Alex didn't already have enough problems to worry about without adding an overprotective witch of a queen to her list. Didn't Niida realise that Alex would give anything to *not* be there? She didn't *want* to have to train with Roka. She didn't *want* to have to prepare herself to fight Aven—a fight that would likely only have one outcome, that being Alex's death. She didn't *want* to have to figure out how to save her best friend, knowing that, no matter how much hope she manifested, the odds weren't in Jordan's favour. She didn't *want* a part in any of this, and yet she was stuck right at the centre of everything.

So, *no*. She wouldn't back down because of the queen's high-handed threats. Whether or not Niida wanted to believe it, everything Alex was doing was to *save* her son. To *save* her husband. It was Roka and Astophe who Aven would be coming for first, after all. His royal status could only be reinstated if the king and rightful heir were out of the picture, which would then automatically grant Aven rulership over Meya.

And that was something that could *never* be allowed to happen.

"Alex?"

Jumping at least a foot in the air, she whirled around just as Roka clapped his hands three times, illuminating the room with a soft light originating from an unknown source.

"Jeez, give me a heart attack, Roka!" Alex cried, raising her hand to her chest.

"I knocked on the door before I let myself in," he said, looking at her with concern. "Twice."

Fingers still trembling from her encounter with the queen, she ran them through her hair to hide her nerves. "A Meyarin knock or a mortal one?"

Roka cocked his head. "What's the difference?"

"One I'd be able to hear, the other I wouldn't."

Sending her an apologetic smile, he said, "Ah. My mistake. I'll remember that for next time."

"How about we aim to not have a next time?" Alex said pointedly. "What are you doing in here, anyway? It's nowhere near dawn yet."

"I was worried I'd wake you, but I can see that's not the case," Roka said, his tone questioning. When Alex didn't offer a reason for why she was standing awkwardly beside her bed—

and had been for some time—he continued, "I have an idea I want to run by you, but to do that I have to ask you to come somewhere with me, preferably without Zain or Kyia knowing."

Alex looked at him suspiciously. "Why the secrecy?"

"Because I don't believe they would approve."

She waited a beat, and when he gave no forthcoming details, she said, "You're not exactly selling this idea to me."

Roka's gaze was steady on hers when he said, "Have I ever given you reason not to trust me?"

"Why do I have a feeling my answer is going to mean I lose more sleep tonight?" Alex mumbled.

"That's the spirit," Roka said, beaming. "Follow me to the *Valispath*, Alex. We shouldn't be gone too long."

She looked at him inquisitively when he held a hand out for her to precede him. "Can't we just take off from in here?"

"There are certain rooms in the palace that are warded against direct *Valispath* use—like the throne room and dining hall, for example," he said. "For those rooms, we have to arrive outside them and enter or exit normally through the doors." He gestured around her room. "Your suite is one of the warded ones, so we'll have to come and go from the hallway in order to access the Eternal Path."

Nodding her understanding, Alex motioned for Roka to lead the way and she followed him out the door, grumbling about impossible princes pulling her from bed and ignoring his quiet snort of amusement.

The moment he halted and drew her closer to summon the *Valispath*, Alex knew she was going to regret not having asked Kyia if there was a way to lock her bedroom door. First the queen, now this.

"Are you planning on telling me where we're going?" she yelled over the icy wind as the Path led them out of the palace and into the city.

Roka quickly reached out and activated the shield to protect her from the elements. "Sorry, Alex. It can be easy to forget you're human."

Not sure if that was good or bad, she rubbed some heat back into her arms and replied, "No biggie. But seriously, Roka— where are you taking me?"

He didn't respond straight away. Instead, he looked her over with a furrowed brow and muttered, "I didn't think this through very well."

"Roka—"

"Here," he interrupted, unclasping his black cloak and handing it to her. "Put this on."

Frowning, she did as he requested, belatedly realising how unsuitable her nightgown was for their midnight escapade. "Ro—"

"The reason Zain and Kyia wouldn't approve of what we're doing tonight is because we *shouldn't* be doing it," Roka said, answering before she could get the question out again. "I have informants in the city who have been keeping an eye out for signs of Aven. They've discovered that he's somehow communicating with his remaining *Garseth*—his Rebels. We need to know how he's doing that. We need to know where he's hiding, or at least how he's managing to avoid anyone discovering his whereabouts. We need to know *anything* that will help us better understand what we're facing."

Alex raised her eyebrows at his unspoken implication. "How exactly am I supposed to help with that?"

The *Valispath* moved through the side of a building and sailed to a stop in a large foyer-like room made out of what looked to be black crystal. The walls, floor and ceiling were fully constructed out of the shiny dark substance.

Acting on a hunch, Alex asked, "Is that Shadow Essence?"

"No. It's unrefined *traesos*, pulled directly from the *abrassa* and shaped by the power of the great Aes Daega herself. This place—we call it *Taevarg*—is a prison; the only one in this world that can contain an immortal being indefinitely."

Alex had to take a moment to absorb his words. But even then, she was at a loss. "I have no idea what you just said, other than the prison part. Let's focus on that, since it seems important."

"Zain told me that when you and your friends first came to Meya, he dragged a prisoner up from here because he believed you were affiliated with Aven," Roka said. "A *Garseth* named Niyx. Do you remember?"

Alex knew exactly who he was talking about. She made a face and said, "That guy was a jerk. He made everyone think I was one of Aven's Rebels. I mean, who does that?"

"Focus, Alex," Roka reprimanded softly. "We don't have much time."

"Is that why you brought me here? Because of Niyx?"

"Of all my brother's followers we've captured over the years, he's the most renowned," Roka said, a tinge of bitterness coating his voice. "I'm certain he knows something, despite being locked away since Aven's banishment, but he refuses to tell us anything. I'm hoping your presence might unsettle him. Perhaps enough that he'll let something slip."

"My presence?" Alex repeated. She arched an eyebrow. "Don't sugar-coat it, Roka. Don't you mean my scent? Aven's scent? Whatever it is that makes me smell like one of the *Garseth* because I share his blood?"

At least Roka had the grace to look sheepish. "I was trying to be vague and ease your level of discomfort, knowing how sensitive you are to this topic."

Alex snorted and drew his cloak tighter around her body. "I guess it's the thought that counts."

"Will you do it?" Roka asked. "Will you talk with him?"

She shrugged, deliberately pushing aside her apprehension. "Sure. What's the worst that could happen?"

"Nothing," the prince promised, a little too quickly in Alex's opinion. "And I'll be with you the whole time."

"Then by all means, lead the way."

Seven

Niyx looked exactly the same as when Alex had last seen him. Despite his scruffy appearance, complete with dirty, ripped clothes, he was still unfairly handsome. His choppy, black hair contrasted starkly against his pale skin, and his amethyst eyes drew Alex in, holding her gaze captivated—at least until he spoke.

"Well, if it isn't my mortal friend," he said, his soulful voice washing over her and causing her to shiver. "I must say, I was expecting to see you sooner." His eyes flicked to Roka and he smirked. "But I guess your keeper has had you on a tight leash."

Roka didn't respond, yet his body language was anything but relaxed. Alex had sensed his growing tension ever since he'd led her down a dark staircase—made of the same black *traesos* stuff as the rest of the prison and lit sparingly with dim lanterns—and through a maze of cells, stopping at one with an impossibly thick door blocking it. To open it, Roka had inserted a stylus-like engraved Myrox key into a small indent in the door. There was an inscription etched into the metal—a flowing language Alex hadn't been able to decipher.

"The only power greater than darkness is light," Roka had translated for her, turning the key until the lock clicked open. "Even the smallest star can brighten the blackest of nights."

Alex had merely raised her eyebrows at the philosophical inscription before following him into the cell.

"Nice place you've got here," Alex said, having no idea where to start but also refusing to rise to Niyx's bait. "Cosy. Quaint. Could use a little colour, but hey. Black works for you, right?"

Given that the entirety of his cell was constructed out of the dark *traesos*, his accommodations were undoubtedly rather bleak. He was sitting on a thinly cushioned pallet resting against one side of the wall, and other than a few books, there was nothing to offer him any kind of entertainment. Alex couldn't imagine being in his position, locked in the one small room for thousands of years with barely any social interaction, only let out a few times a day to use the amenities and stretch his legs. It was a wonder he hadn't gone mad.

"It's the colour of my soul, so it seems fitting," Niyx said. "But you didn't come all this way to talk about the décor, did you? Speak your cause and be on your way."

Alex crossed her arms. "What's the rush?" She looked around pointedly. "It's not like you have any pressing engagements."

"Or so you'd like to believe." He turned to Roka with his taunting smirk still in place.

"Fine," Alex said, drawing his attention back to her in an effort to keep her escort from doing anything... rash. Taking a small step closer to Niyx, she said, "You seem like a smart guy—"

"Do I?"

"—which means you've probably figured out why we're here—"

"Have I?"

"—so we'd appreciate it if you would be willing to cooperate with us—"

"Would you?"

"—and answer some of our questions," Alex finished, her eyes having narrowed further and further with each of his interruptions.

Niyx, on the other hand, seemed greatly entertained. "What did you say your name was, young mortal? Aey-something?"

"I didn't tell you my name," she said. "But it's Alex."

"Alex," he repeated, drawing the two syllables out with clear amusement.

"Niyx," Roka snarled, losing patience.

The prisoner waved a lazy hand in the air. "Ask your questions," he carelessly offered. "My time is, apparently, all yours."

Surprised by his easy—perhaps *too* easy—acquiescence, Alex turned to Roka. He too looked suspicious, but he moved a step closer and asked, "Tell us what you know about Aven's current plans. Where he's hiding. How he's communicating with the *Garseth*."

Immediately Niyx threw back his head and burst out laughing.

"Look around you, *my prince*," he said between guffaws, still managing to add venom to the mocking title he afforded Roka. "Does it seem like I'm in a position to provide any of those answers?"

Roka stepped forward again. "I know he's been communicating with you. And you with him."

Niyx raised one dark brow. "Is that so?" He turned to Alex and asked, "What do you have to say about this, my young friend?"

"I say you need to stop calling me that," she replied instantly. "I'm not your friend. I never have been, and I most definitely never will be."

Niyx's unique purple eyes danced with dark humour. "I find it fascinating that you, of all people, would say that. Especially given our... history."

Shaking her head—in pity or bewilderment, she wasn't quite sure which—Alex said, "Niyx, I met you once for a total of about five minutes, tops. That hardly counts as history."

If anything, his humour only increased. He turned to Roka and said, "I'll make you a deal, *kregon*. Give me five minutes alone with her and I'll answer one question. That's all you get—take it or leave it."

"No chance," Roka said, voice hard. He reached for Alex and said, "I was wrong to bring you here. Let's go."

"Roka, wait," Alex said, digging her feet in as he started dragging her from the room. "Maybe we should—"

"Alex, no," Roka said firmly. "I refuse to leave you alone with him."

Biting her lip, Alex looked from Niyx, who was reclining casually and looking more like a king in his palace than a prisoner rotting in a cell, to Roka, who was as cold and rigid as the *traesos* walls surrounding them. It wasn't right that her friend was so tense while their enemy was so relaxed. Niyx wasn't supposed to have it easy. *He* was the bad guy.

"You brought me here for a reason," she whispered to Roka, releasing herself from his pincer-grip on her forearm and giving him a reassuring squeeze. "Let me do my job."

"Alex—"

"You keep reminding me to trust you, Roka," she said, holding his concerned, golden gaze. "Now it's time for you to trust *me*."

"But—"

"And besides," she interrupted again, "you'll be just on the other side of the door. You'll be able to hear if I need you."

Roka shook his head. "The *traesos* is nearly soundproof. Even with my hearing, I'll only be able to hear murmurs, not actual words. Five minutes is a long time. I won't have any idea if you're in trouble."

"Sure you will," Alex said, mustering up a quirky grin that she didn't quite feel, given the knots in her stomach. "If you stop hearing the murmurs, you'll know we've stopped talking and he's probably trying to kill me." She patted him on the chest, bringing her point home. "*That's* when you step in."

"Alex—"

"Roka, we need this," she told him, determined. "You said it yourself. So stop babying me and let me do this so I can go back to my ridiculously comfortable bed and get a few more hours of sleep before you haul me out again to dump me in a forest. Okay?"

The prince's jaw was hard for most of her mini speech, but towards the end his muscles relaxed and his eyes began to lighten. "You know," he mused, "I believe my brother just might be in more trouble than I've anticipated."

"I'll take that as a compliment."

Roka chuckled softly, and the sound made Alex feel as if she'd won an almost-but-not-quite-Meyarin-of-the-year award.

"Go, Roka," Alex said, giving him a nudge towards the door. "And you'd better think up a good question. Make my time worth it."

He sent her one last look of concern before he hustled out the door, sealing it closed behind him.

"Finally," Niyx muttered, jumping to his feet with cat-like agility. "I thought he'd never leave."

Nerves zinging, Alex held up a hand as he prowled towards her. "I'd prefer it if you stayed where you are."

"I'm sure you would, kitten," he said, still moving closer but, thankfully, stopping a few feet away. "Unfortunately, if there's one thing I've learned in the last few millennia, we seldom get what we desire."

"Why did you want to talk to me alone?" Alex asked, edging out from around him and walking slowly across his cell, deliberately putting space between them.

"I remember you, you know," he said. "I shouldn't, but I do."

His voice held a strange tone, strange enough that Alex stopped trying to distance herself and paused, even as he stepped closer to her again.

"I remember it like it was yesterday."

Considering it was only three months ago when they'd first met, Alex would have been worried if he *didn't* remember her.

"I remember you too, Niyx," she said carefully, not entirely sure how mentally stable the Meyarin was after all.

He let out a quiet, mirthless laugh. "No, you don't. Not like I remember you. No one else does, either. Only me."

Alex decided that it was a good time to back away from him again. But she hadn't realised that she'd been retreating towards a corner—a corner that she was now boxed into.

"I was out hunting, you see," Niyx continued, his amethyst eyes on hers but his mind clearly elsewhere. "I was attacked by what you call a Hyroa and its blood was poisoning my body." His gaze became even more unfocused. "There was foreign blood in me. Blood not only my own. No one remembers, no one except me."

With those senseless words, he closed the remaining distance between them until they were toe to toe. He reached out a grimy hand, trailing it down her cheek to rest along the underside of her jaw.

Alex was frozen to the spot. Despite her confident words to Roka, she was now most definitely out of her comfort zone. She knew the power of the immortal race—one slight adjustment and the Meyarin could easily snap her neck.

As if reading her mind, his hand flexed, tensed and curled around her flesh.

"Do you have any idea what it would solve?" he whispered, his eyes staring unfocused at his hand on her neck. "All I have to do is tighten my fingers. It would change everything. Fix *everything*. Tell me, do—you—have—any—idea?"

"Niyx..." Alex was terrified of saying the wrong thing lest she provoke the clearly out-of-his-mind Meyarin. "What is it that you want from me?"

At her softly spoken words, he blinked once, twice and seemed to snap back to himself, releasing his grip and taking a quick step backwards.

"A life for a life," he whispered. "I'm now absolved of my debt."

Alex's whole body was trembling. She didn't know what to say. She didn't know what to do. All she knew was that something was happening, something beyond her understanding. Something that, even compared to everything else she'd experienced in Medora, didn't make sense.

"Our time is nearly up, young mortal," Niyx said, appearing normal again. Or at least as normal as he'd been when Roka had been present. "I've already told you more than I should. But I'll give you a bonus for old times' sake."

Alex wanted to tell him he was crazy. But she thought it best to at least wait until she had reinforcements before she did so.

"I'm listening," she said, pleased when her voice didn't come out as the whimpering croak she'd expected.

"Hear me, mortal," Niyx said, leaning in once more and trapping her in his hypnotic gaze. "With the lashing of the branch, the time will be at hand. All will change." He blinked, breaking the trance, and quirked his head to the side. "Or rather, nothing will."

At that, the door to the room opened and a highly agitated Roka stepped into the cell. Seeing Alex cornered with Niyx so close, the prince's handsome face hardened to stone and he rushed forward, his movement so fast that, to Alex's human sight, he was like a blur.

"Easy, *norot*," Niyx teased, raising his hands and stepping away from Alex. "We were only chatting."

Roka moved Alex to shield her behind him.

"You've had your time with her," Roka said. "Now uphold your end of our bargain."

"Go on then, Prince," Niyx said lazily, lounging back onto his pallet. "Ask your question."

Roka didn't need to be asked twice, clearly desiring to leave.

"Aven's goal, we know, is to take the throne of Meya so that he'll have ruling control over the citizens and the *Zeltora*, which he will then use to wipe out the human race of Medora," Roka said, painting a very bleak picture in Alex's mind. "We know he's been seeking out any *Garseth* who evaded capture and remained loyal to him all these years, meeting with them in secret to devise a plan to infiltrate the palace and finish what he started millennia ago."

"Was there a question in there somewhere?" Niyx asked dryly. "Because I must have missed it while you soliloquised me to a wakeful death."

Roka took an angry step forward, but Alex placed her hand on his arm, holding him back.

Accepting her hint to not let Niyx get to him, Roka inhaled deeply and said, "I want you to tell me the name of one of those *Garseth* loyal to him, one whom he has sought out upon his return. That is what I ask of you. To give up one of your own."

Niyx's relaxed demeanour didn't change, but his eyes flashed. "I'm flattered that you think me capable of such knowledge, given my... unique circumstances." He looked pointedly around the cell.

"Don't try to fool me, Niyx. You and I both know you have an answer."

Alex hoped Roka knew what he was doing. She would have been more inclined to ask what Aven's strategy was, or better yet, when he planned on carrying it out. Did Roka *want* to be looking over his shoulder every moment for his brother's impending attack? She didn't understand how knowing a random *Garseth*'s name would help their cause. Unless of course Roka was able to use it to follow the trail directly to Aven... in which case, it actually made sense.

"One name," Roka said again. "I'm certain you know many; just give me one and our bargain will be fulfilled."

When the prisoner remained silent, the prince barked out, "Answer me!"

"Very well, *kregon*," Niyx said, his voice low. "I will answer you." He leaned forward from his seated position and held Roka's gaze. "*No.*"

Sensing the need to intervene before Roka lost his patience entirely, Alex jumped in. "What do you mean, no?"

"No means no, mortal," Niyx repeated, leaning back again, his face smug. "In any language or race."

She frowned at him. "But we had a deal."

"I said I would answer one question," Niyx replied. "An answer is, by definition, a response. The response I gave was 'no'... Ergo, your question has been answered."

This time Alex didn't keep Roka from hauling Niyx up and slamming him into the crystalline wall.

The Meyarin prisoner laughed darkly. "You're off your game, Roka. Better luck next time."

Alex closed her eyes tightly in resignation and then moved forward, reaching out for the prince. "Let him go. He's not going to help us."

Roka hesitated, his grip still firmly grasping Niyx's shoulders, but when Alex squeezed his arm he gave a terse nod and released the prisoner, taking two steps back.

"You're right," Roka said to her. "This was a waste of time."

Not sparing Niyx a second glance, Roka spun around and marched back towards the door, all but dragging Alex along behind him. She glanced over her shoulder one last time just before they exited the dark room and found the prisoner smirking at her.

"I'll see you soon, my mortal friend," he called after her with a secretive, knowing smile. "But not as soon as you'll see me."

"He's crazy," Alex said when she and Roka were travelling back to the palace on the *Valispath*. "Like, certifiably."

"I'm sorry I put you through that," Roka said, and he truly did look sorry. "I really thought... Well, it doesn't matter now."

"Hey," Alex said, her tone comforting. "Don't worry about it. It was worth a shot, right?"

"I should have expected he would never hold up his end of the bargain," Roka said, clearly unwilling to let go of his ire so quickly. "I never should have left you alone with him."

Alex held her arms out to her sides to show that she was none the worse for wear. "I'm still here and in one piece. That's all that matters." She decided it was best not to mention Niyx's 'life for a life' comment, just in case Roka decided to turn around and exact retribution for the prisoner's implied death threat.

"What did he want with you, anyway?" Roka asked.

Alex looked off into the distance, allowing the sight of the glimmering waterfalls floating down from the Golden Cliffs to soothe the ragged edges of her nerves.

"Just some weird stuff about remembering me. Nothing he said made any sense." She shook her head and turned back to Roka. "Like I said, he's crazy."

Roka ran a hand through his tousled dark hair. "Well, if nothing else, at least we know there's no point in seeking him out again. Niyx has nothing to gain by helping us. He's imprisoned for life, so long as my father rules Meya. His only hope is for Aven to free him."

Alex nodded, agreeing with Roka's assessment. "What were those things he called you? 'Kreg'-something and 'nor'-something?"

Roka furrowed his brow before realising what she was referring to. "*Kregon* and *norot*?"

"Yeah, those."

His face relaxed and a hint of a smile touched his lips. "I was planning to teach you some of our language, but not, perhaps, the kind of vernacular Niyx practises. You might say that *kregon* and *norot* are somewhat… derogatory terms. And not appropriate in a public setting."

"He was insulting you?"

Roka's smile widened for some strange reason. "He was. And rather crudely. *Kregon* alone makes reference to the rear end of a—"

Alex held up her hands. "Nope, stop. I don't want to know."

Roka chuckled but did as she requested and ceased speaking.

"I don't get it," Alex said. "Why do you seem so happy about him calling you rude names?"

"Because I figure if you're asking me about Meyarin curse words, you're probably not too traumatised by the events of this evening."

Alex blew out a frustrated breath. "Roka, seriously, I told you I'm fine."

"And now I believe you."

She shook her head at him and mumbled, "You're going to have to get over your protective tendencies if you want to train me properly. You know you have to attack me, right? That's the whole point of teaching me how to fight like a Meyarin."

"When you have a confident grasp on your abilities, *little human*,"—he sent her a sideways grin at his use of Zain's mocking nickname—"I'm sure my 'protective tendencies' will dissipate. But until then, you're going to have to accept that I'll be watching out for you."

The *Valispath* had entered the palace while Roka had been speaking and it was now swiftly moving them upwards towards her room. When they came to a halt outside her door, Roka turned to face her and quietly said, "I know this past fortnight can't have been easy on you, Alex, not with your worry over Jordan and your fears about Aven. I admire your strength more than I can say. As long as I have it in me to give, I will *not* allow that strength to crumble by any hand. If that makes me overly protective, then so be it. Zain and Kyia, too—we're all going to remain by your side, holding your hands until this dark threat has passed."

Alex tried to swallow through her suddenly clogged throat.

Roka's shoulders relaxed and he reached out to pull her into a comforting hug.

"I know you didn't want any part in all this," he whispered to the top of her head. "But never forget that you are stronger than you realise and more capable than you could ever imagine. Of that you have my word."

"Stop, Roka, you're killing me here," Alex whispered back, her voice croaking.

The prince released her and stepped back, his serious demeanour lightening as he smiled teasingly down at her. "Well, we don't want that now, do we? Not before you embark on the *varrungard*, at least. You'll need to stay alive if you want any chance of surviving tomorrow's adventure."

Relieved as she was that their emotionally charged moment had passed, Alex still narrowed her eyes at him. "You told me it's not dangerous."

Roka laughed once and turned her around, pushing her towards her door. "I said no such thing. Get some sleep, Alex. I'll see you in a few hours."

Eight

"Crash course in Meyarin wilderness survival," Kyia said early the next morning.

The sun had barely begun to crest over the Golden Cliffs when the female Meyarin had dragged Alex out of bed and helped her into a fur-lined outfit that would, hopefully, keep her alive in the wintry forest. Then, still half asleep, Alex had been shoved onto the *Valispath*, only managing to remain upright because she'd spent the entire journey propped against Zain, who had, for the most part, been highly entertained by her humanness.

"Any running water you can find in the Silverwood is pure and safe to drink," Kyia said, and Alex forced herself to pay attention, knowing it was important if she wanted to survive the *varrungard* and make it back to the academy the following night. "It might be the thick of winter, but the streams run straight from the mountains, so they shouldn't be frozen over."

"Water, safe," Alex recited between yawns.

Zain chuckled and Kyia's green eyes sparkled.

"That's right, Alex," the female Meyarin said. "Now, onto food."

She reached into her cloak and pulled out a handful of what looked to be uniquely shaped nuts and coloured fruits. Having not had any breakfast, Alex's stomach grumbled at the sight of the Meyarin food and she reached forward, but Kyia snapped her fingers closed around them.

"They look appetising, don't they?" When Alex nodded, Kyia continued, "They probably taste as good as they look, but if you eat them, they'll also be the last thing you ever consume."

Alex jerked back. "What?"

"The Silverwood is home to many dangers, Alex, not the least of which is a hungry stomach," Zain told her. "There's a reason why the endurance stage of the *varrungard* trial takes place out here."

Wishing she had taken a doggy bag from dinner, Alex lamented, "So you're saying I have to go hungry for the next two days?"

Kyia shook her head. "If we had more time, I'd be able to teach you the difference between safe and poisonous berries, if nothing else. But we don't have long enough for you to learn anything with the confidence needed to take appropriate risks. However, all *Zeltora* initiates know the basics of woodland survival before they embark on the *varrungard*, so I don't believe it's fair for you to go in blindly unprepared, especially considering you haven't grown up in these forests."

The Meyarin dropped her lethal handful to the ground and glanced around the snow-covered clearing where they'd landed, her eyes searching for something. When she found what she was after, Kyia motioned for Alex to follow her over to a large tree. Like the rest of the surrounding forest, the tree had shimmering charcoal leaves and a shining silver trunk, with roots spread across the snowy ground.

"You'll find that *laendra* grows in abundance in these parts of the forest," Kyia said, pointing to a batch of flowers nestled between the upraised roots of the tree. "As you experienced yesterday, it's primarily used for healing purposes. But it can also be substituted for nourishment over short periods of time." She plucked one flower up by the stem and handed it to Alex. "Eat. It will quench your hunger and strengthen you for the day."

Alex looked at the flower in her hands. As silver as the drink version she'd downed the day before, the flower itself glowed from within, almost pulsating with life. It was so beautiful that she almost felt sad that Kyia had ripped it up, but she could see that the Meyarin spoke true about its abundance. Now that Alex knew what to look for, she spotted the *laendra* growing at the bases of trees all around them.

Not sure how to go about eating a flower that was almost the size of her hand, she looked to Kyia for guidance.

"Peel the petals from the bulb and eat them one by one, crunch into the body like a piece of fruit, then chew on the stem." Kyia shrugged. "That's how I eat it, anyway."

Alex followed her instructions, overwhelmed once more by the caramel-vanilla taste that danced on her tongue. After just a few petals, she was warmed from the inside out, feeling revitalised and ready to take on whatever the *varrungard* might throw at her.

"If you happen to become wounded for any reason," Zain said, "cut open the bulb and spread the juice directly onto your injury. The healing will occur faster that way."

Alex bit into the bulb just as he made his statement, seeing for herself just how juicy the body of the flower was. Silver liquid trickled down her fingers and onto the snow, leaving a glowing trail at her feet.

"I seriously love your food," Alex said, now chewing the stem. "Everything tastes so good."

"We *have* had thousands of years of agricultural experience," Zain said dryly. "You'd hope that's enough time to get a few things right."

Before Alex could respond, Roka blurred into the clearing.

"Sorry I'm late," he said by way of greeting. "I must have slept in."

He sent Alex an amused grin, fully aware that she hadn't been afforded such a luxury.

"You're lucky I just ate a magical flower and feel like I could stay awake for the next three hundred years," she told him. "Otherwise I think I'd kick you right now."

He chuckled lightly and turned to Kyia and Zain. "Is she ready?"

"Probably not," Zain muttered under his breath, and Alex couldn't help but agree.

Kyia sent Zain a warning look. "She'll be fine."

"Of course she will be," Roka returned confidently. He looked at Alex. "You understand what you have to do?"

"Find my way back to Meya," Alex recited. When they looked at her as if expecting more, she raised her eyebrows. "That's all, right? Or have I missed something?"

Roka shook his head. "No, you're perfectly correct. You just make it sound so… simple. But I suppose the first part *is* that simple. It's only when you reach the end of the journey that you'll face some of the more challenging complications, when your energy is at its weakest after lasting through the endurance phase. But until then, you're right: simple." His smile was too innocent for Alex's liking, and she pursed her lips in response as he finished, "You don't have any questions?"

Alex scoffed. "Of course I do. Like, 'Do I really have to do this?' And, 'Can't I just jump back on the *Valispath* with you?' Or how about, 'Can I at least have my ComTCD back so I can GPS the quickest route out of this forest?'"

Her final question earned her confused stares so she sighed heavily and turned to Zain. "If D.C. or Bear call, make sure you remind them that I'm okay and not to worry."

"I will, little human," he said, patting his pocket where he'd placed her ComTCD after taking it from her, claiming it would be considered 'cheating'. "But I did warn them you wouldn't be in contact until you see them tomorrow evening."

"Just in case," Alex said, and he nodded in agreement.

"You won't see us, but we'll check your progress at frequent intervals over the next two days to make sure you're safe," Roka said. He placed a steady hand on her shoulder and bent down to look her in the eyes. "To make it through the *varrungard* in the allocated time, you have to think like a Meyarin, Alex. Open your senses, *listen* to what is around you. Move like one of us. If you do all that, you will easily reach Meya by sundown tomorrow."

"And if I don't?"

"Then we'll simply collect you on the *Valispath* and bring you home," Zain said, reaching over to tussle her hair in that big brother-like way of his. "And you'll have enjoyed a nice, quiet holiday in the woods."

"In other words, I'll have failed," Alex deduced.

"The *varrungard* is nothing more than an aptitude test for you," Kyia reminded. "It's not an attempt for you to join the *Zeltora*. Your mission is to try to allow your Meyarin characteristics to flow through you. And who knows? Perhaps you will even enjoy yourself."

"Have I mentioned I don't like camping?" Alex mumbled under her breath, before she inhaled deeply and tried to muster some enthusiasm. "Right. Someone point me in the right direction."

Kyia swivelled Alex until she was facing what could have been north, south, east or west, for all she knew. Having never been a Girl Scout, she had no idea how to find her bearings. And even if she could, she was in a whole new world, so it would likely have done her little good, regardless.

In other words, she was *so* screwed.

"Any last advice?" she asked, trying to delay their leaving.

Zain smirked at her. "Don't let your toes fall off."

Instead of being concerned by his comment, Alex grinned and lifted one of her fur-lined, knee-high boots. "Have you seen these babies? It's like I'm wearing hot water bottles on my feet."

It was true. The clothes Kyia had forced the drowsy Alex into were fully insulating her from the cold. Her pants were made of a windproof, leathery material that was impossibly supple, and her thick, wrap-around tunic dropped to mid-thigh, keeping her nice and toasty. Her outfit was white and laced with thinly threaded Myrox, which—according to Kyia—was why Alex felt so comfortable despite the winter chill. It also meant Alex blended in effortlessly with the snow-and-silver woodland.

"I'm pretty sure my toes will be okay," Alex continued to Zain. "It's the rest of me that's up for debate."

"Then we'd better get you started," the burly Meyarin said, clapping her on the shoulder so hard that her knees buckled. "Travel swift, little human. You'll be back with us before you know it."

He stepped away and Kyia followed suit, sending Alex an encouraging smile. Roka, however, moved closer.

"If you lose your way, follow the path of the sun," he said. "It will lead you directly to Meya. The endurance stage of your *varrungard* trial will end the moment you reach the Golden Cliffs." He leaned in and whispered, "You're not technically allowed a weapon, but since A'enara isn't here in physical form right now, we won't consider it cheating. But don't forget your blade, should trouble find you."

Alex's eyes were wide when he pulled back. "Exactly what kind of trouble might 'find me', Roka?"

"You would be extremely unlucky," he said, answering but also not answering. "I'm sure it won't be a concern, I merely wanted to… remind you. Now go, Alex. And remember: think like a Meyarin."

"*Think like a Meyarin,*" Alex muttered grumpily to herself later that afternoon, her tone deeper in imitation of the prince. "*Think like a Meyarin, Alex.*" She relaxed her voice to its natural pitch, "Well, *sure*, Roka. Because I know how to do that *so* well."

On the whole, her *varrungard* experience wasn't going wonderfully. She was tired, thirsty, and despite her Myrox-lined clothes, beginning to feel the sting of the cold as the sun began its retreat beyond the horizon. She likely would have had blisters all over her feet too, if not for the healing properties of the *laendra* that she snacked on whenever she came across the glowing flower. But while it pumped her body with renewed heat and invigorated her energy levels, the sweet plant did little to actually fill her stomach.

"This sucks," she whined, panting heavily as she waded her way through a blanket of particularly deep snow. She'd mostly been able to travel through the forest unhindered, but wherever she was right now was laden with the thick powder, making it nearly impossible for her to get anywhere fast.

In fact, speed was becoming a very real problem for Alex. No matter how hard she tried, for some reason she just wasn't able to tap into her Meyarin abilities. She'd done it before—back when she'd been with Aven and Jordan just before Kaldoras. With her life threatened, she'd somehow managed to run through the forest with super speed before escaping through a Shadow Essence portal.

Looking down at her bare fingers, Alex mentally cursed Zain for confiscating her Shadow Ring. Had she still been wearing it, she would have been sorely tempted to instantly transport herself back to Meya, aptitude test be damned.

It took another hour before Alex stumbled across her first source of water for the day, and considering she'd been hiking for hours, she was about ready to throw herself bodily into the slowly trickling stream if it meant soothing her parched throat.

She'd been tempted to suck the snow as she trailed, but with the dying sun, she hadn't wanted to risk lowering her core temperature further. Not that the icy water was going to be much warmer.

Drinking until she was satisfied, Alex sat back on her heels, glancing up at the silvery-charcoaled canopy above her. Very little light was filtering through the trees now and she knew the sun had almost completely set.

The human part of Alex told her that the wisest thing she could do was find shelter and bunker down for the night. Unfortunately, even if she was struggling to utilise her Meyarin blood, she could still hear Roka's 'think like a Meyarin' encouragement in her mind. A Meyarin, Alex knew, wouldn't stop for the night. A Meyarin had super senses and super speed and would likely already have made it back to Meya by now. But in the event that they were still out in the forest, there was no way they would pause their *varrungard* trek to take a rest. They would keep going, all night if they had to. So that was what Alex would do.

As much as she dreaded being out in the cold, darkening forest, Alex was determined to pass her trial. Part of that was because she felt like she owed it to Roka, Zain and Kyia, who all believed in her; part of that was because of the snotty council members, who *didn't* believe in her; and part of that was because she, more than anyone, knew what was at stake. She had to get a handle on her Meyarin instincts if she wanted even the smallest chance of surviving another encounter with Aven. And if this *varrungard* test could help unlock her newfound senses in any way, then she needed to give it her all.

Inhaling deeply, Alex pushed up from the stream to her feet and closed her eyes.

"Listen, Alex," she whispered to herself. "Just listen."

With her eyes firmly closed, she concentrated on her breathing, on the sound of air moving through her lungs and out her nose. She could hear her heartbeat in her ears, so she focused on that as well. *Ba-dum, ba-dum, ba-dum.* Then she expanded her hearing outwards. She heard the trickle of the water flowing along the stream at her feet. She listened to the crunch of the snow when she shuffled her feet and the whistle of the wind as it blew through the trees. Far in the distance she heard the sound of birds bedding down for the night, creatures rustling in the underbrush, scavenging for their evening meals. She heard the soft paw prints of a larger animal wading a path across the snow, along with the pitter-patter of smaller paws trailing close behind it; cubs with their mother, perhaps.

Keeping a tight hold on the sounds, Alex focused on her other senses. She felt the cold breeze kiss her face, she smelled a faint scent of earth buried deep beneath the snow at her feet and she tasted the freshness on her tongue from the mountain-crisp water, as well as the faint aftertaste of *laendra*.

Finally, she opened her eyes.

Alex stood motionless as she took in the sights around her, as if seeing the world for the first time. Everything was brighter; everything was clearer. When the heavens opened up and flurries began to trickle down on her, Alex watched them in slow motion, seeing the intricate details of each individual snowflake. She held her hand out, watching as the ice melted on her skin, experiencing everything with microscopic clarity.

Fully in control now, Alex pulled her senses inward. She felt her blood pumping in her veins, her muscles tense and ready for action. She was overwhelmingly aware of the power in her body and the strength at her disposal.

Shifting forward slightly, Alex felt every tendon and ligament yield with supple expectation. And when she used her heels to push off from the ground, she wasn't surprised when she moved straight into a sprint where her feet barely touched the snow as she tore through the forest, blurring through the trees at an impossible speed.

It was exhilarating; intoxicating, even. Alex hadn't been able to enjoy the experience when she'd been running from Aven, but now, even with the wind slashing at her face and bringing tears to her eyes, Alex couldn't help but feel truly free for the first time in what felt like forever.

Maybe this varrungard *thing isn't so bad after all*, she thought, closing her eyes and knowing that her other attuned senses would keep her from ploughing headfirst into a tree. *Because I sure could get used to this*.

Alex ran all night, following a trail of moonlight through the forest and continuing on well into the next morning. She stopped only when she had to—if she came across new streams to drink from or when she felt the faint stirrings of hunger. She wasn't sure if it was the Meyarin blood in her veins or the repeated ingestion of *laendra*, but her energy never failed her, nor did her new abilities. Granted, each time she ceased running, she had to take a considerable amount of time to centre herself and 'listen' before she was able to take off again, but on the whole, she was extremely proud of her progress. In fact, she had travelled so far that the leaves of the trees had just begun transforming from glimmering charcoal to glistening honey, showing that she had now reached the forest forming the boundary around Meya. At the speed she was moving, it wouldn't be long at all until she reached the Golden Cliffs and came to the end of her *varrungard*. It was perhaps even possible that she would be back in time for lunch.

Oh, how she hoped Gaiel and Riza would be at the palace to see her triumphant return. She'd sure show them what it meant to be 'durable for a mortal'.

Increasing her speed in anticipation of her arrival, it was just as she broke through a tight copse of trees bordering a large clearing that she was brought to a sudden, staggering halt. And that was because an agonised roar bellowed out from somewhere close by, causing her to bend at the waist while slapping her hands protectively over her ears.

The sound was unlike anything she'd ever heard before. To her Meyarin-sensitive hearing, it felt like needles were being shoved into her ear canals. Through watering eyes, she looked up just in time to witness the source of the sound fall from the sky above the golden trees and come to a skidding, sliding stop at the edge of the clearing.

Forgetting her pain at the sight before her, Alex scrambled backwards until she hit a tree and froze to the spot.

"No freaking way," she gasped out.

What she was looking at wasn't real. It couldn't be.

Because in front of her, barely thirty feet away, lay a dragon.

Nine

The beast was a pitch-black colour, easily twice the height of an elephant and three times its length. Its scaly hide rippled when its muscles contracted as it fought against the glowing net it was ensnared in, a net that had tangled its wings and legs, pulling it from the air and trapping it on the ground.

Hot puffs of air blew from its huge nostrils, melting the snow near where it lay. A keening cry emitted from its throat, one that spoke to Alex of both pain and fear.

She had no idea what to do. On one hand, she was looking at a *dragon*. A mythical creature capable of eating her without so much as having to chew first. On the other, she couldn't condone the senseless entrapment of such a magnificent creature. But what if…

Alex didn't get to finish her thought before the beast tensed and turned its majestic head her way. Its eyes gleamed like orbs of blue fire, yet the pupils were dilated with terror.

"Please don't eat me for this," she whispered, cautiously moving towards the creature. Its gaze remained locked on her the whole time, tracking her steps. If anything, it looked increasingly more fearful the closer she approached. Its keening transitioned into a high-pitched wail as it struggled fiercely against the bonds.

"It's okay," Alex found herself saying when she was just a few steps away. She was bending slightly, her weight in the balls of her feet, her hands raised in a calming manner. "I'm not going to hurt you."

She closed the remaining gap between them and the dragon's eyes widened further. Its breathing turned even more haggard, the panting bursts complete with alarming sparks of blue fire liquefying the ice at Alex's feet.

"Take it easy, big fella," Alex said, keeping her voice soft, willing her hands not to shake even though she was, perhaps, more scared than the beast. "Let me take a look at you."

Upon closer inspection, Alex recognised the substance the netting was made out of—thin strands of Moxyreel.

"This complicates things," she murmured, knowing that the only thing that could cut through Meyarin steel *was* Meyarin steel. She didn't allow her mind to consider why, exactly, the dragon was caught in a Moxyreel net, nor who was to blame for bringing down the creature. Instead she tapped her finger against her lip and wondered how best to try and free it.

"*Abrassa.*"

Alex jumped backwards, nearly slipping on the melted sludge at her feet. She turned stunned eyes to the creature. "No way! You can *talk*?"

"*Abrassa,*" the creature said again, his voice deep and male but also sounding young, like an adolescent. "*Abrassa…* closing… Hurry."

"*Abrassa?*" Alex repeated, her nerves slightly hitching at the word. "I don't know what that is."

"*Abrassa…* Void."

Alex shook her head, not understanding.

The dragon let out a frustrated, spark-free breath and Alex had to resist taking another step back. The last thing she wanted was to anger the creature.

"*Abrassa…* Void… Must return."

His disjointed sentences made little sense to Alex.

"Just try to stay still," she said, reaching forward to inspect the Moxyreel, figuring the best thing she could do was release him so he could return to wherever he came from. "I'll try to get you out of this."

"Pulled... between. Through *abrassa*," the dragon said, his words remaining nonsensical.

"Sounds painful," Alex said, giving up on trying to understand his broken attempts at speaking her language. She hesitantly threaded her fingers underneath a strand of Moxyreel, surprised when they brushed up against the dragon's black scales only to find his thick hide oddly soft to the touch.

"Painful..." the dragon said. "Golden One cause... much pain."

"Mmm-hmm," Alex said distractedly while tugging at the Moxyreel. She wished Zain hadn't taken everything from her, since she would still be wearing her Myrox bow-and-arrow necklace. But then she remembered something he *hadn't* taken from her. Something he *couldn't* take.

Raising her palm outwards was all it took for the ice-like blade to appear in her hand—a dagger that, not so long ago, she would have cringed away from. Now, however, she was oddly comforted by the weight of A'enara between her fingers.

The dragon stilled as he took in her weapon, his brilliant cerulean-coloured eyes growing wider than before.

"I'm not going to hurt you," Alex told him again, realising how it might look.

But for some reason, he didn't seem afraid. He appeared... awed.

"This net is made of Meyarin steel," Alex said, just for something to say but not sure how much he understood. "Supposedly only Myrox can cut through it, but I'm hoping..." She trailed off and gestured to her weapon with a shrug. "Just don't freak out, okay? I need you to stay still so I can try and cut the net without hurting you."

The dragon nodded his large head against his constraints. "Cut… Hurry."

"Uh-huh," Alex replied, carefully sliding A'enara between the dragon's scales and the Moxyreel. "This *abrassa* thing is closing, right? Don't worry, I'll be as quick as I can."

"*Abrassa* closing… But not why hurry," the dragon said. "Golden One come… More pain come… Must hurry."

Alex froze as an impending sense of dread settled over her. "Golden One? Do you mean… You're not talking about Aven, are you? The banished Meyarin prince?"

"Golden One… Bad… Pull Xiraxus through *abrassa*… Must return before…"

Every muscle seized in her body as she glanced anxiously around the clearing. "Before what?"

"*Before.*"

Shaking her head at her frustrating lack of comprehension, Alex tried not to panic at the idea of Aven coming their way. She could think of no one else who matched the description of 'Golden One'. And if he was the one whose net ensnared the dragon, then he was surely en route to retrieving his prize; something Alex absolutely did not want to wait around for.

"I hope this works," she said quietly, pressing the sharp edge of her blade against the netting. Relief flooded her body when it cut through as easily as if carving through water. Alex didn't even care that A'enara wasn't made of Myrox and therefore shouldn't have been able to damage the Moxyreel. She'd long since come to understand that the weapon had its own secrets.

Slicing through strand after strand of the netting, Alex made short work of freeing the beast. When she managed to cut the final threads binding his taloned forearms to his torso, the dragon let out a roar of triumph and rose onto his hind legs, spreading his impressive wings out to the sides, making him seem even larger than he already was.

Daunted by his sheer size, Alex quickly scrambled backwards. But when his roar mellowed out into a whimpering sound, she halted her retreat.

"Are you—Are you hurt?" she asked as he hunched over, curling around himself protectively.

"Fly..." the dragon said. "Need... fly..."

Pushing the worry of Aven's whereabouts from her mind, Alex took charge again. "Here, let me see."

The dragon seemed to hesitate as if deciding whether or not to trust her. But then his eyes landed on A'enara still in her hands and he seemed to come to a decision. He lowered himself back to the ground and carefully extended his wing. It was then that Alex noticed the jagged slash across the thick muscle near to what she presumed was the elbow joint, with sticky golden liquid splashing across the membrane and dripping down onto the snow. Blood, she realised, strange as the colour was.

"Need... fly..." the dragon repeated, his words urgent. "Golden One come... *Abrassa* closing... *Need fly!*"

Thinking quickly, Alex told him to wait there and she took off into the trees closest to them, returning to his side with her hands full of fresh *laendra*. Following Zain's advice, she used her dagger to cut into the bulb of the flowers, releasing the concentrated juice inside. She then let go of A'enara so that both her hands would be free, and the weapon vanished from sight again.

"This might sting," she told the dragon. "I'm not sure. But, uh, just in case."

Once again, she found herself mentally chanting *'Please don't eat me'* as she reached out and smeared the *laendra* nectar onto the wound.

The dragon hissed and Alex felt her heart skip a beat, but he settled again and let her finish her ministrations. As she watched, the wound began closing before her eyes and she smiled with satisfaction.

"There," she said when the injury sealed completely, no longer oozing golden blood. "All better."

She patted him on the chest, forgetting for a moment that she was dealing with a dragon and not a dog, then she stepped back.

"We both better get out of here," she said, casting another anxious glance around the clearing. "Especially if—"

"*Golden One come!*"

Startled, Alex tripped backwards and onto the ground as the dragon reared up on his hind legs, wings snapping out to the side.

Her Meyarin senses switched on as adrenaline flooded her body, and Alex could suddenly hear exactly what the dragon was referring to—loud, running footsteps moving swiftly through the forest towards them.

"Xiraxus fly... Save from Golden One..." the dragon said, beating his powerful black wings, causing the snow to dust up around Alex like tiny ice missiles.

On all fours, she scrambled backwards, her face stinging from the strength of his air gusts. Not sure if she was more terrified of Aven's approach or the magnificent beast preparing for flight, Alex decided to run. But as soon as she got to her feet, the dragon launched from the ground and then swooped down at lightning speed to snatch her up in one of his massive talons. With her torso firmly clasped in his powerful grip, the dragon burst out of the clearing and up, up, up into the skies above them.

Too winded by his claws to muster up a scream, Alex could only watch in silent horror as the canopy of the forest below became smaller and smaller the higher they rose.

"*Abrassa*... closing..." the dragon repeated, his voice reaching Alex through the mighty wind. He sounded panicked, terrified. "No... time..."

If it was possible, the dragon increased his speed. Alex couldn't breathe, so harsh was the air pummelling against her body and so tight was his hold on her. She felt as if her ribcage was cracking under the pressure of his talons as she lay dangling helplessly in his grip. Agonising pain rippled over her as black dots sprung around the edges of her vision. Just as it all became too much and she knew she was going to pass out, the dragon put in one final surge forward.

"*Abrassa*," the dragon roared. "Hold... on..."

Alex had nothing to hold on to. She was barely able to keep her eyes open anymore. But before they rolled into the back of her head, she saw a shimmering cloud of energy spring into being, like an explosion of ink bleeding across the sky—ink that the dragon flew them straight into...

... and then Alex knew no more.

Ten

When Alex regained consciousness, it wasn't a peaceful, slow awakening. Instead, she shot up with a gasp, heart pounding as she took in her surroundings. Only when she realised she was safely back in her canopy bed at the Meyarin palace did her thumping pulse begin to calm.

Turning her head to her balcony, she was soothed by her view of the city shining in the early afternoon sunshine. Her hands tentatively moved to her chest, feeling for broken ribs or internal bleeding, but there was nothing, not even any lingering pain.

"Did I dream it all?" she wondered aloud, just as the door opened and Kyia walked into her room.

Alex leaned back against her pillows and turned wide eyes to the female Meyarin, blurting the first thing that came to mind. "Please tell me excess consumption of *laendra* has hallucinogenic properties, Kyia, because, no joke—I was just flying with a dragon."

Kyia paused mid-step, her head cocked to the side as she looked at Alex.

"*Laendra?*" Kyia repeated, approaching again until she was next to the bed.

"I ate a lot of it on the *varrungard*," Alex explained. "Like, *a lot*, a lot. So it's either that, or I really did save a dragon from a trap set by Aven and ended up with a free ride for my troubles. I'm sure you can see how I'm hoping it's the former rather than the latter, even if it means I'll have to fess up to my parents and tell them I unintentionally overdosed on what was probably the Meyarin equivalent of magic mushrooms."

Kyia's forehead bunched in apparent confusion. "*Varrungard?*"

Alex raised her eyebrows at the Meyarin's strange behaviour. "Yeah, Kyia. The *varrungard.*" She gestured an arm around the opulent room. "I'm guessing I didn't make it back on my own, which sucks. I was so close, too. But then..." Alex shook her head. "What happened, anyway? Did I pass out from the hallucination? Who found me?"

Just then the door opened again and Alex's stomach moved straight to her throat at the sight of the Meyarin who entered.

In an instant she was on her feet with her arm outstretched, mentally summoning A'enara. The weapon appeared in a flaming blaze of light, the pyrotechnic display surprising Alex enough to nearly drop it. She quickly tightened her grip, even when flicks of blue fire travelled from the blade along the pommel and halfway up her arm, harmlessly caressing her skin.

Startled, but with far more important things on her mind than the now fiery sword, Alex's free hand reached out to drag Kyia backwards as she began a hasty retreat towards the balcony, putting as much distance between them and the new arrival as possible.

"Aven," Alex hissed. "What are you—*How* did you get in here?"

Before anyone could say or do anything, Kyia yanked herself free from Alex's grip and quickly backed away from her.

"Kyia!" Alex cried, stretching for her again but the Meyarin skipped out of reach. "What are you doing? It's *Aven*! Get away from him!"

But Kyia didn't listen to her. Instead, the female Meyarin looked at her with wariness and moved directly to the banished prince's side.

Alex's mouth dropped open when Aven protectively pulled Kyia close.

"*Lenasa sae de la frayon?*" he said to her, his voice soft, almost gentle.

Without Alex knowing how, the words translated instantly in her mind: 'Did she hurt you?'

Blinking in astonishment, Alex felt her hands shake as she took another step backwards, now out onto the balcony with the sun streaming down on her from above.

"What the hell, Kyia?" she demanded, her voice sounding betrayed even to her own ears.

Before she could come to any kind of understanding, the door opened again and Roka walked in. Not sure if she was relieved or even more terrified, Alex called out to warn him, "Roka—it's Aven!"

The dark-haired prince glanced at her in muted curiosity as he strode fearlessly towards Aven and Kyia and said, "*Varria trae fraeden de senus rayos.*" Again, the words translated instantly in Alex's mind: 'It appears I missed the introductions.'

"Apparently we did too, brother," Aven replied in the lyrical Meyarin language. His eyes were on Alex, his lips quirking as if amused. But his smile was different. It wasn't as... dark. It seemed strangely genuine. "As always, our fame precedes us."

"She may know of us, but I've never seen her before," Kyia said with a shake of her head, also speaking her native language which Alex was somehow able to understand. "And I would remember, given that she shines with the binding of a draekon."

"That is indeed curious, as is the weapon she wields," Aven said, his gaze focused on A'enara. "That's no normal blade. If I didn't know any better, I'd say it was—"

Full body trembles assaulted Alex's frame and she interrupted in a whispered voice full of disbelief and confusion, "Is this some kind of joke? What is *happening*?"

"What language is that she speaks?" Aven asked, peering at her intently.

Roka was looking at her with renewed curiosity. "It's the common tongue. It would seem she is… confused."

Kyia snorted. "I don't need to understand her language to see that, Roka. The poor thing looks terrified. And she likely has reason to, since we found her half dead at the base of the Golden Cliffs."

Aven chose that moment to step forward, his hands raised in front of him as he approached Alex. "It's all right," he told her, the melodic language nearly hypnotising. "You're amongst friends here."

Eyes wide, Alex retreated with every step closer he moved until she was backed up against the knee-high railing of the balcony. She glanced over her shoulder and wobbled slightly at the sight of the ground far, far below. Making sure to keep her weight leaning *away* from the dangerously low balustrade, she warned, "I don't know what's going on, Aven, but I swear—"

Her threat was cut short when an almighty roar sounded from above. Alex clapped both her hands over her ears, and with A'enara no longer pointing at Aven, he took the opportunity to rush towards her. She swiftly aimed her weapon in warning again and scampered away from him, but in doing so, her feet slipped on the smooth surface of the balcony. Arms flailing uselessly, she took in Aven's horrified expression as he lunged for her. But he wasn't fast enough, and Alex fell backwards— straight over the railing.

A bloodcurdling scream tore from her throat as she plummeted down the length of the spiralling palace towers and towards the radiant city below. But before she could fully comprehend that she was about to die, a hulking shadow blurred through the air until it sailed directly under her.

Recognising the dragon, Alex banished her blade and reached out to grab onto him. She wrapped her legs around his shoulder blades just over his wing joints and her arms tight around his neck, holding on for dear life as he gave a mighty push upwards, stopping their free-fall and heaving them back up into the air.

Hold on, Alex, she heard clearly in her mind, the dragon's familiar voice sounding so close that she jerked in surprise, almost losing her grip on him.

"You're in my *head* now?" she all but screeched as he flew them straight up and over the waterfalls of the Golden Cliffs and the forests beyond.

I'll explain everything in a minute, he told her, his words no longer broken but instead forming complete sentences. *I promise.*

Alex was about a second away from hyperventilating as they soared over the Silverwood, her near-death experience and encounter with Aven wreaking havoc on her adrenaline levels. She forced herself to count backwards from twenty, attempting to focus only on the numbers and nothing else. Then she did it again. When she was nearing the end of her third countdown, the dragon slowly crested an arc, turning on his wing until they gradually spiralled to the ground and landed smoothly.

Ha! How awesome was that! His triumphant voice cheered in her mind. *I think I'm going to be great at this bonding thing—you didn't even jostle. Go me.*

Quite sure she was having a stroke, Alex unclenched her limbs and slid bonelessly to the ground where she collapsed to her knees, her wobbly legs unable to hold her up. She noticed they were back in the Silverwood somewhere, but bizarrely, there was no snow. None. Zip. Nada. In fact, judging by the heat of the sun overhead, wherever they were, it wasn't even winter.

In a trembling voice, she again asked, "What is going on here?"

You don't look so good, the dragon said, leaning his huge face closer until he was barely a handbreadth away. Had she not been frozen in shock, she definitely would have scurried backwards when his hot breath tickled her eyelashes. *Should I find you some water or something?*

Alex shook her head. Then she shook it again. "How can you—I don't—" She had too many questions and didn't know where to begin, so she settled on asking, "How can I hear you in my mind? And so clearly?"

The dragon sat back on his haunches and said, out loud this time, "I'm Xiraxus."

Alex blinked. "Xiraxus?"

"You can call me Xira," he offered.

"Zeera?" Alex repeated his pronunciation.

Xiraxus bobbed his head. "You're Alex. You wield the Sword of the Stars."

"I—What?"

"The Sword of the Stars," Xiraxus repeated. "The Bringer of Light. The Blade of Glory. The Weapon of the Ages."

Alex looked blankly at the dragon. "Let's ignore A'enara for the moment and go back to you being a talking dragon who can speak in my mind."

Xiraxus let out an annoyed snort. "Draekon," he said. "Not dragon. Draekon."

Making a mental note, Alex said, "Fine, a *draekon* who can speak in my mind. And that would be because…?"

If it was at all possible, Xiraxus actually looked guilty. His big body squirmed and his blue eyes looked away from her, reminding her of a puppy who was aware it had done something wrong. "I may have… panicked slightly."

Alex moved from her knees to cross her legs underneath her, not ready to test her shaky limbs just yet. "Panicked? Yeah, I got that with all your incomprehensible '*abrassa* closing, Golden One come' mutterings. What was all that?"

"The *abrassa* is the Void Between," Xiraxus told her. With his words, a picture forced itself into her mind of the ink shimmering into the sky; darkness they had flown straight into.

Alex gasped. "Did you do that?" she asked, referring to the invasive image she certainly hadn't conjured on her own.

Xiraxus nodded and said, "Unbound mortals can't survive travelling through the *abrassa*. But I was scared. The Golden One was nearly upon us. You were kind to me. You saved me. I couldn't let him hurt you. But I didn't have time to drop you off anywhere else."

"So you took me with you through the *abrassa*," Alex deduced.

He nodded again. "Your heart nearly stopped halfway through the Void. I had to enact *vaeliana* with you. It was the only way for you to survive. But even with the bond, I lost hold of you when we came out this end. The *Zeltora* found you on the outskirts of the Great City and they took you back to the palace before I could get to you."

Alex frowned and repeated, "'When we came out this end'—what does that mean?"

"The Golden One pulled me through the *abrassa*," Xiraxus said. "He pulled me from here. From... before."

Alex just stared at him. "You're going to have to start making more sense." But even as she said it, her heart began picking up speed again, because deep down she already knew what he was implying. Unless she'd entered a parallel universe—which was not impossible given what she'd experienced in Medora so far, but it was still unlikely—there was only one way Kyia and Roka would have peacefully been in the same room as Aven. There was only one explanation for why Kyia allowed Aven to pull her close, why Aven called Roka 'brother' in such a fond voice, why none of them had recognised her—why none of them but Roka even understood her language.

"Xira, this *abrassa* thing... this 'Void Between'... What is it *between*, exactly?"

Fidgeting slightly, the draekon said, "Space. Worlds." He huffed out a gust of air and admitted, "Time."

Time.

Flipping heck.

Alex closed her eyes tight. "This has *got* to be a nightmare. Any minute now I'm going to wake up."

"The bond between us allows me to understand your language so we can freely communicate," Xira said, unaware that she was on the verge of a breakdown and couldn't handle much more. "You'll also be able to translate all of the dialects I know, which is why you understood Meyarin."

This is madness, Alex thought, rubbing her temples.

"I know you nearly as well as you know yourself," Xira went on. "I know your thoughts and how you think. So I believe it will help if you consider the *abrassa* to be like a black hole. It's a tear in the space-time continuum. The Golden One—the future Aven Dalmarta—found a way to open it and pull me through to your time, which is forbidden. We're not supposed to mess with time." Xira's nostrils flared nervously. "Mother says bad things happen when you mess with time."

Alex tried to keep a grip on her budding horror as he confirmed what she feared was true. "You're saying we're in the past? That's why everything was messed up back at the palace—why Aven wasn't on a murderous rampage and none of them knew me?"

Xiraxus bobbed his head again. "Yes. The *abrassa* brought us both back to my time."

Alex wasn't sure if she wanted to throw up or pass out. In a weak voice she said, "You know, on the list of weird things that have happened to me—and believe me, it's *not* a short list—this tops the chart." Her vision started to go fuzzy so she forced herself to inhale a deep, calming breath. "Okay, so I'm in the past. But this isn't a problem because you can just take me back home using your *abrassa* thing again. Stranger things have happened, right?" She quickly amended, "To someone else— stranger things have surely happened to someone else."

Yeah, doubtful.

She shook off her thoughts and stood to her feet, pleased to discover they were only a little unsteady underneath her. "After you fly me back to my time, I say we act like none of this ever happened for the sake of both our sanities. Agreed?"

"Uh…" he said, shifting nervously. "There's one problem."

Alex felt certain she wasn't going to like what he was about to say. But she didn't get a chance to hear it before a bellowing cry came from overhead, echoing throughout the forest.

"Uh-oh," Xiraxus whispered, hunching his body with his tail between his legs.

"What was *that*?" Alex demanded.

"Zaronia." Xira curled even tighter into a ball. "My mother."

That was all the warning Alex received before a mass the size of a small house fell out of the sky and landed with an earth-shaking thud in the clearing. Alex had thought Xiraxus was huge, but compared to the deep purple draekon before her, he looked like a kitten beside a lion.

"Xiraxus, what have you done?" the purple draekon— Zaronia—all but shouted in a clicking, scratching, rumbling language that Alex effortlessly understood.

"I'm sorry, Mother, I had to," Xiraxus replied in a whimper. "Alex saved my life."

The purple draekon stilled and repeated in a deathly quiet voice, "Alex? You know its name?"

Without waiting for a response, Zaronia stretched her massive neck forward until her hulking face neared Alex.

Oh my gosh, she's going to swallow me whole, Alex thought, frozen to the spot.

Zaronia jerked with shock, reared back and turned startled eyes from Alex to Xiraxus. "You bonded with her," she said aloud in the common tongue, with something like fear threading through her surprised words. "I can hear her mind—I can see the evidence on her skin—You bonded with a *mortal*! What were you *thinking*?"

"Mother, I had to," Xiraxus said again, sounding everything like a petulant teenager. "She would have died in the *abrassa* otherwise. We travelled too far back for her to survive the time jump on her own."

Zaronia's fiery eyes widened even further at that. She released a furious sounding growl. "You brought her through the *abrassa*?"

"I panicked!" Xiraxus said, jumping to his feet and causing the ground to tremble under Alex. "The Golden One—he pulled me through to her time. He was going to hurt me. But she saved me. I couldn't let him capture her, but I didn't have time to move her to safety *and* make it back through the Void. So I… brought her with me."

Alex had to clap her hands over her ears when Zaronia roared so loudly that the trees all around them shook down to their roots.

Turning on her massive hind legs, Zaronia stomped away from them, only to spin once more and pace back. Three times she did this, huffing with ill-disguised rage.

"Mother—" Xiraxus tried, but he was cut off abruptly when Zaronia snapped her frighteningly large teeth at him.

Suddenly the purple draekon was in front of Alex again—

one moment she was pacing, the next she was stationary and *way* too close for comfort.

"I can't think with the air so thick down here," Zaronia said. "The girl must come back with us. I'll decide what to do with her—what to do with both of you—once we return."

"Um, sorry to interrupt," Alex said, speaking up for the first time. Her voice was as shaky as the rest of her, but she felt it imperative to put forth her opinion. "It's just, I have to get back to my, uh, time. It's certainly been... *memorable* meeting you both, but I'm hoping Xiraxus won't mind opening up that *abrassa* thing again and sending me home." When both draekons looked at her without so much as blinking, she added, "Any minute now works for me."

Zaronia turned to Xiraxus. "You didn't tell her?"

"I was going to," he said in a small voice. "I hadn't made it that far before you got here."

The purple draekon released what sounded very much like a weary sigh as she turned back to Alex. Like her son, Zaronia's eyes were a brilliant blue colour that began to glow with an inner light, a sight so hypnotic that Alex was lulled to drowsiness.

"Sleep, mortal," Zaronia commanded in an oddly soothing voice. "When you wake, you shall have answers."

And without giving her body permission to do so, regardless of where she was or the fact that she was alone in the woods—and in a different time period—with two massive, mythical carnivores, Alex's eyes drifted shut, her legs gave way and she fell into a sweet, blissfully dreamless sleep.

Eleven

Mortal, it's time to awaken.

"Mortal!"

Alex's eyes snapped open to see a reptilian face the size of a small car barely inches from her own. Incapable of thinking let alone controlling her reaction, she screamed so loudly, so shrilly, that it hurt even her own ears. It certainly surprised the hulking beast who jerked backwards in alarm.

Alex scampered away but her retreat was halted when she bumped into a jagged rock wall. She sat pressed up against it, panting in terror, while her mind slowly began to clear enough for her to remember that, at least so far, the creature in front of her hadn't eaten her. It was therefore *possible* that she just might not be in as much danger as she had believed upon her shocked awakening.

"Zaronia?" Alex said. "What…" She trailed off, not wanting to offend the massive draekon by shouting, 'Does the phrase 'personal space' mean anything to you?' Instead, she said, "You, uh, gave me a fright there. Sorry for screaming in your face."

"It's been a long time since my kind has been so near a human," Zaronia said. "I forgot how fearful your race can be. It is I who must apologise—I didn't mean to startle you." The draekon tilted her head slightly. "Please, come with me."

Alex used the rock wall to push up on her wobbly legs, noting somewhere in the back of her mind that it looked like they were in a cave. As she began following Zaronia through a large channel hewn into the rock, she noticed the intermittent torches of the rainbow-flamed *myraes* lighting their path.

"Are we underground?" Alex asked, somewhat stupidly since she had already deduced they were at least in some kind of cavern.

Zaronia, surprisingly, let out a rumbling chuckle. "I suppose you could say that. However, I doubt you will in a moment."

Raising her eyebrows at the draekon's vague answer, Alex continued onwards in silence until a stronger brightness at the end of the tunnel came into view, the sunlight flooding the darkness.

"No human has ever stood upon our lands before," Zaronia said, moving her shadowing bulk out of the way. "Welcome, young mortal, to Draekora."

Eyes wide and mouth gaping, Alex barely heard the draekon's words, so consumed was she by the sight in front of her.

"We're, um—" She cleared her throat. "We're definitely not underground, are we?"

Way to state the obvious, Alex thought, looking out over the cluster of islands floating above the clouds. It was like… It was like… Alex didn't *know* what it was like. She had nothing to compare it to. No visual imagery to her recollection could match the impossibility of the view.

At least a dozen islands were spread out as far as her eyes could see, suspended mid-air as if by invisible strings. One or two were barely the size of football fields, but others were large enough to hold entire mountain ranges. A few even had smoking volcanoes, with molten lava trickling steadily down the sides.

The floating mass to Alex's left contained a dense jungle that hugged a large lake filled with the clearest blue-green water she had ever seen; water that tumbled over the edges of the land and straight into the thick cloud cover below. The island to her right was covered in snow and icy glaciers, while another further on from that was overcome by desert, with cracked earth and rugged sand dunes.

There was no rhyme or reason to the nature of the islands, but they were, without a doubt, the most magical, fantastical sight Alex had ever seen—and she'd seen a number of amazing things since her arrival in Medora.

"How are they floating?" Alex wondered aloud, unable to muster much volume in her awe.

"The Draekoran Isles are largely made out of a lightweight metamorphic rock not native to this world," Zaronia answered. "When we arrived here long ago, we brought a fraction of our lands with us. The natural gravitational pull of Medora's atmospheric pressure enables our home to remain above the clouds, exactly where we draekons belong. As you can see, up here we are free to be ourselves."

Alex could see that. Because it wasn't just the islands that captivated her. It was also the multitude of draekons inhabiting them.

The magnificent creatures were everywhere. Some were soaring lazily through the skies, some were bathing in the lakes and waterfalls splashed across the islands, some were napping in the sunshine—draekons of all sizes and colours filled her vision.

"Does the rest of Medora know you're up here?" Alex asked, amazed that such a place could exist.

"The Meyarins are aware of our existence, though few have the privilege of ever seeing Draekora for themselves," Zaronia said. "We tend to value our privacy. However, we do allow them to partake in the collection of the *Ter'a Ora Vorren*—the Pool of Tears—twice a year to replenish their supplies."

Before Alex could ask what supplies the Meyarins could possibly need from the Draekorans, let alone from something called the 'Pool of Tears', a shadow emerged from beneath the cave's edge, causing Alex to skitter backwards.

With a muted *thump*, Xiraxus landed on the outcropping of the cavern tunnel, his tail aloft and helping him keep his balance on the precarious ledge.

"Alex!" he greeted, sounding overjoyed to see her. "I came as soon as I felt you were awake."

Knowing the only explanation for his stalkerish statement was the bond that was supposedly now between them, Alex asked, "Any chance you want to explain this bond that keeps getting mentioned? Kyia—one of the Meyarins—also said something about me 'shining with the binding of a draekon', or something like that. What are you all talking about?"

"All will be answered soon," Zaronia said, outstretching her wings and prompting Alex to duck lest she wanted to lose an eye. Then the great purple draekon launched herself off the edge of the cavern and into the sky.

"Come on," Xiraxus told Alex, circling carefully on the cavern edge until his side faced her. "Everything will be explained at the Kyvalon. Everyone's waiting for us there."

Alex raised her eyebrows, wondering who 'everyone' was and what 'Kyvalon' meant. Her inner translator appeared to be letting her down on the word's interpretation.

"Hurry, Alex, or Mother will return," Xiraxus said, lowering his torso to the ground, stretching his wing out, and gesturing with his head for her to climb aboard.

"You've got to be kidding me," she said, unthinkingly.

Xiraxus said, "You've flown with me before—why is this any different?"

"Uh, maybe because I didn't have any choice the last two times?" Alex pointed out.

"The Kyvalon isn't on this island," Xiraxus told her. "We can only get there by flying."

"I'm usually okay with heights, but this is asking a lot," Alex said, sliding closer to Xiraxus and peering out over the edge of the island to see nothing but clouds beneath them. She still couldn't believe she was *this close* to what she'd call a dragon, not to mention being about to fly with him through the sky—again.

"Good thing you're not the one keeping us in the air, then," Xiraxus said. "Now jump on, Alex. We don't want to keep them waiting."

Certain she was out of her right mind, Alex reached out and grabbed hold of the rough black sinew of Xiraxus's wing to help her balance. Even while lowered to the ground, his shoulder was still significantly higher than her head, so she had to manoeuvre herself up by first placing her foot on his forearm and stepping up to push off his elbow, jumping to grip the spiky scales at the base of his neck and pulling herself onto his back.

Panting from the surprising amount of effort it took, she said, "Is there an easier way to do that?"

"When I'm a little older, my wings will be strong enough for you to run straight up them," Xiraxus answered as she settled herself into a somewhat secure position just in front of his wing joints. "Until then, we'll just have to practise. But don't worry, you'll get used to it. The only way to get around Draekora is by air."

"How old *are* you, Xira?"

"I'm still a hatchling," he answered, rising to his feet and causing Alex to clamp her thighs around him and grab a tighter hold of the scales at his neck. "Only eighteen of your mortal years."

"Eighteen is considered a hatchling?" Alex said, surprised. That was the age most humans were considered adults.

"Hold on, Alex," Xiraxus said, bunching his hind legs underneath them. "It's time to fly."

And with that, he pushed off from his haunches and propelled them up into the air.

The moment they left the solid, stable ground—which was ironic, since it was technically a floating hunk of rock in the middle of the sky—Alex closed her eyes, figuring it was best to remain oblivious for the duration of their journey. But Xiraxus wouldn't have any of that.

Open your eyes, Alex, he called mentally. *You won't want to miss this. Trust me.*

Peeking first with one eye and then the other, Alex let out a sound of amazement at the sight before her. Xiraxus had flown them high up above the islands, affording her a view over the entirety of Draekora spread out underneath them. She looked back to see their original island was a wasteland full of craggy rocks and hidden caves, and she again marvelled at the differences in the isles.

With the sun on her face, the wind in her hair and the postcard-perfect view all around her, it was impossible for Alex not to get caught up in the wonder of the moment.

Xira, this is amazing, she called out in her mind, testing if their mental link worked both ways.

You haven't seen anything yet, he responded, his tone laced with humour. Then his voice turned pensive. *I suppose we can be a few minutes late. Hopefully no one will notice. Because you* have *to see this.*

With no other warning, he pulled his wings in close to his body and with nothing left to keep them aloft, they plummeted through the air. Down, down, down they dropped, a scream tearing from Alex's vocal chords, partly in terror, partly in exhilaration. Together they fell between two large islands and continued downwards until Xiraxus flung his wings out to catch an air current, thrusting them back up again.

Alex released a laugh of pure joy and threw her hands up above her head. "That was *incredible!*" she cried, her voice nearly lost in the wind.

The ride's not over yet. Xiraxus sounded just as thrilled.

He dipped his body, circling once before he nosedived again towards an island almost entirely consumed by and overflowing with water but for a rocky mountain cresting the edge of it.

Hold your breath, Alex, Xiraxus told her, not pulling up despite the fact that they were falling closer and closer to the surface of the island. He stroked his wings back as if to push them faster downwards. *And whatever you do, don't let go!*

Alex had only a wide-eyed moment to suck in a lungful of air and reinforce her grip on him, just as he dove them straight into the massive body of water.

This far above the clouds, she expected the water to be painfully frigid, but it was nothing of the sort. Instead it was almost warm, pleasantly so. But all this she only noted with half a mind because Xiraxus wasn't guiding them back to the surface—he was swimming them deeper under the lake.

As beautiful as the crystal clear water was with rays of sunlight streaming into its depths, Alex began to panic when Xiraxus made no move to resurface.

Uh—I'm human, remember? Oxygen is not only important, it's vital! Alex called out to him when they kept moving further down.

We're almost there, he replied nonsensically. *I promise, it'll be worth it.*

Not if I'm dead! Alex countered. But at that very moment, he moved his nose upwards and with a bubbly *swoosh* of his great wings he propelled them into an underwater tunnel. The passageway led upwards and, within a few more pushes of the draekon's wings, they broke out of the water and flew straight up what Alex recognised as the dried magma chamber of a dormant volcano. Bright gemstones veined along the walls of the rock as they flew straight up the channel and broke through the surface of the mountaintop, surging out into the sky.

Beyond words, Alex just laughed again, whooping in delight as Xiraxus soared back downwards and then spiralled underneath the water spilling over the edge of the great island, further drenching them in the spray.

See, flying's not so bad, is it? he said in a semi-smug tone.

It's wonderful, Alex admitted. *I had no idea what I was missing.*

What you're both missing is a very important meeting, came the irritated voice of Zaronia as she glided up alongside them, startling Alex both with her presence and her mental link.

Sorry, Mother, we—uh—we got lost, Xiraxus said feebly.

Alex watched as Zaronia's gaze swept over their waterlogged selves and, in a deadpan tone, the older draekon repeated, *You got lost.*

Even I could have come up with something better than that, Alex whispered to Xiraxus, hoping only he could hear.

Bite me, he returned, startling a laugh out of Alex.

Now, now, hatchlings, Zaronia said, showing that she could hear everything between them. *Play nice and follow me.*

Just how much of my language did you learn? Alex asked Xiraxus as he turned on his wing to follow obediently after his mother.

Everything you know came instantly with the bond, he replied.

And the same for me in reverse, Alex said, marvelling anew that she could now understand the Meyarin language. She wondered whether her new translation skills would remain with her when she returned to her time.

Yes, he confirmed. *And because my race is mentally linked like a—what would you call it? A hive mind?—because of that, you can now also understand and be understood by all draekons. The knowledge of your language flows from you through me to them.*

Then why does your mother sound so much more... proper than you do?

Somehow Xiraxus managed to turn his head but remain flying on course, pinning her with a telling look. *Because Mother is nearly an Ancient, Alex, and I'm the equivalent of a teenager, just like you.*

Are you implying that I'm 'uncool', Xira? Zaronia cut in.

Alex pressed her lips together in an attempt to suppress her laughter. Just hearing the word 'uncool' from the great draekon seemed wrong somehow.

Not at all, Mother, Xiraxus said quickly. *You're not uncool, you're...*

Sensing he needed help, Alex offered, *Dignified.*

Yes, dignified, Xiraxus said with a nod of his head. *Dignified and sophisticated.*

Definitely too dignified to use phrases like 'bite me', Alex finished, stifling a laugh when she felt Xiraxus's body vibrate with a grumble.

Hmm, Zaronia said, but she left it at that.

Just then they flew through a flurry of clouds and out the other side, bringing a new island to Alex's vision. This one was like a rocky, open-air auditorium, a huge amphitheatre made out of glossy black stone. The jagged edges of the crystalline surface gave the island a foreboding feel, or perhaps it was the small group of draekons waiting restlessly upon the variously sized black outcroppings interspersed like viewing platforms around the amphitheatre.

Is that traesos? Alex asked, recognising the rock.

You know what traesos is? Zaronia asked back, sounding surprised.

Alex shook her head even though the draekon wasn't looking at her. *Just that it's some kind of black rock.*

It's not just a rock, Alex, Xiraxus said in a familiar eye-roll tone. *It's pure darkness, pulled straight from the* abrassa *and solidified into crystal form.*

You're saying this stuff is basically, like, congealed black hole matter?

Pulled from one, yes, Xiraxus answered as they began to glide down into the centre of the amphitheatre. *The only thing that can destroy it is pure light energy from beyond the stars, otherwise it's completely impenetrable. To us, it symbolises the ages—those that have been, those that will be—because even when we have long since passed, it will still remain.*

Struck by the poetry in his words, Alex imagined she could almost feel the power of the *traesos* as Xiraxus landed on a stage-like ledge right beside Zaronia.

Not entirely sure what she was supposed to do, Alex remained astride Xiraxus waiting for instruction and tried to ignore all the glowing eyes staring at her. Every single draekon around the amphitheatre was watching her intently, some of them with curiosity, others with barely suppressed hostility. It was because of the latter that Alex kept a firm grip on Xiraxus, wondering what she'd gotten herself into this time.

Zaronia took a step forward and, in a loud voice that echoed throughout the rocky auditorium, she spoke in her earlier language of clicking, scratching and rumbling sounds that Alex unconsciously translated to, "I, Zaronia, born leader of Draekora, call this Kyvalon to order."

Your mother's the leader of the draekons? Alex asked Xiraxus, wincing a little at the strange, almost gritty sounds of the Draekoran language. *What does that make you?*

One day I'll inherit her position, he answered. *But not for many ages.*

When Zaronia began welcoming the different draekons in attendance, Alex asked, *Can they all hear us speaking like this?*

No, just me, Xiraxus answered. *Mother too, since I'm of her blood, which gives her a partial linking to our* vaeliana, *but it requires great effort on her part to listen in so she won't do it without cause. The others can't hear our mind-speak.*

Alex found that a small comfort. After all, she was still adjusting to having someone else in her head—she didn't want to think about a whole herd of draekons invading her thoughts.

"This Kyvalon has been called to address the enactment of *vaeliana* between Xiraxus of Draekora, and his mortal, Alexandra of Freya," Zaronia said in her harsh, guttural language.

Alex frowned at that and asked Xiraxus, *What's she talking about? What do they need to address?*

"Draekoran law states that it is forbidden for a draekon to bond with a mortal," Zaronia said before Xiraxus could answer. "Furthermore, it is equally forbidden to travel with any other race through the *abrassa*. It is up to this council to decide if the punishment for these crimes shall be enforced, and if so, to see it through."

Punishment? Alex asked. *What punishment?*

"After their defence has been stated, we shall put it to a vote," Zaronia said. "If the council does not rule in their favour, the mortal shall be executed. Immediately."

Twelve

"Xiraxus, you may now state your case before the Kyvalon," Zaronia said.

Xira, you need to tell me what's going on, right now, Alex pleaded, digging her fingers into the ribbing of his neck.

It'll be okay, Alex, Xiraxus told her. *I won't let anything happen to you. And neither will Mother, despite how indifferent she sounds.*

His easy confidence calmed Alex enough that she loosened her frantic grip, moving with him as he stepped forward to address the crowd.

"Respected elders," he said, also speaking the scratchy language of his race that translated effortlessly to Alex's ears, "I ask that you would open your minds and allow me to share my memories with you. You will see why I had no choice but to enact *vaeliana* with Alex. Do you consent?"

Alex was surprised by how formal Xiraxus sounded while speaking to what Zaronia had referred to as the draekon council. Perhaps it was only when he spoke her tongue that he sounded like the teenager he technically was.

When the general consensus came back with those in attendance willing to share Xiraxus's memories, the draekon whispered in her mind, *This might feel strange. Just go with it.*

And with that as the only warning, images assaulted her mind—images of Xiraxus flying lazily through the clouds around Draekora before being suddenly yanked upwards and into the *abrassa*. The memories played out as if on fast-forward, showing him being flung out the other end where everything was a blur of distressed flashes, as if he was skipping over parts of the memory. But then the images cleared again to reveal his panicked spiral to the earth, only just managing to slow his descent in time to avoid hitting the ground. It was there he saw the 'Golden One'— Aven—waiting with a small group of Meyarins. On Aven's order, the *Garseth* launched the Moxyreel net at Xiraxus, who roared in fright as he became ensnared. He was able to untangle part of his wings and fly a considerable distance away from immediate danger before his exhaustion from both the *abrassa* and the strangling net caused him to fall to the earth again. That's when Alex entered his memories, and it was fascinating for her to watch their encounter from his point of view, especially given his inability to fully understand her words. Until then, his knowledge of the common tongue had been limited to the teachings of other draekons, and since none of them had spent much time amongst humans, their comprehension was basic at best.

What followed were the memories of a visibly terrified Alex freeing him and healing his injury—whereby all the draekons in attendance broke into disbelieving murmurs at the sight of A'enara—before he sensed Aven's approach and the closing of the Void, taking to the air with Alex in his grip. As Alex lost consciousness, they entered the *abrassa* and were enveloped by darkness. Sometime later a blinding light lit up the darkness as Xiraxus recited a string of melodic words in another foreign language. All Alex knew was that they translated to say, 'Heart I give you, soul to share, strength and mind, both here and there. Forever and always, *vaeliana*.'

Then everything went black again, to the point that Xiraxus himself must have passed out, because his next memories were of him waking up in the midst of the Silverwood, with no Alex in sight.

She then learned that their bond allowed him to find her at the base of the Golden Cliffs being rescued by a group of Meyarin *Zeltora,* who forced *laendra* nectar down her throat to heal her talon-crushed abdomen. After they took her away, he flew around the city in frustration until he saw her fall off the balcony of the Meyarin palace and swooped in to save her.

"As you just saw, Alex rescued me from the one known to her as Aven Dalmarta, currently a prince of Meya, but in her time he is disinherited after having been banished from the Great City," Xiraxus explained to the group of now noticeably agitated draekons. "In the future I visited, he is… very evil. If Alex hadn't helped me, I would have been captured and unable to reopen the same space tunnel I journeyed through. I had only seconds before the original *abrassa* would have been lost to me. Without her help, I would have never been able to make my way back home."

He took a gusty breath and continued, "Because of that, I panicked, and yes, I entered the *abrassa* with a mortal. I could not—*would not*—leave her there for Aven to find, not after seeing the fear on her face at my mere mention of him. I didn't think my actions through, and when she nearly died during the trip through the Void, I truly believed the only course I could follow was to create the bond between us and share my life force."

Relatively calm up until that moment, Alex jolted at his words. *I'm sorry—can you repeat that last part? I think I must have heard you wrong.*

Um… Surprise? he responded as his mother stepped forward again.

"The laws of our race dictate that no draekon shall bond with a mortal owing to the fact that, when the mortal dies, the *vaeliana* link is severed, meaning that the draekon dies, too," Zaronia said, giving Alex even more unwelcome information about their bond. "With Xiraxus inheriting leadership over Draekora in the coming years, this is a concern for all of us."

"We cannot execute the mortal," called out a rusty-coloured male draekon with vibrant aqua eyes. "If she dies, he dies. Better to keep her alive and seek out a way to break the bond without harming Xiraxus. Just because it has never been done before doesn't mean it cannot be. She is young—if we keep her safe up here, we will have many years to find a solution."

Safe up here? Alex repeated. *I can't stay here, Xira! I have to get back to my time!*

"Kriidon has a point," said a ruby red female. "As far as I'm concerned, Xiraxus acted foolishly, but he did it from a noble heart. Neither of them should be punished for his actions. The mortal shall remain with us until we determine our next course of action."

"Thank you for your opinion, Vesaphina," Zaronia said. "Anyone else?"

One by one the draekons all agreed that no punishment should be set for Alex—or at least not the deadly kind, anyway. Every single one of the council members opined that she should stay firmly put on Draekoran soil for the rest of her life, which was something Alex simply couldn't abide. It was only when it appeared everyone was getting ready to finish up and disperse that she realised it was up to her to offer a different view.

"Excuse me," she called out, sliding down from Xiraxus's back and ignoring his low rumble of warning. She, of course, spoke the common tongue, but she also knew that, thanks to the *vaeliana*, they now all understood her, loud and clear. "What you're all forgetting is not only that I don't belong in this era and need to get back to my real time, but it's actually better for Xiraxus—for all of you—if I do." Her voice gained confidence as she explained, "You see, I'm not technically born yet—not for another few thousand years, if my timeline knowledge is correct. If you keep me here, I'll have maybe seventy or eighty more years to live, at best. Probably less, knowing my luck. But if you let me return to my time, Xiraxus will have a few extra *millennia* to live."

The draekons muttered amongst themselves, restlessly considering her words. Then a loud voice spoke up in a melodic language reminiscent of the one Xiraxus had uttered to create the *vaeliana* between them. It wasn't Draekoran, nor was it Meyarin, but something else entirely. Whatever tongue it was, Xiraxus must have been fluent in it since Alex could easily understand what was said.

"The girl must return to her time. If she doesn't, all hope for the future of this world will be lost."

Feeling shivers of foreboding, Alex repeated those ominous words in her mind. She couldn't see who had spoken them, but the voice was strangely familiar, as absurd as that sounded.

I don't believe it, Xiraxus said, craning his neck. *It's Aes Daega.*

Aes Daega? Alex asked, the name recognisable, though she couldn't put her finger on why. *Who is that?*

Before he could answer, a figure robed in white walked into the centre of the amphitheatre and up onto the dais where Alex stood between Xiraxus and Zaronia. A weathered hand pulled back the hood, revealing the face underneath.

"Lady Mystique?" Alex said in a disbelieving voice, finally understanding her sense of familiarity. "What on Earth are *you* doing here?"

The woman had the wisdom of the ages in her deep, fathomless eyes as she peered intently at Alex. "Lady Mystique, you say?" she asked in her foreign, lilting language. "Hmm. I do like that."

The woman still looked as old as time, if perhaps slightly less wrinkled and hunched over compared to when Alex had seen her at Raelia a fortnight ago.

"What *are* you?" Alex breathed out, even knowing that her phrasing was possibly considered highly impolite. "You have to be immortal, but you don't look like a Meyarin."

Strike that, her last phrase was impolite. She'd basically just called the old crone unattractive in not so many words. And even if it *was* true, Alex hadn't meant to say it so openly.

Fortunately, Lady Mystique laughed heartily in response. "Oh, I can see why I will come to like you, Alexandra Jennings. You are a delight."

"Great Aes Daega, what did you mean by saying Alexandra must return to her time?" Zaronia asked.

Lady Mystique—or Aes Daega as she was apparently known here—turned to the leader of Draekora. "If she does not return, all life in this world will be destroyed. I have seen it—then and now."

Alex heard a panicked ringing in her ears at the old woman's words, and the mutterings of the other draekons reached fever pitch to the point where Zaronia had to bellow out a roar in order to calm the assemblage.

"You are sure about this?" the purple draekon asked.

"I am certain," Lady Mystique said. "Her return is imperative if there is to be even the slightest possibility of this world's survival. Even then, the outcome will still largely depend on her choices in the days to come. But she *must* be there to make those choices."

No pressure, Alex thought miserably, forgetting that Xiraxus was listening in.

Sucks to be you, he returned. Somehow his blatant stating of the obvious caused Alex's lips to twitch.

Good to know you've got my back, 'forever and always', she replied, her tone light.

Let's consider those words more like guidelines rather than hard and fast rules, shall we?

Alex actually snorted. *Don't tell me you're giving up on us already, Xira? Where's the loyalty?*

"Ahem," called Lady Mystique, reminding Alex that she should probably be paying attention to the woman who was somehow knowledgeable about both the past and the future.

"As I was saying," the woman said, giving Alex a pointed look, "the girl must return to the future, *exactly* when she left it—not a moment sooner, not a moment later. The only one who can make that happen is the one who was already there with her: Xiraxus. He is also the only one who can keep her safe on the return journey through the *abrassa* due to their bond."

"Sounds good to me," Alex said. "When do we go?"

Lady Mystique furrowed her brow and looked up at Xiraxus. "She does not know?"

"She's had a lot of other questions," Xiraxus defended, twitching his tail. "I was getting around to it."

"Would someone like to tell me what everyone keeps *not* telling me?" Alex asked.

Lady Mystique turned back to her. "Opening a pathway through the *abrassa* takes a tremendous amount of power, no matter how relative the time difference. There are only two races in all the worlds that can create the pathways—draekons being one of them. But they can only manage two jumps at a time without needing rest to build their strength up again."

Alex frowned in confusion. "I'm sensing there's a problem, but I'm not sure what it is. Xiraxus was pulled through to my time against his will, right? So it wasn't his power that was used."

"He was indeed pulled from this time against his will," Lady Mystique confirmed. "It was the power of another that opened the *abrassa* that transported him to your time. But the only reason Xiraxus was able to return here was because a shadow of the original pathway lingered—a mapped route, you might say—allowing him to retrace his steps through the Void. To do so, he had to re-open the *abrassa* using his own power."

Alex saw the problem straight away. "You're saying he's technically used one jump, meaning he only has one left in him until he regains his strength?"

Lady Mystique nodded. "That is correct. And before you ask, he cannot take you back to your time and remain with you there while he recovers. He is needed here, perhaps as much as you are needed there. And in order for him to return to the exact time in which he leaves, which he *must*, he will need to jump straight back through the same pathway to return home."

Alex ran her hands through her lake-drenched hair, tugging at the drying roots in an effort to relieve stress. "How long will I have to stay here before he's strong enough for the double trip?"

It was Zaronia who answered. "If he were an elder, it would only take a few days. But he is just a hatchling like you."

"So...?"

If it was at all possible, Zaronia actually seemed to give her a pitying look. "It will take weeks at the minimum. Possibly a month or more."

"A *month*?" Alex cried. "But—I—What—" She didn't even know what to say. "What about everyone back in my time? They're going to lose their minds if I just up and disappear for *weeks*!"

Lady Mystique waved a careless hand through the air. "They'll never even know you're gone."

Alex sent her a look that spoke volumes. "Forgive me if this makes me sound conceited, but I'd like to think *someone* would notice if I went missing for that long. My friends, my parents— jeez, even *Aven* would be better than no one."

"What I meant was," Lady Mystique said, "as I mentioned before, Xiraxus will be returning you to *the precise moment* in which you left your time. That is why only he can take you back, rather than Zaronia or any of the other draekons. It is not just because your bond with him will keep you safe, but also because the odds of anyone else returning you to the correct time are not in your favour. And for there to be any hope at all, you *must* return to your correct time."

"Yeah, yeah, yeah—survival of the world and all that," Alex said, beyond the point of freaking out and well into denial.

Lady Mystique remained unruffled despite Alex's flippant attitude. "To you, weeks may pass," she said. "But to those in the future, not even a second will go by."

Alex shook her head, trying to control her rapidly growing dread. "This all seems crazy. What exactly am I supposed to do here for all that time?"

"You'll do exactly what it was you were planning to do back in your time."

"What?" Alex gave an unamused laugh. "Train with the Meyarins to learn how to fight Aven?" When the old woman just looked at her, unflinching, Alex raised her eyebrows and said, "In case you missed it, I'm not sure that'll go down so well in this time period. They all seemed pretty buddy-buddy to me and will probably take offence if I try to attack one of their own."

"That is why, as unfortunate as this event might seem to you, it's also rather perfect."

Looking at her blankly, Alex said, "Come again?"

"I have seen into your future, Alexandra Jennings," the old woman said. "The Aven you know is not the Aven who currently is. Right now, there is an opportunity for you to get to know him, to learn who he was before he came to be the Aven of the future."

"That sounds… rather devious."

"Are you not intrigued?" Lady Mystique asked, her ancient eyes almost daring. "Here you'll have the chance to get inside the mind of the one who forced his way inside yours. You may even discover what leads him onto his dark path."

"You can see what that was?" Alex was quick to correct, "Or, uh, *is*?"

"I can witness events outside of time," Lady Mystique said vaguely. "I know what was, what is, and what may be, but not *when*. As such, I cannot tell you how far Aven has already travelled on his journey to becoming the Meyarin of your future. But perhaps you will catch a glimpse of him as you spend your remaining time here in the Great City of Meya."

"Wait—she's not staying with us?" Xiraxus cut in.

"No, hatchling," Lady Mystique said. "Her place is with the Meyarins, for the moment. She must build her stamina and learn how to consistently utilise the Meyarin blood in her veins. For her survival, and yours in turn, she *must* train with the Meyarins."

"That's not the first time you've said something like that to me," Alex said with a resigned sigh.

"I know," Lady Mystique said, speaking Alex's language for the first time, her eyes twinkling. Then she clapped her hands once, breaking the moment, and reverted back to her strange, foreign dialect. "Now, some important things to note. Firstly, no one in Meya can know you're mortal."

"What? Why?"

"Because while humans and Meyarins have a trade agreement in place, they do not mingle other than when they exchange their wares. There is no way the Meyarins will include you as one of their own if they know you are mortal. That, and you can barely pass for one these days, Alexandra. You would simply make them ask too many questions." Lady Mystique shook her head. "No, it's best for everyone if you allow them to believe you are a Meyarin like them."

"Uh, problem," Alex said. "Appearance-wise, there will be some pretty obvious discrepancies." *Like the fact that they're all drop-dead gorgeous*, she thought to herself. "Not to mention, they have more grace in their little toes than I have in my whole body. I think they may realise that I don't quite fit the stereotypical Meyarin mould."

Lady Mystique actually chuckled. "You just might surprise yourself, child. And even if what you say is true, thanks to the *vaeliana*, they won't be able to see past your appearance to notice any lingering humanness in you."

Alex wasn't sure which part of all that alarmed her the most. "I'm sorry—what?"

"Look at your skin, Alexandra."

Still covered head to toe in the wintry Myrox-threaded outfit Kyia had helped her into for the *varrungard*, Alex raised her hands in front of her face since they provided the only visible skin easily accessed. Doing so, she could see nothing out of the ordinary. She wasn't even all that dirty despite her overnight trip in the woods, not to mention travelling through time and spending however long in a gritty cave.

"What am I supposed to be looking for?" Alex asked, squinting at her flesh.

"Stop acting like such a mortal," Lady Mystique scolded. "Take a proper look."

Alex resisted the urge to point out that she *was* mortal and instead tried to centre herself, calling forth her Meyarin abilities. It took her a few moments longer than when she was on her *varrungard*, but she was eventually able to expand her senses and focus her sight.

She took a startled step backwards.

"*What the…?*"

"You may find that the *vaeliana* has produced some unexpected changes to you," Lady Mystique said, sounding way too amused for Alex's liking. "No doubt you already know about the sharing of thoughts and languages, but you'll also be pleased to note that your bond with the Draekoran heir has overpowered all traces of Aven's scent in your blood. The Meyarin abilities still evidently linger in your veins from his forbidden ritual, but no one in this time or any other will recognise the smell of the *Garseth* upon you."

Alex was too dumbstruck by what she was looking at to appreciate the enormity of what Lady Mystique had just told her—or how complicated her time stuck in the past could have become if the Meyarins had noticed the scent of Aven's blood in her veins.

Clearing her throat, Alex said, "And this?" She waved her hands around, her voice verging on hysteria. "I look like I've fallen into a vat of toxic waste!"

Lady Mystique cocked her head. "I do not understand the reference."

"I look *irradiated*," Alex all but shrieked. "I'm *glowing*!"

And she was. Her skin was gleaming with a soft golden sheen—nothing her human eyes had been able to notice, but her enhanced Meyarin sight couldn't miss the unnatural radiance.

"As I said," Lady Mystique stated, "there may be some unexpected changes as a result of your bonding."

Alex gaped at her. "What about when I get back to my time? I think someone—say *Aven*—may notice something has changed about me, don't you think? Normal one day, glimmering the next?"

"That's not something you need to worry about right now, Alexandra."

Alex just shook her head mutely at the old woman, lost for a response but realising that perhaps Lady Mystique was correct. One problem at a time. And speaking of—

"Do I need to be worried about some kind of butterfly effect?" Alex asked. Seeing the woman's questioning expression, she explained, "How careful do I have to be to avoid changing the future—my real time—by accident? Like, if I squash a bug here, it could erase an entire species—that kind of thing. You get me? How can I keep my future safe when I'm not supposed to be here and could stuff up everything I know just by breathing wrong?"

Lady Mystique's face cleared with understanding. "You being here *contributes* to the future you will experience, but since you have already lived that future, there is no need to worry about what you do here in the past, for you cannot change events that have already occurred."

Alex had to repeat that mentally—twice—before she got her head around it. "So, you're saying that whatever I do here in the past is *supposed* to happen in order for the future I know to become a reality?" At Lady Mystique's nod, Alex stated with perfect honesty, "That's messed up."

The old woman gave a wrinkled smile. "Nevertheless, it is true. So do, or don't do, whatever you wish while you're here; it will change nothing—and everything."

Alex pressed her fingers to her forehead. "I think I'm going to have a headache for the next few millennia after all this."

"One final thing, child," Lady Mystique said, "and perhaps it will ease some of your concern."

Alex looked at her hopefully.

"When you leave here, I will make it so none who you meet in this time will remember your face, nor will they recall having met anyone in this time who is shining with the bond of the *vaeliana*."

Raising her eyebrows, Alex said, "You'll do *what*?"

"The Meyarins of the future never recognised you, did they? And yet, since your time here impacts the future, how can they *not* have sensed some familiarity? I can only presume it is because I am to step in and make it so. This will allow you even more freedom to make the most of your time here."

"They won't remember me at all?" Alex asked.

"They'll remember *someone*," the woman said. "But not vividly, only... impressions, you might say. Everything you do while here will be recollected as having been done by a vague, blurry face by the time your future arrives. So do not be concerned about your actions or fear your presence complicating the future."

"Because it's already happened," Alex confirmed, not sure if she was amazed or disturbed by the possibilities. She didn't question how Lady Mystique could do such a thing because if the old woman could make an entire bookshop disappear, altering memories was probably as easy as snapping her fingers together and saying *abracadabra*.

"What happens now?" Alex asked.

"You'll return to the Meyarin palace and begin your training," Lady Mystique answered, making it sound so much simpler than Alex was sure it would be.

Shuffling on her feet, Alex admitted, "Uh, I may have burned that bridge slightly when I woke up, freaked out on them about Aven and fell off the balcony. Not to mention, took to the skies on the back of a hulking beast. They probably think I'm a crazy person."

"Have no fear, child, for all will work out just as it should," Lady Mystique said softly, switching back to the common tongue. "Now bid farewell to the heir of Draekora and we shall depart."

Alex raised her eyebrows, wondering how the old woman planned to get them down to the ground from the middle of the sky without a draekon's assistance. Last Alex checked, she hadn't sprouted wings, regardless of the 'unexpected changes' wrought by the *vaeliana*.

With little option but to follow Lady Mystique's order and see what would come next, Alex turned to Xiraxus. "I guess I'll, um, see you around?" She felt a stirring of sadness at the thought of being separated from him, since even though they'd really only just met, she was comforted by his strong presence.

Xiraxus lowered his face towards Alex, enough that she reached out a hand to touch his smooth black brow, stroking him like one would a horse.

"I'll come visit you soon," he promised, speaking her common tongue again. "And try not to worry, Alex. Everything will be okay—you'll see."

I sure hope you're right, she whispered to him in her mind.

I'm always right, he responded confidently. *You'll learn that soon enough.*

"Come, Alexandra," Lady Mystique said, holding out her hand. "Time waits for no one."

Alex had to purse her lips together when the old woman wheezed out a laugh at her own words, obviously entertained by the irony.

Grabbing hold of the weathered hand, Alex spared a glance around the amphitheatre once more, taking in Xiraxus, Zaronia and all the other striking draekons still in attendance, before her eyes travelled out over the view of the floating islands of Draekora. That was all she saw before Lady Mystique's grip tightened almost painfully and the world around her flashed into a blinding light. Only when it faded did Alex come to see they were no longer in Draekora.

Instead, they were in the throne room of the Meyarin palace where, seated before her on a raised dais, were King Astophe and Queen Niida.

… With both Roka and Aven standing by their sides.

Thirteen

The Meyarin royal family was staring at Alex with unveiled surprise. But then, to *her* surprise, Astophe and Niida rose to their feet and bowed their heads in a clear sign of respect, with Roka and Aven mirroring the gesture.

Baffled, Alex wasn't sure what to think, not until the king spoke.

"Great Aes Daega," he said in his deep voice, speaking the Meyarin tongue. "You honour us with your presence."

"High King of Meya," Lady Mystique greeted, no longer speaking her foreign, lilting language, but instead using Meyarin words. "Thank you for your welcome. I shall not intrude upon you for long, I merely wish to return someone who I believe, for now, belongs with you."

Lady Mystique nudged Alex forward and she stumbled up a step. Both Aven and Roka were studying her closely, their faces openly intrigued.

"This is Aeylia," Lady Mystique said, concealing her real name. "She was abandoned in the forest as a babe and grew up amongst humans, only recently finding herself bonded to a draekon, as you can see."

Alex ignored the woman's false abandonment claims and just clenched her teeth at the reminder of her circus-freak skin.

"I believe she may have had a somewhat… *traumatic* episode which was witnessed by the young princes earlier today,"

Lady Mystique continued, nodding towards Roka and Aven. "Please be assured that won't happen again—she was merely overwhelmed by her unexpected surroundings after having been through a recent personal upheaval."

Alex coughed lightly into her hand. It was either that or snort with incredulity at the overly simplified description of recent events.

"Due to her upbringing away from Meya and its denizens, Aeylia has had little experience with your kind," Lady Mystique said. "I believe it is time to remedy that."

King Astophe looked at Alex thoughtfully. "What would you have us do, Aes Daega? You need only ask and it shall be done."

Alex was amazed by what she was hearing. Who, exactly, was Lady Mystique, and how did she command such respect from both Meyarins and Draekorans alike?

"She has no knowledge of what it means to be one of you," Lady Mystique said, clueing Alex in to where she was going with all this. "She needs to be taught—your language, your history, your physical prowess. I wish to leave her in your hands so that you might teach her how to be who she is *supposed* to be. It is time for her to embrace the Meyarin blood in her veins."

Goose bumps rose on Alex's skin and she fought the urge to rub her arms.

"We will consider it a privilege to take the youngling in," Queen Niida said, surprising Alex with the soft, compassionate look she offered her. With only that one glance, it was clear this queen was nothing like the cold, harsh Meyarin of Alex's time. "My sons will see to her education personally, making sure she receives the best instruction available."

Alex felt her blood freeze. Roka, she was okay with, but Aven? How could she possibly handle spending any length of time with the future murderer without giving away how much she detested him? As it was, she struggled just to look in his direction, let alone fathom the idea of *learning* from him.

"That is very kind of you, Queen Niida," Lady Mystique said. "I'm certain Aeylia will be a quick study. As soon as she is competent, she will leave Meya and return to Draekora to be with the draekon she is bound to—the Heir of the Sky Kingdom."

Alex had to admit, that was a pretty cool title for Xira's position. It didn't even matter that the old woman lied about Alex's eventual return to Draekora. She of all people understood why Lady Mystique didn't explain to the Meyarin royals where Alex would truly be returning to. Or rather, *when*.

"She's bound to the Draekoran *heir*?" Aven asked, his tone full of wonder. Alex tensed automatically at the sound of his smooth voice, but she quickly forced her body to relax. "That's a powerful claim. No wonder she shines as brightly as she does."

"I'm sure our sons will be adept teachers," King Astophe cut in, spearing his youngest son with a look Alex couldn't interpret. "Across all areas of her training."

"Of that I have no doubt," Lady Mystique said with a wrinkled, knowing smile. "In fact, I can think of no one better to instruct her."

Queen Niida clapped her hands together and beamed at Alex—actually *beamed* at her. "Then it's settled. Aeylia shall stay with us while she learns how to be—well, one of us, I guess we can say." She appeared flustered for a moment at her clumsy statement but then sat up straighter. "Roka? Aven? Will you kindly show Aeylia to her room? It's nearly dinnertime and I'm sure she would like to freshen up before joining us."

Alex's stomach lurched at the idea of enduring *another* meal with the Meyarin monarchs—not to mention at the thought of being alone with Aven and Roka so soon. She sent a pleading glance to Lady Mystique, but the old woman only smiled at her in encouragement and, with a token farewell to the king and queen, the great Aes Daega disappeared in a blinding flash of light, leaving Alex on her own in what she truly believed to be a den of wolves—immortal, deadly wolves.

Despite her trepidation, Alex willed herself into a state of pseudo-calmness when Roka and Aven gestured for her to follow, silently trailing after them as they led the way from the throne room.

"Are you all right, *Lasa* Aeylia?" Roka asked as they walked up a Myrox and gold-lined spiral staircase.

Surprised by his unexpected use of the common tongue, Alex almost missed a step. His pronunciation wasn't quite as eloquent as the Roka she knew of the future and he had a slightly lilting accent, but she appreciated his effort more than she could say.

"We were all concerned when you fell from the tower," he continued, "even after you were rescued by your draekon."

"I'm fine, Ro—uh, Your Highness," she replied quietly, almost forgetting that she technically didn't know him yet and should therefore remain formal. "Thank you for asking."

He bowed his head slightly in acknowledgement of her gratitude.

"What did you ask her?" Aven asked in Meyarin. "And what did she say?"

"I enquired about her wellbeing," Roka answered. "She claims she is fine."

Aven let out a disbelieving huff of amusement. "She fell from the palace balcony at the sight of me; you saw it, don't deny it. Even now, look at her—she seems terrified of me."

Turning into a long, narrow hallway at the top of the staircase, Alex felt Roka's eyes on her as if checking to see if Aven's claim was true. She forced herself to appear as relaxed as possible, not wanting to fuel any further suspicions.

"I saw it, yes, but as Aes Daega explained, she'd just awoken to unfamiliar surroundings and was overwhelmed by whatever events had led her to us," Roka said. "And wouldn't you be nervous, too, brother, if you suddenly found yourself in the presence of two Meyarin princes after having been away from your people for your entire life? Let's allow her to settle in and get used to us before we jump to conclusions about her being afraid on a personal level."

"As always, Ro, you are the voice of reason," Aven said.

Alex would have expected such a statement from Aven to be filled with scornful mocking, but there was none to be found. His words sounded shockingly sincere.

She knew then that it was going to be difficult to come to terms with the fact that this Aven truly wasn't her Aven. He wasn't evil—not yet.

"Why not call forth the *Valispath*?" Aven said to Roka. "Her room is quite a distance from here, and you know how Mother is if we're late to dinner. Especially when the council is in attendance."

"Until we teach her how to access the Eternal Path, she will need to know how to reach her room by foot. We don't want her feeling trapped while she is our guest."

Even the Roka of the past was thoughtful, Alex realised, feeling a surge of gratitude towards her future friend. At least some things hadn't changed.

She made sure to pay attention to the corridors and staircases they passed through, since even in her time much of the Meyarin palace remained a mystery thanks to the *Valispath*. It really was the best method for moving around the palace, especially considering it was such a vertical building. The spiral towers went up and up and up—this she knew from the view on the outside, and of course from falling off the balcony—and her legs were beginning to cramp from all the stairs they ascended.

She made certain not to give any indication that she was labouring like a mortal, though. Neither Roka nor Aven looked the least bit strained from the effort as they finally moved off the stairs and strode along a lush hallway that Alex recognised led to her allocated bedroom. She spared a thought to wonder about the chances of being given the same quarters both in the future *and* the past just as Roka opened the door and gestured for her to precede them both inside.

The room looked no different from earlier that day—and thousands of years in the future. There was even the colourful *myraes* flaming in the hearth, sending a wave of nostalgia over Alex. Before she could wonder who lit it, she turned her head to see Kyia sitting on her bed.

"Your mother told me you were on your way," Kyia said to Aven and Roka in the Meyarin tongue. "She mentioned our flying acquaintance had returned to us." She arched her golden eyebrows. "It's weird, right? That she needs to be taught something that should be as natural as breathing?"

"She was raised by humans, Kyia," Roka said, his curt tone surprising Alex. "It makes sense that she only knows how to live and act like them. And look at her—she can't be much younger than we are."

It was only with his words that Alex realised he was right about how similar they all now looked, at least age-wise. In all her shock of falling back through time, she hadn't been able to look too closely at the young Meyarins. But the truth was, the three of them *did* look different, at least slightly. Instead of seeming in their late twenties as they were in her future, they now all looked to be around Alex's age, perhaps a year or two older at most. The difference wasn't obvious, but it was there, if only because there was a certain youthfulness about them. It was odd to think that in the next few thousand years they would only physically age about a decade.

"Yeah, I get it," Kyia said. "But it's still weird."

"What I want to know," Aven said, "is how are we supposed to teach her anything if she can't understand us?"

"I can speak the common tongue well enough to hold a conversation," Roka said. "I guess that means I'll be in charge of her language lessons. But I'd like to point out that I've repeatedly told you both to consider studying with me, especially given our trade agreement with the humans."

"It's not as if Father is letting us take part in any of the trade negotiations," Aven said, sounding disappointed. "If he has his way, we're never going to meet any mortals, let alone have cause to speak with them."

Alex felt her body turn to stone, understanding from Aven's words that he hadn't even *met* a human yet, nor had he witnessed the delegation of them that, according to D.C., led to him demanding the king end the Meyarin-Human alliance— the results of which then spiralled further downward into the mess of the future.

As utterly bizarre as it was for Alex to realise, none of that had actually happened. Not yet, at least.

"It matters not," Roka said, waving a dismissive hand. "This is the perfect opportunity for you both to learn, so I suggest you take advantage of it. And besides, I can't be around translating for you every minute of her training. It's a simple language—it took me less than a week to learn enough to be proficient."

"Why not just focus on teaching her our language—*her* language?" Aven asked. "Surely that makes more sense?"

"We'll do that at the same time," Roka said. "Regardless of whom she was raised amongst, she has Meyarin blood, so she will learn as fast as us. She'll be conversing naturally in our tongue by this time next week."

Alex had to force herself not to react outwardly to that, lest they realise that she could already understand them. She didn't want to show all her cards just yet, not when she might be able to learn something without them realising. But it was hard for her to keep her face blank at the idea of becoming fluent in a foreign language in just a week. It had taken her at least a month just to get a handle on Pig Latin when she was twelve years old and staying at a dig site with other kids travelling with their working parents. All the same, she was fascinated by the idea of accelerated learning, if her blood truly was capable of affording such a feat.

"How about we discuss our teaching strategy further at a time when we're not late for dinner?" Kyia put in. "That was the other reason your mother sent me here—she thought Aeylia might like some clean clothes. Perhaps something more appropriate to dine in."

Alex almost wilted with relief at the idea of finally getting out of her wintry attire. She honestly had no idea how she hadn't expired of heat exhaustion yet. But as strange as it was, even though the outfit had kept her warm in the snow and she wasn't overly comfortable in the currently summer-like conditions, she also wasn't terribly *uncomfortable*. It was almost like whatever insulation had helped her to remain alive on her icy *varrungard* experience was also keeping her internal temperature relatively stable despite the change in weather and seasons.

"Why don't you introduce me to her officially and then we can all start getting ready," Kyia suggested.

Both Roka and Aven's expressions flashed with guilt as they realised they hadn't even introduced *themselves* to her yet.

"I mean," Kyia went on, not noticing the princes' expressions, "I know she said all our names earlier today, so someone obviously must have told her who we are or what we look like or whatever, but I still feel like a proper introduction is important. Don't you agree?"

Roka cleared his throat and turned to Alex with apologetic eyes. Switching to her language, he said, "I'm terribly sorry,

Lasa Aeylia. We've been speaking amongst ourselves all this time without including you. Our behaviour has been deplorable and we would beg your forgiveness."

"There's nothing to forgive," Alex reassured, marvelling at his rather poncy words. While Aven in the future still tended to be somewhat formal in his speech patterns, Roka had always seemed more casual. That said, given that he'd learned her language in a single week, he'd surely be able to relax into it with very little effort. Perhaps that was something she could help him with.

"I believe you already know who we are, but just to be sure, I am Prince Roka Dalmarta, firstborn son to King Astophe and Queen Niida, heir to the Meyarin throne." He quirked his lips up in a smile and said, "But I insist you call me Roka. I'm not a fan of formalities."

Alex bit her cheek to conceal her grin, since he'd said the *exact* same thing to her once before.

"This is my brother, Prince Aven Dalmarta." Roka clapped a hand on Aven's shoulder and then gestured towards Kyia to finish, "And our final companion is *Lasa* Kyia Tarennia. I speak for all of us when I say we are very much looking forward to getting to know you."

"And I you, Roka," Alex returned, sending him a small smile in return and doing her best to keep it on her face as she offered it to both Kyia… and Aven. "You're very kind to take me in and teach me the ways of your—*our*—people."

Alex winced internally at her near stuff up. She would have to be more careful.

"The pleasure is ours, let me assure you," Roka said, still looking at her warmly. "My brother and I will now leave you in Kyia's safe hands and she will walk you downstairs when you're ready to join us."

After Roka turned to his brother and Kyia to translate his words, Aven nodded and smiled at Alex before leaving the room with Roka.

"Sure, leave me alone with the draekon girl who can't understand me," Kyia muttered in Meyarin, apparently not having expected the princes to take off without her. She moved towards the large walk-in wardrobe at the side of the room and continued under her breath, "Because that makes *loads* of sense."

Alex almost felt sorry for her—but she also couldn't help feeling amused by her future friend's grumblings.

After changing into a figure-hugging tunic and knee-high boots over the Meyarin equivalent of tights, Kyia escorted Alex back down to the dining hall entrance.

"Go on in," Kyia said, making a shooing gesture with her hands to supplement Alex's supposed lack of understanding.

When Alex didn't move, mostly because the idea of walking into the dining hall again was enough to cause her to break out in hives, Kyia placed her hands on Alex's shoulders and literally pushed her inside. It was a gentle push, sure, but a push all the same. Apparently it was Kyia's mode of communication when words failed her, and it certainly worked because every eye in the hall instantly came to rest on Alex—the piercing golden gaze of Aven amongst the avid stares.

Her first reaction was to run. She wasn't sure she could handle this. In fact, she was certain she couldn't. But before she could convince her frozen legs to move, Kyia gave her another 'gentle' nudge forward and promptly closed the doors between them.

Fourteen

To Alex's relief, dinner wasn't the nightmare she feared it would be. There were so many Meyarins in attendance that, even after her awkward entrance, none of them were able to keep their attention on her for long with all the conversations breaking out around the table.

Roka had kindly insisted that Alex sit by him so she would have someone to converse with, but barely five minutes into the meal he and the king were called away on urgent business, leaving Alex to fend for herself. Or at least that was the case until Aven swapped seats, moving into the one his brother had vacated.

Every muscle in Alex's body tensed, but he did nothing other than smile kindly and continue eating his meal. He didn't try speaking to her, likely presuming she wouldn't understand anyway. He seemed happy to simply keep her company, as if to make her feel she wasn't alone in the crowded room. His actions truly baffled her. She honestly couldn't reconcile *this* Aven to the one she knew in her time. How was it possible that the simple matter of him taking offence to the inferior trade dealings of a few humans could turn him into the Aven of the future? It just didn't make any sense.

Just after the last course was served, Roka returned to the dining hall, but Astophe wasn't with him. The prince strode directly over to where Aven and Alex sat, his face tight and his tone grim. "Father would like a word."

Aven's expression turned concerned. "Is everything all right?"

"He's in the reception hall," was all Roka would say. "You'd better not keep him waiting."

At that, Aven's lips quirked up in a grin. "At least he's not in the throne room. That's where he orders me to meet him when I'm in *real* trouble. Things can't be as bad as your face claims, Ro."

Roka relaxed his furrowed brow, shaking his head in what looked like resigned amusement. "You're impossible, Aven. Please do us all a favour and start choosing your friends more wisely."

"Ahh." Aven stood to his feet. "I have a feeling I know what this might be about. But fear not, brother, I'll have it all sorted before you can say 'disinherited'."

Alex jolted, but quickly covered her reaction by reaching for her goblet, downing the remainder of the beverage in a few large gulps as Aven confidently ambled from the room. Whatever his father had to speak to him about wasn't causing him any anxiety, that much she could clearly see.

"Are you finished, *Lasa* Aeylia?" Roka asked Alex, switching to the common tongue.

"Please, Roka," she said, standing to her feet in confirmation. "Call me Aeylia. Like you, I'm not big on formalities." Plus, she didn't like the way the presumed title reminded her of the snotty *Lasa* Riza of the future.

"'*Lasa*' is merely a gesture of respect," Roka told her, leading the way from the room. "As is '*Loro*' for the males. The terms don't imply any kind of formal nobility, they're more like the common tongue equivalent for 'sir' and 'madam'."

Alex pulled a face. "You've been calling me madam all this time? Eugh. That makes me feel so old."

Roka laughed heartily, the sound so reminiscent of his future self that Alex's body relaxed properly for what felt like the first time since she'd arrived in the past.

"I apologise then, Aeylia," he said. "Stars forbid you ever feel old."

"Just don't let it happen again," she said, going along with the playful moment.

"I'll spread the word," he promised. "No more '*Lasa*' for you."

Alex smiled widely. "I'd appreciate that."

He came to an abrupt stop in the centre of the hallway. "If you're feeling up to it, we can begin your education tonight—but only if you want. I know you've had a rather trying day."

Alex figured the sooner she started, the faster she'd learn—just as she'd come to accept with the future version of Roka training her—so she nodded her head enthusiastically. "I'm ready when you are."

He looked at her carefully, as if gauging the veracity of her statement, and nodded in return. "What would you like to begin with? Language, history, or the more practical physical capabilities at your disposal?"

If she were in her time, she wouldn't have been given the option. All she needed then was to learn how to utilise her physical Meyarin abilities. But there must have been a reason why Lady Mystique specifically asked that she be educated in the other areas while staying in the past. She just didn't know what the reason might be.

"You're the teacher," Alex said, leaving the decision to Roka. "Whatever you think is best."

The prince tilted his head thoughtfully. "I suppose our priority should be teaching you the Meyarin language so that you can communicate with others who will then be able to assist with your training."

Alex couldn't resist the urge to scrunch up her face, not particularly eager to learn a language she, for whatever reason, already understood. Sure, it might come in handy being able to speak it, but for now, she was content with no one knowing she could comprehend their words.

Apparently reading her disappointed look, Roka chuckled and said, "Or we could start with something a little more exciting before heading to the library, if you'd like? How about a quick sparring match to see what kind of skills you already have?"

"That sounds perfect," Alex said, even if she was somewhat apprehensive. She'd fought Roka once before—the first time her Meyarin abilities had ever kicked in—and she knew without any doubt that he'd been easy on her at the time. She wasn't sure how *this* Roka would treat her, especially since he was under the impression that she was an actual Meyarin.

"The palace has a number of training rooms, some more private than others," Roka told her. "I'm guessing you probably don't want an audience, so we'll head to one of the more isolated rooms. It's located at the top of the east tower, so to save us time I'll introduce you to the *Valispath* and we'll use it to take us there."

Alex stood up a little straighter, excited to learn more about the invisible rollercoaster.

"The *Valispath* is also known as the Eternal Path, and all those with Meyarin blood can access it as a means of transportation."

That wasn't *entirely* true, since Alex hadn't been able to access the Path in the future despite Aven's blood being in her veins. That was only because he was disinherited though, which in turn invalidated his Meyarin heritage. But here in the past, Aven wasn't yet banished, which meant Alex should, theoretically, be able to use the *Valispath* like any other Meyarin.

"The Eternal Path was a gift from the Tia Aurans, long ago," Roka said. "You'll learn more about all that in your history lessons, but all you need to know for now is that they are a race of beings powerful beyond compare. To this day, despite what research we have carried out on the Path, not even our greatest minds can comprehend how it works or what fuels it. The *Valispath* simply *is*. It has been a source of great frustration for many intellects of our time, but I personally believe it is one of those things that is beyond our understanding and should stay as such. If the Tia Aurans had wanted us to know how it worked, they would have told us."

His gaze became unfocused for a moment before he came back to himself. "But I digress. You need not concern yourself with any of that. For tonight, you need only enjoy the ride and experience the power of the Path beneath your feet. In due time you will learn how to call it forth and control it."

Alex made sure to act surprised when the ground moved out from underneath her as Roka activated the *Valispath*. Truly, it wasn't hard for her to feign shock, since he hadn't given her so much as a heads-up. But that also meant that she didn't look like a graceless Meyarin fraud when she fell back against the invisible barrier. While it was such a *mortal* thing for her to do, she had an excuse thanks to Roka's lack of warning. And for that she was grateful.

The Path took them around, up and through the corridors and walls of the palace until they came to a stop in a large training room—the same one in which she'd fought both Zain and Roka in back in her time. And when the prince started leading her across the padded mat-covered floor, Alex knew exactly what to expect next.

"Just in case someone comes in and you get nervous, this will help keep you from becoming distracted," Roka said, crouching to the ground and tapping a pattern into the floor. An impenetrable Myrox enclosure rose up around them, sealing them in a bubble-shaped dome, hidden from all eyes and ears.

Alex watched as Roka unclasped his cape and threw it to the side. He was wearing similar attire to what she wore—leather tunic, trousers and boots—but his were more masculine and, well, warrior-like. He also had a myriad of weapons strapped to his belt; weapons she knew he didn't need since he was lethal enough without them.

"Now," Roka said, "I want you to attack me."

Alex blinked at him. "Just like that?"

He opened his arms in invitation. "I need to see what raw material I'm working with, so go for it."

Chewing her lip, Alex took a tentative step forward, then another. "I'm not entirely sure I'm comfortable with—"

"If you can't directly attack the heir to the Meyarin throne," Roka interrupted, sending her a roguish grin, "at least try to defend against me."

And in a blur of movement, he ran forward.

Alex barely had a microsecond to release a startled yelp as she shied to the side, avoiding his reach.

"Good reflexes," Roka said. "But can you dodge this?"

She swivelled her torso away from him again, but he turned at the last moment and went low, kicking her legs out from the floor.

"You didn't even try that time," Roka admonished.

"Maybe if you'd give me a second to prepare myself," Alex said, rising back up to her feet and rubbing a hand against her bruised behind.

Roka cocked his head. "What's there to prepare?"

"You know, to centre myself and—" She bit down on her tongue, hard, as she remembered that Meyarins wouldn't *need* to centre or prepare themselves. If only Alex had that luxury. She needed to concentrate in order to activate the capabilities of her blood.

"Never mind," she told Roka. "Just, uh, if you don't mind, can I just have a quick moment? Just to sort of, uh, mentally psyche myself up to attacking the royal prince, and all that."

Listen, she encouraged herself, closing her eyes. *Just listen*.

And as she had done all through the *varrungard*, Alex slowly expanded her senses outwards. She hit a block at the Myrox barrier but it didn't matter, because when she opened her eyes, she knew she was back in the game.

"Okay, I'm ready," she said.

Roka arched an eyebrow but, taking her word, he came at her again, faster than lightning. This time she was able to trace his movement almost as if it was in slow motion, and rather than jump out of the way, she raised her arm to block his attack. Her other arm moved to block his next, equally powerful counter-blow. She then decided to jump on the offence and drop to the floor, throwing her leg out to swipe his feet, but he evaded her by leaping into the air at the last second. Seeing his intent to strike now that she was in a vulnerable position, Alex sprung upwards and executed a backwards handspring to escape his range—something she had no idea she was capable of doing.

"Excellent," Roka said, his voice ridiculously smooth to her now heightened hearing. "You're much better than I anticipated, considering your lack of training. You're a natural."

Alex laughed at that, the sound strange to her Meyarin ears.

"Let's see how you fare with a weapon," Roka said, pulling his sword from its scabbard and raising it between them.

When he made no further move, Alex pointed to his blade and asked, "Do I get one of those?"

Roka's brows rose. "You wield the Sword of the Stars, Aeylia. I recognised your blade earlier today, as did Aven and Kyia, though none of us had ever before laid eyes on it. The Bringer of Light is but a legend, or so we thought. I'm certain no weapon I can offer you would compare."

Alex was surprised. Mostly because she wondered how—or *when*—A'enara ended up coming into Aven's possession if this past version of him had never even seen the weapon before. It was, after all, the blade he'd tried to kill Alex with, so he kind of needed it in order for her future to play out. She hoped when she got back to the academy in her time that she'd hear from Kaiden, who had offered to research the strange weapon for her. She could certainly use some answers to her mounting questions.

At an encouraging gesture from Roka, Alex held out her hand, mentally summoning the blade. Just like earlier that day, it arrived in a dazzling blaze of light, surrounded by blue fire that danced along Alex's arm.

"Why is it doing that?" she asked, entranced by the spiralling flames.

Roka sounded surprised when he asked, "Hasn't it always?"

Alex shook her head. "No. This is definitely new."

The prince stepped closer to inspect the flames. He reached out a finger to touch them but withdrew his arm quickly.

"Stars above, that's hot," he hissed, shaking his hand. When he held it out to show Alex, she could see a raw, blistering burn mark. It was healing quickly thanks to his immortal blood, but it still looked painful.

"I can't feel it at all," Alex marvelled, moving her free hand into the flames where they tickled her skin. There was perhaps a slight comforting heat, but nothing more.

"That's because you're as much a part of the weapon as it is you," Roka said. "Where you go, it goes. You are bound to it, as it is to you."

"I sort of already knew that," Alex said, which was true, if not in so many words. "It's been the case for a few months now, but I'm telling you, this fire thing is new. As in, new *today*."

Roka seemed to contemplate that, but then his gaze travelled over Alex. She followed his eyes to the bare skin on her non-flaming arm, and since she was still using her Meyarin senses, she could easily see the glimmer from her bond with Xiraxus.

Roka motioned to her golden-hued skin. "Have you called forth the blade since enacting *vaeliana* with the Draekoran heir, Aeylia? Or was today the first time?"

Alex swallowed. "You don't think…?"

"Legend claims that the Weapon of the Ages was also wrought by the Tia Aurans," Roka said. "The draekons have a long history with the race beyond the stars. I wouldn't be surprised if the blade is merely recognising your bond and reacting to it."

"So, it's like…" Alex searched for the correct word as the blue flames curled around her wrist. "An upgrade?"

Roka chuckled. "Sure. That works. Consider your weapon upgraded. While in your grasp, not only can it pierce flesh, it can now also burn sinew. Congratulations—you are the proud owner of the Blade of Glory."

Alex sent him a challenging look, half amused, half serious. "Are you sure you still want me to attack you with this?"

"I must admit, I *am* having second thoughts." Roka reached behind him and pulled a second sword from the sheath strapped to his back. He passed it to her and said, "Perhaps until I've determined the level of your skill, we might practise with comparable weapons after all. I'm rather fond of my limbs and wouldn't want to risk the flame of the stars burning through them."

Alex grinned at him and, with a flick of her wrist, banished A'enara. "Is that what that was? Star fire?"

Roka looked very much like an excited child. "Wasn't it incredible? I've never seen it up close before. Or felt it. I can't say that I *want* to feel it a second time, either. But still— incredible."

His demeanour turned purposeful again when he raised his sword between them once more, gesturing for Alex to make the first move. She shuffled from foot to foot as she found her centre of gravity, weighing the foreign weapon in her hands. It was much heavier than A'enara, not as sleek, and it felt cumbersome in her grip. But she knew that to a Meyarin, none of that should make much of a difference—not its weight, not its length or shape. So she brought it in front of her and, without hesitating, lunged towards Roka.

He sidestepped, so she lunged again. And again, and again, and again as he continued dodging her attacks.

"What's the deal, Roka?" she asked, lowering her weapon. "I thought you wanted to fight me?"

"Finally," he said. And, having apparently waited to catch her off-guard, he made his move.

She only just managed to bring her sword back up in time to meet his blade in a screech of steel that was painful to her heightened hearing.

Left, right and left again, he thrust his blade towards her as she barely managed to keep up against his attack. It was only because she'd done this with him before—and while blindfolded—that she was able to hold her own, if only *just*. It also helped that she knew he wasn't really trying; she could see it in the way he hesitated a fraction before every lunge, as if making sure she would be able to meet his attack without injury. Her mortal eyes never would have picked up on the tell, but her Meyarin sight revealed it clearly. And Alex was beyond grateful, because partway through their fight she realised something that could have had catastrophic consequences.

Her blood wasn't silver. It was red.

Stumbling over her own feet, she narrowly missed losing her hand to Roka's blade as she cried out, "*Stop!*"

Her voice sounded fearful to her own ears, aware that if he so much as nicked her with his sword, her guise as a Meyarin would be over before it even began.

"I—I, uh, think I've had enough for tonight," she said, panting from both exertion and the terror zinging through her nerve endings.

"But you were doing so well," Roka said. "Definitely a natural."

Alex was shaking her head. "You were going easy on me."

"That doesn't make my words any less true. Are you sure you want to stop?"

"Absolutely," Alex said, handing back his sword. "Maybe, uh, maybe we can give it a go another time."

Roka was watching her closely. She tried to keep her sudden panic off her face, but she wasn't sure if she succeeded.

"If that is what you wish," he said slowly, "then I guess we'll just practise again tomorrow."

Alex wilted with relief. Now all she had to do was find an excuse between now and then in order to avoid the inevitable outing of her mortality.

"You have good speed and instinctual reflexes at your disposal already," Roka went on, "as well as a keen awareness. But your technique could use some work, as well as your confidence and skill with a blade. I truly do believe you are a natural, as I said, but there is plenty of room for improvement."

What really sucked was that if this were the future, she'd be all over Roka teaching her how to strengthen her fighting skills. In fact, up until her internal freak out a moment ago, she'd even been looking forward to the Roka of the past teaching her. But now it was impossible—there was no way she could put herself in a position where he might discover the truth, which would happen if she so much as skinned her knee from falling to the ground too hard. She couldn't believe Lady Mystique hadn't considered the problem of her blood—because it *was* a problem.

"We might as well head to the library and get a few hours of language lessons in before bed," Roka said, bending to tap the ground and lower the Myrox dome around them again.

With Alex's adrenaline scoring through her veins, her Meyarin senses were still activated, so she was able to see the faintly glowing disc imbedded into the mat at their feet. How Roka knew what pattern to press into it was another matter, but at least now she could see more of what was once invisible to her human eyes.

It was also a great surprise when she literally *saw* the *Valispath* solidify around them, presumably at his mental summons. It was still mostly transparent, but she was now able to see a blurry outline of the rectangular barrier. Just like the disc on the fighting mat, there was a similar glowing plate at chest level—likely what the Meyarins of her future used to alter the Path's settings and make it more comfortable for humans.

Before Alex could inspect it further, the Path dropped them off in a vast room lit with numerous ancient bookcases and *myraes*-lit sconces.

The Meyarin palace's library was like a medieval fantasy come to life. The walls were lined with thousands upon thousands of books, with ladders leaning against the cases to provide access to the tomes on the higher levels. And there actually *were* levels to the bookshelves. While the middle of the library was hollowed out straight up to the domed ceiling, there were second and third floors of books accessible by ladders, with narrow bridge-like paths circumnavigating the border of the room in between.

"I think I'm in love with this room," Alex said as Roka led her to a polished table made out of timber from the Silverwood and held a chair out for her.

"The library is one of my favourite places in the palace," Roka admitted. "The knowledge of the ages can be found in here. You could read for a lifetime and still not make your way though all the tomes on offer."

Given that the Meyarin lifetime had no limit, barring early death, Alex knew that was quite a proclamation.

As if reading her thoughts, he grinned and sauntered over to one of the bookcases where he withdrew an armful of books, bringing them back to set down on the table.

"We'll cover the basics tonight," he said. "Our language is in your blood, regardless of whether you've grown up hearing it or not, so it shouldn't take long for you to master it."

Alex wished she could be as confident as he sounded.

Roka took a seat beside her and said, "Let's start at the beginning."

Fifteen

Hours later, Alex collapsed onto her bed, exhausted after Roka's seemingly unending language lesson.

The prince had taught her simple words like 'no' (*naha*), 'yes' (*sesu*), 'you' (*sae*), 'me' (*rae*), 'I' (*trae*), 'please' (*nalahi*) and 'thank you' (*atari sae*). They had progressed through the basics at blinding speed, aided mostly by Alex already understanding the language, and perhaps also by her Meyarin blood-induced accelerating learning. By the end of their session, she'd been stringing together simple sentences like, 'Hello! How are you today?' (*Kendara! Le noran sae risa?*), 'Please help me, I'm hurt!' (*Nalahi suros rae, trae de frayon!*) and 'Would you like fries with that?' (*Koral en* fries *de sae trivva?*). The last was Alex's idea of a joke, even if Roka didn't understand the reference. But still, she felt as if she'd left her mark on the past just by educating the prince about the wonder of deep-fried potatoes.

Happy to finally be in bed after her insane day, she just started to drift off when a voice called to her.

Alex? Can you hear me?

Xiraxus? Alex sat up and turned to squint out over her balcony, seeing the romantic glow of the city at night but no draekon in sight. *Where are you?*

Draekora, he answered, surprising Alex that they were able to communicate so clearly despite the distance between them. *Today was hard on you. I thought I'd check to make sure you're okay.*

Alex felt a bubble of gratitude at the draekon's concern. If nothing else, her sojourn to the past had at least given her a new friend.

Yeah, just tired. Today went beyond my usual kind of weird.

You do feel tired, Xiraxus commented. *I should let you get some sleep.*

Even though he couldn't see her, Alex frowned in confusion. *How do you know how I feel?*

The vaeliana *links me to your emotions. Whenever you feel something strongly, I feel it too.*

Alex wasn't sure if she felt more amazed or violated by the idea of someone—draekon or not—being able to sense her feelings.

You can't manipulate my emotions, can you?

No, Alex, he said with a deep chuckle. *Your feelings are your own—I can just read them. Like how a moment ago you were filled with apprehension, but now you're calming again.*

She let out a relieved breath. *Good to know.*

You'll feel even calmer after a proper night's sleep. I'll talk to you again soon.

Xira? she called before he could 'disappear'.

Yeah?

I just… Alex hesitated, not sure how to articulate what she wanted to say. But then she settled on, *Thanks for saving my life today. I know this whole situation is about a thousand different kinds of crazy and I haven't been quiet about not wanting to be stuck in the past. But the truth is, everything happens for a reason, and I wouldn't be here—alive—without you. So, thanks for bonding with me.*

There was silence for a moment until Xiraxus responded, *Aw, shucks, Alex. We're having a moment.*

Narrowing her eyes, Alex wondered about the fairness of him not only picking up her language through the bond, but also the ability to use it sarcastically. Instead of saying anything more, she sent him a mental image of her whacking him over the head with a pillow. In return, she received a deep belly laugh before she felt his presence vanish from her mind.

After that, she lay back down again and fell asleep with a smile still lingering on her face.

Alex's second day in the past turned out to be much more relaxing than her first.

She was collected early in the morning by Kyia and delivered to a small sunroom to breakfast with the queen, of all people. On her own. That *should* have raised Alex's anxiety levels, but the truth was, this version of Niida seemed nothing but welcoming. This was proven again when Alex took a seat in a cushioned chair and the queen merely reached over and squeezed her hand comfortingly, sending her a friendly smile before returning to sip from what looked like a mug of hot chocolate. Indeed, when Alex's breakfast was brought in on a platter, she too received a serving of the decadently rich liquid.

The queen, seeing Alex's delight at the drink, said in broken words of the common tongue, "It's guilty, my pleasure. Keep our secret, yes?"

Alex hadn't been able to deny Niida a return smile and nod of agreement.

"You can speak my language?" she asked hesitantly, not sure if she was supposed to remain silent or address the queen more formally as befitting her station.

Niida gave a self-deprecating laugh. "Only basic convention."

"Conversation," Alex corrected without thinking.

Fortunately, Niida laughed again instead of demanding Alex's head. "Astophe and Roka more—uh, better?—yes, they better versed in common tongue. But I get by simple. Will learn proper now, to speak you."

"You already speak it very well, Your Highness," Alex semi fibbed, touched by the queen's gesture. "And I'm grateful for you making the effort."

They ate the rest of their meal in companionable silence, with Alex relaxing even more as the sun streamed through the windows of the room and thawed her lingering tension.

But the relaxation couldn't last forever, and all too soon the queen had to excuse herself to go about her royal duties. Left alone, Alex wasn't sure what to do, not until Aven walked in.

Forcing her body language to remain unruffled, she even managed to partly return his smile of greeting, ignoring the twist of her insides as she did so.

"Good morning, *Lasa* Aeylia," he said, standing before her and surprising her with his perfect use of the common tongue. Then he winced and switched to Meyarin, saying, "Forgive me, I forgot that Roka mentioned you'd prefer to remain informal." He shook his head as if at himself. "I know you probably have no idea what I'm saying, even if my brother informs me that your language lessons are coming along well. But he wrote this for me to give you anyway."

Aven handed over a scrolled piece of parchment with a silvery-gold shine to it, and she realised it must have been made from the trees in the forests surrounding Meya. It was very pretty, as far as paper was concerned.

Unrolling it, Alex read Roka's words inscribed in a running calligraphy, perfectly written in the common language:

Aeylia,
*I'm sorry for not meeting you in person this morning, but
my father requires my assistance regarding a matter of
urgency. Being at the beck and call of my people is but
one of the perks of inheriting an immortal kingdom.*

At that, Alex could imagine the prince she knew rolling his eyes and she had a feeling this Roka would act the same. She smiled to herself and continued reading.

I should be back early this evening to continue our lessons, but until then, my brother will take good care of you.

Alex had to still the sudden trembling of her hand.

I've informed him that you have caught on well to our language but your knowledge is rudimentary and needs much improvement. Don't worry; he won't try to engage you in scintillating conversation just yet. I believe he has plans to show you around the city so that you may acquaint yourself with the glory that is Meya. I only hope you will have enough energy left for our evening lessons upon my return.

Again, Alex could pick up a note of dryness to Roka's tone, and it helped ease the knots in her stomach at the idea of spending the day playing tourist with Aven.

Don't be afraid to ask questions in both your tongue and ours. At my urging, Aven began his own language lessons last night and, like you, will soon be fluent. Enjoy your outing, and I'll see you tonight,
Roka

Alex read the note slowly a second time just so that she had time to stifle her panic before meeting Aven's eyes. He was looking directly at her, waiting, it seemed, for her reaction.

Giving herself a mental pep-talk, Alex reminded herself that this was not the evil Aven of the future and it was at least possible that she might make it through the day in his company without being threatened, stabbed or Claimed. Having little option but to go with it—the alternative being to scream and run for the hills—she summoned her courage and gave him a tentative smile.

The beaming grin he offered in return was so dazzling that she was momentarily dumbfounded by his radiance.

"Don't look so scared, Aeylia," he told her in Meyarin, clearly seeing through her attempt at courage. "I'll look after you today. You have nothing to fear."

Deciding to show some spine, Alex quietly lied, *"Atari sae, Aven. Genada torra kin de sae."* Meyarin for, 'Thank you, Aven. That's very kind of you.'

The startled look on his face was well worth her words. "Roka was right—you *are* a quick learner."

Since his words were more complicated this time, she sent him an apologetically puzzled expression and acted like she couldn't understand.

"I guess something is better than nothing," he murmured, holding out a hand and switching to her tongue. "Follow me, Aeylia. Meya awaits."

With nothing left to lose—except, well, *everything*—Alex stood to her feet. She couldn't quite bring herself to take his proffered arm, so she busied her hands by smoothing down the fabric of her outfit instead. She wasn't sure how she felt about the ensemble Kyia had laid out for her that morning. If her parents were around, they would say it was very 'elf-like', since it looked like something one would expect a mythical being to wear. It was stunning, for sure, with a full-length, pale green skirt that fell from her hips and flowed to the floor to meet a pair of strappy flats that were equally pretty. That part was lovely; it was more the top half Alex was uncertain about, since the clothing began only partway up her ribcage, leaving a great deal of midriff bare. Cutting almost horizontally across her upper chest, it also left her shoulders and collarbones exposed, and the short sleeves wrapped around her upper arms like coiling bracelets. What little material the bodice held was embroidered with intricate lace designs, all of it matching the summery colour of the skirt.

It was a beautiful outfit, like something fit for a Meyarin princess. But Alex was uncomfortably aware that her exposed skin was freakishly shimmering thanks to her bond with Xiraxus. It wasn't noticeable to anyone standing more than a few metres away, but to anyone within that range with Meyarin sight, her bioluminescence was impossible to miss.

Unfortunately, there was nothing she could do about her golden sheen, so with a feeling of resignation—for many, many reasons—she silently followed Aven as he led the way out of the sunroom.

When they reached the hallway, he held out his hand for her again—*persistent, much?*—and this time she had no excuse that wouldn't seem downright rude. So, with the trepidation of a mouse poking a tiger, she tentatively placed her non-scarred palm against his. When the world didn't instantly implode, she looked up to find Aven glancing at her curiously.

"You're a jumpy little thing, aren't you?"

Like before, Alex thought it best not to let on how much she understood. And besides, what was she supposed to say to something like that? 'Only around you, you psychopathic murderer'? *Yeah, right.*

Curling his fingers securely around hers, Aven pulled her closer. She made a startled noise at their sudden proximity but thankfully it was mostly drowned out when he activated the *Valispath*. Within moments they were outside the palace and soaring swiftly along a route of Aven's choosing.

When they came to a stop, Alex took a quick step back, extricating herself from his hold and avoiding eye contact by glancing around at their new surroundings. It appeared Aven had brought them to the edge of Meya, right where the land dropped off to meet the river containing the deluge falling from the cliffs surrounding the city. The stunning aquamarine water was captivating, with ripples glinting as they reflected both the light of the sun and the Myrox from the nearby buildings.

"Beautiful, isn't it?" Aven said in her language, and when she turned to him, it was to find him staring intently not at the water, but at her. "We call it *'De la sondrae tella de fora'*." He gave a rueful shake of his head and switched back to Meyarin. "But that's meaningless to you without me knowing the translation in the common tongue."

He turned away, clearly frustrated. But Alex didn't need his translation.

De la sondrae tella de fora. 'The light that falls from the stars.'

It sounded as lovely as the view in front of them deserved, with the water lit up like a thousand rays of starlight dripping from the heavens to the earth. Alex almost considered communicating with Aven that she understood, given how upset he appeared to be by their language barrier. But before she could decide, a voice called out, diverting her attention.

"Aven! Finally! By the stars, where have you been? You were supposed to meet me over an hour ago!"

Alex's breath hitched as the owner of the impatient voice stepped out from the balcony of what looked to be some kind of waterside bistro with a sign calling it *De Talen*—'The Edge'. She knew her expression showed her surprise, but she couldn't help it. He looked so different from when she'd seen him just a few days ago. No longer grungy and dressed in millennia-old prison rags, Niyx was as youthful and full of vitality as Aven. His amethyst eyes were sparkling, his black hair was still choppy but shining with health, and replacing his pale skin was a glowing tan.

"I mean, I get it—you're the prince and blah, blah, blah," Niyx continued, approaching them, "but seriously, with all that trouble we caused the other day, I thought maybe—" He cut off abruptly, seeming to notice Alex for the first time. "Oh. I see." He raised a cocky eyebrow and sent a knowing look to Aven before turning back to her. "Well, *he-llo* there. And who might you be, gorgeous?"

Aven made a derisive sound. "Save it, Niyx. She doesn't yet know enough to understand you. And trust me when I say that's to her benefit. Tone it back a notch, would you? Some of us want to keep our breakfast down."

Niyx's second eyebrow rose to join the first. "Ahh, can this be the lovely *Lasa* Aeylia you've told me so much about?"

Alex twitched, and Niyx caught the movement, his brows rising a fraction higher.

"She only arrived yesterday," Aven argued, drawing Niyx's attention back to him. "I've hardly mentioned her at all."

"Exactly. I'm reading between the lines of how much you *didn't* say."

Aven's gaze narrowed. "I don't know what you're talking about."

"She's very pretty, especially with the *vaeliana*," Niyx said with a smirk, eyeing the now excruciatingly uncomfortable Alex from head to toe. "That's one of the things that you didn't say. Would you like me to list the others?"

"Enough, Niyx," Aven said through his teeth. "I'm sorry I was late, all right? I was on my way here when Roka waylaid me to ask if I'd look after Aeylia for the day. I get it; you're unnaturally punctual and you're annoyed I was so late. But this game isn't necessary."

"Game?" Niyx was clearly amused. "Who said anything about a game?"

"I mean it." Aven's face was serious. "Whatever you're thinking, about me, about her, about *you*, stop it right now."

Niyx crossed his arms, his smirk still in place. "I'll let it go—for now. But only because we're being shamefully rude." He turned to Alex and, to her disbelief, spoke the common tongue with perfect fluency. "Apologies for being so discourteous, *Lasa* Aeylia. I'm *Loro* Niyx, firstborn son and heir to House Raedon of the High Court. I also happen to have the misfortune of calling this brute my best friend." He jerked a thumb towards Aven. "He's not so bad once you get to know him, but—nope, who am I kidding? He's a pain in the ass most of the time. But you'll learn to love him."

Alex could do nothing but gape from the confident manner in which he conversed.

"What did you say to her?" Aven demanded, grabbing the arm of his friend to pull him away from Alex.

Niyx casually dislodged his hand. "Relax. I was just introducing myself."

Aven looked extremely disgruntled and asked, "Tell me again why I decided not to learn the common tongue with you?"

"Oh, I don't know. Maybe because you're a narcissistic jackass who cares about nothing and no one unless you stand to benefit in some way?"

Alex inhaled sharply, startled by Niyx's candid declaration. But while Aven again missed her unchecked reaction, Niyx caught her every move—and this time his eyes narrowed with curiosity that bordered on suspicion. She, however, was too busy wondering if Aven was going to throw a punch at him to worry about what she might have inadvertently given away.

As it was, she needn't have been concerned. Because instead of lashing out with anger, Aven burst out laughing.

The sound was beyond anything Alex could have imagined. She'd heard him laugh before, but nothing like this. Nothing that sounded so clean and pure and *light*. More than anything else, it was the melody of his laughter that convinced her that he was not—*yet*—her Aven.

All of a sudden Alex wondered if perhaps Lady Mystique had been right—if being in the past was an opportunity to not only learn the skills to defeat him, but to also discover who he was now, who he *could* have been, rather than who he would one day become. Maybe she might even see a fraction of that transition taking place, enough that it might give her some leverage in the future, something to help fight him and *win*.

The idea was so convoluted that it made her head hurt, and when she looked up again, both Aven and Niyx were looking at her in question.

"*Vassa rae,*" she quickly apologised. She turned her eyes to Niyx and said, "Uh, I tuned out for a moment there. Did you ask me something?"

"So you *can* speak," Niyx returned with a perfect white grin. "I was worried for a moment that you might be all looks, no brain. Imagine my relief."

Unsure how to respond, Alex settled on, "You, uh, speak the common tongue very well, *Loro* Niyx."

He shrugged aside her compliment. "It's not a hard dialect to learn."

"So I've been told," she returned, still reeling over how fast the Meyarins were able to pick up new languages.

Aven cleared his throat pointedly and Niyx shot him an annoyed glance before turning back to Alex. "The royal brat wants to know if you'd like a drink?"

Alex blinked, wondering what else she'd missed during the scant seconds she'd been lost in her thoughts. "Uh, sure." Deciding to play nice, she addressed Aven directly, "*Sesu, nalahi. Atari sae.*"

A hint of a smile touched Aven's lips as he nodded at her, and after throwing what appeared to be a warning look in Niyx's direction, he walked off towards the balconied bistro.

When he was far enough away, Niyx snorted and Alex turned back to him to ask, "What's funny?"

"'*Yes, please. Thank you*'—overkill, much? Just how thirsty are you?"

She wrinkled her nose at him. "Hey, I only started learning last night. Give me a break."

At that, he laughed outright. "You know, I almost believe you."

She hesitated a shade too long before schooling her face into puzzlement and asking, "What do you mean?"

"What I *don't* believe," he said, acting like she hadn't spoken at all, "is the story about you being abandoned and left to live with mortals for most of your life. Even if that were true, you would have been born here. *Someone* has to remember you, surely." His eyes trailed over her from head to toe again and he lowered his voice to finish, "*I'd* remember you, I can promise you that."

Alex's entire body solidified at his words. Not at the teasing innuendo behind them, but at the words themselves, and at the memory they called to mind from a few days earlier.

'*I remember you, you know,*' Niyx had told her from his prison cell. '*I shouldn't, but I do... No one remembers, no one except me.*'

And then, as if her subconscious was linking memories, she recalled the first time she'd met Niyx months ago when Zain had dragged him to the palace. '*Come now, kitten... I've missed you these past years.*'

Back then Alex had thought Niyx was just trying to antagonise her, but now...

"Crap on a cracker," Alex whispered, staring at him with incredulity. "You knew. I can't *believe* it. You knew all along, you piece of—"

It was probably for the best that Aven called out and interrupted her then, mostly to stop her from accidentally spilling any secrets to Niyx who looked intrigued by her nonsensical words, but also because whatever name she'd been about to call the future prisoner was likely not appropriate in public, regardless of the fact that no one other than him would have understood her.

"Drinks are up," Aven announced loudly, walking from the indoor bar towards a set of chairs on the café's balcony overlooking the water. "Come and get them."

Niyx looked at Alex with a curious yet challenging expression on his face. "I'd give a lot to hear what you were about to say, but I know our princely friend has a royal lack of patience. Fear not, Aeylia—we can continue our discussion later."

And with those promising words, he motioned with one outstretched arm for her to precede him to the table where Aven was waiting for them.

Mind still reeling, Alex did exactly that, desperately trying not to show how shaken she was with every step she took.

Sixteen

Alex wasn't sure how it happened, but somehow she survived her morning.

While drinking a fruity nectar that again proved the Meyarins had the best food in Medora, Alex listened in silence as Niyx and Aven conversed. It was surreal for her, since everything they said was so *normal*; just two friends catching up over a drink. She couldn't get her head around Aven asking Niyx how his father was, if his mother was still determined to marry him off by the end of the year and if his sister was pleased her *varrungard* results allowed her to join the *Zeltora*. Their conversations were so... mundane.

Even Niyx's return questions to Aven were borderline boring, mostly with him asking about the upcoming end-of-season banquet. Apparently Aven was tasked with planning the annual celebration to farewell the summer. The prince claimed the event was coming along nicely and was on track to be the grandest festival in Meyarin history. But according to Niyx, Aven said that about every event he had a hand in planning, such was his cocky confidence.

As the two of them chatted, Alex truly felt like a fly on the wall, eavesdropping on her future enemy and his best friend. Whenever Niyx tried to draw her into the conversation by mockingly offering to translate for her—his dry tone always just a shade too amused for her liking—she repeatedly told him she was happy being left to her own thoughts.

'Happy' was a stretch of the imagination, because ever since realising that the Niyx of the future knew about Alex's trip to the past, she couldn't stop thinking about what else he'd told her inside his cell. At the time she'd thought he'd been spouting the inane ramblings of a mad Meyarin left alone too long, and she'd barely paid him any attention. But there was something he'd said at the end, something that had sounded like a warning, if only she could recall it. The best she could manage was a reference to change, or perhaps a lack of change. None of that helped her now, though, and anything else he'd said was lost to her subconscious.

She spent most of the time at *De Talen* torn between sipping her drink and straining her memory as she half listened to the two Meyarins catch up as if they hadn't just seen each other yesterday. Putting two and two together, Alex realised Niyx had been involved in whatever 'urgent business' had called Roka and Astophe away from dinner last night—the same business that had prompted Roka to suggest Aven be wiser when choosing his friends.

Given what Alex was learning of the insouciant Niyx—both past and future versions of him—she wholeheartedly agreed that he was trouble with a capital T. But there was also something about him that intrigued her. He was so cavalier, so casually lackadaisical that she almost envied him. Even when Aven told him straight up to stop flirting with the clearly flustered Alex—which happened every time he swapped over to the common tongue—Niyx simply laughed outright and obscenely replied, "Fine, but only because you saw her first." He then misinterpreted the expression Aven threw his way as disbelief and laughingly added, "By the stars, I swear it, Aven. You have my word. She's all yours."

Alex, for her part, had wanted to throw her drink at the both of them for talking about her as though she was nothing more than chattel. Not to mention, doing so within hearing range. But of course she resisted, suspicious that Niyx was trying to provoke her into revealing her deceit.

At the anticipated language-learning rate, she figured she had maybe two more days of acting like she was oblivious to anything but the basics. So, on the off chance she might overhear something of worth, she ignored the byplay between the two Meyarins and continued sipping her beverage, only *imagining* throwing it in their faces.

When they were all finished with their drinks, Niyx excused himself by turning to Alex and saying in Meyarin, "Until next time, gorgeous. And hey, if this one strikes out with you"—he jerked a thumb at Aven—"then I'm always happy to step up and give it a shot. You never know; you might just find me charming. One way or another, I can *guarantee* we'd have a good time."

The roguish wink Niyx sent her was so implicitly wicked that Alex had to dig her nails into her palms to keep from blushing.

She was grateful when Aven diverted his attention by shoving him in the shoulder. "You'd better thank the stars she can't understand you, *kregon*. And for the record, I'm not going to 'strike out' with her because I won't be attempting to strike *in* with her. Aes Daega tasked Roka and me to teach her the ways of our people, nothing more. By the light! What's the matter with you?"

While they bickered back and forth, Alex tried to revisit her mental happy place rather than linger on the idea of Aven trying to strike *anything* when it came to her. That was just… There were no words for how wrong that was. She only managed to keep a grip on her sanity by distractedly wondering why '*kregon*' wasn't able to translate fully. All she could tell was that the future Roka had been right about it impolitely referencing the rear end of *something*, she just wasn't sure what. Not that she particularly wanted to know.

Lost in thought, she missed Niyx whizzing off on the *Valispath* and only realised she and Aven were alone again when he called her name in question.

"*Vassa rae*," she said again, apologising for tuning out and offering a weak smile as her heartbeat hitched now that it was just the two of them once more.

"That's all right, Aeylia," Aven said, his common tongue pronunciation hesitant but clear. "You must have been quite"— he searched for the correct word—"bored listening to Niyx and me. I apologise for negating you."

Alex's brow furrowed at his last sentence before she realised what he'd meant. "Do you mean neglecting me?"

Looking sheepish—and that was an expression Alex *never* would have imagined seeing on Aven's face—he said, "Neglecting, yes." He sighed to himself and muttered in Meyarin, "It's like the blind leading the blind. What a nightmare."

Unable to help agreeing with him, at least for the last part, Alex actually had to bite her cheek to keep from laughing at the ridiculousness of it all.

"Come, Aeylia," Aven said in his native language as he motioned for her to follow him, "and I shall introduce you to the wonder of our fair city."

Quelling her apprehension—for the most part—Alex stepped up beside him and allowed him to lead her through the streets of Meya.

With frequent use of the *Valispath*—which to Alex was comparable to a 'hop on, hop off' bus tour—Aven went about showing her around his favourite parts of the city. He took her high up onto the Golden Cliffs to offer her the best view of the stunning metropolis laid out across the valley and reaching high into the heavens; he took her to the base of one of the waterfalls so she could dip her feet in the clearest water she'd ever seen;

and he took her into the heart of the city where Meyarins were bustling around and going about their daily lives, running errands, trading wares, even practising combat as if for street performances. It was all so normal, but with the picturesque backdrop of something only found in an epic Hollywood blockbuster.

No matter where Aven took her, Alex could only marvel at the architectural phenomenon that was the citadel. The spiralling buildings with their arcs, curves and graceful flowing lines seemed to pay tribute to the simplicity of nature in a way that enabled Meya to defy the ages and remain timeless. Trees of both silver and gold grew in abundance around the shining Myrox-lined buildings, making it seem like the city was both part of, and separate to, the surrounding forest.

Every step Alex took brought a new wonder, a new miracle of design, and she was surprised to realise she was genuinely enjoying her day, regardless of her company. Perhaps even *because* of her company, given that the language barrier meant she and Aven remained mostly silent during the sightseeing trip, which enabled her to fully appreciate the experience without distraction.

Everything was going so well until Aven used the *Valispath* to transport them to what appeared to be the entrance of the city.

It was early in the afternoon and, having just eaten a delicious lunch Aven had purchased for her from a street vendor—some kind of sweet, grainy bread filled with toppings she couldn't recognise—Alex was more content than ever. In fact, she was fully relaxed and at peace, almost charmed by the gentlemanly behaviour he'd consistently displayed throughout the day. She should have known better than to be lulled into a false sense of security. Because given everything she'd experienced in the last few days, nothing was *ever* going to be as easy as enjoying a day out in a foreign city with her sworn enemy without catastrophe striking.

And strike it did.

Because when they arrived near the city's entrance on the outskirts of a large pillared courtyard, Alex knew something unexpected was happening. Something not even Aven had known about, given the inquisitive look on his face.

The courtyard appeared to be hosting some kind of market event, with Meyarins bartering left, right and centre for goods. In the middle stood a small group of people who were gathering the most attention. It was strange seeing their horse and cart laden with goods, mostly because after everything Alex had encountered that day, the display seemed rather primitive.

She glanced at Aven, wondering how to ask without actually asking, and was struck by the look on his face as he gazed upon the group in the middle of the square. She'd never before seen such open wonder splashed across his features.

Interest piqued, Alex turned, and with the force of an incoming freight train, her stomach lurched violently as understanding washed over her.

The people Aven was watching weren't Meyarin—they were *human*.

She automatically reached for Aven's arm, wanting to drag him somewhere—*anywhere*—away from there. But he was too entranced to notice her feebly grabbing for him.

"You there," he called to one of the Meyarins walking by. "What's going on here?"

The male Meyarin paused, his eyes widening in recognition before he bowed deeply. "Prince Aven! What—I mean, uh—It's an honour to meet you, Your Highness!"

Impatient, Aven repeated, "Do you know what's happening here?"

The Meyarin turned to follow the direction in which Aven pointed. "It's Market Day, Your Highness. The mortals have come to trade."

Aven looked puzzled. "But humans rarely ever come here. Normally my father leads a delegation to meet them in Tryllin."

The other Meyarin tugged at his collar, clearly not knowing how to respond.

Seeing he was of little further use, Aven dismissed him with a quiet note of gratitude and, with another deep bow, the Meyarin disappeared back into the crowd.

Throughout the encounter, Alex had struggled to stay silent while panicked thoughts screamed in her mind. All she knew was that this was bad. As in, very, *very* bad.

Aven's face was lit with excitement when he turned back to her. "I've never seen a human up close before. Let's go meet them."

"No!" Alex cried. "*Naha*, Aven!" But he was on a mission and didn't seem to hear her urgent plea, nor did he pick up that she'd understood his Meyarin words. Instead, he grabbed her hand and pulled her after him, his steps buoyant with purpose.

No, no, no! Alex thought, tugging uselessly against his grip. If the account D.C. had once told her was true, meeting mortals for the first time was what prompted Aven's initial hatred for them. Alex was literally about to witness history in the making, and that absolutely terrified her. What was he going to do? What was *she* going to do? Lady Mystique had said nothing could change the course of the future, but the idea that Alex was about to watch events set in motion that still affected the world thousands of years later was enough to make her want to curl up in a ball and hide for all eternity.

"Hello, mortals," Aven said upon reaching the small group at the centre of the courtyard and dragging the reluctant Alex closer to his side. "How are you all today?"

Alex had to give it to him, he at least *sounded* like he understood the common tongue. But when a short, portly woman stepped forward and began to speak, it was clear Aven was lost within seconds.

"It's a mighty fine city you've got here, sir," she said in a deep voice with a broguish accent. "All this shiny My-whatsit stuff sure is pretty in the sunshine. It's like lookin' at starlight, only in daytime. I don't know how you lot get anythin' done 'round 'ere. I'd be too busy lookin' about to do anythin' productive."

When Aven turned wide, pleading eyes towards Alex, she sighed deeply and took pity on both him and the human by stepping forward.

"Uh, hi there. I'm Ale—uh, Aeylia," she said to the woman, catching her name just in time.

The woman appeared to be starstruck as she gawked at Alex. "Bless my socks, but you are somethin' to look at, ain't you? Much more natural than most of these other folk, yet still just like 'em."

"That's, um, very kind of you," she replied, brushing hair behind her ear in an effort to draw attention away from anything that might reveal her humanness. "Might I enquire of your name?"

"There I go again, forgettin' me manners," the woman said, pulling the beret off her head to reveal frizzy grey hair. "Name's Bensie Hayes, and this rusty lot are my companions, Chadwick, Hestor, Dunstan, Emerson and Lilith."

The humans each nodded their heads respectively as Bensie said their names, finishing with Lilith giving Alex a curtseying bob.

"It's a pleasure to meet you all," Alex told them, while internally screaming at them to run before they screwed up everything. "Can I ask, is someone looking after you here?" She motioned to the courtyard, wondering if the group was simply left to fend for themselves.

"Aye," Bensie said. "One of your womenfolk has been translatin' for us. She's just run off on that enchanted path of yours but said she'd be back in a—"

At the sudden appearance of a new Meyarin appearing out of what seemed like thin air on the *Valispath*, Bensie let out a startled oath before offering an apologetic glance to Alex and finishing, "Uh, looks like she's back now."

Alex had to hold back a smile at how terrified Bensie and her companions appeared. Not so long ago, Alex, Jordan, Bear and D.C. had visited Meya for the first time and they'd probably looked even more fearful than this motley group.

"Apologies for leaving you alone, mortals," said the female Meyarin whose back was to Alex, her tone brusque. "The king has agreed to the trade and permitted me to make the exchange on his behalf."

The Meyarin turned and, seeing Aven, her eyes lit with recognition. Because of that, she missed Alex's doing the same, but towards *her*.

"Vaera, can you translate for me?" Aven asked. "I want to ask them a few questions before you finalise their affairs."

Alex was trying so hard to rein in her shock that she missed whatever accepting words the female Meyarin replied with.

Vaera.

Alex had seen her before—just once, on her first trip to the Lost City. At the time, Vaera had been one of the guards stationed at the front archway entrance into the palace along with Zain. Like everyone else Alex knew in the future, this version of the Meyarin was more youthful looking, but her glossy black hair still hung in waves down her back and her steel-grey eyes were as intense as Alex remembered.

"This is Prince Aven, second-born son to Royal House Dalmarta of the High Court," Vaera told the humans, whose eyes widened as they each proceeded with more bowing and an even deeper curtsey from Lilith. "The prince offers his apologies for not yet being fluent in the common tongue, and he has asked if I would stand in as translator, provided that you don't mind."

"Not at all, sir—uh, Your Highness, sir," Bensie said to Aven, twisting her hat nervously in her hands. "We're happy to answer anythin' you've a mind to ask."

No, no, no, Alex thought frantically, but all she could do was watch in muted horror as Aven through Vaera began to question the humans about the wares they had brought to trade.

Bensie and her crew seemed delighted by the regard of the prince and they responded eagerly to his questions, telling Aven all about the items in their possession. With every description, Alex found herself wincing more and more in line with Aven's darkening face.

The humans had brought medicinal herbs, but the Meyarins didn't need them since they couldn't get fatally sick and they had abundant access to *laendra* for the healing of any other injuries. The Meyarins also didn't need the spices that were offered, since their food was already decadent enough. Textile fabrics were unnecessary when the clothing of the immortal race was silkier and sturdier than anything the mortals could yet produce. The soaps and perfumes, while pleasant, were valueless to the people of Meya who, from Alex's experience, seemed to permeate their own naturally pleasant aromas. The wax candles were entirely redundant due to the advanced *myraes* that needed nothing in order to burn. The handcrafted trinkets—blown glass jewellery, pottery and wood sculptures— were nothing beyond ordinary to the eye. Even their cases of bottled wine likely paled in comparison to the liquor already available to the immortal race.

Quite frankly, Alex could actually *kind of* understand why Aven looked like he was about to throw a fit. But it only became worse when he asked Vaera what the humans were receiving in return for their wares.

Her answer astonished him—and Alex too, even if she had already known that Meya provided the humans much of what made them into the future version of themselves. But that didn't mean she wasn't still surprised by the detailed inventory of what Meya was giving the humans. Everything from medicines to weapons to practical knowledge that helped with the mortals' advancements in technology was offered to them, all traded in return for a handful of useless wares and some art that even the eclectic Pablo Picasso himself would turn his nose up at.

Alex wasn't surprised when, without so much as a word of farewell, Aven stormed away from the humans, activated the *Valispath* and took off for the palace. The reason she wasn't surprised was because that's exactly what D.C. said had happened. Right this moment, Aven was on his way to demand the king cease the trade alliance with the humans, claiming that they were earning everything while the Meyarins received nothing in return. Which was, essentially, true. But, if D.C. was correct, Astophe would turn Aven down, saying that 'he would understand one day'. That, in turn, would prompt Aven to begin meeting in secret with other young Meyarins, eventually leading to the mass slaughter of the next human trade delegation to set foot in the city, followed by his attempted murder of Astophe and Roka right before his pending banishment.

Knowing how it was all going to play out and that there was nothing she could do to stop him made Alex feel sick. Because of that, she pushed aside her nausea and focused on her more immediate concerns—like the fact that Aven had left her on her own, with no way to get back to the palace.

"Crap," she muttered, looking about the courtyard at the Meyarins going about their business.

Vaera was the only one around who might be willing to take her back to the palace, but before Alex could interrupt her to ask for a ride, Vaera nodded her head at the humans, handed them a sealed scroll, took a step away and vanished on the *Valispath*.

"Double crap," Alex said, louder this time.

Hearing her curse, Bensie walked over and said, "'Twas a right nice pleasure meetin' you, m'lady. Please share our farewells with your prince as well. A fine gentleman, that one. We don't oft visit your grand city, but perchance we'll return next moon cycle and happen upon him again."

"No!" Alex blurted out.

Startled, Bensie asked, "M'lady?"

"I, uh, I just mean…" She stumbled over what to say. "Meyarins—my people—we value our privacy. It's, um, probably best if you wait until we come to you next. Allow us some time to grow comfortable with the idea of you visiting us."

Eyeing her shrewdly and likely reading the panic on her face, Bensie slowly nodded her head. "As you wish, Lady Aeylia. We won't return 'til we're invited. Does that comfort you?"

Alex felt shaky with relief. "Indeed it does, Madam Hayes. Thank you."

Bensie offered a crinkled smile, her weathered features like brushed leather. "Not at all, m'lady, and while it's a fine thing to hear you callin' me Madam, I'm but a humble tradeswoman. 'Bensie' is all you need call me."

"Well then, Bensie," Alex said with a smile that seemed to enchant the old lady. "It seems you've lost your translator again—did she say when she'd be back?"

Bensie shook her head. "Lady Vaera won't be returnin'. We've already settled our business for the day." She waved the scroll in her hands and pointed to her companions who were packing up the horse and cart. "We'll be leavin' soon. 'Tis a long walk home."

At that, Alex's shoulders dropped. If Vaera wasn't coming back, then she truly was on her own, since she doubted she was at the top of Aven's list of priorities right now. The only comforting news was that Roka was expecting to continue her Meyarin education that evening, so worst case scenario, if she failed to show up for her lessons, he would hopefully search for her. But that was still hours away.

"I won't take any more of your time," Alex told Bensie, realising that they likely didn't have Bubbledoors invented this far in the past, and wondering just how long it would take the humans to walk to wherever they were settled. "It was a pleasure meeting you."

"Mayhap we'll meet again, Lady Aeylia," Bensie returned with a wrinkled wink. "I'll chance lookin' forward to that day."

Please don't, Alex thought, but outwardly offered another smile and a bob of her head, before turning on her heels and walking away from the last humans who would ever visit Meya and make it out alive.

Seventeen

Hours later, Alex stumbled through the dark streets of Meya, shivering from the storm that had blown in earlier that evening. Drenched to the bone, her summery clothes offered little protection from the stinging rain and unseasonably cold wind. A deluge of water streamed from the sky that lit up with unending lightning flashes—flashes that reflected off the citadel's Myrox-lined buildings, leaving Alex in a constant state of near blindness. And yet she continued onwards, determined to make her way back to the palace; back to at least an illusion of safety.

It was only when a vein of lightning struck a golden tree barely twenty feet away, cleaving it in half and leaving a smouldering wreck of nature behind, that Alex realised perhaps she was best taking a breather and waiting for the storm to pass.

The alleyway she was in was much darker than the other streets she'd travelled that night, but she'd chosen it because it kept her on a straight path towards the palace. And given how visually impaired she was from the storm, she needed all the help she could get if she wanted to make it back to the palace before dawn.

Meya, she was realising, was *not* a small city. Despite her best efforts to activate her Meyarin blood so she could run with the speed of the immortal race and thus shorten the time of her journey considerably, Alex was still too keyed up after everything that had happened with Aven to concentrate enough to make the change occur. That meant she'd been stuck walking for hours and felt as if she'd barely made any headway.

An ear-splitting crack of thunder overhead prompted Alex to hustle over to the nearest inhabited dwelling, opening the door and stepping quickly inside. Attempting to wring the water from her clothes rather than drip it all through the place, Alex cast her eyes around and noted that she had entered some kind of poorly lit tavern. Grateful as she was for respite from the storm, she didn't want to judge it based on her initial assessment, but the truth was, she doubted the pub—with a scrawled sign calling it *Narsae de Trigon*, or 'The Scarlet Thief'—was the kind of establishment many upstanding Meyarins frequented, given the ragtag patronage. Regardless, she was willing to take a chance with the dubious-looking clientele and ignore their flagrant debauchery if it meant she'd be allowed a moment of rest from her journey.

Glancing around, Alex saw an empty stool at the bar and slowly made her way over to it. She kept her gaze low and avoided all eye contact with the current patrons as she passed their tables and booths, ignoring the skin-crawling feeling of them watching as she walked by, dripping water all the way.

The moment she pulled herself up onto the stool, a gruff-looking Meyarin sauntered over to her from behind the bar.

"*Terin doro trae melana sae?*" he asked. Meyarin for, 'What can I get you?'

Having no currency of any kind, Alex shook her head and politely declined service, "*Trae osso, atari.*"

The barman leaned closer, his stance somewhat threatening. "*Naha coran, naha vestu.*"

Swallowing thickly as she translated his 'no drink, no scat' policy, Alex moved to stand, figuring that she might be better off trying her luck with the storm after all. But before she could make it fully to her feet, a calloused hand came down on her bare shoulder, pushing her none too gently back onto the stool.

"I've got this exquisite creature covered, Tohro," came a raspy sounding voice at her ear, the Meyarin words dripping with smug confidence. "A round for both of us. Actually, make that two."

Alex crinkled her nose at the repugnant smell emanating from the male Meyarin sliding into the stool beside her. It was as if he'd bathed in enough liquor that the smallest spark of flame would set him alight. And yet, he didn't seem drunk. His black eyes were sharp, his speech clear and steady.

"I think you've had enough fun for the night, Skraegon," said the barman, Tohro, glancing between the stiffly alert Alex and the newcomer Meyarin watchfully. "Why don't you go back and finish up with Faluh? She's looking impatient to retreat to your room."

"Faluh can wait," Skraegon said, his gaze trailing lazily over Alex. "And I've not had anywhere near enough fun yet tonight. But I'm about to, aren't I, my sweet?"

Skraegon reached a hand out and traced it across Alex's shoulder and down the skin of her arm. Feeling violated, she snatched at his fingers and shoved him away from her. She then jumped to her feet so fast that her stool fell over with a crash, drawing the attention of all those around them.

"You've got fire, I'll give you that," Skraegon said, standing more slowly. "I like that in a girl."

Not at all comfortable with the eager look on his face, Alex decided that enough was enough. Being struck by lightning was surely better than this. She spun on her heel and made a hasty retreat towards the door, but she barely made it halfway across the room before her arm was grabbed and she was yanked violently backwards.

"Where do you think you're going?" Skraegon demanded, blowing liquor-scented breath into her face. "We haven't even started to play."

Mind blank, Alex couldn't come up with any Meyarin words to yell at the foul beast. So she stuck with the language she did know and hissed, "Unhand me right now, or I promise you'll regret it."

She, of course, didn't know *how* she would make him regret it, since he was easily a foot taller than her and at least twice her weight.

Skraegon's eyes narrowed with his lack of comprehension. "What did you just say?" When she didn't respond, knowing he wouldn't understand her anyway, he shook her roughly enough to cause her to wince with pain.

"Let me go!" Alex screamed at him, struggling in earnest now. Reacting from fear, she fisted her free hand and brought it up to smash it into his face, causing him to stumble back a few steps, releasing her in the process.

It seemed as if the entire tavern turned silent and sucked in a collective breath, waiting to see what would happen next.

"Skraegon," Tohro called, scurrying out from behind the bar and quickly approaching the Meyarin who was looking at Alex with scorching disbelief. "I'm sure she didn't mean it. You just startled her. Look—Faluh's still waiting for you. Why don't you go and enjoy your time with her? Your next drinks are on me."

Skraegon ignored him and raised a hand to his face where Alex had hit him. In a low, burning voice he asked, "Do you like to play rough, youngling? Because I can do rough."

In the blink of an eye he had her thrown across the room and pushed up against a wall, her arms pinned above her head, his body pressed firmly against hers to trap her in place.

Panicking now, she struggled fiercely against him, but his hold on her was unyielding. She bucked her torso to no avail.

She kicked out at him, but he just moved to the side. She even tried head-butting him, but he just laughed and swiftly moved out of range. In her horror-stricken state, she couldn't begin to try tapping into her Meyarin abilities, and her human weakness meant she was entirely at his disposal.

"Keep fighting, sweet," his greasy voice whispered into her ear, sounding sickly satisfied by her miserable attempts to free herself.

"Let go of me!" Alex shrieked in his face again. Then, appealing to their riveted audience, she yelled, "Please! Someone help me!" Knowing her common words were useless, she managed to call up what Roka had taught her last night and cried, *"Nalahi suros rae!"* But still, no one moved to intervene, not even Tohro, who had slunk back behind the bar and was wiping glasses to avoid her pleading gaze.

What was *wrong* with these people? Why were they just allowing this thug of a Meyarin to attack her in front of them?

She heard the door to the tavern blow open just as Skraegon grabbed both of her wrists in one hand, freeing his other to wander sleazily down her body.

Repulsed by his touch, Alex renewed her frantic struggle against him, but still to no effect. She sucked in a shuddering, horrified lungful of air and screamed one more time straight into his face, as loud and shrill as she possibly could, "LET ME GO!"

And then suddenly she wasn't propped up against him anymore, because he was ripped away and tossed into a table across the room.

"It appears the girl wants to be released, Skraegon," the rain-soaked newcomer said, his voice low and furious. But more than that, it was *familiar.*

He had his back to her, but even dressed in sodden, tattered clothing, Alex would have recognised his dark-skinned, bulky physique anywhere.

"Zain?" Her voice was barely a whisper, but it was enough for his Meyarin ears to catch, and he turned back to look at her in puzzlement. Her eyes widened as Skraegon took advantage of his distraction and leapt forward. "Zain, look out!"

Her future friend turned back just in time to duck Skraegon's attack. What proceeded next was the bar brawl to end all bar brawls, with suddenly everyone jumping in on the action. The Meyarins moved like flashes, so fast that Alex was unable to track them with her human sight, but she was still too freaked out to try and calm down enough to access her heightened senses. More than ever, she wished she'd had more training on how to act like a Meyarin, because instead of grabbing Zain and fighting their way out of there together, she was stuck cowering in the corner, waiting and hoping that they would both make it out in one piece.

A crackle of thunder roared so loudly from outside that Alex had to clap her hands over her ears, along with many of the fighting Meyarins who had to pause mid-attack to do so. A heartbeat later came a lightning strike so close and full of energy that her hair stood on end, but that wasn't all that happened. Somehow the strike caused the low-lit *myraes* illuminating the tavern to splutter out as if blowing a fuse. Instant darkness surrounded them, with unending surges of lightning from outside keeping the well-seeing Meyarins nearly as blind as Alex with her mortal sight.

When someone grabbed her in the dark, she didn't hesitate to throw her free hand out in a solid uppercut to what she presumed was her assailant's jaw. A low curse came in response, and recognising the tone of Zain's voice, Alex cried out, "Crap, I'm sorry!"

He uttered another terse oath and started dragging her after him in the pitch-black, lightning stunned tavern.

She followed without question, even when he led her outside onto the stormy street and started jogging down the alley.

She kept up as best as she could despite the blinding flashes, deafening thunder and piercing rain, only managing to do so because he wasn't using Meyarin speed.

When they were what Alex judged to be about three blocks away from The Scarlet Thief, Zain yanked her to the side of the road and kicked open a doorway, pushing her inside ahead of him.

Gasping for breath in the shadowy room, Alex bent at the waist, placing her hands on her knees to steady her raging heartbeat. A light bloomed into existence when Zain lit a sconce of *myraes* and shadows flickered around the dilapidated room they were in, bouncing across his uncharacteristically scruffy and rain-drenched features.

"Thanks so much for your help back there," Alex told him wholeheartedly, wiping her scraggly wet hair off her face. Seeing his questioning look at her use of the common tongue, she repeated what she could in broken Meyarin, "*Atari sae... suros... Narsae de Trigon.*"

"How do you speak the tongue of mortals so well and yet you do not know your own language?"

Alex blinked at him, stunned. "You know the common tongue?"

Zain crossed his massive arms and water fell from the creases in his shabby clothes. "Much of my time is spent amongst mortals. It helps if we can understand each other."

Confused and quite frankly feeling out of her right mind, Alex said, "But... how can you spend much time with them if you're busy leading the *Zeltora*? Don't you have responsibilities with Roka?"

The look Zain levelled towards Alex made her feel as if she were a few too many seeds short of a strawberry.

"Roka? As in, *Prince* Roka?" Zain let out a burst of laughter. "He'd call for my imprisonment before so much as *thinking* of allowing me into his precious elite guard." He snorted, still amused but why, Alex had no idea. "What is this nonsense of which you speak?"

"But... If you're not with Roka or the *Zeltora*... Then..." Alex looked around the empty room in helpless confusion. "Didn't he send you to come find me tonight? Isn't that why you saved me?"

Zain shrugged carelessly, more water sloshing with the movement. "*Narsae de Trigon* might not be the most reputable establishment, but you learn to ignore the regulars after you've tasted their *glaeron*. You won't find a finer brew anywhere else in the city."

"Wait... Are you saying...?"

"I was on my way there for a drink when I heard your screams from down the street," Zain told her. "It's suicide to call the *Valispath* in a storm like this, otherwise I would have made it to you sooner. But you at least looked like you were holding your own when I arrived, I'll give you that."

It was Alex's turn to snort. "I don't think so. That Skraegon guy was about to—about to—" She couldn't finish the sentence, not allowing her mind to go there.

"Skraegon is a bully," Zain said, his voice harsh. "Tonight wasn't the first time he and I have scrapped. And since he continues to ignore common decency, it likely won't be the last."

"Scrapped?" Alex repeated, incredulous at his choice of description. "That's what you call what happened tonight?"

"Tonight was nothing." Zain brushed aside her concern with a wave of his hand, flinging more water everywhere. "But back to the prince—you seem under the impression that he sent me after you like some hound doing his master's bidding, but you're wrong. I just happened upon you at the right time to hear your distress, nothing more."

Reeling from the idea that Zain and Roka weren't, well, *Zain and Roka*, all Alex could do was nod and offer her gratitude again. "Well, thank you, Zain. I really appreciate you stepping in for me."

Eyeing her thoughtfully, Zain's lips pursed at what he saw. He raised his hands to unclasp his cloak, swinging it from his shoulders—again, with water flying everywhere—and then stepped determinedly towards Alex, handing it to her. "Here. It's only wet on the outside. If I didn't know better, I'd say you look like you're freezing."

That's because Alex *was* freezing—from the rain and wind, but more from the shock of the last twenty minutes. However, she also knew Meyarins were supposed to be hardier than humans. A little storm shouldn't have caused her to be so shiveringly cold, regardless of how minimal her clothing was.

"Thanks again," Alex said quietly, throwing his bulky cloak around her, pleasantly surprised to discover his words true since it offered instant, dry heat.

"You can thank me properly by telling me two things," he returned, his dark eyes watching her closely. "First, why would the crown prince send his *Zeltora* after you?"

That was easy, at least.

"I'm a guest of the palace," Alex answered. "I was meant to meet with Roka tonight but I spent the day in the city with Aven. He, uh, had to take off unexpectedly, leaving me to walk back. I figured since I didn't make my meeting with Roka that he would have found out what happened and sent someone to come find me."

"Why didn't you use the *Valispath*? The storm didn't begin until after sundown. You could have activated it anytime before then."

"I'm new to Meya," Alex said, mentally adding, *this one, anyway*. "There's a lot I don't know, including how to call upon the Eternal Path."

Zain's eyes narrowed. "How can you be new to Meya if you are Meyarin?"

"I grew up with humans," Alex said as casually as she could manage, neither accepting nor denying his assertion of her race. "I don't know anything about Meya or the ways of Meyarins—including how to activate the *Valispath*. Roka and Aven have just started to teach me."

Zain placed his hands on his hips, his stance wide, his features alert. "That brings me to the second thing you're going to tell me."

"And that is?"

"You know me," he accused. "You called my name back in *Narsae de Trigon*, but I've never seen you before. I want to know how you know who I am, and I want to know right now."

Alex stilled, and all she could think was, *Well, triple crap.*

Eighteen

"You called me by my name," Zain repeated when Alex remained silent. "Without hesitation, like you knew exactly who I was."

She quickly tried to recover from her unnatural stillness and lack of speech, figuring her only option was to lie. "No, I didn't."

His lips thinned. "You said it twice in the tavern; once just my name, the second time you yelled, '*Zain, look out!*'"

"You're name's Zain?" Alex asked, playing dumb. "That's so weird—I was actually calling out 'rain' since the door was open and the rain was blowing inside from the wind. Half the benches in there were wood which would have ended up wet and rotting, and no one wants to sit on rotting wood, don't you agree?" Reading his expression, she cleared her throat. "So you must have heard me wrong. But nice to meet you, Zain. I'm Ale—Aeylia."

His voice was dripping with disbelief when he repeated, "Ale-Aeylia?"

At the second stuff up of her name that day, Alex wondered what the chances were of her stepping outside and convincing the lightning to strike her. Given her lack of fortune to date, it would be more likely to strike everywhere else and she'd still be left facing the irate Meyarin across from her, only surrounded by more water and wind than the dark, abandoned room they currently inhabited.

"That's right," she said, rallying. "But mostly I'm known here as Aeylia. Fewer syllables. Easier to say. You know how it is." She almost tacked on a question about whether 'Zain' was short for anything, but she figured she was already pushing her luck.

She was right.

"Well, *Aeylia*," Zain said, his tone as hard as his features, "even if I believed for one second that you called out, '*Rain, look out!*' back at the bar—which I *don't*—then how do you explain two minutes ago when you thanked me by name?"

Flipping heck. Alex *had* done that.

"I'm a mind reader," she blurted out, wincing internally at how stupid she sounded.

Zain shook his head. "Try again."

"No, really," she said, rolling with it. "Right now, for example, you're thinking I'm crazy."

"And right *now* I'm thinking those might be the only true words I've heard you say all night."

It seemed they were at an impasse. Zain's stance was unwavering, but Alex couldn't give him what he wanted to hear. She let out a deep sigh, her shoulders slumping.

"Zain, please," she said in a quiet voice. "I know you have absolutely no reason to trust me, but I'm asking you—I'm *begging* you—please let this go."

He held her gaze, his own eyes roaming over her face, reading her. She forced herself to maintain eye contact, only blinking again when he gave one short, terse nod.

"Fine," he said. "I'll let it go, but only if you swear by the stars that you'll answer one day."

Alex bobbed her head emphatically. "That I can do." One day in the far, *far* future she would do exactly that.

"Swear it."

Unsure exactly what to say, Alex made it up on the fly. "Uh, I swear by the stars that one day I'll tell you how I know your name."

Jaw clenched, it was Zain's turn to sigh, and Alex wasn't sure if it was in frustration, acceptance or both.

"It sounds like the storm's fading," he said, holding to his promise to let it go. "You should be fine to head back out there now."

Alex mustered up her best cutesy-cute expression and socked it to him. Apparently even immortal, badass Meyarins weren't immune to her doe-eyed, 'please-help-poor-little-old-me' expression, since he sighed again, much deeper this time.

"The *Valispath* should be safe again," he said, stalking past her and towards the door. "Hurry up and I'll get you back to your prince."

"He's not *my* prince," Alex stated, rushing after him through the lingering drizzle of rain, the lightning now flashing far off in the distance.

"I don't care who he is as long as you're his problem, not mine."

Alex didn't deign to respond, but she *did* pull a face at Zain's back.

"Move, Aeylia," Zain barked. "I don't have all night."

She jumped, thinking he'd caught her immature gesture, but realised he was just eager to be rid of her. Rolling her eyes at this younger but decidedly crabbier version of Zain, she hurried over to his side and braced herself in preparation for the ground moving out from underneath them. But it didn't help, as she still went slamming into the barrier.

Ignoring Zain's disdainful look, she glanced around as they zoomed through the weather-beaten city. The damage was nowhere near as bad as she would have imagined in the storm's wake. There was hardly any indication that there had been any kind of severe meteorological event at all. Clearly the city was

192 · Lynette Noni

not only architecturally beautiful, but also structurally sound. No wonder it lasted so well throughout the millennia—as Alex could attest to first hand.

When the *Valispath* came to a stop outside the grand archway entrance to the palace, Alex turned to thank Zain when another voice jumped in before she could speak.

"Aeylia! Thank the light!"

Alex glanced over to see Roka jogging in her direction, soaked from head to toe. The relief on his face was stark as his eyes took her in, assessing her physical state. He then turned to Zain and his features tightened.

"If you hurt her, I swear—"

Zain's face darkened. "Calm yourself, princeling. Your precious Aeylia is safe. You should be grateful I happened upon her at The Scarlet Thief when I did, otherwise I likely wouldn't be able to offer the same assurance."

Alex shuddered, knowing his words were true.

All eyes flicked to her, noting her reaction to words she shouldn't have comprehended, so she covered by unclasping Zain's cloak and handing it back to him.

"Thanks for this," she said.

He didn't respond other than reaching for the material, and she wondered if perhaps he didn't want Roka to know he'd understood her use of the common tongue.

Casting one last piercing glare at the prince, Zain took off on the *Valispath* again.

Roka watched until he was out of sight before turning to Alex. "I've been looking for you everywhere. Aven said—He told me—" Roka broke off, swiping his drenched dark hair off his face. "Stars, I'm sorry, Aeylia. I don't know what he was thinking leaving you out here on your own. I *never* would have asked him to look after you today if I thought he'd abandon you."

"Hey, it's okay," Alex said, placing her freezing fingers on Roka's arm. Feeling his wet but warm skin, she quickly retracted her hand in renewed realisation that a Meyarin wouldn't be as cold as she was. "I'm good, see? No harm done."

He looked at her incredulously. "No harm done? How can you say that when I found you standing at the entrance to the palace with one of Meya's most notorious criminals?"

Zain, a criminal? Alex couldn't help it, she burst out laughing.

Roka looked at her in concern. "Come, let's get you inside. I can't imagine how you ended up at *Narsae de Trigon* but you've clearly had a traumatic evening. You should rest."

"Could this place get *any* weirder?" Alex asked between guffaws as the *Valispath* zoomed them straight to her bedroom. When they came to a stop in the hallway next to her door, she laughingly added, "Next you'll be telling me that you and Kyia hate each other."

Roka's brow furrowed. "Hate is a very strong word. But I'm surprised you picked up on that—usually we try to hide how we feel about each other when we're around others."

That brought Alex up short and she immediately sobered. "Wait, what?" At Roka's questioning look, she added, "Aren't you two betrothed?"

It was the prince's turn to burst out laughing. His head fell back and everything, so great was his mirth. "By all the stars in the sky, where did you hear *that*?"

Alex felt like everything she knew was crumbling around her. "But you're... You're..." She paused, gathered her thoughts, and tried again. "You're Roka and Kyia. That's who you are."

Roka was still laughing as he shook his head. "We put on a good front in public, since both of us grew up in court and know how to play the political game. But we can barely stand each other, Aeylia."

Seeing the truth all over his features, Alex wasn't sure if she wanted to cry or hit something. *The past sucks*, she thought, wondering how everything could be so wrong. How could Zain, Roka's right-hand man, leader of the *Zeltora*, be a criminal? And a notorious one, at that? How could the almost sickeningly in-love Kyia and Roka not be a couple, let alone not be able to stand one another? How were both Aven and Niyx—Rebel Leader and Rebel Underling of the future—what Alex would almost consider *nice*?

When her thoughts lingered on Aven, Alex knew she didn't want to ask. Really, she didn't. But she had to know what she was dealing with, so she sucked up the courage to enquire, "Is your brother all right?"

When Roka's jaw tightened, she knew the answer wasn't good, even if all he did was repeat, "He never should have left you."

Alex waved her hand. "Let's move on from that. Is he okay after whatever caused him to take off in such a hurry?"

Roka gave a short shake of his head. "My brother is many things. Disillusioned is now perhaps one of them. His eyes have been opened to some truths he was not prepared to discover and he has yet to accept the way things are. But don't trouble yourself, Aeylia. He will be fine."

Alex could read Roka's body language enough to know he was not at all pleased with whatever happened in the wake of his brother storming back to the palace.

"What about Zain?" Alex asked, jumping topics so swiftly she was surprised Roka didn't get whiplash. "If he's a criminal, why didn't you arrest him?"

Roka's tightened jaw locked even further. He only unclenched it to say, "One good deed deserves another. I'd been searching for you all night, but he returned you to the palace unharmed. I could not in good conscience call the guards upon him."

"He didn't just return me unharmed, Roka," Alex said carefully. "Zain saved my life tonight."

"I'm sure you're overreacting," Roka said, smiling slightly as if to take the dismissive sting out of his words. "*Narsae de Trigon* is not a place I would ever wish you to visit, but that doesn't mean—"

"Do you know a Meyarin called Skraegon?" Alex interrupted.

The fire that lit behind Roka's golden eyes and the air that hissed from between his teeth was all the confirmation she needed.

"Trust me, Roka. I'm not overreacting," she promised quietly, her voice full of meaning. "Zain *did* save my life tonight. Or he at least saved me from a broken life no one should have to endure. Criminal or not, I now owe him."

Eyes boring into her own, Roka asked, "What would you have me do, Aeylia?"

Alex didn't understand his response. "Do about what?"

"You're meant to be under the protection of House Dalmarta, *my* protection," Roka said. "Another member of my House let you down, therefore *I* let you down, so I owe you reparation for that. If you owe Zain, and I owe you, then it leads to the conclusion that *I* owe Zain. So tell me, Aeylia, what would you have me do?"

Alex suddenly realised the position of power she was in. And she wasn't going to waste it, even if she was taking advantage of the situation. "I want you to let Zain try out for the *Zeltora*."

Roka threw back his head again, laughing uproariously once more.

Alex stood with her arms crossed, waiting for him to compose himself. "I'm not kidding, Roka."

"Zain Erraeya would sooner die than be a part of my elite guard," Roka said, humour still in his eyes as he looked back at Alex. "The *Zeltora* stands for everything he's against. Truth, justice and moral decency."

Alex was shaking her head. "You're wrong. They mean *everything* to him." At Roka's probing look, she winced mentally at her appalling lack of care and quickly added, "From, uh, what I gathered in the few minutes I was with him." She hurried on to cover further by saying, "And just so you know, he's of the opinion that it's *you* who would sooner imprison him than allow him into the *Zeltora*."

"He's not wrong."

"Roka!" Alex cried, annoyed now. "You asked me what you could do. I gave you my answer. Are you going to fulfil your debt or not?"

Roka eyed her thoughtfully. "You're serious, aren't you?"

"Deadly," she answered truthfully.

"You want me to allow Zain Erraeya to attempt the *varrungard*? And if he completes it with the necessary results, you then want me to offer him a place in training to become one of my most trusted warriors?"

"I do."

A muscle ticked in Roka's cheek and he moved away to start pacing, muttering under his breath in Meyarin, "I must be mad for even considering this. But what else am I to do? If he truly did save her from that beast of a Meyarin, then I owe the *kregon*." Roka ran an aggravated hand through his slowly drying hair and continued walking. "All this is Aven's fault. If that *norot* brother of mine causes me to end up with a dagger in my back at the hands of one of my own warriors, I swear by the stars I'll haunt him from my grave."

Alex hid a smile at the thought—both at Roka haunting his brother, which would admittedly be rather funny, and at the idea of Zain so much as laying a hand on his future best friend.

Finally releasing a deep huff of air, Roka moved back to stand before Alex.

"He gets one chance," Roka said firmly. "That's it. If he does anything wrong, he's not just out, I'll lock him up in *Taevarg* myself. Is that clear?"

Alex grinned widely. "Crystal."

Roka made a face that told her just how much he wished she were someone else's responsibility. That only made her smile more.

"Get some rest, Aeylia," he ordered with a resigned grumble. "I need to figure out how to find your new friend and convince him to attempt the *varrungard* since I'm certain you won't take 'no' for an answer from him either, am I right?"

"You already know me so well, Roka. We're gonna get on great."

Judging by the look he sent her, Alex figured she'd pushed her luck enough for the night and moved quickly to open her door.

"I'm not sure what's happening with Aven," Roka said just before she could escape into her room, causing her to glance back at him. "But regardless, you'll have a full day of learning tomorrow. Be prepared, since after I've lost all my dignity by begging a criminal to become a warrior sworn to protect our people, I likely won't go easy on you."

Knowing his threat wasn't idle, she said, "I can accept that. And seriously, thanks, Roka. It means a lot that you're willing to do this. All of it—taking care of me, teaching me, everything."

Roka offered her a small smile but otherwise waved aside her thanks. "Sleep, Aeylia. I'll see you in the morning."

She stepped through her door and had it almost closed before she called out to him one last time, saying, "Just so you know, we're not done talking about Kyia, either. So brace yourself, Roka. If you think I was serious about Zain, just you wait for what I'm going to throw at you about her."

Seeing his startled yet questioning look, Alex quickly shut the door, knowing she would have to tackle *that* particular problem another day. Matchmaking was a whole different ballgame, especially when it involved a couple as important as Roka and Kyia. She needed to be fresh if she wanted to help them in any way, especially if their current relationship status was as bad as he'd suggested. And help them, Alex would. Because even though they were together in her future, who was to say she hadn't played a part of making that happen in the past?

The whole timeline paradox was so messed up that Alex's head ached anytime she considered it. But she was becoming more and more convinced that she was where she was for a reason. She only had to wait it out to see why. And if she achieved nothing more than helping Zain and Roka find their way to each other, then she already considered her time in the past as being well spent. Kyia and Roka would just be an added bonus.

As she was shuffling around and getting ready for bed, Alex checked in with Xiraxus to make sure he and the rest of the draekons had survived the storm, only to discover they hadn't experienced it with Draekora located so high above the clouds. She ended up having to listen to a full ten minutes of him ranting concerns about *her*. The lightning pummelling Meya had stopped him from being able to fly down anywhere near the city, but he'd still felt her distress at the tavern and hated being unable to swoop in and save her.

While he expressed his concern straight to her mind, she made the frustrating realisation that her entire evening could have been prevented if she'd thought to contact him earlier and ask for a lift back to the palace before the storm had set in. She, of course, had never had her very own flying taxi service before, so it was only natural that she hadn't thought of him.

Xira? she called, her slurred word interrupting his vow to hunt down anyone who tried to lay a hand on her again. *I appreciate your concern, but I really need to sleep now.*

Alex wasn't sure what he said in reply, only that his tone quieted enough for her to doze off without waiting to hear his full response.

That night she dreamed vividly, likely as a result of her anxiety-fuelled day. She dreamed of her friends, Jordan, D.C. and Bear, all walking through the forests around Woodhaven, laughing at something Jordan said. She dreamed of her parents, Rachel and Jack, spending the Kaldoras break in their Ancient Egypt Library habitat, inspecting fossilised bat droppings and whatever else they could get their hands on, having a grand old time. She dreamed of her headmaster and friend, Darrius Marselle, along with many of her other teachers, Karter, Finn, Hunter, Caspar Lennox, Maggie, even Administrator Jarvis. She dreamed of her classmates, their faces flashing across her mind's eye. She dreamed of Fletcher, the doctor who did his best to keep her alive even when she made it difficult for him. She dreamed of her Meyarin friends of the future—*her* Roka, Kyia and Zain. And lastly, she dreamed of Kaiden. She dreamed of sparring with him in Combat class. She dreamed of dancing with him at D.C.'s birthday party. She dreamed of his gentle touch, his strong arms, his incredibly, *impossibly* blue eyes.

Every dream she had ended the same way: with a laughing Aven standing triumphantly over their dead bodies.

Jordan, dead.

D.C., dead.

Bear, dead.

Her parents, her teachers, her classmates. All dead.

Roka, Kyia, Zain. Dead.

Kaiden... *dead.*

When she woke up panting in the middle of the night, Alex felt the weight of a thousand lifetimes linger between her and everyone she cared about.

Homesick for a place currently well beyond her reach, all she could do was turn over and try to get back to sleep. When she finally managed to drift off again, she did so with a wet pillow and a single tear still rolling down her cheek.

Nineteen

Almost an entire week passed before Aven showed his face
around the palace again. Until then, the yelling match he'd had
with his father was all anyone talked about—how the prince had
lost his mind and screamed at the monarch about the mortals
who were stealing from Meya. The news had spread swiftly
beyond the palace walls, and anytime Alex wandered the city,
she heard the gossiping voices of Meyarins in the streets. She
did her best to ignore it all, knowing that what would be, would
be, and instead focused on her training.

Roka was a demanding teacher, but Alex would have
expected no less. At her request, they focused primarily on
theory-based knowledge rather than practical experience since
she still had no idea how to get around the problem of her red
blood and stubbornly avoided sparring with him every time he
offered, with her excuses becoming more paltry each time he
asked. The bonus was, within the span of six days she became
nearly fluent in the Meyarin language, began to learn the *long*
history of the immortal people, and, most excitingly, was taught
how to use the *Valispath*.

It turned out the latter was actually rather simple. All she
had to do was *will* it to activate around her and focus on where
she wanted to go and it just sort of… happened. But she also had
to concentrate for the entire trip, otherwise she would end up
somewhere unintended—as she'd learned the hard way during

one of her first solo outings. One moment she was rollercoasting along with her mind on the Golden Cliffs, and the next she'd been wondering why Zain was repeatedly refusing to take up Roka's offer to try out for the *Zeltora*. That led Alex to thinking about the warriors themselves, and before she knew it, the *Valispath* spat her out in the centre of the garrison, right when the elite guards were in the middle of a training drill. All eyes had come to her and she'd awkwardly forced herself to laugh it off, saying in Meyarin, "Well, this sure isn't the kitchen."

Roka hadn't let her live it down for a full day. Niyx hadn't either, since in Aven's absence he'd pulled out the 'best friend' card and was regularly checking in with the royals, telling them their son and brother was fine but needed some time to cool off. Doing that, Niyx was around the palace a lot more than Alex would have presumed normal. Stranger still, he seemed to be on friendly terms with them all—even Roka, who had been the one to counsel Aven on choosing better friends. It was just plain weird seeing Niyx interact so casually with Roka, Kyia, even Astophe and Niida, knowing that, like Aven, he was *not* one of the good guys. And yet, in this time period, he kind of was. Sure, he was a pathological flirt and relentless charmer to boot, but Alex had noticed he was like that not just with her, but with *anything* that moved. Once she came to that realisation, she was much more comfortable being around him. She couldn't forget the threatening future version of him, but as unbelievable as it was, she didn't absolutely detest him in the past. His buoyant personality alone made that nearly impossible.

Other than having lessons with Roka and what felt like daily verbal sparring matches with Niyx, Alex spent much of her time with Kyia, who had been given the task of teaching her about Meyarin customs and culture. It was all frightfully boring, but it gave Alex the chance to carefully scout out how the female Meyarin felt about Roka. Unfortunately, the prince hadn't been playing coy when he implied that he and Kyia didn't get along. In fact, if Alex read their relationship correctly, Roka had severely downplayed the level at which they detested each other. So much so that she wondered if perhaps she was best just letting them get on with it themselves, knowing they would eventually end up together. She was only going to be there for another couple of weeks and came to the conclusion that it might be safer not to make any more waves in the time she had left.

Deciding that was the best plan—unless, of course, opportunities arose where she couldn't resist playing Cupid—Alex kept the ripples at bay by going about her life in an almost perfunctory manner. Every morning she breakfasted with the queen, whose common tongue improved just as quickly as Alex's Meyarin. Other than her desire to converse better with Alex, the queen's official reasoning was that she was housing someone raised by mortals and thought it was a good indication that she should invest in the ability to communicate with the human race. That might have been her official response to anyone who asked, but Alex knew better. One morning Niida had broken down in tears and admitted that she was thankful she had something to do in order to keep her mind off her youngest son who she was deeply concerned about. The love and fear shining out of her eyes had nearly brought Alex to her knees, and she knew without a doubt that the queen was terrified of the changes in Aven. All Alex could do was hold Niida's hand and tell her everything would be okay, offering false hope but true comfort as the queen wept on her shoulder.

When she wasn't lying to emotionally wrecked monarchs or learning from Roka and Kyia, the rest of Alex's free time was spent exploring the copious and extravagant halls of the palace, strolling around the streets of the beautiful city and checking in with Xiraxus to find out how close he was to having the energy to re-open the *abrassa* back to her time. Every day his answer remained the same: not close enough. But still she continued asking, waiting for the day when he would tell her they were good to go. And in the meantime, she was determined that when she finally left the past, her presence would leave hardly any mark at all.

… Other than sorting out Zain.

… And maybe Kyia and Roka, if she could swing it.

But nothing else.

It would be like she was never there.

On Sunday, exactly one week after her arrival in the past, Alex was on her way to her bedroom to freshen up for dinner following a mind-numbing, three-hour session where Kyia lectured her about the seven different Houses of the Meyarin High Court. Dalmarta was obviously one of them, as well as Niyx's family in House Raedon. The five others were Lorenn, Varsae, Fraelorn, Quoris and Tarennia. Each of the Houses had one elected representative who sat on the ruling council, and Kyia had felt it imperative to educate Alex as much as possible on short notice after discovering that all of those council members would be attending dinner that evening.

Head pounding from having to take in so much information in such a small amount of time, Alex's eyes were on her feet when she opened the door to her room, so it was only when she heard a throat clear that her gaze shot up and she saw who was sitting on her bed, waiting for her.

"Aven!" she yelped. "What are—How—I mean—Everyone's been looking for you! What are you doing here?"

Realising he wouldn't have understood her words, she opened her mouth to repeat them in Meyarin when he jumped in first, showing that he had also been practising his language skills, replying perfectly in the common tongue.

"Forgive my intrusion, Aeylia," he said, standing to his feet and running a distressed hand through his messy hair. "I only wished to speak to you without an audience."

Alex had never seen him look so dishevelled, neither in the past nor the future. His clothes were rumpled, his skin streaked with dirt and his eyes lined with shadows, suggesting he'd been without sleep for some time.

"Are you okay?" she blurted before she could help it. *This is your enemy*, she reminded herself. But looking at him now, she simply couldn't dredge up any kind of antagonism towards him. Not when he looked so... lost.

He let out a startled laugh, but there was no humour in it. "Am I okay?" he repeated, his tone as unreadable as his expression. "Aeylia, I abandoned you in the middle of a foreign city without the means to return to safety right before we were hit by one of the most severe tempests the city's ever seen. How, after all that, can you possibly be kind enough to ask if *I* am okay?"

When he put it like that, Alex couldn't fault his reasoning. Shoving a lock of hair behind her ear, she moved hesitantly away from the door and closer to him.

"You seemed pretty upset when you left me," she cautiously said, pressing on even when his jaw clenched. "And no one's seen you in almost a week. Of course I want to know if you're all right. Your mother, your father, Roka—everyone's been so worried."

"Niyx was supposed to relay that I was fine," Aven said, his stance rigid.

"And he did," Alex confirmed. "But it's one thing to hear that you're 'fine' from your best friend, another entirely to

206 · Lynette Noni

believe it. Or so I presume, since your mother has cried in my arms for the last three mornings."

Finally a flash of remorse travelled across Aven's face, telling Alex that Niida's deep love for her son wasn't one-sided.

"Leaving you alone was deplorable of me," Aven said, avoiding Alex's words and going back to his original topic. "I did it because, at the time, I was consumed by a need for justice. That desire is no less strong in me now, regardless of my failed attempt to serve my people. But for the moment, that's beside the point." He inhaled a breath. Released it again. "I'm here to apologise, Aeylia, for my inexcusable behaviour. I can't offer you a sound reason for abandoning you, but please know that for this past week, I've been filled with a deep regret over what I did. I am truly sorry."

Everything from the look in his eyes to his slumped shoulders told Alex that he meant every word he'd said. But she didn't need his apology. While that night had sucked, mostly because of the foul Skraegon, if Aven hadn't left her alone she may never have bumped into Zain and thus never have had the chance to coerce Roka into giving him a shot at the *Zeltora*—which was something Zain was *still* refusing to do, but Alex maintained that he just needed time. None of that would have happened if Aven hadn't run off on her. And seeing him so down about it had a strange effect on Alex—almost like she felt *bad* for him. So she did the only thing she could.

"I accept your apology," she told him quietly—and genuinely. "And I appreciate you offering it, Aven. It means a lot. But now that we've done this, I want you to promise me something."

He took a step closer to her, his eyes losing some of their bleakness as hope replaced the dark emotions. "Anything."

"I want you to let it go," Alex told him. When the shutters came down on his expression, she sighed internally and decided that she would take what she could get, qualifying her statement by saying, "I want you to let go of your regret about abandoning me." It cost her, but she continued, "Whatever your crusade for justice is, that's your call. But as for us, why don't we just… start over?"

"Start over?" he repeated, his face looking dubious but hopeful again. "You would consent to that?"

Alex shrugged, mentally wondering what the hell she was thinking. "I'm sure you've picked up on the fact that I've been uncomfortable around you since we first met"—in both the past and future, that was true—"so I figure it might be a good idea for us to wipe the slate clean and start anew. What do you think?"

Alex knew—she *knew*—what she was doing was risky. Lady Mystique had said it was impossible to change anything in the future, since the events had already happened and therefore *would* happen. But maybe, just maybe there was a way Alex could leave a mark on Aven that somehow softened him towards mortals. Even if he would still follow through on his awful massacre the next time the humans visited—and she prayed that would be many, many years away yet—perhaps if she spent enough time with him she could sow a seed that might one day allow her to break through his hatred of mortals and…

Well, she didn't know the 'and' part of that just yet. All she could do was hope that her presence in the past might do *something* good for the future. Because right now, all she had was hope. And that hope would have to be enough to get her through the next few weeks.

"If you are willing," Aven said quietly, moving forward until he was close enough to reach out and grasp her hands, "then I would like that very much."

While Alex had offered the olive branch, she was nowhere near psychologically capable of not reacting adversely to his touch, but she managed to only slightly stiffen when his fingers linked with hers and gave a gentle squeeze.

It was then his brow furrowed and he lifted up her left hand until it was at eye level where he opened her palm and frowned at her flesh.

"By the light, what manner of wound could leave such a mark on you?"

Alex snatched her hand back, curling it protectively at her chest and backing away quickly.

"Aeylia," Aven whispered questioningly, his face flooding with concern—and the irony of that was not lost on Alex.

"I—It—Really, it's nothing," she told him, mentally screaming at herself to settle down. But her heart was racing just from his quiet enquiry about the scar on her hand, something that no one else had yet noticed in her time there. "Just a nasty cut, that's all."

Aven looked sceptical. "I've seen many wounds caused by blades, but none that *laendra* couldn't heal."

"Raised by mortals, remember?" Alex said, trying to offer him a quirky smile that probably came out more like a grimace. "I had to heal like one of them. No *laendra* for me."

Half of that was true—the *laendra* part. The other part was a lie, since the wound had sealed closed almost as soon as Aven had sliced her with A'enara and completed his forbidden Claiming ritual. Fletcher had tried to get rid of the glowing, silvery scar, but to no effect. The same was true for the entry wound on her back where the blade had sunk into her flesh. Fletcher had admitted to wondering whether the instant healing of both wounds and resulting scar residue was because of Aven's Meyarin blood or perhaps merely due to A'enara itself. To this day, Alex had no answer to that question, and she'd come to accept that it might remain a mystery forever.

"That does make sense, however it must have been quite the injury for you to not naturally heal entirely from it," Aven pressed, watching her carefully.

"It got infected," Alex said without thinking. At Aven's baffled look, she realised that, since Meyarins couldn't get fatally sick, it was likely they couldn't get blood infections either. She quickly tacked on, "I mean, the blade was laced with Hyroa blood and it made it really hard for me to heal."

Aven continued looking at her quizzically, causing her to remember that his race had a different name for the snarling beasts and their incapacitating blood. Straining her memory, the name came to her and Alex cried it out, perhaps a little too loudly, "Sarnaph!" She cleared her throat and in a much more normal voice went on to finish, "The blade was laced with Sarnaph blood. That's why I had such trouble healing from it."

The horrified look on Aven's face told her that her lie was a believable enough reason to explain her scar and she felt her body relax again—slightly.

"That must have been a traumatic experience for you," he said, his tone showing just how much he meant it. "I've never heard of anyone surviving Sarnaph blood poisoning without *Menada dae Loransa* being performed on them."

Not even Alex's new translation abilities could fully interpret the phrase he used, so she repeated it in a question. "*Menada dae Loransa?*"

"The Claiming of Life," Aven told her, causing her body to lock instantly. "It was once a procedure used by healers under the most dire of circumstances. It allowed them to bind the life of another Meyarin to themselves, enabling them to share energy, almost like the *vaeliana* connection you have with your drackon."

Everything inside Alex trembled at his words, and it only became worse as he continued.

"The ritual was prohibited long before I was born largely due to the side effects of the bond when activated by someone unwilling to Release the recipient after their life had been saved."

Alex managed to force two words through her stiff lips. "Side effects?"

Aven nodded, his face dire. "While the connection was in effect, the will of the injured party was no longer their own. They were fully under the control of the healer until they were Released from the bond."

Hardly daring to hope, Alex asked, "How did—How did they Release them?"

Aven looked at her curiously, almost like he could read her barely restrained desperation to hear his answer. "From what I understand, the bond allowed the creator of the connection to issue mental and verbal commands to those who they had performed the ritual on. All the creator had to do was command the injured party to accept their freedom from the bond after their shared energy had healed the wound, and upon acceptance, the link was severed instantly."

Could it possibly be as easy as that? Could Jordan be freed from Aven by a single command?

"Of course, that's why it was so important to outlaw the ritual, since there were cases where those who performed it became consumed by the power they had at their fingertips and refused to Release the will of whom they had bonded with." Aven shook his head in sadness and disgust. "What they did was reprehensible. To steal someone's will... That would be a fate worse than death. I can't imagine the kind of monster who would inflict such suffering on another."

Oh, dear sweet irony.

Aven shook off whatever dark path his mind had wandered down and focused on Alex again. "I've truly not heard of any

Meyarin surviving the taint of Sarnaph blood without *Menada dae Loransa*. And since it is forbidden, I know you can't have undergone the ritual. So how is it that you stand here today, Aeylia?"

Thinking quickly, all Alex could come up with was, "The mortals I was staying with, they had a really good doctor—healer, I mean. I was lucky, the blade was only lightly coated with the Sarnaph blood, so barely any entered my system, just enough to make me very sick for a few days and stop the wound from healing as quickly as it should have. The healer used herbs and poultices on me, kept me hydrated and got me through it."

Aven made a derisive noise. "Herbs and poultices." He shook his head, anger blazing in his eyes. "Mortal methods. You're fortunate they didn't kill you out of ignorance."

"They're not all bad, Aven," Alex whispered, even knowing it was of little use. Seeing his eyes darken, she tried for a more jovial tone when she said, "Let's face it, if someone like me can manage to survive as long as I did with them, then they must have *something* going for them. Don't forget, you've seen me on the *Valispath*."

Aven's expression lightened as humour filled his features. "You do seem to have a surprising lack of grace for one of our kind."

"Hey!" she cried with mock indignation, mustering her courage and punching him lightly in the bicep, just as she would Jordan or Bear. "We can't all move like we're floating on air."

"And yet, the rest of our kind do, so clearly we *can* all move like that," he returned, a grin on his face. "You appear to be the single exception to the rule. Congratulations."

"Yeah, yeah," Alex muttered, acting playfully grouchy. "Don't you have somewhere else to be now? Someone else to bother?"

His grin only widened further at her fake attitude. "I do, but so do you." When she looked at him blankly, he reminded, "Dinner with the council. I'm presuming you're attending?"

Her eyes widened as she wondered how much time she had lost with Aven and how long before they were both due downstairs. Then her eyes roamed over his unkempt appearance and she reacted automatically.

He uttered a startled chuckle as she spun him around, placed both her palms flat against his back and forcibly pushed him towards the door.

"You need to clean up, like, right now," she said, shoving him forwards. "Your mother will die if she sees you like this."

Aven chuckled again. "I should hope not, since I visited her before coming to your room."

"Then I'm guessing she was too happy to see you to notice you look like a deadbeat. If you turn up at dinner as you are, I doubt your luck will hold."

There was a pause. "I admit, I've learned much of your language in the past week, but the term 'deadbeat' is beyond my comprehension."

"It's a—You know what, never mind," Alex said as they reached the exit to her room. She took her hands from his back and opened the door, tapping her foot impatiently when he just looked at her, highly entertained.

"I find you fascinating, Aeylia," Aven said, golden eyes lit with humour.

"That's fantastic. But how about you maybe do that later instead of right now? Otherwise we're *both* going to be late."

Aven laughed lightly and, catching her off-guard, reached out and affectionately stroked her cheekbone before activating the *Valispath* and disappearing from sight.

Alex stood frozen to the spot for a moment before she shuddered and closed the door again.

This is what I need to happen, she reminded herself, pushing aside her unease.

If her plan to soften him towards mortals was going to be effective at all, they had to be friendly enough to share their opinions. To do that, she had to get over herself and accept the Aven of *now*, rather than the one she knew in years to come.

Friends with Aven, she thought, shaking her head as she proceeded to get ready for dinner. *I must be crazy.*

All she could do was hope that it would be worth it.

Twenty

If dinner that evening was strained due to Aven's reappearance and the full council in attendance, Alex hardly noticed. She was barely aware of the three members she already knew from the future: *Loro* Gaiel of House Varsae, *Lasa* Riza of House Fraelorn, and *Loro* Roathus of House Lorenn. While it was certainly interesting to see them in the past, especially the wise, old Roathus—not to mention, having Gaiel and Riza no longer look down upon her—Alex was too distracted to pay much attention to any of them. And that was due to the presence of another council member, the representative for House Quoris; the family Queen Niida was born to before marrying into the Dalmarta House. The council member for Quoris was her father, Roka and Aven's grandfather, and his name was Eanraka.

As in, the founder of Akarnae.

For the entire first half of the meal, Alex struggled to take her eyes off him, so awed as she was by his presence. She simply couldn't believe she was eating dinner with the Meyarin who created the academy that would become her home thousands of years into the future. It was only when dessert was passed around that he spoke to her directly, causing her starstruck self to become even more enraptured.

"So, Aeylia, is it?" Eanraka said, his turquoise eyes spearing her from across the table. "I hear you grew up amongst mortals. Is that true?"

Alex quickly swallowed the sip she'd taken from her goblet and replied in perfect Meyarin, "Yes, *Loro* Eanraka. I only arrived here a week ago."

"Who were your parents, youngling?" asked *Lasa* Naelin of House Tarennia—Kyia's aunt.

"Aeylia was abandoned as a babe," Roka said from Alex's right before she had a chance to respond, his firm tone telling the whole council to be cautious with their next line of questioning.

"I'm intrigued to hear how you managed to survive amongst humans for so long," said Niyx's father, *Loro* Cykor of House Raedon. He shared his son's dark hair and rugged good looks, but instead of Niyx's amethyst eyes, Cykor's were a magnetic grey that shone with a deep, cunning intelligence.

Again, Alex wasn't able to answer before someone else spoke up first. This time it was Eanraka.

With a snort, the founder of Akarnae said, "You make the mortals sound like savages, Cy."

"For all we know, they might be just that," Cykor returned with a careless shrug. "After all, Ean, you're one of the few at this table who has interacted with them for any length of time. And even then, the ones you allow into that school of yours are hardly a representation of the majority, if I understand correctly. What is it you call them again?"

"Gifted," Eanraka replied. "As you well know by now."

"It's been nearly three hundred years since you named that place after yourself and yet you still haven't given up on them," Gaiel put in, a sneer in his tone. "Why do you bother, old friend?"

Eanraka dug into a sponge-like pudding and raised the spoon to his mouth. "You have your hobbies, I have mine."

Alex felt an unpleasant stab in her stomach at the idea of humans like her being considered a mere hobby by the Meyarin responsible for banding them together, and she couldn't keep her face from showing her distaste.

"It seems I've offended you, Aeylia," Eanraka said, watching her closely.

She thought carefully about her response before saying, "It's difficult for me to look upon humans in the same manner as most of you. To me, they aren't savages or hobbies, they're people who cared for me when no one else would, Meyarin included. Forgive me for taking offence; I'm still learning the ways of your—*our*—people."

Something flashed in Eanraka's eyes, a spark of pride or approval, Alex thought, but then his expression blanked again and he said, "I can understand how you would find yourself indebted to them. It's only natural, given your upbringing."

"Let's move on from the subject of mortals," King Astophe said diplomatically, careful to keep his eyes from drifting to Aven who surprisingly kept his own views on the topic quiet. "Eanraka, tell us your latest happenings with *Soraya de lah Torra*."

The words Astophe used weren't Meyarin, but they had the familiar lyrical cadence of the language Lady Mystique had spoken. Translated mentally thanks to her bond with Xiraxus, Alex understood them to mean 'The Light of the Worlds'. But what Astophe was referring to, she had no idea.

"And of course," the king continued, "you must also tell us how fares the young Freyan who had just used the *eiden* paths to travel here when last we saw you."

Having been in the middle of taking another sip from her drink, Alex nearly sloshed the liquid all down her front, so startled was she by his enquiry.

'Freyan' was a word she needed no translation for.

Eiden in the unknown lyrical language meant 'doorway'.

Connecting the dots, Alex suddenly realised what *Soraya de lah Torra*—The Light of the Worlds—referred to.

Astophe was talking about the Library.

How could I be so stupid? Alex berated herself, lowering her trembling hand until the goblet was resting back on the table. For seven days she'd been in the past, and not once had she considered seeking out the Library, not even after she'd mastered the use of the *Valispath*. While she couldn't know for sure, it was entirely possible that if the Library was capable of transporting her from Freya to Medora—between two entirely different worlds—then perhaps it was also able to bend time and return her to the future.

In fact, until this moment, she had also never given any thought to other Freyans ever having visited Medora, although she vaguely recalled Bear and Jordan once telling her that she was the first to arrive in thousands of years. That meant at some stage before her, someone else had journeyed from her world to Medora. Wondering if perhaps this person Astophe had asked about was the predecessor her friends had been referring to, Alex turned her full attention back to the table.

"*Soraya de lah Torra* shows itself to be more magnificent every time I wander its halls," Eanraka answered with a contented smile lighting his face that, with his dark hair and sharp features, made him look like an older version of Roka. The family resemblance was uncanny. "There can be no doubt that it truly is the Jewel of Medora, and I can see now why it was fought over for so long by other races of this world. Akarnae would not be what it is without the Great Library offered as its foundation."

"And the Freyan?" Niida asked her father. "What of him?"

Eanraka let out a rumbling chuckle. "Enoch is his name, and what a story he has. It's been surprisingly difficult for me to learn his dialect, and for him to learn the common tongue enough to comprehend little more than a basic understanding. But from what I gather, he claims that one day he was walking with a friend and then suddenly he was no more."

"He was no more what?" Niida asked.

Eanraka spread out his hands. "Those are the only words he used."

"That must have been when he travelled the *eiden* paths and found his way through to Medora," Roka guessed, and his grandfather nodded.

"Indeed," Eanraka confirmed. "And I must say, Enoch is a rather intriguing mortal. He's already lived much longer than the lifespan of the humans who inhabit our world, and yet he is still considered young in Freya. He has an inquisitive mind and, rather than desiring to return to his world, he is content to remain here until the time comes for him to travel to what he calls *ha adar haleah*."

Judging by the looks all around the table, Alex wasn't the only one unable to understand the phrase.

"'The Great Beyond'," Eanraka translated for them all. "I believe, despite our language barriers, that he was referring to death."

"Jeez. Morbid, much?" Alex muttered under her breath, forgetting that there were now at least five people around the table who understood the common tongue—Niida, Astophe, Roka, Aven and Eanraka. Given Roathus's and Cykor's twitching lips, she gathered that they too understood her softly spoken words.

Eanraka's eyes were sparkling when he said, "He's a pleasant sort of human, young Aeylia, morbid or not, and he seems content to enjoy his hours wandering the hallways of *Soraya de lah Torra* as his days move toward their final conclusion."

"Otherworlders are so strange," Aven spoke up for the first time all night. "Regardless of where they're from."

"Be that as it may, we're hardly ones to judge, given our origins," Roka said curtly, causing Alex's ears to perk up, curious as to what he meant. But she would have to wait for

Kyia to cover it in her lessons since it hardly seemed appropriate to ask while the council was in attendance.

As the conversation dwindled to less interesting topics and the table cleared of food, Alex thought over everything she had learned that night and wondered when she might sneak away to Akarnae. But as it happened, she needn't have worried about devising a plan because when they all began to depart the dining hall, Eanraka sought her out directly.

"Aeylia, I thought perhaps given your background that you might be interested in joining me for a tour of my school?"

His words were perfectly clear in the common tongue, and at the risk of sounding too eager, she answered, "I'd love that! When can I come?"

"How does right now suit?" He tugged at the collar of his double-breasted vest as if he couldn't wait to be away from the palace. "Unless you have other plans?"

"Not at all," Alex said enthusiastically. Roka cleared his throat pointedly and she sent him a pleading look. He rolled his eyes and waved his hand, allowing her to skip whatever lesson he had planned for the night. She beamed back at him and he shook his head in amusement, walking out the door with the other Meyarins and leaving her with his grandfather.

"Shall we?" Eanraka said, gesturing for her to follow as they moved out of the warded dining hall. The moment they were in the corridor, he activated the *Valispath* and they took off, zooming out of the palace and away from Meya.

Faster and faster they soared through the gold and silver forests before the trees transformed into the normal green and brown variety. She had travelled this path before with Zain, but it was no less remarkable thousands of years in the past than it had been that night in the future.

Before long, the Eternal Path began to slow down and Alex looked on with wide eyes at the familiar shape of the academy's

Tower building silhouetted against the night's sky. As she stepped off the Path and onto the base of the medieval structure, she glanced around in awe. The grounds were the same, from the stunning Lake Fee mirroring the starry sky to Mount Paedris in the distance and the moonbeams bouncing off its snow-capped peak. But as for the buildings of the academy, *those* were definitely different to the future campus of Akarnae. Other than the Tower and two large structures that were in similar locations to the future dormitory and food court buildings, there was nothing else familiar. There were no Stable Complex, Arena or Clinic. Most notably, there was also no General Sector building, and without Gen-Sec, Alex wondered where most of the theory classes were held, let alone where the Medical Ward was situated.

Amazed by the similar but oh-so-different academy laid out before her, Alex trailed her eyes over the landscape before turning back to find Eanraka studying her closely.

"I daresay it looks much different to what you're used to. Am I right, Alexandra Jennings?"

Alex gaped at him. She couldn't even muster up a denial, so confident was his statement.

She must have looked as alarmed as she felt because he reached out and placed a comforting hand on her shoulder, smiling gently at her.

"It's all right, Alexandra. I'm not going to tell anyone."

"How—How—"

"I didn't bring you here tonight to give you a tour of an academy you're already familiar with," Eanraka said, using his hand on her shoulder to guide her into the Tower building. "I brought you here because I was *asked* to do so."

In a high-pitched, disbelieving voice, Alex squeaked out, "By who?"

Eanraka chuckled and led her towards a familiar downwards staircase. "Who do you think?"

"The Library told you about me?" she asked, throwing her best and only guess out there. "You were sent to get me?"

Eanraka nodded as they descended the staircase together. "Collecting you was the only reason I travelled back to Meya tonight. I abhor those council meetings and the pretentious House representatives. They're eternally stuck in their ways. My people might be advanced as a civilisation, but sometimes we can be anything but civil—especially to other races."

He led the way across the Library's grand foyer and towards the second downward staircase.

"I don't know what happens in the future, Alexandra, and I won't ask you to tell me. But what I will say is this: don't forget why you're here, because therein lies your strength."

Waiting a beat for more information that didn't end up coming, Alex hesitantly said, "By 'here' do you mean the past?"

Eanraka pulled her to a halt, his face stoic. "Medora, Alexandra. Don't forget why you're in Medora."

"I..." Alex trailed off, uncertain. "I'm not sure I understand. I'm in Medora because the Library brought me here from my world."

"That's the 'how', not the 'why'."

Alex thought for a moment and finally admitted, "I'm not following."

"You were Called, Alexandra," Eanraka said, using a term she hadn't heard for a while. "And you were Chosen."

As if there was some kind of speaker system within the stone walls, Alex heard the whispered replay of a faded memory.

'Many are Called, but few answer the Call. Fewer still respond to it and follow where it leads... And that's why you're not only Called, but also Chosen. Because you'll continue to walk through the doors, no matter where they lead.'

"As I told you, Alexandra," Eanraka said as the Library's replayed words came to an end, "I don't know what the future brings. What *your* future brings. But I do know you were Called to Medora—both past and future—for a reason."

Another whispered memory sounded in her ear, as if confirming his words. *'Because you are Chosen… And you are needed, for such a time as this.'*

Alex was shaking her head, not sure if in fear, denial or confusion. "I don't know what I'm supposed to do," she said in a quiet voice.

"I didn't bring you here to tell you what to do," Eanraka replied just as quietly. "But if it helps, be encouraged in knowing you will never be required to face more than you are capable of handling."

Regardless of the moment holding great solemnity, Alex couldn't repress a quiet snort. "I'm sorry, but have you seen the mess that is my life?"

"What I see is you standing here before me," he said. "Since you are still breathing, one could conclude that you have indeed been capable of handling every situation you've yet experienced in life."

"You make a valid point," Alex reluctantly acknowledged. "But that doesn't mean I'm handling things *well*."

Eanraka's mouth stretched into a smile. "That's not the encouragement I offered you."

Alex let out a huff of laughter. "Well played, you sneaky elf."

Cocking his head to the side, Eanraka said, "I shall assume I'm better off not asking the meaning of that term, given the context in which it was used?"

"That's probably wise," Alex agreed, still grinning.

"Perhaps I'll remember to hunt down Enoch sometime to ask him," Eanraka mused.

At that, Alex's laughter was much more genuine. "Good luck to you, since I doubt they had many pop culture references in

Freya back in the… whatever year this is. There are probably dinosaurs roaming the earth, for all I know."

"I guess I'll have to leave it as a mystery then," Eanraka said. He moved a step closer to Alex and placed both his hands on her shoulders, tilting his head down to meet her eyes. "It has been an honour to meet you Alexandra Jennings of Freya, but this is where I must leave you."

She looked at him in bafflement. "What? But— "

"I was asked to collect you, nothing more," he told her. "From here, you're on your own." He squeezed her shoulders once and let her go. "May the stars shine ever brightly upon you, and the light be your guide forevermore."

With those strange blessing-like words, Eanraka offered a final smile and disappeared back up the stairs, leaving Alex on her own.

Giving herself a mental nudge, she followed the spiralling stairs downwards and, making sure she had a clear picture in her mind of where she wanted to go, she willed a doorway to open before her.

Stepping into the blackness beyond, Alex fell through the dark until she landed in a cavern divided by a river rushing between two fissures in the rock walls on either side of the large space.

Alex wasn't sure why she'd chosen the cave as her destination; perhaps it was merely a sense of nostalgia and the desire to be comforted by its familiarity. This was the place where she'd first conversed with the Library, the place where she'd had to make a choice whether or not to stay in Medora or return to her world. It was symbolic, Alex felt.

"Excuse me, Library?" she called out, standing to her feet and moving closer to the river, watching the luminescence wax and wane as if the light itself was alive.

"*I was wondering when you would come visit me, Alexandra,*" the Library responded, "*And when you didn't, I thought perhaps a little motivation might be in order.*"

"Thanks for that," Alex said sheepishly. "I don't know why I didn't think to come here sooner."

"*I daresay you've had a lot on your mind.*"

If that wasn't an understatement, Alex didn't know what was.

"Can I ask a question?"

"*You can always ask me anything.*"

Alex only just refrained from pulling a face as she clarified, "Let me rephrase. Can I ask a question that you'll answer in a way I'll understand?"

The Library chuckled, the sound soothing to Alex's ears. "*Why don't you ask and we'll see?*"

Well, it wasn't a 'no' at least.

"How do you know who I am?" she asked. "We technically haven't met yet."

"*I knew you long before you were born, Alexandra.*"

She waited for more, but when the Library said nothing else, she prompted, "That's great and all, but again, technically I haven't been born yet."

"*You would have a hard time standing here and speaking with me if that were true,*" the Library said in a strangely wry tone.

Alex's brow furrowed. "Did you just… Was that sarcasm?" When no response came, she added, "You're a Library. Since when do you have a sense of humour?"

"*Apparently since I decided to ask Eanraka to collect you tonight.*"

Eyes widening, she cried out, "There! You just did it again! Who are you and what have you done with the Library I know?"

"*I am what I was, just as I am what I will be,*" the Library said. "*I am the same yesterday, today and forever.*"

Alex blinked and tried to get her head around that. "Right. Well speaking of, uh, forever, let's get back to how you know me."

"*Let's instead move on to why you're here,*" the Library returned.

"You know why I'm here, otherwise you wouldn't have sent Eanraka after me," Alex said. "But still, I need to know. Are you able to return me to my time?"

Heart thumping, Alex waited for an answer, the sounds of the rushing water filling her ears as she strained to hear the Library's voice again.

Finally, it came, but not with the response she was after.

"*I will answer you, Alexandra, but first I want to show you something. It's the reason I called you here tonight.*"

Interest piqued, Alex said, "You have my attention."

She jumped in fright when the river suddenly quieted and three familiar boulders rose to the surface, offering a bridge to a new doorway that appeared. It was open, but Alex couldn't see where it went.

"Is it wishful thinking to hope that will lead back to where I'm from?" Alex asked, making her way over the boulders.

"*It will lead you nowhere,*" the Library said, "*or perhaps somewhere. Only you can decide.*"

"I really hate it when you speak in riddles," Alex said with a sigh.

"*Step through the doorway, Alexandra, and you will soon understand.*"

With a promise like that, what am I waiting for? she thought, sucking in a deep breath and stepping forward. *Here goes nothing.*

Unlike every other time she'd walked through the Library's doorways, this time she felt it as if it were a physical thing, like oil coating her skin, stumbling through a spider web, or wading through water—perhaps all three at once. When she came out the other side, she had to shake her head a few times before her vision cleared, and then she stumbled back a step at the sight before her.

She was in Tryllin, the capital city of Medora.

Or what was left of it.

Standing before her was the smouldering wreck of a once thriving metropolis. The centre of the city was nothing more than a smoking crater, with the majestic palace half destroyed and the rest collapsing in on itself. There was fire everywhere, with people running through the streets, screaming in pain, crying for help.

Alex just stood there, frozen in horror.

"What happened here?" she whispered to herself—or so she thought.

"This is the future, Alex."

She woodenly turned her head to the owner of the voice as he stepped up beside her. He looked exactly the same as when she'd last seen him, his stunning blue eyes captivating her own as she mouthed his name in disbelief.

"Kaiden?"

"This is the future," he repeated, "or it will be, if you fail."

Twenty-One

"You're not real," Alex gasped out. "None of this is real, it can't be."

"It's not real yet," Kaiden told her. "But only you can stop it from happening."

"How are you—*What* are you?" she demanded.

He stepped around to face her. "I'm a manifestation you've called forth from your subconscious as a guide."

She blinked at him. "You're a what now?"

His lips quirked up at one corner. "You're in a simulation, Alex. A virtual reality created to show you the plausible future that may occur should you be unsuccessful in defeating Aven."

Alex looked out at the burning city. "So I was right—none of this is real. It's just a… hypothetical possibility."

Kaiden reached out and wrapped his fingers around Alex's upper arm. The moment he made contact, the world swirled around them and suddenly they weren't in Tryllin anymore, they were at Akarnae.

Alex wasn't sure if she was more shocked that she had felt Kaiden's touch, or at the newest sight in front of her.

Akarnae was a wasteland. If it weren't for Lake Fee and Mount Paedris, Alex never would have recognised where they were, even though the lake was the colour of blood and the mountain spewed ash high into the sky. But that was nothing compared to the academy itself where all that remained were some crumbled buildings surrounded by destroyed forests.

"Hypothetical or not, I'm here to show you what may become of our future."

Alex turned from the devastating sight and asked, "Why you?"

Kaiden met her eyes. "You chose me."

Alex spluttered, "Excuse me?"

"You feel safe with me."

"I *what?*"

A confident light came into his eyes. "Go on, Alex. If you can't admit it to yourself, who can you admit it to?"

"You're a figment of my imagination," Alex hissed out. "*Literally.* I'm *so* not having this conversation with myself."

He chuckled, and the sound was so lifelike, so similar to that of the real Kaiden that Alex actually felt a shiver travel down her spine.

"What I said was true," he claimed. "Your subconscious knew that what you're going to see here will be traumatic, and that you would need someone you felt safe with to guide you through it."

"There are plenty of people I feel safe with," Alex said. "Why are you at the top of the list?"

"Name one," Kaiden challenged.

"Jordan," Alex returned instantly, saying the first name that came to mind.

Shaking his head, Kaiden said, "Not true. With him currently Claimed by Aven, your subconscious knows you wouldn't be safe anywhere near him."

"That was a bad example," Alex admitted. "What about Bear? D.C.? I know both of them way better than I know you."

"And at the moment, after having lost Jordan, you would never have one of them go anywhere with you if it left the other alone for any length of time, virtual scenario or not."

Alex was unwilling to concede just yet. "What about my parents?"

Kaiden shook his head again. "You wouldn't put them in any kind of danger, even if it was all in your mind."

"Darrius. Fletcher. Roka, Kyia, Zain—hell, even Hunter and Karter. I trust all of them."

"You do," Kaiden agreed. "But it's with me you feel safest." He couldn't hold back a self-assured grin when he said, "Deny it all you want, we both know the truth."

Alex pulled a face at him. "You're annoying."

He burst out laughing. "I'm not real, remember?"

"That just makes you more annoying."

After a moment he sobered and his expression turned serious. "We don't have long here. Are you ready?"

"To see what might happen in the future if I let the whole world down?" Alex asked, her tone only slightly bitter. "Sure. Lead the way."

Taking Kaiden's hand, she observed with growing horror as he showed her not just destroyed cities and mass graves, but also specific—and vividly detailed—events.

She saw the empty eyes of Astophe and Roka, both lying in pools of silver blood. She saw the triumphant King Aven standing above their lifeless bodies, commanding his *Garseth* and the *Zeltora* to kill any mortals they could find.

Houses were demolished.

Families were slaughtered.

Villages were decimated.

And it wasn't just humans who Aven targeted. He massacred entire races, from the tree-dwelling Jarnocks to the amphibious Flips to numerous other beings Alex had never encountered. Not even the powerful Shadow Walkers were able to survive his tyranny, their city of darkness and all its inhabitants burning amid the chaos.

If seeing all that wasn't bad enough, Alex also witnessed the deaths of her friends.

Bear was first, his family dragged from their home in Woodhaven and strung up in Myrox cages outside the Meyarin palace, left to die slowly and painfully from starvation. Simulation or not, Alex would never forget their whimpered pleas or the look of their malnourished, neglected bodies for the rest of her life.

Next she had to watch as Aven Claimed D.C. and ordered the princess to kill her own parents before turning her blade on herself—and all in front of a crowd of horrified onlookers who were then forced to bow to their new immortal ruler.

Then came Alex's parents, having left the safety of the Library only to be captured by a group of scouting *Garseth*. Rachel and Jack were tortured first before the Rebels discovered their connection to Alex, and only then were they delivered directly to Aven. His laughter was almost as loud as their final screams as he slowly, so slowly drew out their deaths.

On it went as one by one, the lives Alex held most dear were taken from her; the goodness in the world snuffed out like a candle. Leaning on Kaiden more heavily with each passing frame, she could do nothing but try to detach herself from what she was seeing, telling herself it wasn't *real*.

But it *was* real. Or rather—it *could* be real.

Everything came to a head when Jordan was handpicked by Aven to lead the final attack on Akarnae, presenting the worst of everything Alex was forced to watch. Her classmates, her teachers, the academy itself went to war against Aven's immortal force. Even the Medoran military was there, led by General Drock and Major Tyson. The Wardens battled alongside them, with Kaiden's sister, Warden Jeera, shooting Stabiliser blasts at Meyarin attackers from all angles, but to no effect. The mortal weapons barely phased the immortals, if they even managed to land a hit.

The humans gave as good as they received, fighting back with everything they had. But ultimately, they were destroyed.

Darrius, dead.

Fletcher, dead.

Karter, Hunter, Finn, dead, dead, dead.

Drock, Tyson, Jeera, all dead.

Declan, dead.

The other Combat boys, dead.

Mel, Connor, Blink, Pipsqueak and the rest of her classmates and teachers, dead.

Everyone—*dead*.

It was also at the academy where Jordan himself fell.

He was fighting against Kaiden—the real Kaiden—with their blades moving so fast they blurred in the air. Even though Jordan had the advantage of Aven's connection, they were so closely matched that it was impossible to see who would come out the victor.

But then Kaiden paused in his attack and desperately told Jordan, "Alex would forgive you, you have to know that. I was with her at the end, and not once did she blame you. Even now I know she wouldn't. And you do, too."

Something sparked in Jordan's eyes, a burning ember of emotion, but it quickly dissolved into a smug look as his detached voice replied, "You'll know if that's true sooner than I will."

And without any further warning, a sword speared Kaiden's chest from behind, its icy design painfully familiar—as was the hand that delivered the killing blow.

As Aven withdrew A'enara from Kaiden and his body slumped lifeless to the ground, the Meyarin turned to his Claimed underling and in one swift arc, sliced the legendary blade across the base of Jordan's neck.

Shocked, Alex's hands flew to cover her mouth, and the simulated Kaiden had to wrap her in his arms to keep her from collapsing to her knees.

"I felt you hesitate," Aven said in a silky voice to Jordan who was choking on his own blood as it poured forth to stain the soil of the academy. "You have been a constant pain, fighting my will at every moment. I kept you alive to torment dear Alexandra and the rest of your friends, but now that they're gone, you have no further use to me."

Unable to take what she knew was coming next, Alex buried her face in Kaiden's neck, but it didn't stop her from hearing the sickening sound of A'enara hacking into Jordan's flesh, his gurgling groan eventually trailing off into silence.

With Jordan's death, Alex's vision faded to black as the scenery changed, only to leave her standing with Kaiden amid the ruins of a once beautiful Meya.

"What happened here?" she asked, her voice coming out as a hoarse croak. "Isn't this where Aven should be ruling from?"

"In this future, Aven becomes possessed by his desire for unlimited power," Kaiden answered quietly, reaching out to wipe a tear from her cheek and brush a strand of hair behind her ear. "After having razed Medora to the ground, he seeks beyond it, fixing his sight on the humans of Freya."

Alex pulled in a shuddering breath. "Is that because of me?"

"I'm sorry, Alex, but you have to know that the hatred Aven feels for you in this future is unparalleled."

"But *why*?" she cried.

Kaiden shook his head. "I can't tell you that. You have to find out for yourself by following the path you choose and seeing where it leads."

Alex couldn't help it; her eyes welled with tears again. "But it could lead *here*. With Aven in Freya, and everyone in Medora dead."

"Aven's not in Freya in this future, Alex," Kaiden told her gently. "He never makes it there."

She looked around in confusion. "Then… If he's not there, and he's not here, where is he?"

"He's gone. The Tia Aurans learned what he was planning and they stepped in before he could harm anyone else. They saved Freya, but it was too late for Medora."

Tia Aurans… "Are you talking about the people who created the *Valispath*?"

A hint of a smile touched Kaiden's mouth. "They did much more than that, but yes, they are an incomparably powerful race of beings who inhabit a world called Tia Auras. That's where the Meyarins originated from before they were banished long ago to live in Medora."

Head spinning, Alex wasn't sure what to ask first.

"We're out of time," Kaiden said before she could gather a single thought. "I'm sorry you had to see all this, but you need to know what you're fighting for, what the stakes are. You already knew it would be bad, but it's not just a few humans Aven will kill, it's everyone you care for and more. He won't stop until every mortal in Medora is dead."

In a voice barely holding any sound, Alex asked, "What must I do?"

"You're already doing it. Just don't stop."

Her lips trembled as she looked into his tender eyes. "I'm scared, Kaiden. I'm not strong enough for something like this. What if I can't keep this future from happening?"

He let out a soft laugh and stroked her cheek. "Oh, Alex. There's no one stronger than you." He leaned forward and pressed a kiss to her forehead, pausing there to whisper, "I believe in you."

And with those four words, the scenery faded back into reality and Alex found herself lying on the floor of the Library's dark cavern.

She had to take a few moments to calm herself before she was able to rise to her feet, and even then she struggled to form words.

"I don't—" Alex's voice was so rough that she had to clear her throat and try again. "I don't want that future."

"*No one does,*" the Library replied. "*Not even Aven.*"

"Am I really the only person who can stop it?" she asked, feeling the weight of the world on her shoulders.

"*You're not the only one who can defeat Aven,*" the Library said, and Alex felt a shred of hope until the voice added, "*but you are the only one who can put a stop to that future.*"

Closing her eyes tightly, Alex wrapped her arms around her body to ward off the chill of those words.

"Can you take me back to my time?" she asked again.

"*If that is what you want,*" the Library said, opening a door to Alex's left.

She looked through the doorway, her eyes widenening as she watched a live-action replay of her last moments before falling into the past. There her future self was, in the snow-covered forest with Xiraxus, his wings outstretched, ready to take flight and haul her up and into the *abrassa*.

"Why was he there?" Alex whispered. "Why did Aven pull Xiraxus into the future?"

The Library was silent.

"If I leave now, I'm not going to find out, am I?" Alex realised. "I'll leave with so many questions unanswered. Zain being a criminal, Kyia despising Roka, even Queen Niida's personality transplant." Her thoughts continued spiralling until she concluded, "I won't have a chance to try and influence Aven's decisions in any way, to leave any kind of mark on him. I'll be left reacting to future events as they unfold, with not even the smallest hope to sway his mind or his actions in our favour."

Again, the Library was silent.

"Come on!" Alex cried, throwing her arms out. "Give me something here! Anything!"

Still, the Library didn't answer. Not directly. Instead, Alex heard Eanraka's words echo throughout the cavern.

"*... you were Called to Medora—both past and future—for a reason.*"

Trembling inside, Alex realised that was all the guidance she needed. But just as she moved her shaking legs to close the doorway back to her future, the Library spoke again, causing her to pause mid-motion.

"*One thing to consider, Alexandra. I will never again offer you a doorway through time. If you choose to remain now, you will only be able to travel back through the Void.*"

Alex had already presumed as much given the gravity of the decision, but that didn't make it any easier to hear. Regardless, now that she had made her choice, she wouldn't waver from her path.

Squaring her shoulders, she sealed the door with a resolute sound, and seconds later it disappeared entirely.

Alex stared at the now empty space, suddenly overcome by doubt. "Every time I come down here, I end up having to make really hard decisions."

"*Life is full of hard decisions, Alexandra. It's merely evidence that you are alive.*"

"But how am I supposed to know if I'm doing the right thing?"

"*That's not something you'll ever know. All you can do is live in the moment and choose not to worry about what the future may bring. Don't waste today by fearing tomorrow, for tomorrow will come whether you're ready for it or not.*"

Repeating those encouraging words in her mind, Alex finally said, "I think I'm ready to go back to Meya now."

Without having to say more, a new doorway appeared.

Alex took a step forward but hesitated. "Will I be back here again? While I'm in the past, I mean?"

"*You can visit me whenever you need,*" the Library said. "*But remember, I am always with you, even beyond these walls.*"

"So… that's a 'yes' to the stalker Library, but a 'no' to the coming back here anytime soon?"

The Library chuckled. "*Until next time, Alexandra.*"

Knowing a dismissal when she heard one, Alex shook her head with a slight smile and stepped through the doorway, landing inside a familiar mushroom-circled forest clearing.

"And I'm back to where it all started," Alex whispered, glancing around Raelia as the doorway disappeared behind her.

"You certainly took your time."

Alex jumped as a silhouette approached her in the dark. The moon was hidden behind the clouds, so the only identifier was his voice.

"Aven! What—um—" Alex squeaked. "Why are you out here?"

She couldn't help her suddenly racing heart. Despite her mission to befriend him, it was only a few moments ago that she'd witnessed him murder her friends and family.

"I heard Grandfather invited you to that school of his," Aven answered, moving close enough that Alex could see the outline of his features. "I figured he wouldn't be able to resist showing you *Soraya de lah Torra*, and rather than traverse back here using the *Valispath*, it was likely you'd return through one of the *eiden* paths." Aven shrugged, trying to play off his waiting presence as nothing. "The Library doesn't open its doorways any closer to the city than here. I thought I'd meet you and accompany you back to the palace."

He looked uncomfortable, like he was embarrassed, though Alex couldn't imagine why. "That's very thoughtful of you, Aven. Thank you."

His mouth quirked up at the corner. "I'll admit, my actions weren't entirely altruistic."

Alex raised her eyebrows. "How so?"

He rolled his shoulders as if shaking off tension. "I needed some fresh air after dinner. It was... difficult, sitting there and keeping my thoughts to myself."

Alex asked the question she'd wondered earlier that night. "Then why did you?"

Aven's tone was dry when he replied, "I figured it best to avoid another yelling match with my father, especially since the council was there."

Against her better judgement, Alex said, "It sounded to me like some of them would have taken your side."

Aven cocked his head. "And what side is that, Aeylia?"

Wow, foot in mouth, much? Alex thought, mentally regrouping. She sent him a teasing grin and said, "If you don't know, then you've got more problems than you think."

He chuckled lightly and stepped closer, activating the *Valispath* around them. "Come on, let's get you home."

Zooming through the Silverwood, Aven didn't speak, which suited Alex perfectly given her distracted thoughts. It was only when they stopped outside her bedroom that he broke his silence.

"Thank you, Aeylia."

Alex looked up at him, surprised. "What for?"

"For not judging me. For not telling me what I should think or what I should believe. For not forcing your opinions on me when I know you disagree with where I stand."

Seeing that he was waiting for a response, Alex carefully said, "What right do I have to make you believe anything? At the end of the day, your values are your own. No one should tell you how to feel." She meant every word she'd said, despite wishing for the opposite.

Aven closed his eyes in what looked like relief. "It means a lot to hear you say that."

To lighten the suddenly heavy moment, she offered a quirky grin and said, "Well, you may think so now, but watch out, princeling. By the time I'm done subtly schooling you in the ways of mortals, you'll be so in love with humans that you'll want to ride off into the sunset with them."

Aven let out a surprised laugh, which was thankfully the reaction she was going for, rather than the opposite, which could have happened just as easily. "Is that so?"

"It sure is," Alex said with joking confidence.

"I could be wrong, but I think subtlety flies out the window when your declaration comes as a warning."

"Well, darn," Alex said, playing dumb. "And here I thought I was being oh-so-sneaky."

Aven laughed again and gave Alex a nudge towards her door. "You need to leave me before your mortal infatuation becomes contagious."

"Meyarins can't get deathly ill," Alex reminded him smugly. "So that leads to the conclusion that whatever you catch will only make you better. Like a new and improved version of yourself. Aven Two-Point-O."

Rolling his eyes, he firmly said, "*Goodnight*, Aeylia."

"Don't worry, I'm sure we'll have plenty of time to talk about this again tomorrow," Alex told him with a jaunty grin. "And the day after, and the day after, and the day after, and the—"

"Star's light, make it stop," Aven muttered, interrupting her unending diatribe. He nudged her forward again, this time not so gently, and pushed her through the opened door. After making sure she was clear, he promptly closed it in her face.

It was then that Alex did something she never thought she'd be capable of doing after an encounter with Aven.

She laughed.

Twenty-Two

The next day, Alex was in the palace library studying the extensive but monotonous history of the Seven Houses when she closed her book with a loud *snap*.

"I just don't get it," she said to Kyia, whose brows rose in question. "It's *Roka*. What can you possibly not like about him?"

"Everyone else may be willing to coddle you by speaking your language, but that doesn't mean I am. You need to practise your Meyarin," Kyia replied.

Alex made a frustrated sound. "Come on, Kyia. You now know the common tongue as well as anyone."

When Kyia remained silent, Alex rolled her eyes and switched languages.

"Fine," she said, somewhat belligerently in her now fluent Meyarin. "But if that was your attempt to get out of answering my question, think again."

"And what question is that?"

Alex pinned her with a knowing look. "*Roka*, Kyia. I don't understand your problem with him."

Kyia stood to her feet and moved to the nearest bookcase, absentmindedly perusing the shelves. "Why are you so insistent about this? It feels like every day I have to argue my case all over again."

"Because your case doesn't make sense!" Alex cried. "Let me repeat, it's Roka!"

Kyia turned and glared in irritation. "If you think he's so perfect, why don't *you* chase after him?"

Alex made a spluttering noise, not sure if she was more amused or disturbed by the idea. Aside from their absurdly incompatible age differences, there was also the huge fact that they weren't even of the same *race*. It would be like… like pairing up a dairy cow with a prize stallion. The idea of Alex thinking of *any* Meyarin in the way Kyia was suggesting was just plain wrong.

Being unable to properly explain her reasoning, all Alex could do was grin and say, "Trust me, he's not my type."

Throwing her arms up in a rare display of emotion, Kyia said, "Then why can't you accept the same for me?"

"Because you two are made for each other!" Alex returned, slightly desperate in her matchmaking attempt. "You just need to give him a chance, that's all."

Kyia stalked over to where Alex was sitting and slumped back down beside her. "Why would I do that when he's nothing but an arrogant, conceited, overconfident, cocky, puffed up, bigheaded *kregon*?"

By the end of her speech she was on a roll, nearly yelling the words as they blended from one into the next.

"You know," Alex said thoughtfully, "aside from *kregon*, I'm pretty sure most of those words all mean the same thing, give or take."

"Argh!" Kyia cried, throwing her weight back in her chair and shaking her head in annoyance.

"But let no one say she lacks an extensive vocabulary," came the highly amused voice of Roka as he strolled out from behind one of the shelves. "I particularly liked the combination of puffed up *and* bigheaded. Poetry for the ages."

Alex was horrified on Kyia's behalf but she couldn't repress her totally inappropriate snort of laughter. In her defence, the prince's timing was atrociously hilarious, as was his light-hearted reaction to the vicious slander.

"Please don't hold back next time, sweet Kyia," Roka finished, his lips twitching while his eyes sparkled with mirth. "Otherwise Aeylia might continue believing that we are, ahem, *'made for each other'*."

Poor Kyia looked like she was at a loss as to how to react. If it were Alex, she'd be wishing for the power to spontaneously combust, but Kyia had more backbone than most. That, and she'd grown up with Roka, so this wasn't their first experience trading insults.

"You didn't hear anything I wouldn't have said to your face," Kyia said, crossing her arms and folding one leg over the other, her position casually apathetic.

"But so rarely do you favour me with your undivided attention," Roka replied, not missing a beat. "I thought I was beneath your regard, but I now see that you've thought long and hard about your passionate feelings towards me. I'm touched, Kyia. Truly."

Alex bit down hard to keep from laughing again at Roka's unbridled sarcasm. But she still must have made a squeak of noise, since Kyia turned narrowed eyes in her direction.

"I can see exactly why you think so highly of him, Aeylia," she said, her sarcasm just as clear. "He's a real charmer."

"You can add that to my long list of virtues," Roka said with a wink. "Slot it in before *'kregon'*."

Must not laugh, must not laugh, Alex chanted, with little success. She only half managed to turn her amusement into a cough and quickly spoke before Kyia could throw a book at her head.

"I thought you were busy with the king until later tonight?" Alex questioned Roka, switching over to the common tongue out of habit.

"It turns out Father has no need of me for the rest of the day, after all," Roka answered. "I thought perhaps you both might like to take the afternoon off as well."

Alex perked up at that, happy for any excuse to set aside the never-ending lessons about the Meyarin High Court.

"Aven sought me out earlier," Roka went on. "He suggested we could all benefit from a break and that we should spend some time together away from the palace. Get away from it all."

"This is Aven's idea?" Alex asked. When Roka nodded, she said, "Are you, um, okay with that? With spending time with him, I mean. After everything that went down last week when—"

"I know what you're speaking of, Aeylia," Roka interrupted gently. "I may struggle to understand his fervent opposition towards mortals, but no matter what grievances Aven and I hold, he'll always be my brother, my closest confidant."

Alex had to turn away so that he wouldn't be able to read the look in her eyes. *Oh, Roka. If only you knew.*

"Besides," the prince continued excitedly, "cliff jumping is the perfect way to bring people together."

"Cliff jumping?" Kyia repeated, and even she sounded uncharacteristically eager. "Why didn't you say so sooner?"

"If I'd led with that, I would have missed out on your ebullient recitation of my vastly underrated personality traits."

Kyia opened her mouth but Alex got in first.

"At the risk of cutting off what I'm sure would be a perfect example of scathing wit," Alex said, tipping her head with mock respect towards Kyia, "can I just say, Roka, that I've known this language my whole life and not once have I heard anyone use the word 'ebullient' in a sentence. I'm not sure if I should applaud you or to tell you to stop reading the common tongue dictionary in your spare time and get a life."

Kyia burst out laughing, and even Roka let out a chuckle, proving yet again that he truly was the perfect prince by not taking her words to heart.

"I'll keep that in mind, Aeylia," he said in a humour-filled voice. "Perhaps right when I'm about to push you off the Golden Cliffs."

"Actually, I'm glad you've come back to that," Alex said, standing to her feet. "What exactly did you mean by 'cliff jumping'?"

Not at all liking the gleam that entered Roka's eyes, Alex didn't have the chance to retreat as he reached out to pull her closer to him. Kyia took that as her cue and jumped up as well, moving alongside them. One of the two—presumably Roka—activated the *Valispath* and it took off from beneath them.

"I'm not entirely sure I'm comfortable with whatever is going on here!" Alex called over the howling wind, but all she received in response were matching grins full of anticipation.

When the *Valispath* soared to an end atop the cliffs at the place where Aven had taken Alex sightseeing, she tried to steady her breathing so as to not give away just how apprehensive she was. Like her first visit, the view offered the perfect panorama of the city. But looking at it in removed appreciation was much, *much* different to looking at it and wondering if 'cliff jumping' meant exactly what Alex presumed it meant.

"I thought you'd never get here, brother," Aven said approaching them from behind.

When Alex turned, she saw he wasn't alone; Niyx was with him as well. Both of them, like Roka, were the most casual Alex had seen them, wearing lightweight pants and shirts, their feet bare. They wore no armour, held no weapons. They appeared almost exactly how Alex would imagine Jordan and Bear to be like in the future. Minus the jeans, of course, but she couldn't imagine *any* Meyarin wearing something as common as denim. It would be as odd as seeing a draekon sporting a polka dot onesie.

Kyia and Alex, on the other hand, were both clothed in summery dresses that Alex had become used to wearing over the week. Dainty, pretty material most definitely not suited to jumping off cliffs.

"Lovely Aeylia," Niyx greeted in a singsong voice, boldly slinging his arm across her shoulders. "I was hoping you wouldn't wiggle out of coming this afternoon. My day just turned even brighter."

She tried to slide out from underneath his heavy limb, but he just tightened his grip and drew her closer, so she resorted to frowning pointedly. He sent her a cheeky grin—an expression Alex was used to seeing given the relentless cat-and-mouse game he so loved to play.

"Do you have a quota you have to reach?" Alex asked him, placing her hands on his hard torso and giving a hefty push, for all the good it did. He barely even jolted.

"A quota?" he repeated in question, looking down at her with sparkling amethyst eyes.

"You know, like a specific number of girls you have to hit on each day before you call it quits."

His eyes brightened all the more. "Don't worry, kitten. Quota or not, I'll always have time for you. I know seeing me is the highlight of your day and I'd never deprive you of that."

"Eugh, gag," Alex said, making a face. She ignored the laughter of those around them and shoved against him again, only succeeding because Aven stepped in to help.

"Points for punching above your station, Ny," the younger prince said, effortlessly prying Alex away from his friend. "But I'm guessing from the unnecessarily detailed reports you've given me of her spurning your advances this past week that perhaps you might be better off looking for your next fling elsewhere."

Niyx sent a wicked grin in Alex's direction. "She'll cave to my charm. It's only a matter of time."

"Seriously," Alex said, "I think I just threw up a little in my mouth."

If anything, everyone just laughed louder—Niyx included.

"Come on," Aven said, leading her by the hand closer towards the edge of the cliff.

She dug in her heels and tugged against him. "Actually, can someone please explain to me why we're up here? Roka said cliff jumping, but surely we're not..." She trailed off at seeing the excited expressions the four of them wore. Casting her gaze outwards, she took in just how impossibly high they were above the city. "Hands down, you're all crazy if you're thinking of jumping off this cliff."

Niyx snorted. "Don't be ridiculous, Aeylia, that would be suicide." She felt her muscles relax, at least until he finished with, "We're jumping from over there."

Following the line of where he was pointing, Alex felt her heart leap into her throat at the sight of the massive waterfall.

A tremor of fear ran through her body. "Uh-uh. No way."

But before she could put up any further argument, everyone stepped close and the *Valispath* activated, transporting them to a boulder smack bang in the middle of the raging cascade. The force of the wind was so strong that it sprayed water straight back up the cliffs, soaking Alex within seconds. The sound thundered in her ears and the rocky platform beneath her feet rumbled with the violence of nature at its most terrifying.

"You're all insane!" Alex screamed over the sound of the torrent, yanking fiercely at Aven's hand. He wouldn't let her go though, and she was pinned into place when Niyx, on her other side, reached for her free hand, his grip gentle but firm enough to keep her locked between them.

"We won't jump until you're ready," Aven told her, leaning in close to her ear so she could hear him above the roar of the water.

"You don't get it!" Alex yelled. "I've done this before! Waterfalls and me *don't* mix well!"

Granted, Alex had never jumped from a cliff so high, but she *had* fallen off a huge waterfall inside one of the Library's oil paintings during her first year at Akarnae. That had been one of the scariest moments of her life. This, however, went way beyond that.

"I can't do this!" Alex cried, trying to pull away from both Aven and Niyx.

Aven, standing on her right, turned her away from Niyx until they were face to face, curling his free arm around her waist so he could lean in even closer. It was a mark of how scared she was that she didn't even have the presence of mind to consider him her future enemy and put space between them.

"You have my word, Aeylia, nothing bad will happen," he said into her ear, his hand at her waist giving a gentle squeeze. "You're one of us now. Let go of your mortal fears and embrace this moment as a Meyarin. You'll never feel more free."

Seeing that she was still unconvinced, he said in a voice only for her, "Live in the moment, Aeylia. I promise you won't regret it."

Alex wasn't sure if it was his gentle tone, his sincere eyes, or his absolute confidence, but something in her gave into his words, the same words the Library had said to her just last night. *Live in the moment.* It was a frightening thought, but maybe, just for one afternoon, that was exactly what she needed to do.

Xira? she called in her mind. *Can you hear me?*

It took barely a second for him to respond. *Everything okay, Alex? You feel... anxious.*

If I was to jump off this—she sent him a mental image of just how mammoth the falls were—*what's the chance I'll survive?*

Xiraxus's rumbling chuckle echoed in her ears even above the sound of the torrential cascade. *That depends.*

On what?

Whether you can swim.

Alex made an annoyed sound and somehow managed to translate it into her thoughts. *If I understand correctly, when I die, you die. I'm sure I don't have to remind you that it's in your best interests to be honest with me right now.*

The draekon just chuckled louder, but he thankfully also gave her a straight answer. *Jump as a mortal and you'll be in trouble. Jump as a Meyarin and you should have a blast. But jump either way, Alex. The flight will be good for you.*

Alex instantly remembered soaring with him above the clouds around Draekora and the feeling of impossible freedom that came with the experience.

Soon, he said, reading her thoughts. *We'll fly together again soon.* And with his promise, his presence fled her mind.

Mustering her courage, Alex looked down the line from Roka on her far right to Kyia then Aven, jumping over to Niyx on her left. She wondered how she had come to be hand in hand with such an unlikely group of friends. And she realised with startling clarity that that was exactly what they were. Niyx and his playful arrogance, Kyia and her cynical derision, Roka and his thoughtful intelligence, and the biggest surprise of all, Aven and his unexpected affability. They really *were* friends, as bizarre as it was. And Alex trusted them to keep her safe, mortal or not.

With an unexpected pang of emotion, she couldn't help imagining what it would be like standing atop the falls with Jordan, D.C. and Bear beside her. Jordan and Bear would no doubt be grinning from ear to ear with the thrill of adventure while D.C. would likely share Alex's concerns and say they were all mad if they were thinking about jumping. But Alex knew the truth—the princess would leap right alongside them, even if it meant she'd be screaming the whole way down.

Sudden homesickness slammed into Alex, a feeling that was as ridiculous as it was painful—ridiculous because she wasn't technically *missing* anything. Her friends were all frozen in time, unaware they were even waiting for her return. But for Alex, time was still moving forward, and if she wanted to see them again, she'd first have to survive the next few harrowing minutes of her life.

Taking a moment to centre herself, Alex allowed her heightened senses to slide into place. It was like embracing an old friend or slipping into a bubble bath, so comforting as it was for Alex to allow her Meyarin abilities to take over. And when she opened her eyes, the view before her was even more magnificent.

And also much more terrifying.

Determined to embrace the wonder of the moment, she managed to paste a semi-realistic grin on her face and, with her voice only slightly shaking, said, "Let's do this."

With jubilant cries, Roka, Kyia and Aven all linked hands, and both Niyx and Aven strengthened their grips on Alex.

"One!" Roka called out.

Alex's heart was beating like a hammer in her chest.

"Two!" Niyx followed.

She wondered if she would pass out before they made it over the edge.

"*Three!*" Aven yelled.

And, with their hands connected, the five of them leapt off the Golden Cliffs and plummeted down the cascading water into the valley below.

Screaming at the top of her lungs, all Alex could think was that Aven had been right: she had never before felt freer than she did right now.

Twenty-Three

If someone had told Alex that she'd enjoy spending an afternoon jumping off waterfalls and splashing around in rocky plunge pools with the future psychopath Aven, his right-hand man Niyx and the would-be-betrothed-but-were-currently-hating-each-other Roka and Kyia, she would have never believed it. But the truth was, Alex couldn't remember the last time she'd had more fun. For just a few hours she felt free of her worries, free of her cares. She simply lived in the moment, exactly as the Library—and Aven—had encouraged her to do.

And. It. Was. *Brilliant.*

After they dragged their soaking, laughing selves back to the palace and gobbled down a late dinner, the five of them all but crawled from the kitchen to their rooms. Alex barely had enough energy to change out of her wet clothes and into a silky nightgown before she collapsed onto her bed, her exhaustion sending her to an instant sleep.

But despite how tired she was, she still awoke with a start a few hours later when someone shook her shoulder and quietly called her name.

"Easy, it's just me."

At any other time, hearing Aven say those words in the dead of the night would have had Alex reaching for A'enara and swinging with all her might. But after their enjoyable day together, she couldn't find it in her to call up any apprehension whatsoever.

"Wha' 're you doin' 'ere, A-A-Aven?" she asked, slurring half the words and yawning his name. "'s the middle of the night."

"I'm sorry it's so late, but I want to show you something."

"Why don' I haf'a lock on m'door?" Alex grumbled, rolling over and burying her face in her pillow.

"Aey-lee-uh," Aven called, tauntingly drawing out her name. "Trust me. You won't want to miss this."

Alex made an annoyed sound in the back of her throat and rolled over again, squinting up at him to grouch, "This better be worth it."

He grinned in triumph and handed her a steaming goblet. "Drink up, you'll feel awake in no time."

True to his promise, after only a few sips of what Alex recognised as warmed *laendra* nectar, she felt as if she'd slept for days and was now ready to take on the world.

After making Aven leave her room so she could change into what she considered a night-time escapade outfit—tights, boots and a dark tunic cinched at the waist, coupled with a hooded cloak—Alex met him out in her hallway. Without a word, he pulled her close and activated the *Valispath*.

"Do you mind telling me what's going on?" Alex asked as they soared out of the palace and into the city.

"I already did," Aven replied, sounding distracted. "I told you I want to show you something."

"You could be a tad more specific."

But there was no need for him to reply because the *Valispath* brought them to a halt in the dark alley outside The Scarlet Thief.

With a groan, Alex said, "*Narsae de Trigon*? Really, Aven?"

Seeming surprised, Aven asked, "You've been here before?"

"It's not a memory I want to relive," Alex said. "Why are we here?"

"I know it's not the most… hygienic of places, but I promise there's a good reason for us being here."

"Hygienic isn't the word you're after," Alex replied as he led the way towards the entrance.

"No, it definitely is," Aven said with the hint of a smile. "We might not be able to get terminally sick, but if a plague was ever to break out amongst our people, I'm certain it would start here."

Stepping into the grimy, low-lit tavern, Alex couldn't help but agree. Being human and therefore susceptible to illness, she also set herself a mental reminder not to touch anything. Eww.

"Tohro," Aven greeted the burly barman eyeing them from behind the bar. He appeared to be expecting Aven, but showed definite surprise to see Alex.

She too was surprised, though not at seeing him again. Rather, she was surprised to see no one else in the room. The place was empty.

"They're all out back," Tohro told Aven. "I closed the place down early like you asked. Make sure you lock up when you're done."

Aven gave a nod of agreement and guided Alex deeper into the tavern, his steps long and buoyant.

"Seriously, Aven," Alex said, a trickle of apprehension crawling along her skin. "Why are we here?"

He stopped at a wooden door that had seen better days, covered as it was in suspicious stains and gritty bar filth.

"I need a favour, Aeylia."

Alex looked at him, intrigued.

He fixed his eyes on hers and said, "Just for tonight, I need you to forget you grew up with mortals."

Alex's heart skipped a beat. "What?"

"I know you have a high regard for them due to your upbringing, but for tonight, all I ask is that you keep an open mind and just... listen. Maybe see things from a different perspective."

"Aven—"

"It's really important to me, Aeylia," Aven said quietly, the golden flecks in his eyes burning like embers. "Can you do that for me?"

"You're asking a lot," Alex told him, only half truthful, since he was asking the impossible.

"I know I am," he replied instantly. "But it's just one night. You can leave whenever you like, but I hope that you'll stay for at least a little while. And then you're free to go back to your human-loving self again."

Not sure how to respond, Alex gestured towards the door. "Who's in there?"

"Just a few of my friends."

Her trepidation instantly skyrocketed as comprehension hit her like an anvil falling on her head. "And... uh, what are they doing?"

A secretive smile stretched across his face. "Waiting for me."

And with that, he opened the door to what Alex knew without a shadow of a doubt was a meeting of *Garseth*—Aven's original Rebels.

Considering the fact that she was witnessing one of the early get-togethers of a bunch of future murderers, Alex found there was nothing all that revolutionary happening. There were no ceremonial slaughters of innocents, no calls for violent rioting and thankfully, no blood-bonding rituals of faithfully blind devotees. It was simply a bunch of young Meyarins in a room,

chatting over drinks and suspicious looking appetisers—
suspicious because Alex figured Tohro had supplied the food,
and as Aven had said, *Narsae de Trigon* was hardly the most
sanitary of places.

After his grand entrance was met with boisterous excitement
from the Meyarins, Aven had left her in the corner with an
apology, saying that he had to make his rounds. But she kept
her eye on him, fascinated by the way he spoke to them, how he
gave his full attention, treating them as if whatever they said was
the most important thing he'd ever heard. Darrius had once told
her that Aven was gifted with an almost unnatural amount of
charisma, and after seeing him work the room, Alex had to agree.

He was really quite spectacular.

Regardless, she was starting to get fidgety, still unsure why
she was there.

"You look like you could use a drink."

Alex spun around at hearing words in the common tongue
and felt her heart sink. "Zain?" *No, please no.* "What are you
doing here?"

Still looking as shabby as the last time she'd seen him,
Zain raised a Myrox shot glass to his mouth and threw back
its contents. "What does it look like?" he said after swallowing.
"I'm drinking."

He reached out to grab two full goblets from the tray of a
passing Meyarin, shoving one into Alex's hands.

"*Glaeron*," Zain said. "The finest brew around."

"This just keeps getting better and better," Alex said, not
touching the drink even when Zain started swigging large
gulps from his. "Not only are you a criminal, but you're also a
functioning alcoholic. Perfect."

"Everyone has a role to play," Zain said, his eyes scanning
the room, strangely alert. "Mine just happens to be one of the
more enjoyable ones."

"What are you *doing* here, Zain?" Alex demanded again.

His eyes came back to her. "I could ask you the same question, *Aeylia*."

"And I could ask you both, but I already know the answer," came a new voice.

Alex turned just in time to see Niyx swagger to her side.

"Lovely Aeylia," he greeted, seeming to have decided on her nickname for the day. "A pleasure, as always."

"I saw you a few hours ago, Niyx," she told him, following his lead and speaking Meyarin, figuring it was best to avoid sounding like a mortal given their company. "Surely there's someone else you can bother?"

"Oh, how my heart bleeds," Niyx said, raising a hand to his chest. "How ever shall I survive such a painful rejection from my one true love?"

Jeez, he was laying it on thick. All Alex could do was roll her eyes while trying to suppress a smile. Despite how blatantly ridiculous his flirting was, he really was entertaining to be around.

"I'm sure you'll get over it," Alex told him.

"You know, I think you may be right," he said, snapping out of his lovey-dovey charade. "And besides, it's not *you* I was wanting to speak with." He turned to Zain. "First time seeing you here. Glad you could make it tonight."

Zain gave a slight nod and took another swig of *glaeron*.

Seeing his new target wasn't one for words, Niyx turned back to Alex. "Did you know Zain here is Meya's most notorious illegal trafficker?"

Alex felt her stomach lurch. "Trafficker? You don't mean…" Her eyes jumped up to meet Zain's. "You don't traffic people, do you?"

Zain's lip curled. "I do many things, but I draw the line at smuggling live goods."

That, at least, was something. But still… "What *do* you smuggle, then?" Alex asked.

"Whatever he can get his hands on," Niyx said, clapping Zain heartily on the shoulder and ignoring the bulky Meyarin's look of disdain. "He steals from the rich and sneaks his wares out of the city, bartering with desperate mortals who will pay an arm and a leg for anything Meyarin-made. Myrox designs in particular are always in high demand, am I right, Zain?"

Again, Zain remained silent as he threw back the dregs of his goblet and liberated Alex of her own.

"You want to go a little easy with that?" Alex said pointedly. "You're a big guy, but I can smell those fumes from here. If you pass out, I'm sure not carrying you home."

"It would take much more than a few flagons of *glaeron* to knock him out," Niyx said with a knowing grin. "He could drink all night and still find his way around the city backwards with his eyes closed. Trust me on that."

"Don't encourage him, Niyx," Alex said with a frown. "We want him to stop drinking, not to drink more."

Niyx let out a bark of laughter. "Good luck with that, sweetheart. Prying Zain from his drink would be like asking him to give up his commercial exploits. It's not going to happen."

"It *could*," Alex argued. "If only he was willing to try something new."

Ideally, this would be the time to ask Zain why he continued to refuse Roka's invitation to join the elite guard, but with Niyx listening in, all she could do was stare at Zain meaningfully, knowing he was aware of what she wasn't saying.

Finally, Zain spoke. "It would appear, Niyx, that you've managed to find the only Meyarin more irritating than you."

"Hey!" Alex cried indignantly.

"She is rather magnificent, isn't she?" Niyx said, lips twitching. "But be warned, this kitten has claws."

"Kittens are harmless even with their claws," Zain returned, his eyes roaming until they deliberately narrowed in on Aven. "It's the snakes you need to watch out for. You never know when they might strike."

Alex couldn't miss the underlying tension and wondered what had caused the rift between the two Meyarins.

Throwing back the last of Alex's drink, Zain abruptly announced, "I need a refill." He didn't wait for a reply; he simply disappeared into the growing crowd.

"Pleasant sort, isn't he?"

A bubble of laughter rose out of Alex. "Yes, he's the life of the party. I can see why you invited him."

"To be fair, he's not here because of his social skills," Niyx said. "Aven thinks he'd be a good ally, considering his access to mortals and his contacts within other trade circles."

"Aven reached out to him?" Alex asked, relief washing over her. "You're saying Zain's not here because he believes in… What everyone else here believes?"

Niyx cocked his head. "What do you think everyone here believes?"

"I'm not a fool, Niyx. I know this isn't a birthday party."

His eyes searched her face. "How much has Aven told you?"

Alex wasn't sure what the correct response was, so she settled on a half-lie, half-truth. "He's told me enough."

"And yet, you're still here?"

"I agreed to have an open mind."

Niyx burst into laughter. "This I have to see."

"In all seriousness, what are we actually doing here?" Alex asked.

Still highly amused, Niyx said, "I'm guessing he didn't tell you much, after all."

She crossed her arms and turned away, deciding it best not to respond.

He chuckled again but reached out to turn her back around to face him. "I'll tell you, but only because I figure if Aven brought you, then he must be fine with you knowing. The most important thing you need to realise is that tonight must be kept a secret. No one who's not here can know. That means Roka, Kyia and anyone else you spend time with." He paused for a beat and reiterated, "Roka especially."

Alex sent him a bland look. "I kind of gathered it was hush-hush when I was pulled from bed at an ungodly hour and brought to the shadiest tavern in the city."

Niyx shrugged. "One can never be too careful. This group has only been meeting for a week; the foundation isn't strong yet, despite Aven's magnetic leadership."

A week. The *Garseth* were only a week old. That meant Aven must have started recruiting almost straight after his altercation with the human trade delegation. He sure hadn't wasted any time amassing his group of Rebels. There were already at least thirty young Meyarins in the room.

"As for Aven's purpose here..." Niyx continued, reeling back her attention. He trailed off, though, when Aven himself stepped up beside them, his eyes alight with fervour.

Before the prince could say anything, another Meyarin entered their circle—someone Alex already knew. She automatically took a step away from the brutal thug, Skraegon, only to run into the solid wall of the tavern.

"I'm only saying you should consider it," Skraegon said, continuing whatever conversation he'd been having with Aven, his focus wholly centred on the prince. "Just think about it— if *you* were on the throne, you could do as you please without having to answer to anyone."

Chilled by his words—and wanting to seal his lips shut—Alex imagined Skraegon to be a perfect candidate for the *Garseth*. And when his eyes finally drifted to her, she felt her stomach sink as they narrowed with recognition.

"You!" he bellowed, lunging towards her.

Trapped against the wall, Alex had no room to retreat. But she didn't have to, since both Aven and Niyx reacted instantly, with Niyx leaping protectively in front of her and Aven grabbing Skraegon by the ruff of his collar and hauling him through the now silent crowd and out of the room.

"Well, that was dramatic," Niyx said, turning back to Alex as those around them resumed their conversations. "There's never a dull moment with you, Aeylia."

Alex looked at him with wide eyes, startled by how quickly the scene had transpired.

"I'm sure there's an entertaining reason for what just happened, but as long as you're all right, I'd better go and make sure they're not killing each other out there," Niyx said, tilting his head in the direction Aven had dragged Skraegon.

There was genuine concern in his normally carefree eyes—concern for *her*—so Alex quickly reassured him, "I'm fine, really. Go make sure Aven's okay."

Looking at her carefully, Niyx nodded, and his untroubled features fell back into place. "Back soon, kitten."

He jokingly reached out to stroke the top of Alex's head as if she really were a cat and took off in the footsteps of Aven and Skraegon, leaving the room. She scowled after him, patting her mussed hair back down.

Alone again, she thought about what Skraegon had said. '*If* you *were on the throne, you could do as you please…*'

Burdened by dread and fatigue, Alex wondered if anyone would notice if she left. But before she could slip out, Aven re-entered the room, followed closely by Niyx and a skulking Skraegon.

The prince moved directly to the small stage area towards the front of the crowd, his voice loud enough for everyone to hear.

"My friends, thank you for coming tonight," he said with a welcoming smile that somehow managed to feel personal despite the public space. "I apologise for the late hour, but as you all know, for the moment we must guard our secrecy. In due time our cause shall be considered just and we'll no longer have to hide in the shadows."

"Hear, hear!" cried a Meyarin towards the back of the room.

"I've spoken with many of you already tonight," Aven went on, "and I'm pleased that we stand in one accord. We're here because we agree that the mortal blight threatening our city should no longer be given power over us. The humans are thieves, stealing that which is ours and trading it for paltry and useless trinkets of no worth. I ask you—what need have we of human medicine?"

"None!" the crowd shouted, causing Alex to jump.

"What need have we of cloth and spices?"

"None!"

"What need have we of art, perfume and the foolish things of humans?"

"*None!*"

"*None*, I tell you!" Aven all but screamed, stirring the crowd. "They offer us nothing we don't already have—nothing we will ever need. And yet, my father"—his expression turned grim—"your *king*, is determined that we give them the best of our wares. We trade Myrox for manure, weapons for wax and advanced education for the clinking of seashells tied around leather strings. We give everything and receive *nothing*. And I for one have had enough!" Chest heaving, Aven vehemently bellowed, "I will no longer stand by and allow our proud race to yield to an infestation of mortal vermin!"

The shouts of agreement around the room were just as passionate as those of their leader.

"It may be early days," Aven went on, "but it's up to us to take a stand. If we can gather enough voices to our side, the king will have no choice but to consider our words. And if he doesn't—"

A gloved hand suddenly latched around Alex's waist and a second slapped over her mouth, forcefully yanking her from the room and Aven's horrifyingly captivating speech.

Her cries for help were muted by the taste of her assailant's leathery glove as she was pulled through the dimly lit tavern and into the balmy night air. Even her best attempts at breaking free of the impenetrable grip holding her were useless.

Just as Alex was about to call out for Xira's aid, she was hauled into a shadowy alleyway where her abductor swiftly released her. She stumbled away, drawing her hands up in a defensive position as she turned back to face the cloaked figure.

"Who the hell are you and what do you want with me?" she demanded in terse Meyarin.

The figure threw back his hood and stepped into the moonlight.

"Roka?" Alex gasped out, reverting to the common tongue. "You scared the crap out of me!"

"By all the stars in the sky, what in the name of the light do you think you're doing here, Aeylia?" Roka asked, looking aghast to see her.

"Me?" Alex cried, her voice pitched high. "What about *you*?"

Roka glanced around the cobblestoned street and reached for her again, pulling her closer. "Come. We'll talk back at the palace. It's not safe here."

They rode the *Valispath* in silence until it delivered them directly outside Roka's sitting room. It was, to Alex's distracted eye, styled similarly to how it looked in the future.

Tearing off his cloak, Roka threw it onto his desk, sending writing implements and parchment flying. He began pacing like a caged animal, his agitation palpable in the loud silence.

"What's going *on*, Roka? What were you doing out there? How did you know about that meeting?"

"My brother's exploits aren't as quiet as he would like others to believe," Roka responded, still pacing. "And not all of his followers are as fanatically devoted as he claims. I—and they— have been keeping an eye on him all week, ever since he began this asinine crusade against humankind."

"You've been watching him?" Alex asked, surprised.

"Of course I have," Roka said, in a tone that implied her question was ridiculous. "If our father hears of the insurrection Aven is stirring, he'll lose his royal mind. I need to make sure I understand what my foolish brother is planning ahead of time so I can put a stop to it."

Looking at the agitated prince, Alex felt a wave of sadness. "You really do love him, don't you?"

"He's my brother, Aeylia," Roka said. "And his rebellious side will cost him our father's respect if he doesn't soon come to his senses. As long as it's within my power, I'll do whatever it takes to keep my family together. Even if that means I have to sneak around and eavesdrop on his supposedly secret meetings."

Alex let that sink in, not sure how she felt about the fact that while Roka was determined to save Aven from Astophe's ire, he'd yet to mention anything about his brother's actual anti-mortal cause.

"Forgive me for pointing this out," Alex said carefully, eyeing Roka's restless movements across the room, "but judging by the tracks you're making, it looks like you're worried about more than Aven's deteriorating relationship with your father."

Roka's steps stuttered to a halt as he paused, almost as if he only just noticed his agitated footsteps. Running a hand through his uncharacteristically dishevelled hair, he released a long, weary breath and collapsed into one of his cushy chairs.

"What's on your mind?" Alex asked quietly, taking the seat opposite him.

Roka swallowed thickly and, in a voice almost too low for Alex to hear, he said, "What if he's right?"

Alex felt the ground shift out from underneath her. "What?"

"About the mortals," Roka went on, as if not having heard Alex's whispered exclamation. "What if he's right and Father is wrong? If nothing else, Aven's words are true—we *are* giving them more than they give us. The trade agreement is an insult to everything we are, yet my father believes it's our responsibility to assist those lesser than ourselves. I thought I agreed with him, but I can't deny that Aven's cause holds merit. I almost feel as if I should step in and appeal to our father alongside him, offering a united front in his stance against mortals."

Feeling sick to her stomach at the idea of Roka—good, kind, compassionate Roka—feeling anything negative towards mortals, Alex barely managed to get her next words through her horrified lips. "You can't seriously think it's okay to kill humans, can you?"

Roka jerked backwards at her words. "Kill them? What are you talking about?"

Realising that she'd stuffed up, *big time*, Alex swiftly backpedalled. "Not, like, *kill them*, kill them. I just meant..." She scrambled to find a valid response. "If Meya ceases trade with the humans, it means you'll—*we'll*—stop giving them aid, right? Essentially we'll be cutting off our support and, well, some of them will likely die as a result."

Roka thankfully seemed to accept her lame reasoning. Either that, or he was too distracted by his own thoughts to realise she'd hardly put forth a stellar argument.

"Be that as it may," he said, "any mortal fatalities would be unintentional on our part."

"Death is death," Alex said in a hard voice. "Whether at the hand of a weapon or by old age, accident or disease, it can't be undone. If the cost to save innocent lives is so insignificant to Meya, then what reasoning can you possibly offer to rationalise your negligence?"

Roka stared at Alex for a moment before his mouth quirked up into a grin. "You really do love those mortals of yours, don't you?"

"There's a lot to love," Alex returned, thinking of her friends, her family.

A pause, and then Roka quietly said, "Thank you, Aeylia."

Uncertain, she asked, "For what?"

"For reminding me that there is always a larger picture, a grander perspective. A single pebble dropped into tranquil waters can ripple out into waves of change for the whole pond." His gaze turned inward as he finished, "We are the pebble; we mustn't forget to consider the pond."

A surge of affection rushed through Alex. He may have experienced a moment of doubt, but this was the Roka she knew. The prince she trusted.

"I'm sorry you were abandoned as a babe, Aeylia," he told her tenderly. "No one deserves that. But if nothing else came of it, I'm glad you had the chance to get to know mortals well enough to fight for them. Stars above, they'll need all the help they can get if Aven continues his campaign against them. They're fortunate to have a Meyarin with a heart as strong as yours on their side."

Alex wasn't able to look at him when she quietly admitted, "Sometimes I feel I'm more human than Meyarin, Roka."

Instead of rebuking her, the prince smiled, not taking her honest moment seriously. "Sometimes I feel the same."

He rose to his feet then, stepping forward to offer his hand.

"The hour grows late," he said. "Allow me to see you back to your quarters."

After they parted ways outside her room and she crawled into bed for the second time that evening, Alex stared unseeingly out at the glowing view of the city over her balcony.

Xira, you there? she called.

Always, Alex, he returned almost instantly. *What troubles you?*

Suddenly overcome with emotion, she asked, *How long until I can go home?*

There was a reluctant pause. *Soon, Alex. But not yet. I'm sorry.*

Alex already knew that was the answer. She asked him almost every day, but still, she could hope. Not for the first time, she wondered if she should have just stepped through the Library when she'd had the chance.

Why are you upset? You felt joyous earlier, but now you're... distressed?

Alex let out a bitter laugh. 'Distressed' was the perfect word for how she was feeling. *I just had a rough night*, she answered. *I'll be okay after I've had some sleep.*

Do you want me to help?

Alex was about to ask what he meant when suddenly her mind was awash with images. She felt her body relax as, from Xiraxus's view, she soared through the air as his own memories played out before her eyes.

Before long, she was so lulled by the swooping feeling of the wind brushing against her scales and the power of her wings capturing the air currents that she drifted off into a peaceful sleep, still soaring through the skies as she slumbered through the dreamscape of her mind.

Twenty-Four

After her breakfast with the queen the next morning, Alex slowly made her way to the palace library, wondering how she might get out of whatever history lesson was in store for her. It wasn't that the lessons weren't interesting, it was just that what she learned wasn't exactly relevant to her immediate—or future—troubles. It also didn't help that her mind was elsewhere today—specifically the upcoming end-of-summer banquet Niida had been excitedly talking about.

When Alex entered the library, she was surprised to find the grand room empty. Usually her tutors, Roka or Kyia depending on the day, beat her there.

Glancing around warily, she approached her usual study table to find a note written on silvery parchment.

Aeylia,
I'm terribly sorry, but the bane of my existence
needs someone to hold his hand for a few hours, so I
have to leave you on your own this morning.
(Don't worry, I'll make sure His Royal
High-handedness regrets asking for my help.)
We'll be back after dinner, so enjoy your day
today and we'll see you later tonight.
Kyia.

Underneath Kyia's neat script was another message, this one also in familiar writing.

A,

As you can see, Kyia is thrilled to be spending the day with me in service to the crown. You might as well start planning our wedding now, since I have it on good authority that she's a sure thing.

R.

Laughing at Roka's dry humour, Alex set the parchment aside and glanced around the library, wondering how she'd spend the day. She could explore more of the city, of course, or do a myriad of other things. But what Alex really wanted was knowledge. And for the first time since arriving in the past, she found herself alone and surrounded by exactly that.

Striding over to the nearest walled bookshelf, she began scanning the titles, remembering that Roka had once said the tomes were sorted into alphabetised categories around the room. Alex first hit up the section labelled *Ascorava*, which held all the Meyarins' written knowledge relating to weaponry, and then she found the ancient history section where she picked out several particularly old-looking books. Lastly, she stepped up one of the ladders until she reached the third floor bookshelves and scanned the category that she was most interested in—*Vanorias*, or as it translated in the common tongue, 'Healing'.

Teetering down the ladder and wobbling to her table with her arms laden with books, Alex wasn't sure how she managed to avoid breaking her neck. She dropped her heavy load onto the desk, taking a seat and pulling the closest book towards her.

It took four hours, five return trips up the ladder and eighteen more medical books before Alex finally found what she was after. Rubbing her strained eyes, she sat up with a jolt when she found the miniscule font hidden in the appendix of an impossibly thick tome. She leaned forward and squinted to make out the fine writing, her breathing coming quicker with each sentence.

Menada dae Loransa, she read, before mentally translating as she went along:

> *The Claiming of Life creates a bond between one living being and another, enabling them to share energy in the most dire of physical health conditions...*

Anxious to get to what she needed, Alex skimmed a chunk of the summary that Aven had once described—not to mention Alex had experienced firsthand—and jumped right to the part she was after. With shaking hands and a thumping heart, she read on:

> *When the ritual is first performed, it is a battle of wills, where the strongest mind wins out. Since the bond is used as a means of healing in extreme situations only — for those nearing death with no other option but to bind their life force to that of another — the healer will almost always be in a position where their will reigns supreme over the individual in need.*

Head spinning, Alex frantically eyed the page for anything that might help to free Jordan from the bond.

> *To complete the ritual and Claim the life of another, there must be a direct blood link between the giver and the receiver — between the healthy and the injured. A simple cut on the hand is the most common practice, however any open wound will suffice.*

Joining their blood, the performer of the ritual must impress their will onto the mind of the recipient by mentally commanding the words —

"*Trae Menada sae.*" Alex then repeated the command in the common tongue, her voice barely a breath of sound. "I Claim you."

Was that really all it took? It seemed too easy, too simple.

Shaking her head, Alex skimmed over the next part detailing the Claimed's everlasting obedience to the creator and the technicalities of how the link transferred life forces. What she was *really* looking for was right at the end, a single sentence confirming what Aven had already told her:

Once the Claimed has returned to good health, the creator of the bond may terminate the connection by joining blood again and mentally calling the words —

"*Trae Gaverran sae.*" Alex's voice hitched as she read the phrase that spilled like written hope across the page. "I Release you."

After the Claimed willingly accepts their Release from the bond, neither party will retain any lasting effect. They will each be an individual entity once more, with no further connection between them.

Alex felt tears well in her eyes. She still had to find a way to convince the Aven of the future to willingly Release Jordan, but at least there was now hope that it truly was possible to free him. If she found the right leverage, perhaps Alex would be able to barter for his life. Aven had little use for her best friend other than as a means to hurt her. All she had to do was find something the Meyarin wanted *more*, something he was willing to trade in exchange for Jordan. Perhaps Alex herself, it if came to that. Though, she quickly realised that might very well lead to the catastrophic future the Library prophesised.

Ideas coming to her as swiftly as she swatted them away, Alex brushed a hand across her wet cheeks, drying her tears, and turned to read the final entry at the bottom of the page, this one written in a different hand:

> ADDENDUM: As of the third month in the year of the Desteroth, let it be known that any and all blood-bonding rituals are hereby forbidden. To perform such an act on a living being will result in immediate execution.

"That's some heavy reading you've got there, Aeylia," teased a voice in her ear.

Startled, Alex snapped the book shut with a loud *whump* and spun around to find Aven directly behind her. She knew her eyes were wide and she could feel her heart thumping wildly in her chest, but her reaction wasn't uncalled for. Just how long had he been standing over her shoulder? How much had he read? What if—

"Still curious about *Menada dae Loransa*?" he asked, moving beside her to lean casually against the table. "I can understand your fascination, especially given what you went through."

Seeing she was lost for words, Aven reached out and took her left hand in his, uncurling her fingers until he could see the silvery scar slashed across her palm.

"It doesn't seem fair that you had to suffer the agony of Sarnaph poison when a simple bonding ritual would have healed you in a matter of minutes."

"You know what they say," Alex managed to choke out. "What doesn't kill you only makes you stronger."

"In your case, no truer words can be said," Aven replied. Softly, oh so softly, he traced his fingers over her scar before releasing her hand altogether. "How you lived with those people for so many years, I'll never know. Your inner fire is something I envy, that strength of will within you."

Taken off-guard by his gentle—almost *intimate*—touch, it took a moment for Alex to focus on his words.

"Last night was interesting," she offered, directing their conversation away from the danger zone of the Claiming ritual. "You have a lot of… friends. I didn't realise there were so many other people willing to rebel against the king's consideration for mortals."

A wondering light glistened in Aven's eyes. "Willing to rebel?"

Alex looked at him strangely. "Uh, yeah. Isn't that what you're all doing?"

"You're saying we're rebels?"

"Aven, what…" She trailed off as the translation washed over her and she realised just how ridiculous this moment was in the paradigm of time.

"I like that," Aven mused in the common tongue, not waiting for her to finish her question. "Rebels. We are the *Garseth*."

Alex wasn't sure whether to laugh incredulously or punch herself in the face. Who would have thought it was she who originally gave Aven the name for his followers? She might as well have offered to have her teeth pulled out one by one, so acute was the horror of what she'd just done.

"But, yes," Aven continued, "essentially that is what we are. Ignoring your brief, unpleasant run-in with Skraegon—"

Unpleasant run-in? Alex scoffed to herself, remembering the brute lunging for her. And that was *after* he'd suggested Aven take the throne for himself. 'Unpleasant' didn't quite cover how she would describe their encounter.

"—I'm glad you were able to see last night what we stand for; that our cause is just and valid. Can you disagree with that?"

"I can," Alex said instantly. Aven's fervour dimmed and his expression morphed into disappointment, so she explained, "There's a saying amongst mortals: 'Don't bite the hand that feeds you.'" She paused to let that sink in and then continued, "If you were to place a wolf cub in the care of a herd of sheep, that cub would grow up loving the sheep, not seeing them as its next meal. And if another wolf was to come along and threaten the cub's adopted family, can you blame that cub for doing whatever it could to protect its sheep? To protect its family?"

Aven's face softened again. "We're your family now, Aeylia."

Unwilling to let his declaration sway her, Alex responded, "That's what the new wolf would likely say to the cub, too."

They looked into each other's eyes for a long while, but soon Aven's lips moved up into a reluctant smile.

"Such loyalty," he said, sounding awed. "Yet they'll never know how fortunate they are to have a cub like you protecting them."

"I still have to manage that feat," Alex said. Sensing it was time to let go of the heavy metaphor that meant more to her than Aven could yet know, she poked him lightly in the ribs and finished, "And that's something I have a feeling you and your merry bunch of Rebels will be making increasingly difficult for me."

With a chuckle, all Aven said was, "It will certainly be interesting to see if the wolf or the cub end up winning the battle for the sheep."

Like an icy droplet of water, a shiver ran down her spine at the strikingly valid analogy.

Aven pushed off the table, standing to his full height as he looked down at Alex, his expression thoughtful.

"You know, all this talk of wolves and sheep, it does beg the question," he said, reaching out to trace his fingers across the cover of the book Alex had slammed shut upon his arrival.

Following his actions closely with her eyes, she asked, "And what question is that?"

"What if the sheep spent so much time with their cub that they started to think they'd rather be wolves themselves?" Aven asked, his tone pensive. "What if the real wolves had to find a way to control the sheep, to make sure they didn't try to become something more than they were? A sheep can never be a wolf, no matter how much it might wish to be." He gazed thoughtfully down at the closed book. "What if the wolves discovered a way to keep the sheep in line, if they found a way to…" He trailed off, his brow furrowed in thought.

"Aven," Alex breathed, her heart heavy with dread. "Are we—Are we still talking about animals?"

Just as quietly he returned, "You know we were never talking about animals, Aeylia." A fire lit in his eyes as he continued looking at the book, his expression calculating. "I have to admit," he said in a voice so hushed Alex had to lean in to catch it, "if it wasn't forbidden, I'd be curious as to the effect the *Menada dae Loransa* would have on a mortal. I don't believe it's ever been tested."

It was then that fear took complete hold of Alex, "That would be—You can't—It's not—" She couldn't finish a single sentence, so acute was her distress at the idea that she might have been the catalyst for the future Aven's decision to start actively using the forbidden blood-bonding ritual.

Sensing her anguish, Aven hastily laughed off his words. "Of course, no Meyarin would ever be immoral enough to attempt such an act. The stealing of one's will…" He shook his head. "I can't imagine anything worse. But it's a curious thing to hypothesise the potential influence on mortals, even if we'll never know the answer." He resolutely pushed the book away. "Now, Aeylia, it seems I've been entirely distracted from the reason I originally came to find you."

Feeling cold all over, Alex managed to pull herself together to ask, "And what reason is that?"

"The best reason there is," he returned. "Food."

"Food?"

"I'm starving," he explained. "I'm meeting Niyx at *De Talen* and between you and me, I'd much prefer your added company." He winked at her and she forced herself to dredge up a smile, despite the ice still flooding her veins.

"I'm not sure..." she said, looking at the books laid on the table and hoping they would provide an excuse to avoid spending time with him. What she really needed was to get her thoughts in line and come to grips with just how badly she might be responsible for future Aven's deplorable actions.

"I won't take no for an answer," he said, his dark mood all but gone in the face of his renewed cheerfulness. "You look like you're in desperate need of a break."

Alex didn't doubt it. In fact, she felt so lightheaded that she wondered if she just might pass out.

"I—"

"And I'll make you a deal," Aven interrupted, cutting off her next attempt at a refusal. He picked up another heavy book from the pile, one of the ancient history texts she'd collected. "I'm guessing you pulled this out for a reason?"

She hesitantly nodded, unsure what he was getting at.

"Well, here's something you don't know about me." He leaned down to whisper, as if it were a secret, "I'm *obsessed* with history. I've read every book in this library on the subject. So I'll tell you what; if you come out to lunch with us for a little while, take a break from all this research, then I'll come back with you afterwards and answer any questions you have. That'll save you poring through book after book to find whatever you're looking for. Sound good?"

Judging by his expression, there was no way Aven was going to accept an excuse. He actually *wanted* to spend time with her, as mental as that was. So she might as well take advantage of his offer.

"I suppose I could have a short break," Alex said, shoving aside all thoughts of forbidden rituals as she stood to her feet. "But I'll warn you, I expect some quality answers when we get back here."

"You have my word," Aven said, his voice lowering to finish, "I'll be all yours."

Twenty-Five

Hours later, Alex was back in the library on her own again. True to Aven's word, after a casual and admittedly fun lunch with both him and Niyx, the prince had returned Alex to the palace and spent the afternoon answering her questions. For the most part, she had been curious to finally learn something about the reference she'd heard only in passing—Tia Auras.

Unfortunately, despite Aven's vast knowledge of history, he wasn't able to help her much because there was very little he knew himself regarding the world from which his people had originated.

Alex had found that difficult to believe at first, certain the Meyarins would have a long account of how they had arrived in Medora—and why. But Aven's frustration was clear when he admitted to wishing he knew more. Apparently all records dating back to when his race was banished from Tia Auras were shared by word of mouth only and held as closely guarded secrets known only to the most ancient of Meyarins.

Both fascinated and disappointed, Alex still managed to learn at least a few things from Aven. Like how the Meyarins referenced the 'stars' and 'light' as verbal exclamations because, while they didn't hold to a higher religious belief per se, they acknowledged the supreme power of light and its ability to break through darkness. Even after Aven's explanation, Alex wasn't entirely sure if he'd been speaking figuratively or not.

She was also surprised to learn that the Library—*Soraya de lah Torra*—was built by the Tia Aurans. Or perhaps, like the Meyarins, it was originally from Tia Auras. Aven was a tad sketchy on which version was true, again claiming his otherworldly history to be limited. But either way, the Library of Legend was also known by a second name in the lyrical language of the Tia Aurans: *Tu'eh L'randae ess Relana*. Aven translated it to mean 'The Cascade of Light', but thanks to Xiraxus, who apparently spoke fluent Tia Auran, Alex internally corrected the name to actually mean, 'The Fountain of Life'. Regardless of which was more accurate, neither made sense to Alex since the Library wasn't a flowing source of water, light *or* life. Even the Tia Aurans' first name for it—'The Light of the Worlds'—didn't fit. But hey, who was she to judge? So long as the Library continued being a library and didn't suddenly up and transform into a river, she was okay calling it whatever they wanted.

The last thing Aven was able to provide any information on was A'enara. Again, his knowledge was annoyingly limited, telling her much the same as Roka; that the blade was wrought by the Tia Aurans and known by many different titles. He also theorised that when it disappeared from sight, it most likely vanished into the *abrassa*, biding its time until it was called back from the Void. What he couldn't tell her was *how* that actually worked, or why it was bound to her to begin with. Nor was he able to explain how it could change size at will.

As for its new fiery development, Aven presumed, like Roka, that it was linked to her *vaeliana* with Xiraxus. When he asked to hold A'enara to see if he was right, Alex nearly broke out in hives, but she couldn't exactly say, 'No way, José!' and run madly out of the room. So she cautiously passed the pommel over to him by the tips of her fingers, careful not to let the flames burn him. The moment he held it in his hands, the fire disappeared... but A'enara didn't. Nervous for a number of reasons, Alex made up some joking speech about him stealing candy from a baby and laughingly asked for her 'pretty sword' back. He just grinned at her and did as she requested, causing her to twitch with relief the moment the blade was back in her possession and released once again into the Void.

She still had many questions about A'enara and the Tia Aurans, but she would just have to hope that the future might hold more answers for her. Perhaps if Kaiden had already found out something about the weapon, she could trace the information back to the creators of A'enara and why they banished the Meyarins.

It was a long shot, but there were clearly no more answers for her in the past, none easily open to her, anyway. She could, of course, seek out an ancient Meyarin who remembered Tia Auras, but she feared drawing too much attention to herself and thought it best to discourage further unwanted scrutiny.

Regardless of her decision to stop researching the otherworlders, after following Aven to dinner where they had a quiet meal alone with Astophe and Niida, Alex retreated to the library again, deciding that it couldn't hurt to take advantage of all that knowledge while she could. Aven offered an apology, saying he had to be elsewhere—and she knew by his meaningful glance he was off to meet with more *Garseth*.

Alex was deep in the middle of reading about the past recorded instances of known draekon bondings—none of which had occurred in over a thousand years, none enacted with anyone other than an immortal and none of whom were still alive today—when, just as she was turning the page, a hand came down on her shoulder.

Letting out a girlish squeal of fright, Alex reacted on instinct and flew back from her chair, hissing in pain when her fingers slid along the edge of the page as she jumped to her feet.

278 · Lynette Noni

"Sorry, Aeylia," Roka said, laughing as he held his hands up in apology. "I didn't realise you were so out of it."

"Jeez, Roka!" Alex said, her adrenaline spiked. "Make some noise next time!"

She shook her stinging hand through the air and, noticing her reaction, he asked, "Are you all right?"

"It's just a paper cut," she replied, distracted by trying to convince her nerves to settle again from her fright. "It sounds lame, but they hurt worse than stab wounds sometimes."

"I truly didn't mean to scare you," Roka said, full of contrition. "Let me see the damage."

"Really, I'm just being a wuss," she said, turning her finger around. "See? It's barely a scratch. Just stings like hell."

It was a mark of just how much she wasn't thinking that even when Roka's body locked, she still didn't realise the catastrophic enormity of what she had just done.

Before she could offer up more reassurance to the suddenly stricken-looking Meyarin, his hand flashed out to grip her wrist, holding her arm in place.

"Roka, what—" She trailed off when his eyes moved from her finger up to her face and she read the emotions there: Confusion. Fear. *Anger*.

Alex looked back at her hand and gasped loudly as belated understanding washed over her. She violently yanked her arm from his grip and curled her fingers tightly, hiding the miniscule drop of red—so very red—blood from view. But it was too late; the damage had been done.

"Roka," she whispered, feeling her face pale. "Roka, please. I can—I can explain."

His eyes were wild. "What manner of deceit is this?"

"Just—Just give me a second and hear me out," Alex begged.

Roka started backing away from her, but she followed quickly after him.

"This is wrong," he said, his voice low, horrified. "I—You—" He stopped retreating and inhaled a staggered breath. "You're a Meyarin—I've *fought* you as a Meyarin! You're bonded to a draekon and you can call forth the *Valispath*, and yet… your blood… How can this be?"

"Roka, please," Alex repeated urgently. "Just listen to what I—"

His face darkened as his gaze locked on her still tightly fisted hand, betrayal hitting his eyes. "You lied to me. You've been lying to all of us. You're—You're one of *them*, aren't you?"

"Roka—"

"Answer me!"

At his roar, Alex jumped in fright, her hand automatically opening again, allowing his gaze to narrow in on the small smear of red at the tip of her index finger.

The fury blazing in his eyes caused Alex to tremble outwardly as prickles of electricity fired along her nerve endings, so acute was her feeling of dread. She didn't know what to do; she didn't know how to respond in the face of his wrath, in the face of her deceit. She mouthed his name, unable to call up any sound to form a response, and something in him snapped, sending him stumbling away from her. She reached out a hand to stop him, but it was too late. He activated the *Valispath* and disappeared without once looking back.

Shaking fiercely, Alex reacted on instinct. She knew she was too upset to even think about being calm enough to tune into her Meyarin abilities and call up the *Valispath*, so she did the only thing she could. She bolted.

Running through the palace, hurtling past startled Meyarins going about their own business, Alex was blind to everything as she sprinted as fast as her legs could carry her.

Alex! What's happened?

Her steps faltered as Xiraxus screamed into her mind, his voice filled with concern as he registered her fear. Barely keeping from tripping over her own feet, she continued her mad dash along the hallways and spiral staircases, answering him as she flew through the palace.

Xira, I was so stupid! she cried. *I need to get out of here!*

Where are you?

Heart pounding and panting heavily from fear, she answered, *Nearly back at my room.*

I'm on my way.

That was all he said. He was coming for her, no questions, no hesitations.

Almost dizzy from her whirlwind of emotions, Alex tore along the corridors, cursing the enormity of the Meyarin palace and her limited human speed. Without being able to use the *Valispath*, it was a mission to get anywhere in a rush, but Alex still made it back to her room in record time, throwing the door open and slamming it behind her. She skidded to a halt and stood frozen in place, so terrified that she couldn't gather a clear thought as to what to do next.

A massive shadow blocked the glow of the city under the moonlight, followed quickly by a *thump* as Xiraxus landed precariously on the edge of her balcony, his massive body barely able to maintain a foothold. Seeing him there, with his black scales melting into the night and his anxious eyes shining bright in the darkness, Alex didn't hesitate. She darted straight for him, taking a running leap to scramble up the side of his body.

The moment she was secure with her arms gripping tightly at the base of his neck, she screamed, "Go, go, *go!*"

He didn't need any more encouragement to heave his body off the spiralling tower, freefalling until his wings caught a wind current and hoisted them back into the air.

Only when the radiant city was far below them did Alex start to calm somewhat, the trembles running through her frame easing as the distance between her and Roka increased.

Show me, Alex, Xiraxus said gently, soaring them ever upwards through the night's sky.

Somehow he must have known she was beyond words, so she did as he asked and sent him her memory with Roka, still in disbelief over her carelessness. For ten days she had managed to avoid sparring with him so she could keep him from accidentally spilling her blood—and just like that, it was all over. She couldn't believe that of all things to have given away her mortality, a miniscule paper cut was to blame.

I'm such a fool, Alex woefully said to Xiraxus. *I can't believe I did that.*

You'll be okay, he told her. *I promise, everything will be okay.*

She didn't believe him, but she allowed herself to become lost in the sensations of the flight as his powerful wings carried her safely through the sky. Higher and higher they rose until they broke through a cluster of clouds into the clear air above. Alex marvelled at the expanse of stars stretching out across the horizon and released a deep sigh of relief at seeing the floating islands of Draekora again, this time bathed in the light of the moon.

I didn't realise you were so close to Meya, Alex said, trying to keep her mind off Roka and what he was probably doing right now; who he was probably talking to.

We're almost directly above the city, Xiraxus confirmed. *But our lands are too high for even immortal eyes to see from the ground.*

Veering in an arc, the draekon headed straight towards one of the smaller islands positioned to the side. From far away, Alex could see that one half of the land was bordered with a semi-circled ring of snow-dusted mountains, at the base of which the remaining land stretched into what looked to be a multi-coloured glowing valley. When they touched down in the centre of the island, she was delighted to find herself surrounded by rolling pastures full of colourful, bioluminescent wildflowers.

"How beautiful," she exclaimed, sliding off Xiraxus and into the phosphorescent blossoms. Some of them came to her ankles, others rose on stems higher than her hips, but all of them were unimaginably magical.

"I thought you might like it here," Xiraxus said, curling his haunches underneath him and resting his torso on the valley floor, squashing flowers beneath his heavy weight. The kaleidoscopic radiance bounced off his dark hide, creating shards of light that sparkled like glitter.

Inhaling the sweet aroma of the flowers, Alex willed her body to relax as she cast her wandering gaze around the fairytale-like meadow and sat cross-legged in front of her rainbow-lit draekon.

"Everything that could have gone wrong today, went wrong," she admitted quietly, needing to get it all off her chest. "First, I think I inadvertently gave Aven the idea to start Claiming humans—and believe me, Xira, that's not something I want on my conscience—and then I went and gave away that I'm mortal to Roka who's on the edge of deciding whether or not he agrees with his brother's views regarding humans. This is *not* good. It's whatever comes after bad because 'bad' is nowhere near potent enough to describe the severity of the situation."

Xiraxus allowed her a moment to vent, not interrupting, but when she was done he said, "You can't change what happened, Alex. All you can do is decide how you'll react to it."

Alex plucked the nearest flower from the ground and began pulling off its glowing petals. "How am I supposed to react, Xira? What can I possibly do to fix any of this?"

He moved his head closer, his eyes holding hers. "What makes you think anything needs fixing?"

Alex made a spluttering noise. "Did you not see what happened with Roka? Or hear what I said about Aven?"

"Didn't Aes Daega tell you that nothing you do here will change what happens in the future?"

Alex opened her mouth but then snapped it shut again, knowing he was right. Then she said, "Let's not forget I'm still stuck here for who knows how long. What am I supposed to do? Hide in Draekora until we leave?"

"The night before last you told me you made a deliberate decision to remain here when you could have returned to your time," Xiraxus said. "You made that decision not knowing what you'd face in the time you have left here, but confident that this is where you needed to be. Am I right?"

Alex offered a reluctant hum of agreement.

"You can't change what happened with Roka and Aven today," Xiraxus repeated, "but you might want to consider the possibility that the events played out exactly as they were supposed to."

Shaking her head, Alex said, "It sounds like you're suggesting that what's happening here is predetermined, like all I'm doing is following a destiny already laid out for me, blindly walking a path without any say in the matter. But I can't accept that."

"Why ever not?"

"Because it implies I have no authority over my life."

The draekon rumbled with laughter.

Frowning, she asked, "How is that funny?"

"Alex," he said, "you're stuck in the past where your actions *affect* the future but don't *change* it. That means whatever you do here has *already* been done here—by *you*." He laughed again. "I'm sorry to be the one to tell you, but right now, right here, you *don't* have any power to choose what happens. Or rather, you *do*, but the power of choice you have will still lead to the future you know. Nothing you can do will change that, so you might as well embrace your lack of control and try to find some comfort in it."

His words, though frustrating, made sense. That, and his reasoning matched Lady Mystique's as well. But Alex hated the idea that she might be responsible for so much of the pain that Aven would bring upon the future. She'd already provided him with a name for his notoriously murderous group, and given him cause to think about the Claiming ritual; what else was she going to do? And how would he respond if Roka spilled the beans about her being mortal?

"This is such a nightmare," Alex groaned, collapsing back onto the flowers and looking up into the star-strewn sky. Goose bumps covered her flesh from the crisp air but she hardly felt the cold, mostly because her insides were still just as chilled after everything that had happened.

"Nightmare or not, you know what you have to do," Xiraxus said, nudging her foot lightly with his muzzle.

"I have to go back," Alex said in a bland tone. "I know that. I know I have to face Roka and explain. It's just..." She broke off into a heavy sigh before finishing, "Can we just stay here a few more minutes?"

In a gentle voice, Xiraxus replied, "We can stay as long as you need."

Twenty-Six

It could have been minutes or it could have been hours, but eventually Alex decided she was ready to face whatever might be waiting for her at the palace.

She was glad for the time she'd been able to spend with Xiraxus, grateful for his support and quiet counsel. But she knew she couldn't avoid Roka forever. And sure enough, as soon as the draekon landed on her balcony, Alex discovered she wouldn't have to wait long for the dreaded confrontation.

Will you be all right if I leave you? Xiraxus asked, the two of them noting the Meyarin prince sitting on her bed hunched over with his head in his hands, his posture speaking volumes.

She wanted to ask Xiraxus to stay—or to take her back up to the enchanting valley again—but she knew either of those options would only make things worse. *I'll be okay*, she told him, hoping it was true. *But, um, maybe stay close, just in case.*

I'm only a short flight away, he promised, nuzzling her with his big head before launching himself into the air.

Inhaling deeply, Alex hesitantly walked into her room, her eyes on her feet even when she felt Roka tracking her every movement. The radiance from the city streamed in, and that combined with the burning *myraes* in the hearth provided enough light for her to see, but only just. And yet, Roka didn't clap his hands to make the room brighter.

Coming to a stand just a few paces from him, Alex wrapped her arms around herself, swallowed thickly and found the courage to meet his eyes. She expected to find the same emotions from earlier there—confusion, fear, anger. But his face was guarded, making him impossible to read.

When Roka finally spoke, his quiet words felt like they were shouted, so tense was the atmosphere. "I wasn't sure if you were going to come back."

Just as quietly, Alex admitted, "I wasn't sure if I was going to, either."

It would have been much easier for her to wait out her remaining days in Draekora with Xiraxus, but that didn't mean it would have been right.

"Why did you?"

Three simple words from Roka, and Alex struggled to find an answer.

"A lot of reasons," she said. "Mostly because this is where I need to be."

The shadows highlighted the moment he tightened his jaw and also when he forced his muscles to relax.

"I'm sorry, Aeylia."

Alex's body jolted with his apology, so surprised as she was to hear the quiet words from his mouth. "*You're* sorry? What can you possibly have to be sorry for?"

His response was as instant as it was sure. "I shouldn't have taken off on you like that. I should have let you explain. I— You caught me off-guard, but that's no excuse for how I reacted. I could have handled that much better."

Shaking her head the whole time he spoke, Alex said, "Are you kidding? You'd just found out… what you'd just found out. Your reaction was beyond justified."

He looked at her carefully for a moment, seeming to come to a decision. He patted the spot beside him on her bed, gesturing for her to sit. "I'm ready to listen now," he said, "if you're still willing to explain."

It was one of those invitations that wasn't quite an invitation. But still, she was grateful for the illusion of choice, so she offered what little smile of thanks she could muster and took a seat at his side.

Not sure where to start but trusting that since the cat was already out of the bag, she might as well send the kittens on their way too, Alex decided to throw it all out there for him.

"So, here's the thing," she said, keeping her voice low enough that no other Meyarin ears would be able to hear. "I'm not just human, I'm also from the future." She swore she could actually *feel* Roka's body solidify beside her, so she hurried on before she could chicken out. "I was on my *varrungard* when a series of events led to me being accidentally pulled into the *abrassa* with Xiraxus—with the heir of Draekora. Since mortals can't survive the Void, he had to create the *vaeliana* bond with me to keep me alive, but we still became separated coming out this end—which is why, when I woke up here and none of you recognised me, I freaked out a bit." *And fell off the side of the building*, Alex decided not to mention. "Because of my... association with Meya in the future, when Lady Mys—uh, Aes Daega met me in Draekora to explain a few things, she said it would be best for me to spend my time down here in the city until Xira can return me to the future, which will happen as soon as he has the energy to open the *abrassa* again, sometime in the next couple of weeks. You already know the rest—Aes Daega brought me straight from Draekora to the palace where you all agreed to take me in and educate me in the ways of your people."

Alex thought she'd done well to summarise the main points so succinctly, but when she found the courage to look at Roka, she feared perhaps she'd given him too much, too quickly. Indeed, she wondered if he had stopped breathing, so still as he was.

288 · Lynette Noni

"Uh, Roka?" she called. "You still with me?"

"I'm here in the room," he answered, his voice strained. "But that's all I can say."

Okie doke, Alex thought, figuring she should maybe give him a moment.

Inhaling deeply through his nose, Roka eventually gathered his thoughts enough to speak. Unfortunately, what he asked was the one thing Alex was hesitant to answer.

"How can you be human, yet still be able to call up the *Valispath* and fight with the strength and agility of a Meyarin?" he asked. "Not to mention, why were you undertaking the *varrungard* if you're mortal? I assume in your future"—he sounded incredulous just saying that, and Alex could relate— "the trial is still used to decide who will become *Zeltora*? But how could a human ever be accepted into the elite guard?"

Deciding to answer the easiest part first, Alex said, "I wasn't on the *varrungard* to try out for the guard. It was more to test my... Meyarin-ness."

In a dubious tone, he repeated, "Your Meyarin-ness?"

Picking at a thread on the blanket beside her, Alex quietly asked, "Who did you tell, Roka? About what happened today, I mean."

There was a pause before he answered, "No one, Aeylia. After I cleared my head, I decided to wait to hear you out first."

Alex nodded, hoping that would be the case but hardly believing her luck. "If I answer your question, you have to promise, you have to *swear* that what I tell you will go no further than us."

She'd been staring at her fidgeting fingers, but when Roka reached out for her chin and turned her to face him, she didn't resist his gentle touch.

His eyes were steady on hers when he said, "I swear by the stars that I will keep whatever secrets you entrust to me."

Biting her lip, Alex took in his open, honest expression and uncurled her left hand, showing him her scar. "In the future, a... very bad Meyarin is doing... very bad things." *Jeez, I suck at this*, Alex thought, wincing at her lame offering but continuing anyway. "This Meyarin needed something from me but I wasn't willing to help, so he—or she—performed the *Menada dae Loransa* on me, Claiming my will as their own."

Roka's reaction was fierce as horror overtook his features. "But you're mortal!"

"I am," Alex confirmed.

"And blood-bonding rituals are supposed to be forbidden on pain of death," Roka continued. "Or... Does that change in the future?"

"No, the Claiming ritual is still very much forbidden," Alex said firmly. "But this Meyarin no longer lives by the laws of Meya. They are... an outcast, I suppose you could say. Accountable to no one and caring nothing for right and wrong." She let that sink in and said, "And it didn't matter that I was mortal. They started practising the ritual on others of my kind long before my time."

"Others?" Roka swallowed. "You don't mean...?"

"I'm not the only mortal this Meyarin has bonded with," Alex answered. "They were—*are*—actively seeking out gifted humans, people who your grandfather created Akarnae for, because with control over the mortals comes control over their gifts."

"But *why*?" Roka asked, aghast. "What could motivate anyone to do something so inherently evil?"

"From what I understand," Alex said, being very careful with her words, "they thought they were doing the right thing. At least to start with. Now I don't think they care. It's all in the name of vengeance now."

Roka's face was so pale even the shadows couldn't mask his horror. "If this Meyarin is so malicious, how did you get them to Release you from the bond? I know you wouldn't be here freely telling me all this if you were still Claimed."

"No, I'm not bonded anymore," Alex confirmed, answering his unspoken question. "But the Meyarin didn't willingly Release me. In fact, I didn't even know anyone *could* be Released from *Menada dae Loransa* until recently. But I'm hoping—I'm *hoping* now that I do, I'll be able to find a way to free some of the other bonded humans when I get back to my time."

"But if the one who Claimed you didn't Release you, then how—"

"I'm gifted," Alex interrupted. "I'm a student at Akarnae. I didn't know it when the ritual was performed on me, but it turns out I have a supernatural strength of will. My gift was triggered when I was under the influence of the Claiming, allowing my willpower to break the bond between us."

With a voice full of awe, Roka said, "I've never heard of such a thing."

"Trust me, you're not the only one," Alex said, somewhat dryly. "But in a roundabout way, what I'm trying to explain is that something in me changed when the bond was severed. Somehow I ended up absorbing Meyarin characteristics that, even though I'm no longer Claimed, I've still managed to retain."

Roka made a pensive sound. "I bet it's because you weren't willingly Released."

"Sorry?"

"From the bond," he clarified. "From the accounts I've read, whenever a Claimed Meyarin was willingly Released by their healer, the grip of the ritual left them instantly. But since it sounds like you destroyed your bond by sheer strength of will, the life force that was Claiming you left a trace residue behind. Almost like the difference between cutting a piece of cloth cleanly as opposed to ripping it and leaving frayed edges behind."

"Are you calling me a frayed edge, Roka?" Alex asked, a small smile on her face.

His return smile was brief but she definitely saw a flash of it. "Not you personally, Aeylia, but the effect of the Meyarin blood that was in your veins."

"Strangely enough, you and I have already had a similar conversation to this before, though neither of us made the connection to the 'willingly Released' part then. Still, it's good to understand that might be why the Meyarin abilities have stayed with me."

As she spoke, Roka seemed to slump beside her.

"What's wrong?" she asked, alarmed.

"Nothing," he said quickly. "I'm just relieved. That's the first time you've mentioned the future me. I was worried…"

"That you're dead?" Alex guessed.

He let out a startled chuckle. "No. I was worried I might have been the outcast Meyarin Claiming mortals."

It was Alex's turn to stiffen in shock. "Why would you say that?"

His shoulders rose and fell. "Very few people have access to the knowledge of how to perform *Menada dae Loransa* any more. I'm one of them. You can't blame me for being concerned."

Looking at him with undisguised disbelief, Alex demanded, "Do you really think I'd be sitting here with you if your future self had done all that to me?"

If anything, Roka's relief only grew. "I'm guessing since you're so friendly with the others, none of them are to blame, either," he deduced—incorrectly.

"How about you stop trying to guess who it might be," Alex said, her tone stating that it wasn't just a suggestion.

"You're right, I'm sorry," he hastily apologised. "Let's go back to your Meyarin abilities. Is it because of them that Aes

Daega wanted you to stay in Meya? So we could teach you how to utilise them?"

Alex nodded, relieved that he was able to come to the conclusion on his own. "The changes in me are relatively new," she told him. "In my time, you were only just about to start training me; teaching me to be a Meyarin, I guess you could say."

"It's not natural for you, I take it?"

"I have to concentrate really hard," Alex admitted.

"That first day you were here and we sparred," Roka mused, his eyes unfocused. "You needed a moment before we could fight."

"I needed a moment otherwise you probably would have killed me," Alex returned pointedly. "Every time I call up the *Valispath* or do some stupid stunt like jump off a waterfall, I have to first centre myself to trigger the blood in my veins. I have to stop and listen and breathe until it sort of... kicks over from human to Meyarin." She shook her head at herself. "It sounds weird, I know it does. But I don't know how else to explain it."

"Should I ask *why* you need to have the strength and skills of an immortal? Why you need to move and fight like one of our race?"

Trying for a casual tone when she felt anything but, Alex quirked up her lips and joked, "Someone's gotta keep you crazy Meyarins in line."

It was clear the prince saw straight through her act, but he didn't press her, likely guessing it involved the malicious Meyarin of the future.

"Well I guess there's only one thing we can do, then," he said instead.

Alex raised her eyebrows in question.

"We have to follow through with what Aes Daega asked," Roka said, "and teach you how to be a Meyarin."

Not entirely sure if that was a good idea anymore, Alex started to argue, "Roka—"

"Am I correct in assuming that during our first sparring session you panicked, fearing I might draw your blood?"

She nodded slowly.

"And that's why you've been avoiding fighting me ever since?"

"Can you blame me?"

He chuckled lightly and she felt a weight lift off her chest at the hearty, genuine sound. He wasn't forcing it for her benefit. He was just... Roka.

"No, Aeylia, I can't blame you, given how I reacted earlier today."

"About that..."

Rushing to assure her, he said, "I won't tell anyone, I gave you my word."

"It's not that," Alex said, though she was definitely relieved. "It's just... Are you, um, okay? I mean, I *have* been lying to you for the past ten days. And my secret is not something small. I'm mortal, Roka. I'm *human*. That's like... That's like buying a pet dog and going home to find it's really a cat dressed up as a puppy. No one wants to own a cat disguised as a puppy. Most people don't even want to own a cat that looks like a cat!"

Thankfully, Roka chose to ignore her strange analogy and focused on what was more important.

"I don't know what you are, Aeylia," he said, lifting her hand and looking at her scar, then flicking his gaze along her forearm showing the glow of her bond with Xiraxus. "But human, Meyarin, Draekoran, or otherwise, I don't care. Aes Daega wouldn't have asked us to help you without reason, and now that I know the truth, you don't have to hide anymore— not from me. I'll train you here, just as I would have done in the future." He pursed his lips thoughtfully and amended his tenses, "Just as I'm sure I *will* do in the future."

Her eyes swimming, Alex had to blink to keep her grateful tears at bay. "Roka, what you're offering—You don't know—"

"Is it important?" he interrupted. "Your learning how to control your Meyarin abilities?"

"Very," Alex replied quietly.

"Then that's all that matters. There's nothing else I need to know."

With calm determination, he stood to his feet, holding out a hand to Alex.

She looked at it in question.

"Well, come on then," he said, gesturing for her to take it. "You said you'll be returning to the future as soon as your draekon can manage. We don't have any time to waste."

Alex's eyes were wide when she guessed, "You want to start my training *now*? It's after midnight!"

"Are you tired?" Roka instantly returned.

"Well—no," Alex admitted. In fact, she was wired with adrenaline after the events of her evening.

Roka grinned. "Then what are you waiting for? Let's go see if we can turn a mortal into a Meyarin. Are you with me?"

Looking from his open fingers to his bright eyes and, reading the challenge in them, Alex inhaled deeply and said, "Yeah, Roka. I'm with you."

Twenty-Seven

If Alex thought hours of sparring with Roka *every... single... day...* would transform her into a Meyarin fighting machine, she would have been wrong. Very, very wrong. The truth was, as much as she appreciated his instruction, and as much as she was learning from him, she didn't actually feel she was getting anywhere. And as hard as it was to admit it, that was *because* of Roka.

To put it simply, he was babying her. She felt as if every time they fought it was like he walked on eggshells around her, excruciatingly aware of her mortality. Every move he made, every attack, every single motion was carefully controlled so as to not cause even the smallest bruise. Alex wasn't sure if it was because this Roka was much younger or because he'd spent so little time around mortals and didn't want to accidentally harm her, but either way, the next seven days of 'training' benefitted her much less than she would have liked.

A big part of the problem was that he was of the opinion she needed time to 'warm up' and become familiar with her Meyarin abilities before he was willing to outright assault her. She, however, argued that there wouldn't *be* any warming up in a life-and-death situation, and that was what she needed to be preparing herself for. She even mentioned that in the future he had fought her blindfolded—and fully armed—the first time they'd met just to prove that she was able to fight like a Meyarin.

Needless to say, Roka was horrified to hear he'd attacked a 'helpless mortal' in such a way.

Alex didn't speak to him for a day after that remark, though she did feel better after throwing a wooden practice sword at his head. It didn't matter that he reflexively ducked in time; her action was still cathartic.

Aside from her growing frustration at her lack of progress, Alex's week wasn't a complete write-off. Thanks to all the hours she spent sparring with Roka—regardless of how basic those attempts at fighting were—she was using her Meyarin abilities more frequently than ever before, which meant they were coming more naturally to her now. It still took time to 'enter the zone', as she called it, but she was noticeably faster each time she tried.

Despite that, after a whole week of training, Alex was neither comfortable nor confident with her ability to access Aven's blood in her veins, and that royally sucked.

So, to get her mind off her snail-like improvement, Alex spent her downtime with Kyia, Aven and Niyx. Roka, too, when he was free, though with the *Garseth* becoming increasingly prominent on the city streets, the prince was busier than ever trying to play peacemaker with the Rebels and preventing Astophe from recognising Aven's involvement.

Alex didn't know why Roka bothered, since she was certain the king *had* to be aware that his youngest son was at least in cahoots with, if not the leader of, the anti-mortals. But she admired Roka's dedication to keeping his family intact and figured it best to let him remain committed for as long as possible before all hell broke loose on House Dalmarta.

The good news was that disaster wouldn't be unfolding any time soon. The day Roka and Kyia had disappeared turned out to be because they'd visited the ruling human monarchies of Medora—there were four of them in the current time—to ask that they hold off from visiting Meya until the political climate had calmed. The trade agreement was still in place, but until the anti-mortal propaganda quietened, all exchanges of wares would happen outside of the city on human soil.

Since D.C.'s recount of history claimed that Aven's massacre happened in front of the Meyarin palace the next time a trading group of humans visited, Alex was thankful to know she, at least, wouldn't have to witness it happening in the short time she had left in the past.

As for Aven himself, he'd been a constant in Alex's life over the past week. After her daily breakfasts with the queen—a rendezvous Niida seemed to especially treasure—no matter where Alex was or what she was doing, Aven always sought her out for lunch. Most days someone else joined them; Niyx, Kyia or Roka if he could swing it. Sometimes all three managed to come along, and those were the lunches Alex loved the most. She was still homesick for those she'd left in the future, but there were moments when she would laugh so hard at her Meyarin friends' antics that she nearly cried—particularly when Niyx's attempts to be debonair were crushed by Aven's relentless wit. Then there was the equally hilarious development between Roka and Kyia that had only become more noticeable since their day trip around Medora. Now as awkward as a pair of opposing magnets, Alex was certain something must have happened between them. Not that they'd ever tell her. Though, Roka *did* look at Alex appraisingly the first time she badgered him for details, and she hastily retreated after realising that, since he now knew she was from the future, he'd likely put the pieces together.

Other than that particular 'oops' moment, the rest of her week outside of training was reasonably uneventful, apart from Niyx's mysterious disappearance three days ago. When Alex questioned his whereabouts, disguising her concern as mere curiosity, Aven reassured her that he was out hunting in the forest and would be back soon. It was something Niyx often did, apparently, disappearing only to return later with his spoils, just like a cat leaving a mouse on the doorstep of its master.

Alex chuckled at the thought of Niyx slinking back home with a rodent between his teeth. Somehow she doubted that was the kind of hunting he was doing, even if the mental picture was entertaining.

Apart from sparring with Roka, breakfasting with Niida, hanging out with Aven, Niyx and Kyia, and continuing to dine with the whole royal family and whatever council members might be in attendance, the rest of Alex's time was spent helping organise the upcoming, end-of-summer festival. She blamed Kyia for roping her into it, since the Meyarin had claimed Alex was no longer paying attention to her theory lessons, so she might as well do something useful with her time. When Aven, who was in charge of organising the festival, overheard this, he jumped on the idea of Alex's assistance—dragging Kyia along too, much to her disgruntlement.

Aven made it sound as though the whole city would be taking part in the celebration, filling the palace to capacity until the Meyarins spilled into one massive street party. Given the scale of the event, Alex had been apprehensive to help at first, but it turned out that with Astophe and Niida's—mostly Niida's—last-minute decision to finish the banquet with a masquerade ball, Aven needed all the help he could get when it came to the only part of the night's planning he considered to be outside of his expertise: fashion. The rest was covered, from the food to the music and everything in between. But when it came to the clothes that the royal family would be gifting to each and every one of their citizens to wear for the celebration, he was at a loss and happy to delegate that mammoth task to Alex and Kyia's governance.

With neither of them having any idea where to start, they were both relieved when the queen took up the cause alongside them, launching herself into fashionista mother hen mode. Between the three of them—and a host of other helpers, including the king himself at times—within seven days they worked wonders, having the production of thousands of decadently formal outfits and masks well on their way to completion. Feathers and frills, silks and sparkles—their innovative creations stretched the boundaries of fashion, resulting in unparalleled miracles of design.

Aven, in Alex's mind, owed them big time, even if she came to enjoy their haphazard planning sessions surrounded by scrawled drawings and fabric samples. It was the most girlishly carefree she'd felt in a long time, and she revelled in the feeling. With only eight days to go, she knew they were well on their way to experiencing the best dressed festival in the history of Meya, and Alex couldn't wait to be a part of it.

Presuming, of course, that she was still in the past when that time came. Xiraxus had yet to give her a solid idea of when he'd be ready to return her to the future, but every day he assured her he was getting stronger, which meant they were drawing nearer to the time when she'd have to leave her new friends behind—half of whom, in the future, wanted her dead.

But that, she knew, was a problem for another day. As for now, she would live in the moment, enjoying her time in the past while it lasted.

"I have something to tell you," Roka said, ducking his head to avoid the blur of Alex's wooden sword slashing through the air, "and you're not going to like it."

"There are a lot of things I seem to not like," Alex said, targeting his torso this time, "especially when they come with a warning like that."

She parried to the right, to the left and then left again, with Roka effortlessly meeting her attempts with his own dummy sword. It was beyond frustrating considering she was currently keyed into her Meyarin power and *still* she wasn't offering up any kind of worthwhile assault against him.

"Come on, Roka! Attack me!" she cried for what felt like the thousandth time that week.

Everything they were currently doing—or *not* doing—was messing with her psychologically, from the knowledge that Roka would never hurt her to the craptastic wooden swords that wouldn't slice butter. She only hoped the Roka of the future would give her a better run for her money, especially if his past self continued to suck so badly as a teacher.

"Just hold on for a second," he said, relaxing his stance and dropping his sword arm.

"You know, I *can* multi-task," she huffed out. "I'm able to carry on a conversation while we fight—if that's what you want to call what we're doing."

Inside the domed Myrox barrier, no one else could watch or hear them, which was both a blessing and a curse. A blessing because it kept Alex's mortality a secret, but a curse because it kept Roka treating her like she was made of glass. Alex wondered, not for the first time, whether he'd finally take the kid gloves off if she surprised him with a public attack. But since she couldn't risk getting a scratch and exposing her humanity, her hands were tied. At least until she became *really* desperate.

"Maybe I'm the one who can't multi-task," Roka said. "Or maybe I just want your full attention."

"Then say what you have to say so we can get on with it," Alex said, crossing her arms. If she'd held a real blade in her hands, she would have sliced open her stomach with the move, but the wooden toy barely snagged on her outfit, so blunt as it was.

"I'm going to be away from the palace for the next few days," Roka said. "A fresh round of recruits just finished their *varrungard* and have been accepted into the *Zeltora*, and it's up to me to make sure they all start their training on the right foot."

Disappointment washed over Alex. Even if her time with Roka wasn't progressing at a speed she would like, anything was better than nothing.

"Are you sure you're the best person for that job?" she asked, raising a sceptical brow. "Or do you like your elite guards using wooden swords to protect your kingdom?"

Thankfully, he grinned and accepted the dig with grace. "Don't worry, Aeylia. Unlike you, I'm confident they won't trip over their own feet and impale themselves if I let them use proper weapons in their training. It's real steel for them."

"You," Alex said, narrowing her eyes, "are not very nice."

He laughed out loud, and she glared all the more for it.

"Why are you the one who has to start their training, anyway?" she grumbled. "Teaching the newbies doesn't seem like something a prince should have to do."

"Normally the head of the guard would take on that responsibility, but since our previous leader stepped down and we haven't found anyone to take her place yet, the duty falls to me," Roka explained. "I only need to get them settled and then others in the guard will take over their training from there on out. I'll be gone a few days at most, but I wanted you to know so you don't think I've abandoned our mission here."

"Mission aside, you know who would make a great new leader of the *Zeltora*?" Alex said casually.

Roka's tone was wry when he replied, "Let me guess, Zain Erraeya?"

Smiling widely, Alex said, "It's like you read my mind!"

The prince looked like he wasn't sure whether he was more amused or exasperated. "Or maybe it's because you've been saying it for over two weeks now."

"Have I? My, how time flies."

"Aeylia—"

"Roka, has it occurred to you that perhaps since, oh, I don't know, *I'm from the future*," Alex said with glaring emphasis, "that maybe I know what I'm talking about?"

"Of course it's occurred to me," Roka returned instantly. "But short of conscripting him unwillingly into service, there's nothing I can do. He has to *want* to become *Zeltora*. No one can make him. And believe me, Aeylia, with his history, the chance of him ever making that decision seems impossible to me, regardless of what you imply the future holds. He wasn't always a criminal, you know. As much as I disagree with what he does, I can't blame him for travelling down that path, not after everything that happened to him."

Alex didn't like the sound of that at all. "What are you talking about? What happened to him?"

Roka shook his head. "That's not my story to share, nor do I even know the full extent of it. Just trust me when I say I'm doing everything to follow through on my end of the deal to convince him to join the ranks of the guard, but at the end of the day, I can only do so much. The rest is up to him."

While frustrated, Alex nodded reluctantly. "Okay, fine. I'll leave that one with you," she said. "And since you're deserting me, what are my chances of convincing you to fight me properly now, enough that I at least get a bruise to show we actually *fought*? Consider it a gift to apologise for your upcoming negligence. What do you say?"

"Only *you* would consider the idea of me injuring you a gift."

"Punched with love," Alex said solemnly, but she was unable to keep a straight face when Roka rolled his eyes.

"Here's a compromise," he said. "If you can disarm me in the next ten minutes, I'll give you one match with a real sword before we call it quits for the night."

"That's not a compromise," Alex argued. "You know there's no way I'll be able to disarm you."

"Take it or leave it, Aeylia."

"This is a sucky deal," she grumbled in acceptance.

She tried her best to disarm him, but with his strength and agility so completely natural to him, all he had to do was duck and dodge and swivel away from her, keeping her at arm's length the whole time. She didn't come close to separating him from his sword, let alone landing a single hit on him.

With an apologetic shrug at the end of the ten minutes, he promised to dedicate more time to their sparring once he returned. He then squeezed her shoulder, knowing how unsatisfied she was, and escorted her to her room.

Disappointed and edgy with unused adrenaline, Alex knew she wouldn't be able to sleep anytime soon. She needed to go out and clear her head, get some fresh air. Ideally, she would love to go flying with Xiraxus, but when she called to him, he warned her that a storm was coming and unless she wanted to risk ending up on the back of a roasted chicken, she would have to wait until it passed.

Sighing, Alex stepped out onto her balcony and looked off into the night. True enough, far on the horizon beyond the Golden Cliffs and distant forests she saw the tell-tale flash of lightning high up in the sky. But it was still a long way from reaching them.

Coming to a quick decision, Alex grabbed a cloak and stepped out of her room. Still attuned to her Meyarin senses from her time with Roka, she called up the *Valispath*, directing it until she came to a rest atop the cliffs overlooking the city.

Taking a seat on the edge of the rocky precipice, Alex pushed back her hood to feel the night breeze in her hair and brazenly dangled her legs over the side, confident for once in her ability to call up the Eternal Path again should the ledge crumble beneath her.

Looking down, she chuckled at the memory of her first experience using the *Valispath*, when the future Kyia deviously made Alex, Jordan, Bear and D.C. jump off the cliffs and onto the invisible Path. Alex now knew that the stunt hadn't been necessary at all, since Kyia could have easily activated the *Valispath* from atop the cliffs—or even back at Raelia—and saved them all from shaving ten years off their lives from shock alone.

Feeling nostalgic, Alex wondered what her friends would be doing right now if they weren't frozen in time; if Bear and D.C. would be busy concocting plans between classes to rescue both Jordan and herself. She knew they wouldn't give up on either of them, that her friends would travel to the end of the world if it meant the four of them could be together again.

A sick taste entered Alex's mouth as she thought about Jordan and the horrors he'd endured being bonded to Aven for a number of weeks before the showdown in Raelia. More than ever before, she was determined to save him from being Claimed. She just had to figure out how to convince Aven to willingly Release him.

With her thoughts drifting over her parents, her teachers—and lingering perhaps a little too long on Kaiden—Alex sat for what might have been hours, watching the moonlight bounce off the Myrox. Even when the storm clouds started rolling over, the brilliance of the city didn't dim, so radiant was the silvery metal on its own.

When Alex felt a water droplet tickle and roll down her forehead, she knew it was time to head back to the palace, unwilling to linger further and risk having to use the *Valispath* in the impending electrical storm.

Carefully wiggling away from the edge, Alex made sure she was stable enough before she pushed up to her feet. As she did so, the rain started sprinkling, not quite heavy yet, but enough to be a nuisance. Since she'd been sitting there for so long, she had to take a few moments to clear her mind and tune into her Meyarin senses again, and when she did, she was just about to activate the *Valispath* when a noise caused her to pause.

It sounded like a moan, coming from the forest.

Frowning, Alex channelled her inner B-grade-horror-movie skills and called out, "Hello? Is someone out there?"

When no answer came, she figured her imagination had been playing a trick on her, but then she heard it again, followed by what sounded like something crashing through the bushes.

Not sure whether to take off or investigate, she didn't have time to make a decision before a dark figure stumbled out of the dense trees, collapsing in a heap barely ten feet from where she stood.

That was the moment the heavens decided to open, the rain falling down in earnest now as a crackle of thunder rumbled overhead and the storm blew in at an alarming speed. But Alex didn't move, *couldn't* move, because a flash of lightning highlighted with startling clarity exactly who the figure was.

It was Niyx.

And he was covered in blood.

Twenty-Eight

"Niyx!" Alex cried, rushing over to him and sinking to her knees at his side. "Niyx! *Niyx!* Look at me!"

When she rolled him over to face her, she let out a loud gasp as he moaned in agony.

Four long slashes, like claw marks, ripped through his clothes and tore into his flesh. The lines travelled across from his right hip all the way up to his left shoulder, diagonally dissecting his chest. But as gruesome as the injury was, that wasn't what had caused Alex to gasp, nor was it the amount of silver blood spilling out.

No, what caused her to gasp was the murky brown liquid the rain was quickly washing off his body. Because she knew exactly what it was. Heedless of the risk to her own health, she reached out in order to put pressure on the wound and draw him close enough for the *Valispath*, but with a shout of pain, Niyx jerked violently away before she could touch him.

"Don't," he panted out. "Can't... touch... me."

"Niyx, I need to get you out of here," Alex said, talking to him as she would a wounded animal, low and calm. "You need to let me help you."

"Don't... touch," he struggled to tell her. "Sarnaph... blood."

Alex felt a shudder go through her at his confirmation of what the murky goo washing from his wound was. Thanks to

Aven's blood in her veins, if her skin made contact with it, she would be almost as debilitated as Niyx.

"It—It's not as bad as it seems," she lied, reaching for his face instead and running a soothing hand across his cheek and through his dark hair. Even in the rain she could tell he was sweating feverishly, something she had never seen a Meyarin do before. He needed help, and he needed it immediately.

"I'll be right back," she said as an idea came to her, and she tore off into the forest. She was back by his side in a blur of movement thanks to her Meyarin speed, carrying a whole armful of *laendra* with her. Knowing he was beyond able to chew the flower, she summoned A'enara and sliced open a bulb, the sticky liquid within dribbling down her fingers and merging with the ever-increasing rain.

Moving it to trickle onto his wounds, she continued cutting bulbs until the *laendra* coated his chest like honey. She then sliced her final flower and carefully took Niyx's head in her hands, gently lifting his face and urging him to swallow the healing liquid. Hacking and spluttering, he could barely manage a whole mouthful.

"You're going to be fine," Alex told him, steeling her voice to mask how much she was shaking inside.

"Won't... work..." Niyx panted. "Just... helps... pain."

"Don't be ridiculous," she told him, stemming her rising panic at his words. "*Laendra* can heal anything."

"Not... Sarnaph... blood," Niyx said. "Nothing... can... fix."

"Not true," Alex said, trying to come off as confident when she felt nothing of the sort. "I have a friend who was poisoned and he's perfectly fine now."

But Zain *had* nearly died, or so he'd told Alex. It was only because of Fletcher that the Meyarin had managed to survive the arrow to his shoulder. The problem was, Alex had no idea how Fletcher had saved him.

"Look," Alex said, hands shaking, "the Sarnaph blood's all washed away now. I'm going to get you back to the palace—someone there will know how to help you."

She reached under him to pull him up enough to wrap an arm around his shoulders, drawing him close and forcing herself to ignore his agonising moans.

"Can't... save... me," he puffed. "Going... to... die."

Despite her concern, Alex was certain that wasn't true. Niyx remained alive in the future, so she knew—she *knew*—he would survive this.

"You are *not* going to die!" she told him adamantly, giving him a small shake to bring her point home. And yet, it was then with shocking clarity that a memory came to her; the sound of Aven's voice after he first saw her Claiming scar and heard her lie about its cause.

'I've never heard of anyone surviving Sarnaph blood poisoning...'

That wasn't all he'd said. It was his next words that had Alex trembling hard enough that Niyx groaned and tried to pull away from her jostling his injured body.

'I've never heard of anyone surviving Sarnaph blood poisoning,' Aven had said, only to finish, *'without* Menada dae Loransa *being performed on them.'*

Looking down at her rapidly fading friend, Alex was panting almost as hard as he was as she waged a mental war with herself. Was it possible that Niyx truly wouldn't survive the poison... unless she helped him? Unless she shared her life force with him? Unless she *Claimed* him?

It was an abhorrent thought and she couldn't believe she was even considering the idea, especially given that she had firsthand experience with the effects of the bonding. And yet, she also knew he was right. If she *didn't* try to Claim him and share her energy with him... he was going to die.

Maybe if she got him back to the palace, someone else would be willing to do the ritual. Maybe she could convince them to break the law, and maybe they'd be willing to risk execution in order to save his life. But Alex knew it was a long shot. And looking at how quickly Niyx was fading in her arms, she doubted he would last until she found someone to help. His life was literally in her hands.

It was then that another memory hit her, one of him speaking to her from the darkness of his future prison cell.

'A life for a life... I'm now absolved of my debt.'

"I can't believe this," Alex said, looking down at him through rain-blurred, impossibly wide eyes. "I can't believe I'm even *thinking* this."

But despite her disbelief, there was no way she was going to let her friend die, even knowing the murderer he would become. That wasn't who he was, not yet. And if she didn't do everything she could to save him now, then that would make her just as evil as his future self.

When Niyx released a gurgling, ragged breath that sounded disturbingly bloody to her ears, Alex knew it was now or never.

"Please don't hate me for this," she whispered to him as she reached for A'enara. "Or do hate me, if you must, just as long as you stay alive."

Before she could talk herself out of it, Alex sliced the ice-like dagger in a line above the scar already on her palm. She hissed at the pain it caused and steadfastly ignored Niyx's horror-stricken face as he took in her glaringly obvious mortal blood mixing with the rain and flowing to the earth.

"Aeylia... What... *What...*"

"Shh," Alex told him. "Save your strength." Mentally, she added, *We're both going to need it.*

Having only a vague idea of what to do and no guarantee other than her knowledge of Niyx being alive in her future,

Alex reached out her noticeably quaking hand and placed her bloodied palm against the torn flesh over his heart.

"*What…*" he tried to say, but then his eyes rolled to the back of his head and he released one final, gurgling exhale.

"Niyx?" Alex whispered, pressing down hard on his skin, their blood mixing together, dark and light. He didn't respond, nor did he inhale; his chest remained still under her fingers. "No! *Niyx!*"

Knowing she was out of time, Alex didn't think, she just acted. Screaming the Claiming words in her mind, she focused them outwardly in the same way she would call to Xiraxus.

Trae Menada sae, Niyx!

With rain soaking their bodies and lightning streaking overhead, Alex leaned in above his deathly still form. For a fraction of a second she feared it hadn't worked; that perhaps she had to be Meyarin to pull off the ritual. But then her mind suddenly blanked, with her subconsciousness floating out of her like some kind of out-of-body experience, and she was pulled into what she instinctively knew was Niyx's mind. Surrounded by the darkness of his swiftly fading thoughts as he moved closer and closer to death, she repeated her words with more urgency than she'd ever thought possible.

"*Trae Menada sae,* Niyx!" she yelled, impressing her will upon his. "I Claim you!"

In an instant she was yanked from the darkness and back into her own mind as a burning sensation ripped across her torso. The feeling was so intense that she cried out in pain and hunched over his body, unable to hold her weight against the agony shooting through her nerve endings.

A scream tore from her throat as inch by inch, she *felt* her flesh being slashed open, from her right hip to her left shoulder. Her free hand moved to press against her stomach, but all she felt were her rain-soaked clothes. She reached under the material, certain she would discover the gaping edges of shredded flesh, but there was nothing there—no wound at all, just phantom pain. Meanwhile, Niyx's real claw marks began to pulsate with a soft, shimmering glow—a glow that was mirrored on Alex's unmarred skin in four distinct diagonal slashes.

Heaving ragged breaths as strength drained from her body at an alarming rate, the pain Alex felt was excruciating enough to make her wonder what would happen to her future if she died in the past. Unlike with Niyx, she had no guarantee that she would survive to see another day in her real time. For all she knew, she was never going to make it back home. And if that happened, she wasn't the only one whose life would be forfeit.

Alex! came Xiraxus's cry, his voice more panicked than ever. *Alex, what did you do?*

Xira, she called, and even her mental voice sounded weak against the absolute agony rippling through her. *Xira, I'm so sorry!*

She somehow summoned the strength to send him the memory of her actions. In return, he bellowed out a deep, anxious roar.

But that was all she was able to hear from him because a burning like nothing she'd ever felt before scorched across the flesh of her torso, ripping another scream through her vocal chords. The glow of the claw marks intensified to a nearly blinding flash, blending with the lightning now beginning to streak around them.

The last thing Alex saw before she succumbed to unconsciousness was the glow disappearing as Niyx's wounds began to seal. His body convulsed beneath hers, his chest rose with a great, shuddering gasp, and then Alex knew no more.

Alex! Wake up! Wake up—wake up—WAKE UP!

Bolting upright, Alex's heart thudded in her chest as she came to her senses. *Xira! What happened? How did I—Is Niyx—Where—What—*

Her head was throbbing and she struggled to string a complete thought together. All she could tell was that she was back in her room at the palace. The storm was raging over the city, much fiercer now than when she'd been up on the Golden Cliffs, and her clothes were still sopping, soaking through to her bed.

What were you thinking, *Alex? Are you crazy?* Xira demanded.

That's still up for debate, she returned, casting her eyes around the room until they came to rest on the motionless body slumped against the wall beside her unlit fireplace, knees raised, head pillowed between crossed arms.

Alex's pulse stuttered as she quickly told Xiraxus, *Listen, I can't talk right now. I'll check in again later.*

You better, the draekon threatened, *because storm or not, I'll fly down there and make you talk if you don't.* And with that warning, his presence left her mind.

Alex slid off the bed, rising on wobbly legs, and moved towards the figure huddled near the fireplace.

"Don't come any closer."

The words came out as harshly as the crack of a whip in the silence of the room.

"Niyx," Alex pleaded, halting mid-step.

His head came up and he stared straight at her, his eyes like blazing purple fire. Alex had never seen him look so ravaged, like he had no idea what to think, what to feel, what to say or do. Gone was the confident, cocky Niyx she'd come to be so fond of. In his place was someone clearly waging an inner battle.

"You saved my life," he said, his voice brittle. "That's the only reason—" He broke off, swallowed and tried again. "It's the only reason I brought you back here and haven't told anyone what you did. What you *are*."

Alex fisted her hand around her new scar, knowing that her flesh was as healed as it had previously been, but also aware that Niyx hadn't failed to see the red of her blood, even as close to death as he had been.

"Niyx—" she whispered, but he cut her off.

"There's nothing you can say that would make any of this okay."

Alex agreed with him. But she also didn't. She chose to ignore her mortality for the moment and simply said, "I couldn't let you die."

"So you *Claimed* me?" he demanded, rising to his feet, his clawed shirt hanging in tatters. "Are you *insane*? Now we're both going to die! They'll execute us for what you've done—you do realise that, don't you?"

Alex shook her head. "No one has to find out. I'll free you from the bond and no one but us will ever know it happened."

Niyx released a bitter laugh. "If you believe that, you're only lying to yourself. We both know you won't free me, not as long as I know your little mortal secret."

As if being stabbed by a dagger, Alex felt the full force of his words like the blow they were. Because he was *right*. She'd been so consumed by saving his life that she hadn't thought beyond that, hadn't worried about the repercussions of her actions. It was one thing for Roka to know the truth about her; Roka who she had faith in and knew would never do anything to harm her. But Niyx was a wildcard. Not only that, he was Aven's *best friend*. And if the leader of the *Garseth* discovered the truth about Alex… She couldn't bear to think about what might happen.

"I'll Release you," Alex promised, her voice shaking. "Of course I will, Niyx. It's just…"

"Just what, Aeylia?" he asked, a sneer on his beautiful face. "Just that you can't right now? That it's not a good time? Well guess what, sweetheart. That excuse is going to get real old, real fast."

"Niyx…"

"But it won't matter, will it?" he went on, prowling her way. "Because you can make it so I don't care. You can make it so I forget why I'd *want* to care. Stars, you can make me do whatever you want!" He threw his hands up, his fury palpable as he continued stalking towards her.

Sensing it was time to retreat, Alex backed away in the direction of her balcony. "Niyx, please," she said, her tone uneasy. "You know me. You know I won't do anything like that to you."

He paused mid-step. "I *know* you?" he repeated in a low voice. "Do you really think that's your best argument right now?"

A flicker of anger sparked in Alex, but she knew she had to stay calm and reasonable. "Despite the fact that I saved your life, I know you have every right to be mad about what I did."

"Why in the name of the light would I be mad, Aeylia?" he asked, his tone simmering. "Maybe because you *stole my will from me?*"

Alex flinched as he bellowed the words, thankful that the rain was coming down in heavy sheets loud enough to protect them from any eavesdropping, immortal ears.

"You're angry," Alex said. "I get that. Believe me, I do." And she did, having experienced the disturbing puppet-like effect of the bond herself.

"I'm not angry!" Niyx shouted. "I'm furious!"

"Let's just—Let's just take a moment and breathe," Alex suggested in the face of his wrath as she reached the edge of her room. If she retreated any further, she would have to step out onto the balcony into the rain. But Niyx didn't stop his advance, so she raised her hands in front of her, trying to ward him off. "You're in shock. Of course you are. But please—let's just talk about this."

"*Do you have any idea what you've done?*" he roared in her face.

That was when Alex's spark of anger flared, prompting her to yell right back at him. "Stop it, Niyx! Take a breath and calm down!"

She felt it the moment it happened. It was like there was a tugging sensation, an invisible piece of string moving from her scarred palm and attaching to Niyx's chest where she'd created the bond. The effect was instantaneous: he stopped, took a breath and calmed down.

Horrified by what she'd done, even if the result was to her benefit, Alex's hands flew up to her mouth. With wide eyes, she whispered out, "I'm so sorry—I didn't mean—" She bit down on her cheek, stopping her words before she could accidentally say something else she didn't mean.

Raising her fingers to pull at her wet, straggly hair, Alex admitted in a helpless tone, "Niyx, I don't know what to do here."

He just looked at her, his gaze furious but his body perfectly relaxed thanks to her command.

Hating what she'd inadvertently done, Alex softly said, "Please be—um, please be you again." She felt the tugging of her command between them and finished, "Do what you want, say what you want. For the moment, just act like you would if there was no bond between us."

Niyx's eyes flashed with her order and his body immediately tensed with pent up rage. Then, without any warning, he drew his sword from the sheath still strapped to his back from his hunting trip and charged at Alex.

Twenty-Nine

Alex only just managed to leap out of the path of his attack, scrambling backwards onto the balcony and into the rain.

"Niyx, what are you—" She had to cut off her cried exclamation when he came at her again, forcing her to duck out of the way and continue retreating from him.

When the low railing met the backs of her legs, she knew she couldn't afford a repeat tumble off the spiral tower, not with Xiraxus grounded in Draekora because of the storm. So when Niyx swung his sword at her again, she did the only thing she could—she summoned A'enara and met his weapon mid-air. Blade crashed against blade, with blue fire blazing along Alex's arm, swirling around them both with her movements.

"Please don't do this, Niyx," she called to him over a loud crack of thunder, using her free hand to wipe rain-soaked hair from her eyes.

"Is that an *order*, Aeylia?" he demanded, swinging at her again.

"I won't make you stop," she promised him. "But I'm asking you to."

"Then you're going to have to ask nicer," he returned, and with a cry, he lunged towards her again.

She had a fraction of a second to centre herself, but she used that fraction wisely, forcing in a calming breath and just—only *just*—managed to flick the internal switch on her Meyarin senses in time to meet his attack.

It was then that their fight began in earnest.

Niyx was relentless in his assault. Fuelled by uncontrolled rage, he stabbed, slashed, parried and charged at Alex over and over again as she slipped and slid across the slick balcony. She met him almost strike for strike, but only because he was so blinded by fury that he wasn't fighting well—just desperately. It was the only reason she didn't order him to stop; she knew he needed to get it out of his system. The fear of nearly having died, the relief that he was still alive, and the anger that his will was no longer his own. She knew what he was feeling; she'd been there herself.

The skies flashed and thunder deafened their ears, but still their fight continued. Alex hadn't battled many Meyarins in either timeline, only Aven, Roka and Zain, but she could tell Niyx was uncommonly skilled with a blade, even rampaging blindly as he was. She was hard pressed to hold up a defence against him. With the strength of his assault, Alex had no hope of striking any kind of offensive manoeuvre herself, but she hoped to be able to stay standing long enough for him to burn off his wrath and come to his senses.

However, when she slipped and her feet slid from underneath her, Alex knew she was in trouble.

Sprawled out on her back, she looked up through the rain, her Meyarin sight allowing her vision to remain crystal clear as she took in the form of Niyx standing above her like an avenging angel. His sword was pointed down at her chest, holding her in place, his eyes spearing her like shards of purple ice.

"Tell me not to," he dared, his voice ragged, pressing the tip of his blade against her heart.

Her pulse was erratic and she was panting wildly, both from the fight and from her fear, but she shook her head. "I won't."

To prove her point, she released her grip on A'enara and it disappeared from sight.

"*Tell me not to!*" Niyx repeated in a shout.

"*I won't!*" she yelled back at him.

They stared at each other, their furious gazes locked, until Niyx released a savage growl, closed his eyes tightly and stepped away. He spun on his heel and threw back his arm, hurling his sword with all his strength and sending it smashing against the wall of the palace where it clattered to the ground. He then turned back to Alex and, shocking the stuffing out of her, reached down and yanked her to her feet, dragging her roughly back into the shelter of her room.

As if the heavens were playing a great joke at their expense, the rain started to ease and the storm dispersed, leaving them in an eerie silence as they dripped water all over her floor.

"So…" Alex said, needing to fill the silence. "You can fight."

The look he sent her was scathing. "Unlike you, I'm a real Meyarin—of course I can fight."

"Hey, I managed to hold my own out there, didn't I?" she defended, crossing her arms.

"You did," he returned. "And I'd be curious how you managed that if I didn't already know the answer."

"And what answer's that, smarty pants?"

"You've been Claimed before," he said. "And even though you're not anymore, somehow the Meyarin blood has stayed with you."

Her body stiffened. "How—"

"I can feel it," he said, cutting her off. "I can feel your blood in me, like a taint."

Alex chose not to take offence to that, since she was hoping his reference was to Aven's blood, not her mortal blood… Though, she doubted that was the case.

"I can't feel your blood in me," Alex said, and she'd never felt Aven's, either, just the heightened effects of it. "Are you sure you're not being melodramatic?"

His gaze narrowed, reminding her that he was still very much on edge and she should watch her words. "You're mortal. You're nowhere near sensitive enough to feel something so subtle."

"But as you've deduced, I have Meyarin senses."

"Which is not the same as being Meyarin," he rebutted. "And besides, unless I'm wrong, you don't seem to always be using those senses. I had presumed it was because you'd grown up around mortals. Now I know it's because you *are* mortal."

Alex wrinkled her nose, annoyed that he'd managed to notice something like that. "I do suck at being one of you," she admitted. "But I'm trying."

"Why?"

"Why?" Alex repeated, eyebrows rising at his curiosity.

"Why are you trying to be one of us? Why are you even *here*?"

Alex bit her lip, not sure how much she should say. But then again, he was technically bound to her will. She could tell him anything and he'd have to keep it a secret if she asked. The problem was, she didn't want to have to ask.

"I meant what I said earlier," she told him, ignoring his question for the moment, "about knowing what you're going through. You're right—I *was* Claimed by a Meyarin, one who ordered me to do unspeakable things, and I hated every single second of it. You can despise me all you want, Niyx, and I'll deserve that. But please know, I did what I did to save your life, and I'd do it again if I had to."

She lowered her voice to a near whisper. "I can't convince you to believe me, but other than keeping my secret, keeping *our* secret, you have my word that I won't order you to do anything without your permission. Not intentionally. And when I leave Meya, which won't be far from now, I'll Release you before I go."

She held his gaze as she finished, "Everyone has a right to free will. I won't keep yours from you. Not for long, anyway."

He was watching her carefully throughout the entirety of her speech. "You mean it, don't you?" At her questioning look, he clarified. "You're really going to Release me?"

She nodded. "I promise."

"And you won't make me do anything I don't want?"

His eyes remained trained on her, so she kept her face open, showing her honest intent as she answered, "Nothing other than having you stay quiet about my mortality and our bond."

"And if I asked you, right now, to Release me," he said, "and gave you *my* word that I wouldn't tell anyone your secrets, would you let me go?"

Alex hesitated and Niyx saw it, his features darkening in response. She hated seeing the harsh look on his handsome face since it reminded her too much of his future self.

"Wait," she told him before he could take a bite at her. "I'm thinking, okay? It's not an easy question for me to answer."

"A simple yes or no will suffice. You either trust me, or you don't."

"You don't know what's at stake."

"Then *tell* me," he barked at her.

"I'm from the future, okay?" she snapped at him. "When I say there's a lot at stake, I mean there's *a lot at stake*."

Niyx reared back as if slapped. "What did you say?"

Alex huffed and stormed over to sit on her bed, careless that she was making it even wetter than it already was.

Summing up what she'd told Roka a week ago, Alex said, "I'm from the future, I'm human, I was Claimed by a Meyarin, and it's believed by a number of... people... that I'm the only one who can stop that Meyarin from doing all kinds of bad things, which means I have to learn how to fight like an immortal if I want to live long enough to see my real future actually *become* a future." She finished by adding, "Roka's been trying to teach me, but it hasn't been going so well."

"Roka knows about you?" Niyx said, moving to stand before her.

"I got a stupid paper cut, if you can believe it," Alex said. "He knows pretty much everything now."

"And he's been training you?"

"Not very well," Alex admitted, trying not to feel guilty about her lack of appreciation towards the prince. "He's too careful with me, too afraid that he'll hurt me, so he's constantly holding back. Not at all like you." She laughed quietly and pressed a hand to her bruised backside from where she'd fallen hard to the ground.

Niyx's expression was unreadable as he looked down on her.

"How important is it for you to beat this Meyarin of the future?"

Frowning at him, Alex returned with a question of her own. "How are you not wondering how I'm *from* the future?"

Niyx waved a dismissive hand in the air. "Your draekon brought you through the *abrassa*, or so I'm presuming. Probably unintentionally, judging by how lost you were when you first arrived."

"I was not lost!"

"You pretended like you didn't understand our language and you were as skittish as a terrified kitten for days," Niyx shot back.

Alex gaped at him. "How did you know I understood you?"

"Just because the others are exceptionally unobservant doesn't mean I am," he said condescendingly. "I also happen to know more about the *vaeliana* than most, including how the bond allows for language exchange."

"Why didn't you say anything?" Alex asked, but even as she asked it, she remembered the pointed jabs he'd repeatedly made. "Why didn't you tell anyone?"

He looked like he didn't understand why she was arguing with him, and she wondered the same herself. "I figured you had your reasons for wanting it kept secret. And besides, I knew that within days you'd learn our dialect properly and have no excuses, no language barrier to hide behind. Your knowledge wasn't harming anyone, so..." He trailed off in a shrug. "Now it's your turn to answer my question. How important is it for you to win against this future enemy of yours?"

Alex called to mind what the Library had shown her, skimming over blurred images of villages burning, people screaming, death and destruction, until she finally stopped on the image of Meya with its crumbling ruins, abandoned like a ghost city. She didn't realise that she was mentally projecting the memory as she answered, "If I lose and my enemy wins, Medora will be destroyed. Does that sound important enough to you?"

When Niyx didn't respond, Alex looked up to see his slack, shocked face. "Niyx?"

"What was that?" he whispered. "What you just showed me?"

Alex squinted in bafflement. "What I just... what?"

"Was that the future I just saw? Meya in ruins? Medora in flames?"

Her jaw dropped. "You *saw* that?"

We're bonded, Aeylia, his dry tone said in her mind. *That's what happens when you perform forbidden rituals you know nothing about.*

"Holy crap!" she cried, jumping to her feet. "Get out of my head!"

"Take it easy," he said, reaching out to place a steadying hand on her arm and only narrowing his eyes slightly when her words came out as a command.

"Sorry," Alex said, feeling the tug and realising that she'd accidentally broken her promise—except for the caveat she'd given that she wouldn't *intentionally* give him orders.

"I can see this bond of ours is going to be a problem," Niyx said through gritted teeth, before rolling the tension from his shoulders and relaxing again.

Alex, however, was confused. "Don't you—Aren't you going to promise to keep my secrets and ask me to Release you? Isn't that what you said?"

"I questioned what you'd do if I asked you to do that," Niyx corrected. "But you've managed to convince me about your high stakes and the need for secrecy rather well."

"Are you saying...?"

"Keep the Claim on me, for now," Niyx said, to her surprise. "I presume when you mentioned leaving here, you were referring to going back to the future once your draekon is up to the return trip through the *abrassa*?"

Alex was impressed with his deductive reasoning skills. "That's right."

"And you'll still do what you promised and Release me before you take off?"

"Of course," she said. "But... Not that I'm not grateful that you're no longer attacking me over it, but why the sudden change of heart?"

Niyx took a moment to respond, choosing his words carefully. "The future I just saw, I don't know how far away it is, but forever isn't considered long for a race of eternal beings," he said. "If you're the only one who can stop that destruction befalling this world, then I'm going to do what I can to help you, even if that means I must relinquish my free will for the time being."

Alex wasn't sure if she'd heard him right. "You're going to *what*?"

"You said Roka isn't training you properly because he's afraid to hurt you, correct?"

Alex made an affirmative sound, not quite following.

"And as you've clearly seen, I hold no such reservations towards you."

She nodded, still feeling the throbbing of the bruises.

"Then the logical conclusion is that *I'll* train you so that you'll be ready to fight this Meyarin when you return to the future," he said. "Or at least be better prepared than you are now."

Alex couldn't believe the magnitude of what he was offering. It was actually the perfect solution, since she knew Niyx wouldn't hold back like Roka did. And he'd clearly proven himself an expert swordsman. But still—

"I'm going to regret saying this," Alex said, "but since you're making that offer, I'm presuming you'd be equally willing to keep it secret along with everything else you've learned tonight. So why are you okay with me keeping my Claim on you until I leave?"

A strange glint came into Niyx's eyes, part dangerous, part mischievous, as he reached for her wrist and pulled her non-scarred hand towards him. In a flash of movement he drew a hidden dagger from his belt and slashed it lightly across the back of her knuckles.

"Ow!" she cried, yanking her arm back and curling her other hand protectively over the wound. "What the hell, Niyx?"

In response, he held up his right hand. In the exact same spot as where he'd sliced open her skin, he had a matching cut on his flesh; his bleeding silver while hers bled red.

She looked from his hand to hers and back again. In a strangled voice, she asked, "What just happened?"

"The safest way for me to train you, especially if I'm not pulling my punches, is to know how injured you are, how much strength you have and how much further I can push you before you break," Niyx said, tearing off part of his ripped shirt and reaching for Alex's hand, tying the wet material around her cut before repeating the process with his own. "The bond between us will allow me to know all that without the guesswork in between."

"That didn't happen last time I was Claimed," Alex responded shakily. But then again, neither Alex nor Aven had been injured while she was under the effect of his bond. She'd only been stabbed by A'enara *after* she'd freed herself from Aven's Claim.

"It wouldn't have," Niyx said, "because you didn't perform the ritual, it was performed *on* you."

As if to help her understand, he pressed his dagger against his own flesh this time, on the skin further up his forearm. When blood started welling out, Alex turned to look along the line from her wrist to her elbow, but there was nothing there at all.

"I don't understand," Alex said. "Why do you get hurt with me, but I don't get hurt with you?"

"That's just the way the bond works," he said. "It's your life force that's shared with me, not the other way around. That means what you feel, I feel. You healed me when you performed the Claiming ritual, but from what I understand, that's a one-time deal, which is for the best since all that glowing was a bit too weird for me, if you know what I'm saying."

Alex did. She absolutely did. But she still didn't quite understand the rest. Even so, she let it go and summarised, "So if I get hurt, you get hurt, which is how you'll know if you've pushed me too far in the training?"

Niyx nodded.

"And you're willing to give up your freedom just so you can know how much pressure I can take?"

"It's quite noble of me, if you think about it," he said pensively. "Giving up my will in order to save the future of the world."

Alex felt a crushing weight settle on her chest. "Niyx," she said, "about the future—about *your* future…"

She didn't know what she was going to say, but in the end, she didn't have to say anything.

"Don't, Aeylia," he said, reaching forward to press a finger to her lips. "I don't want to know what my future is. I just want to make sure I *do* have one, along with everyone else in Meya. Okay?"

Slowly, she nodded and he took his finger away. He then seemed to brace himself.

"Give the command," he said, the light of the city casting shadows over his face. "Tell me to keep it all secret."

"Ni—"

His voice was resigned but firm when he said, "Just do it, Aeylia."

Knowing it was best for the both of them if she got it over with quickly, she mustered up the courage and ordered, "You won't tell anyone what happened tonight. You won't say a word or communicate in any other way about anything we said or did."

When the tug of the command eased, Niyx gave a stiff nod and stepped back. "That was broad, but I think you covered it all."

"I'm sorry, Niyx," she said.

"You did what you had to, Aeylia. Just don't expect me to be doing cartwheels about it."

The image of him doing a cartwheel sprung to her mind and she had to bite back a smile, certain he wouldn't appreciate the visual as much as she did.

"What happens now?" she asked.

"Now is the easy part," Niyx said. "We both need dry clothes and sleep. It's tomorrow that's going to be hard—for you, anyway."

Brow furrowed, Alex said, "Why's that?"

"Because we begin your training at dawn," Niyx told her. "And I may have accepted this mess you've gotten the both of us into and decided to do the right thing in the face of it all, but that doesn't mean I'm forgiving about it. Prepare to have your ass handed to you tomorrow, Aeylia. And every other day for the foreseeable future."

With those words, he turned on his heel and stormed towards the door, clearly still stung over the command he'd all but forced her to give him.

Knowing that she shouldn't, but unable to resist, the moment he was out her door and presumably on the *Valispath* leaving the palace, Alex called out in her mind, *'Night, Niyx. Sweet dreams.*

His response was instant. *I may not be able to kill you without killing myself in the process, but I can still make you wish you were dead. Trust me when I say my pain threshold is significantly higher than yours, mortal.*

Alex retreated from his mind, not sure if she was shaking because she was amused or because she was genuinely fearful. To get her mind off the spiteful Meyarin she was now bonded to, she called out to the *other* being she shared a connection with.

Xira, you there?

When he responded, she followed through on her promise to explain everything to him. After she was done and managed to convince him *not* to fly down and swallow Niyx whole, she asked the burning question, *If he's now connected to me, does that mean he's connected to you, since you and I are linked?*

No, Alex, Xiraxus replied. *The* vaeliana *isn't a bond of blood and it can't be enacted by anyone but a draekon, regardless of whomever else you might become connected to.*

If it's not a blood bond, then what is it?

It's more a... soul bond, I suppose you would call it, Xiraxus said. *Our connection goes beyond flesh, beyond the heart and the mind. It's founded in the deepest core of who we are. No matter what time or distance separates us, we'll always be linked to one another.*

Alex blinked into the darkness of her room. *I guess it's a good thing I don't have commitment issues, huh?*

Xiraxus gave a rumbling laugh. *Go to sleep, Alex. Dawn isn't far away and if what you say is true, you're going to need all the rest you can get before meeting with your Meyarin in the morning.*

With her stomach churning at the mere possibility of what the early training hours might bring, Alex bid sweet dreams to Xiraxus and was left alone, until finally, overcome by the events of the day and heedless of her soaked clothes, she succumbed to sleep.

Thirty

Five days later, Alex bent over at the waist, trying to draw oxygen into her desperate lungs.

"I... just... need... a... minute," she gasped, holding up a hand.

"You have three seconds," Niyx returned. "One. Two. Three."

And then he ruthlessly came at her again, attacking her with the same vigour he'd managed for the last three hours. Non-stop.

This was what Alex's life had been like for nearly a whole week now. Upon her dawn wake-up call the morning after saving Niyx, he'd dragged her, still yawning, deep into the Silverwood to begin a rigorous training program that would make even her psychopathic PE teacher tremble in his boots. In fact, being taught by Niyx was worse than taking a lesson with Finn, Karter and Hunter—*together*. Part of that was probably due to his own frustration over knowing that at any second, despite her promise, she could strip him of his free will. But another part, Alex knew, was because unlike Roka, who had offered to help because she said it was important, Niyx had *seen* what was in store if Alex failed. And he was determined to have her as prepared as possible to stop that future from happening.

Thus began a regime the likes of which Alex figured a stint in hell itself would be a pleasant holiday in comparison.

In other words, Niyx was true to his threat about Alex's ass being handed to her every... single... day. Multiple times per hour, to be precise. And that was a large reason why they were out in the forest rather than in one of the training halls of the palace—because for what Niyx was making her do, they needed to be near a steady supply of *laendra*.

Basically, he hacked the crap out of Alex. The wounds themselves often needed immediate attention, and even if they didn't, they couldn't risk anyone else seeing her bleed. From small scratches to nausea-inducing lacerations, even unchecked stab wounds and broken bones, Niyx didn't hold back in his attacks, regardless of receiving the same injuries as she did thanks to their connection. Despite him feeling firsthand how Alex was handling those injuries—which was often the only reason she remained alive—he really did have a greater pain threshold than hers. What caused her to double over in pain was comparative to an ant bite to him, for all he reacted. When he'd practically severed her sword arm in one of his attacks, he'd merely ripped off a piece of material as a makeshift bandage for her, saying it was a good excuse for them to practise their ambidexterity. He'd then proceeded to attack her left-handed— his own right hand as gored up as hers—and continued until she'd almost expired from blood loss, whereby he'd shoved *laendra* across her wound and, once healed, forced her to keep training.

What was amazing, though, was that every day Alex started to see improvement in her Meyarin fighting skills, her injuries becoming less and less. And that was largely because of something that happened on her first day of training. The moment they'd landed in the forest, Niyx hadn't paused to offer any kind of safety lecture, he'd just launched straight at her. She hadn't expected the attack and was knocked unconscious almost instantly. When she'd come to, it was with Niyx standing above her, holding a hand to his equally throbbing head and demanding to know why she hadn't ducked. Furious, she'd yelled back just as loud that she needed a minute to tune in to her Meyarin senses before "—some idiot decides to throw a sucker punch at my face!"

After that, she'd explained how she went about calming and focusing herself enough to flick the switch to activate the blood in her veins—to which Niyx had looked at her as if she were crazy. He'd then run a hand through his hair and blown her world apart by saying there shouldn't *be* a switch—that she needed to be 'playing Meyarin' all the time if she truly wanted to become competent enough to face the future. He'd said, if anything, she should have to flick her inner switch in the *opposite* direction, with the option to 'act human' only when she deliberately chose to do so.

So, along with kicking her butt physically, the unrelenting Meyarin set about helping her remain consistently locked in to her immortal senses. That meant she didn't just spend her time avoiding the sharp edge of his blade, but she also did other tasks he set out for her: she had to run through the forest for hours using Meyarin speed, like when she'd been on the *varrungard*; she had to climb up the sheer rock face of the Golden Cliffs, then she had to do it again but by scaling up through a waterfall; she had to hold her breath underwater for impossible lengths of time, and then repeat it in ice water found in crevasses at the top of snow-covered mountains; she had to fall from great distances with nothing to catch her but her own ability to tuck and roll at just the right moment; she had to spend unnatural amounts of time hanging suspended from trees while liberating herself from something similar to a straightjacket—*without* summoning A'enara; and lastly, and possibly the most extreme, she had to handstand-walk around the rim of a crater at the summit of an active volcano.

Niyx had, for that one, recruited Xiraxus's help in 'spotting' Alex in case she lost her balance and began to fall into the magma chamber, since despite her Meyarin blood and *vaeliana* bond, none of them would have survived that. And just to add insult to injury, since the volcano Niyx had chosen was situated on one of Draekora's floating islands—but *how* he knew its location, he refused to say—half the winged beasts had come along to watch the show, to Alex's embarrassment. She'd been forced to look like a total fool walking on her hands around a crater spouting bursts of lava, and they'd practically been calling for popcorn. Even Zaronia hadn't been able to hide her amusement when the sweaty-faced, skin-burned, clothes-on-fire Alex had stumbled back to the base of the mountain and glared at the entertained assemblage.

Suffice it to say, Niyx had put Alex through the ringer over the last five days, pushing her to thrive beyond her limit. Every night she fell into an exhausted sleep, only to be awoken at dawn by the merciless Meyarin who seemed to take great delight in her painful misery. Despite their early sessions, he always returned her to the palace in time for her breakfast with the queen, which the king was joining more often than not these days, too—mostly to get away from the manic fervour of the palace's last-minute festival preparations.

The times the king joined them were surprisingly enjoyable. Astophe, Alex had quickly discovered, had a sharp wit and a keen intelligence. During one of their early breakfasts together, Astophe had asked if she'd like to play a game of Stix with him. Having never played before, Alex had been hesitant, but Astophe had been a kind and patient teacher, showing her exactly how best to understand the game of strategy that turned out to be a mixture of chess, checkers and tic-tac-toe—but the aim was to *lose*, because the first person to have all their pieces wiped from the board was pronounced the winner. Within a few matches, Alex had started giving the king a run for his money, something which delighted him to no end.

When breakfast finished each day—and after at least one obligatory Stix match with the king, or more, if his time permitted—Alex and Niida would meet up with Kyia and spend their mornings overseeing the final production and distribution of the masquerade costumes to the denizens of Meya. Her time with the two of them was like a vacation for Alex because after lunch she was Niyx's to torture again. Roka was still busy training the *Zeltora* recruits, so other than a few fly-by sightings of the prince—where he apologised profusely for neglecting her but promised he'd be back as soon as he could— Alex didn't see much of him. Aven too was a rare sight, thanks to his involvement in organising the festival that was now only three days away. Every time Alex saw the leader of the *Garseth* he looked harried and stressed, determined to make the end-of-summer celebration the best in the history of Meya.

Noticing just how frazzled Aven had been of late, a couple of days ago Alex had stopped him in the hallway and asked if there was anything else she could do to help make his load lighter. Part of that was because he'd looked like he hadn't slept in a week, but the other part, the larger part, was the hope he might give her an excuse to have a few Niyx-free hours. What she hadn't anticipated as a result of her offer was the emotion that had washed over his face. He'd stared at her in a way that had made her squirm with discomfort, before gently telling her everything was under control. Then, before she'd had time to react, he leaned forward and kissed her on the cheek, leaving her frozen to the floor when he whirled away, calling over his shoulder that he'd see her later.

His clear show of affection had brought great alarm to Alex, since even though she was able to accept him as her friend in the past, even acknowledge him as someone she'd come to care greatly about, she couldn't forget who he would become in the future. And that was not someone who she would ever want kissing her—on the cheek or anywhere else.

When she'd shared her concerns with Niyx that afternoon, at least vaguely in the form of 'I'm leaving soon and don't want to inadvertently lead anyone on,' Niyx had just looked at her as if to see whether she was being serious before erupting in laughter.

"You're kidding, right?" he'd said to her in between sword thrusts. "You do know he's been half in love with you since you forgave him for ditching your ass in the city that day?"

Barely avoiding having her spleen punctured by his blade, Alex had gaped at Niyx. "But that was weeks ago!"

"Which means he's had plenty of time to get to know you and even up the other half," Niyx returned, swiping at her head. "You better watch yourself, kitten. My best friend thinks you're Meyarin and he's falling for you—a *mortal*—and falling hard."

Alex ducked and spun, meeting his weapon mid-air as she said, "I think this might be a slight problem."

"A slight problem?" He sounded incredulous. "*A slight problem?*"

"I can't stop him from feeling whatever he's feeling, Niyx, as mental as that is—and believe me, given everything I know, it's *really* mental," Alex said, her mind reeling. "But I sure as hell am not encouraging him!"

Niyx's rebuttal was as quick as his next thrust. "You aren't *dis*couraging him, either!"

Since then, Alex had done everything she could to avoid Aven, not wanting to lead him on further than he'd apparently already been led—as unintentional as that had been. Her efforts had proven effective, as she hadn't seen him since he kissed her on the cheek a few days ago. But that was likely also because she'd spent almost every other hour training to become

Superwoman. It was a feat that Alex could admit was finally paying off.

"What's going on with you today?" Niyx asked, drawing her back to the present as he paused his attack and looked at her with shrewd eyes. "You've been improving a lot lately but today it's like we're right back to where we started."

"I'm sorry," Alex panted. "I didn't get much sleep last night."

"Why not?" he asked, crossing his arms over his bare chest.

During their first sparring session, Alex had learned his preferred state of dress when fighting was minimal—which meant all he wore were boots and long black combat-like pants belted at his waist. The first time Alex had seen him half naked, she hadn't been able to stop staring, but it wasn't because of his ridiculously defined abs; it was because of the silvery claw marks highlighted against his tanned skin, the diagonal scars stretching across his chest.

He'd noticed her staring and had made some flippant remark about her drooling over him, but she'd seen the emotion in his eyes—the fear of his near-death experience, the relief of being alive, the anger at *how* he was alive and the regret that he would always bear the mark of the Sarnaph—and of the Claiming. In that moment, Alex was thankful that her own scars were tiny by comparison, the one on her hand *and* the one where A'enara had lodged into her back. Apparently only the most grievous of injuries were able to mar the flesh of those with immortal blood, and Niyx's claw marks topped the charts.

Alex would never say it to his face, certain that she would receive some ridiculously lewd comment in return, but she thought the scars just added to his overall appearance, as impossible as that should have been. Meyarins on the whole were a tad too perfect, in her opinion. They were almost too unnaturally good looking. But Niyx's scars, even when hidden by clothing, gave him a flaw that made him all the more real.

They were a mark of what he'd been through, a badge of honour and a testament to his decision to help Alex learn to fight no matter the cost.

That was just plain beautiful to her.

"Aeylia!" he barked at her.

She shook her head and apologised again. "Sorry, what did you say?"

His lips pursed. "Why didn't you sleep?"

"That would be my fault," came Xiraxus's rumbling voice as he landed in their clearing with a *thump* that wobbled the ground under Alex's feet and shook the nearby trees of the forest.

"Well, if it isn't my favourite draekon," Niyx said in greeting. His words may have sounded snarky, but Alex knew he'd established a kind of mutual respect with Xiraxus, especially after they'd both laughed so hard together during the volcano incident. "Do I want to know why you kept our little mortal friend here up past her bedtime?"

Alex let the derogatory comment slide over her, since she'd heard much worse from him in the past few days.

"Do you want to tell him, or should I?" Xiraxus asked Alex.

Niyx glanced between them both. "I'm officially intrigued."

"Xira thinks he'll be ready to take me back to my time in a few days," Alex said, still marvelling over what the draekon had told her the previous night. After everything she'd experienced in the past, she found it difficult to wrap her head around the idea of returning home—back to her friends, back to her family.

Niyx looked puzzled by the lack of jubilation in her voice. "This is a good thing, right?"

Alex nodded, more to herself than him. "Definitely. I mean, coming here was an accident to begin with—or maybe not, if you want to read into the whole looping-time paradox. But getting stuck in the past was never in my five-year plan, so I always knew I would have to go home when the time came."

She didn't mention her option to leave earlier through the Library, knowing it would raise too many questions about how she'd stayed to get a better idea of how Aven had become... well, *Aven*.

"I made the best of a bad situation by trying to learn what I would have if I'd been in the future," Alex continued, "and thanks to you, I've come a long way with that." She tipped her head in gratitude. "But I think it's about time I got back to my real life."

Knowing her better than she would like, Niyx asked, "Are you ready for that?"

"Psychologically?" Alex shook her head. "Probably not. Physically?" She grinned self-deprecatingly and shook her head again. "Definitely not. But I'm more ready than I ever have been before, so I'll take that as a win."

He watched her carefully, his eyes alert, and then turned to Xiraxus. "When do you think you'll be up to the journey?"

"The day after the festival, at the latest," the draekon returned, his tail sweeping forest debris in an arc around his hindquarters. "Possibly sooner."

Niyx looked back to Alex. "Then we still have a few days left to practise before you go."

The challenging glint in his eyes caused Alex no small amount of unease as she wondered what agonies he might inflict upon her next.

"Summon A'enara back, Aeylia," he ordered. "If you think I've been going hard on you these last couple of sessions, you haven't seen anything yet."

Thirty-One

Niyx hadn't been lying about taking it easy on her previously, not if the rest of their training session was any indication.

When they eventually called it quits that evening, Alex was barely able to summon the energy to return to the palace, clean up her bedraggled self and stumble down to dinner. Once there, she struggled to lift her fork to her mouth, and she was sorely tempted to ask the queen to feed her like a child. But after a few bites of the delicious meal, along with some hearty swigs of warmed *laendra*, Alex finally felt strength return to her body, enough to look up and properly take in her surroundings.

The moment she did, she froze with her goblet in the air.

For the first time in days, the entire royal family was dining together. Astophe and Niida were there, but so too were Roka and Aven, as well as the addition of Kyia—something which Alex was pleased to note, since the more time she spent in the presence of Roka, the more Alex was certain they would soon fall for one another.

What Alex *wasn't* pleased to note was how oblivious she'd been of her dinner company up until the *laendra* jolted her back to awareness. How had she missed both Roka and Aven being there? The former was barely at the palace at all of late, so busy as he was with the *Zeltora* recruits, and the latter Alex had been deliberately avoiding due to his potentially unrequited feelings for her.

But now… Now everyone was looking at Alex with unbridled amusement.

"Rough day, Aeylia?" Kyia asked, a grin tugging at her lips.

Lowering her goblet to the table, Alex considered how best to respond. They'd all seen her zombie-like self just moments ago so she wouldn't be able to brush aside their observations.

"I feel as though I single-handedly hunted down and fought my way through an entire pack of Sarnaphs."

Her answer produced chuckles all around the table, and given how outrageous her statement was, it had the effect she was after, meaning that no one thought to question the real reason for her exhaustion.

"I hope you still have it in you to practise tonight," Niida said, passing a hamper of pastries over to Alex.

Reaching for a spiced fruit scroll, Alex asked, "Practise for what?"

It was Kyia who answered, taking the hamper from Alex once she was done. "There are only three days left until the ball, and *someone* still doesn't know enough to pass as a Meyarin."

Nearly choking on her mouthful at what sounded very much like an accusation outing her humanity, Alex raised panicked eyes to Roka. He caught her look and gave a slight but meaningful shake of his head.

"Or at least," Kyia continued, not noticing the interplay between Alex and Roka, "you don't know enough to pass as one of us when it comes to dancing."

"*Dancing?*" Alex cried, equal parts relieved and apprehensive. "No one said anything about dancing."

Deadpan, Kyia said, "What exactly do you think happens at a ball? That we all sit around playing Stix?"

"I vote we do that next time," Astophe offered his opinion from the head of the table while reaching for a second helping of honey cake. "It sounds much more enjoyable."

As Alex turned back to Kyia, her eyes flicked past Aven just in time to see a flare of annoyance blaze across his face. She understood the reason for his quickly concealed display of emotion, since she knew he'd been desperately trying to organise the end-of-summer celebration so that it was something everyone would enjoy. The knowledge that his father would prefer to sit in a corner and play a game rather than revel in the festivities can't have been something Aven was thrilled to hear.

"These pastries won't eat themselves, Aeylia," Kyia said, drawing Alex's attention away from Aven by placing another fruit scroll onto her plate. "You need to regain your energy, so dig in."

Not needing to be told twice, Alex did as ordered, wondering how she might avoid the coming dance lessons and instead rest her tired eyes. But one look at Kyia, who was still piling more food in front of her, and Alex stopped brainstorming excuses, knowing that her evening was already planned whether she liked it or not.

After finishing their meals, the king and queen excused themselves, and Kyia took that as her cue to drag Alex from the table and through the palace until they reached a grandiose ballroom.

Staring in awe as she looked around the glass-domed space that was more like an observatory than a ballroom, Alex marvelled at the star-strewn sky and the glowing Myrox city easily seen beyond the transparent walls. There were at least three large balconies leading out into the open air, making the *myraes*-chandeliered room even more magical than it already was.

Craning her neck from side to side, Alex tried to take it all in, but her attention was seized when music began echoing around the space. The sound was classical yet upbeat, using a combination of woodwind and stringed instruments. Where it was coming from, Alex had no idea.

"There are a number of traditional Meyarin dances that you should have at least a basic knowledge of before the ball, so we'll start with the easy ones and work our way from there," Kyia said, just as Aven and Roka ambled into the room.

"Is this really necessary?" Alex asked, brushing her hair behind her ear and feeling all kinds of awkward. "I've danced before." She paused, then admitted, "I may not be very *good*, but I can twirl my way around a ballroom without falling on my face."

She reminisced about Kaiden and his arms around her, guiding her confidently through their waltz at D.C.'s seventeenth birthday party. But even that wasn't her first time properly dancing, since that happened with Bear and Jordan during the previous New Year's Eve Royal Gala at Chateau Shondelle—Jordan's family home.

So much had happened since then.

Wiping her mind clear lest she become lost in her memories, Alex looked back at Kyia and added, "I'm sure I don't need to practise—how hard can it be?"

But half an hour later Alex realised just how ignorant her words had been. Meyarin dancing was *complicated*, full of spins and twists, skips and jumps. And it was also fast. But that wasn't the worst of it—the worst was that Kyia had paired Alex up with Aven as her teaching partner.

Normally Alex would have been thrilled by the arrangement because it meant Kyia herself was practising with Roka, which led to the two of them being in very close proximity to each other as they danced together. But given Alex's desire to distance herself from Aven—and from whatever he might feel towards her—she was supremely uncomfortable being in his arms, despite the fact that it was purely for educational purposes.

"This would be a lot easier if you would just relax," Aven said quietly to her, one arm curled snuggly around her waist, the other hand tangling with her fingers as he tried yet again to lead her through the steps. "You're as stiff as a slab of Myrox."

"I'm perfectly relaxed," Alex lied, looking at anything but him.

Silence for a beat, and then, "What's going on with you, Aeylia? I thought you... I thought we..." He trailed off, sounding lost enough that Alex felt compelled to look at him, only to see not just confusion in his eyes, but also hurt.

It was the hurt that made her wince inside, because this younger Aven was her friend. The last thing she wanted to do was hurt him—there was enough of that coming for the both of them in the future. Her treating him like a pariah now wasn't helping anyone.

"I'm sorry," she answered softly, forcing her body to relax. "I haven't been getting much sleep lately." That much was true, thanks to Niyx's rigorous training demands. "I think I'm just a little stressed and not feeling like myself lately."

"You know you can tell me anything, right?" Aven said, his voice both compassionate and sincere. "No matter what, I'm here for you, Aeylia—always."

Alex wasn't sure if she wanted to laugh or cry, fully aware his statement wouldn't hold true for the future. And she certainly had no idea how to handle her current situation—how to keep him at arm's length but also keep their friendship intact for as long as possible. Niyx had implied that she should consider discouraging Aven's feelings, but short of being a cold-hearted witch, Alex didn't know how else to make it clear that she was never—*ever*—going to be romantically inclined towards him. She still couldn't understand how he could feel that way about her when all she'd done was offer a few non-judgemental words of support. Was he so starved for kindness that her encouragement had claimed such a strong hold on his feelings? Having spent time with his loving family and friends, Alex struggled to comprehend how that could be true.

"Can I ask you something?" Alex asked, step-hop-twirling with him as he led them around the room in time with the music.

His reply was instant. "Anything."

Alex kept her voice low enough that neither Roka nor Kyia could hear when she said, "Do you remember that night you took me to *Narsae de Trigon*?"

Aven's features tightened a fraction and he glanced quickly towards where his brother was dancing on the far side of the room before turning back to Alex and quietly saying, "What about it?"

Biting her lip, Alex said, "When Skraegon came up to us"— Aven's body tensed under her hands—"he suggested that if you—"

"I remember what he said," Aven cut in, casting another wary glance over to his brother, but Roka was too busy laughing at something Kyia had said to be paying them any attention.

"Is that what you want?" Alex asked before she could chicken out. "To take the throne? Your family dead or cast aside?"

She, of course, knew that one day he would try and do exactly that. But the question had been plaguing her for almost a fortnight, ever since that unforgettable *Garseth* meeting. Had Aven been dwelling on it all this time as well? Just how close to being the villain of the future was he?

"Of course I don't want that," came his fast reply, his grip tightening around her. "Stars, Aeylia. What kind of person do you think I am?"

Glancing over his shoulder, Alex made herself finish what she'd started, needing to know exactly where he stood at this point in time. "You and your father are at odds about his

344 · Lynette Noni

support of the mortals. Skraegon might be a disgusting bully, but he's right about one thing—if you were on the throne, you could rule Meya however you wanted."

For a long moment, all Alex could hear was the anxious thumping of her own heart, increasing with the rising crescendo of the music.

When Aven spoke, it was so low that even with her Meyarin hearing, Alex could barely hear him.

"I won't lie to you—I *have* considered his words more than I care to admit," he said, his continued guidance through the dance steps the only thing that kept her from freezing with dread. "As you said, Skraegon is right—if my family were out of the picture, it would certainly simplify matters."

Alex almost dropped to her knees when Aven's tormented golden eyes locked on hers.

"But I could never instigate anything like that, Aeylia," he whispered fervently. "I might not get along with my father all the time, but he's still my *father*. We have our differences, sure, and there are too many of them for us to ever be as close as he is with my brother, but how would I ever live with myself if I decided to… to get rid of him?" Aven shook his head, horrified by the very idea. "And Roka—he's one of the only people in this world who I trust with my life. He'd never betray me, nor I him. He's more than my brother—he's my closest confidant. We tell each other everything. I could no sooner harm him than I could you."

Alex couldn't help jolting in surprise at his mention of her, but the unintentional reflex occurred right as he spun her out in a twirl, effectively concealing her knee-jerk reaction from his watchful eyes.

So much of what he'd said distressed her, mostly because she knew that Roka *wasn't* telling Aven everything—he was hiding the truth about Alex. And if Aven ever found out…

Alex couldn't stomach the thought. Her only comfort was in the knowledge that when the time came for him to finally snap and change so drastically from who he currently was to someone willing to commit murder, she wouldn't be around to witness how and why that came about. All she could do was guess the reason for it.

Perhaps Astophe would push him too far in one of their arguments, or maybe his relationship with Roka would decline over the coming years, enough that when Aven eventually decided to kill the humans, he would be willing to throw his family away.

Whatever the case, with only a couple more days left in the past, Alex decided to cast all the possible scenarios from her mind. She couldn't stop what was going to happen, all she could do was live the hours given to her. Right now that meant focusing on the dance steps she was learning.

It might have been wishful thinking on her part, or perhaps just plain denial. But as she twirled with him around the room and their difficult conversation faded away, Alex decided she was happy enough to live in that bubble for the moment— especially if it meant she could enjoy the little time she had left with Aven as her friend and not as the raging future psychopath who wanted nothing more than to see her dead.

Thirty-Two

"Aeylia."

"Aeylia, wake up."

"Come on, Aeylia, open your eyes."

A gentle shaking made Alex groan as the persistent voice kept calling to her, pulling her out of the deep sleep she so desperately needed.

It was two days since she'd danced with Aven, which meant it was two and a half days since Niyx had learned she would soon be leaving. With her festival duties considered complete once the distribution of outfits had been finalised, all Alex's spare time had been spent continuing her training with the unrelenting Meyarin. True to his word, the sparring she'd done with Niyx in the last couple of days had been about fifty million times more challenging than anything she'd ever experienced before, and her body was paying a price that even her frequent ingestion of *laendra* was struggling to assist with. What she really needed was rest, yet it seemed that her middle-of-the-night visitor was determined to interrupt her favourite part of the day.

"Now s'not a good time, Aven," she mumbled, recognising his voice but unwilling to open her eyes and relinquish her grip on sleep. "Come back never."

He chuckled from overhead. "Don't you mean, 'come back later'?"

"Nope," Alex said, hugging her pillow closer. "Never." She nuzzled her face into the soft material. "Then I can"—she broke off to yawn—"sleep forever."

A gentle tugging that became a firm yanking pried her pillow from her hands.

"I've been trying to catch you for days," Aven said when she finally opened her eyes enough to squint up at him in a glare. "I can't help wondering if you've been avoiding me."

"So you decided to ambush me in the middle of the night—in my *bedroom*?" Alex said, every slurred word waking her up more and more, to her annoyance. "While I'm *sleeping*?"

"It's the only place I knew you'd be," he said, grinning unrepentantly.

Alex was too tired to call up any concern about his feelings towards her, despite the fact that she was in quite a vulnerable position, in bed as she was. She simply didn't have it in her to worry about boundaries right now.

With a reluctant sigh, she pushed herself up to lean against the headboard, knowing that he wasn't going to let her go back to sleep just yet. "Why are you here, Aven?"

His eyes brightened in the darkness as a boyish excitement overtook his features. "It's *Mahna ess L'randae*."

Alex blinked groggily at him. "Marna-who-a-what-ah?"

"*Mahna ess L'randae*," he repeated with a flash of a smile. "It's Tia Auran for—"

"The Giving of Life," Alex said, her inner translator waking up enough for the words to not sound so much like gibberish.

"You've been studying," Aven said with clear approval.

Alex chose not to enlighten him, and instead asked, "But what does it mean?"

In response, he held out a hand. "Come and you'll see."

Alex wasn't sure what made her decide to go with him—whether it was the anticipation in his features or the fact that she doubted he'd leave her alone until she agreed, but either way, she rolled out of bed, careful not to take his hand so as to at least *try* and keep some emotional space between them.

Since she was now used to being woken up in the dead of the night by male Meyarins—mostly Niyx who, on the odd occasion, decided that dawn wasn't early enough to begin her training and dragged her out of bed in the really mean hours of the morning—Alex had gotten into the habit of going to sleep fully clothed in gear appropriate for fighting. Because of that, all she had to do was grab a cloak and she was ready for whatever midnight escapade Aven had planned.

Following him out the door, he activated the *Valispath* and they soared out of the palace, shooting straight upwards. Alex was grateful that Niyx had drilled her so hard in the past week because her automatic setting was now constantly switched over to her Meyarin blood. If that hadn't been the case, she would have gone sailing back into the boundary of the *Valispath* without her heightened reflexes helping her keep balance on the vertical climb. As it was, all she had to do was coolly adjust her footing, returning Aven's surprised smile when he saw that she was much more graceful than any other time she'd travelled on the Path with him.

Upward and upward they climbed, the direction telling Alex exactly where they were headed. It was one thing to travel so high with a winged beast under her, it was another entirely to be travelling on an invisible rollercoaster that made it seem like there was nothing beneath their feet.

"Why are we going to Draekora?" she called over the howl of the wind. Other than her volcano visit with Niyx, she hadn't been to the floating islands since Xiraxus had taken her to the glowing flower field the night Roka discovered her secret. As far as she was aware, it was almost considered taboo for anyone other than a draekon to spend much time in the sky lands.

Zaronia herself had told Alex that the Draekorans valued their privacy, so she wondered what reason Aven could possibly have for taking her there.

"*Mahna ess L'randae* happens twice a year," he called before frowning and reaching out to press his hand to the barrier around them until it sheltered them from the elements.

"Once every six months the draekons welcome Meya to their lands to receive an offering from the *Ter'a Ora Vorren*," Aven continued, his voice at a normal level now.

Alex furrowed her brow. "*Ter'a Ora Vorren*? Why do I know that name?"

"Your draekon probably mentioned it," Aven said. "What's his name again?"

"Xiraxus," Alex answered, distracted because she didn't think Aven's presumption was correct. But then she remembered it was actually Zaronia who had used the phrase. "Are you talking about the Pool of Tears?"

He nodded, his eyes glowing with starlight as they continued upwards. "You know it?"

"I just heard it in passing. What is it? And what's the offering given to Meya?"

Before Aven could answer, the *Valispath* began to slow as Draekora opened up in front of them, the islands bathed in what looked like blue powder under the light of the moon.

"Tonight is a sacred ceremony," Aven told her as they zoomed towards the middle of the floating lands. "Only Meyarins of the royal family or the council are permitted to be here; it's forbidden for anyone else to watch the ceremony."

"Uh, newsflash," Alex said, pointing to herself with raised eyebrows.

"That's why I'm sneaking you in," Aven said. "Believe me, tonight is a night you won't want to miss. Now please, keep quiet for a moment while I figure out the best place to hide."

Sighing, Alex thought it might be wise to send out a quick call to Xiraxus. *How much trouble would I be in if, hypothetically, I was to witness* Mahna ess L'randae?

She followed up by sending a mental image of her current position, soaring with Aven towards the same rocky, open-aired amphitheatre she had been taken to for her trial before the Kyvalon on her first day in the past. The glossy black *traesos* was resplendent in the moonlight, as if the crystalline surface actively *repelled* the light. It almost looked like a barrier of pure darkness surrounded the jagged edges of the variously sized outcroppings. Outcroppings that, just like last time, were acting as viewing platforms for the hulking winged beasts. But this time there weren't just a few draekons in attendance; the entire amphitheatre was full of the multi-coloured creatures.

Please tell me you're dreaming and you're not really here, Xiraxus replied after a moment's pause.

I could do that if it'll make you feel better, Alex offered.

The draekon made a noise that emphasised just how bad on the not-good scale her being there was. *Just make sure you stay out of sight. I want to live past tonight, thank you very much.*

His response validated her misgivings, so Alex promised she'd do her best before focusing back on Aven as he guided them towards a smaller outcropping at the side of the amphitheatre, slightly away from where the bulk of the draekons were. Quite frankly, Alex didn't think they were fooling anyone with their attempted stealth, but if their presence was noted, none of the draekons called attention to it. She could have sworn she saw Zaronia glance over from her raised platform though, which was proven true when Alex heard the leader's resigned-sounding mental voice saying, *I should have known*. Alex, in turn, sent her a sheepish wave before Aven yanked her behind a boulder of *traesos* and out of sight.

"The Draekorans might accept you being here since you're almost considered one of them thanks to your bond with their heir, but our people won't be as forgiving," Aven told her. "Please help me out here and at least *try* to avoid being seen by anyone from Meya."

Alex peeked out around the corner and said, "I can only see draekons out there."

"They'll be here any minute now," Aven replied, moving closer to glance over her shoulder, his front brushing lightly against her back.

Alex attempted to subtly wiggle away from him, but there wasn't enough room to put any more space between them, so she resigned herself to their close proximity—at least for the moment.

"So what's this Pool of Tears thing?" she asked again, since she hadn't received an answer earlier. "And what's the ceremony for?"

"It's said that when our people were banished from Tia Auras long ago, a small number of them were bonded to draekons who also inhabited the world beyond the stars," Aven said. "Not wanting to part with each other, those draekons and a few others left their race behind and followed the ancient Meyarins to Medora, knowing that, having lost everything, our people would need help to survive and thrive in this new place."

"Not to mention, those draekons would have ceased living if their bonded Meyarins failed to adapt on their own," Alex pointed out dryly, and Aven made a sound of agreement.

"Self-serving or not," he said, "the Draekorans contributed their most sacred offering to our people—something they call the *Z'ao*. They taught us how to mould it into architecture to strengthen the foundation of our city, sharpen it into weapons worthy of our best warriors, refine it to combustible dust that requires no fuel to burn and guided us in many other ways to utilise it to ensure the continued evolution of our race."

Alex craned her neck around to look up at him in shock. "Are you—You're not talking about Myrox, are you?"

Aven nodded. "That's what we call the *Z'ao*, yes."

Struggling to wrap her head around the fact that Meyarin steel actually originated from draekons, Alex asked, "And *myraes*, too? The multi-coloured fire?"

"*Myraes* is powdered Myrox," Aven told her, "crushed after the *Z'ao* has solidified but before it has been tempered."

"I can't believe this," Alex whispered, feeling strangely disappointed, like she was discovering that Santa's reindeer were actually buffalo, or that the North Pole was really situated in the middle of the Sahara Desert. She felt a little bit like the immortal race she held in such high esteem had been lying to her, even though they'd done nothing of the sort—it was *her* race who had slapped the 'Made in Meya' label on Myrox.

"Twice a year we're permitted to come and draw the *Z'ao* from *Ter'a Ora Vorren* to replenish our stores," Aven continued his explanation. "It's a power source for Meya, helping us to continue thriving as a race, even providing us with the energy to create the protective wards we use sparingly around the city. Without the *Z'ao*, those wards would fail. We would also have no materials of quality high enough to create new weapons, raise new buildings or even light our paths and hearths. We rely on the Draekorans' continued blessing—the Giving of Life ceremony— for allowing our people to flourish in this new world."

That must be why he pulled me to the future.

The unexpected words caught Alex off-guard. *Xira?* She looked around but couldn't see him anywhere. *What are you talking about?*

Haven't you wondered what possessed him to pull me through to your time? Xiraxus asked.

Of course I have, she replied. *But I'm no closer to knowing the answer.*

There are no draekons in your future, Alex, Xiraxus said, causing the air to rush out of her in a quiet sound of disbelief. *When the Golden One—the Aven Dalmarta of your time—pulled me through the* abrassa, *before I was caught in his snare I saw a dead sea of islands above the clouds. Your Draekora was abandoned long ago. I could sense not even a distant trace of my race in your world. That's when I panicked and fell out of the sky, allowing him to get close enough to attempt my capture.*

Alex watched as Xiraxus showed her a mental picture of the Draekora in the future—the images he had skipped over in blurred flashes during his replay for the Kyvalon weeks ago. His memories revealed a desolate wasteland of islands resting atop the clouds, nothing at all like the vibrant assortment surrounding them now.

But... That means... She focused her thoughts and asked, *What about you, Xira? The future you?*

I don't know, Alex. I can't tell you what happened to your Draekora, he said. *But I'm guessing your Aven pulled me through because he needed a draekon to give him an advantage over the rest of the Meyarins.*

How would having you in captivity help him? she asked.

It was then that a hush fell over the draekon assemblage, pulling Alex from her inner conversation to look at what was happening. She threw a stealthy glance up at Aven who was still leaning in close and peering over her shoulder, relieved to find that he was too busy watching the draekons to have noticed her mental check-out.

"What's happening?" she whispered, barely moving her lips in the silence.

"Our people are coming," Aven whispered back.

Sure enough, Alex's Meyarin eyes picked them up the moment he'd said it, watching as they soared in on nearly invisible *Valispaths*, the seven council representatives landing one after the other in the *traesos* amphitheatre. They all wore identical hooded robes glowing with the familiar shine of Myrox threaded into the fabric, the brightness standing out in stark contrast against the crystallised blackness surrounding them.

"Here comes the best part," Aven whispered into Alex's ear, causing goose bumps to rise on her skin.

"Denizens of Meya," Zaronia called out in the Meyarin tongue, her voice echoing loudly across the space to Alex's heightened hearing. "Tonight you join with all of Draekora to honour those who have been lost beyond the stars."

As if reciting from a script they'd all memorised, in one voice the Meyarins said, "May the light shine always upon on the lost."

Alex was more than a little creeped out, and it only became worse when Zaronia stretched out her wings and flew down from her raised perch until she came to a rest on the ground in front of the Meyarins. In between them was what looked like a large basin forged into the *traesos*, but instead of it being entirely black like the rest of the rock, it had veins of glowing Myrox webbed throughout.

"Light for life," Zaronia said like some kind of pledge—this time not in Meyarin, but in the scratchy, rumbling language of the draekons—as she ducked her head over the basin. As Alex watched, a massive silvery tear fell from her eye and dropped into the bowl.

One by one the draekons flew to the ground, offering the same 'Light for life' declaration before releasing their tears into the steadily growing pool and then flying off into the dark of the night.

I didn't realise Ter'a Ora Vorren *was a literal description*, Alex called to Xiraxus. *It really* is *a Pool of Tears*.

The Z'ao provides the foundation for most of the Meyarins' necessities in life, he responded, repeating what Aven had said as he spoke of what Alex now knew was Myrox in its liquid form—the tears of draekons.

And if there are no draekons in my future... Alex said, jumping back to their earlier conversation.

Then the Meyarins of your world would have no new Z'ao available to them, he answered. *And without access to something so vital to their foundation, for their continued thriving existence, they would, essentially, be slowly devolving. Slowly dying as a race as their stores run out.*

Alex suddenly remembered jokingly asking the Kyia of her time if she could take some *myraes* home with her.

'*Unfortunately, there's very little* myraes *available to us these days*,' Kyia had said. '*It's a rare commodity amongst our race.*'

Alex shared the memory with Xiraxus and followed up by saying, *You think Aven pulled you to the future so you could, uh, cry for him?*

I believe he wanted the tears of a draekon, yes, Xiraxus said. *With a steady supply of Z'ao he would be able to provide weapons for his growing* Garseth*; he'd be able to barter the worth of our tears with any of the other races across Medora and receive anything he wanted in return; he'd even perhaps be able to tempt others in Meya and sway them into his favour, if he was able to offer them something of such significant worth that they'd been living without for so long. People will do anything if they're desperate enough. They will follow anyone, support any cause.*

Alex shuddered as an image of Aven storming the palace came to mind. A few gifted humans and a small handful of faithful *Garseth*, while not good, didn't present much of a threat to the crown. But with the backing of an entire city of desperate Meyarins willing to rise up against their rulers if it meant access to the luxuries denied to them for so long, then Roka and Astophe's lives would be in much more danger. Not even the elite guard could take on a whole city of revolutionists. Aven would barely have to lift a finger to kill his brother and father before claiming the throne as his.

Trembling at the visual, there was still something that Alex didn't understand. *Why you, Xira? Why not some other draekon? And how did he even pull you through the* abrassa *to begin with?*

Only two beings in all the worlds can access the abrassa *to manipulate or travel through space and time*, Xiraxus said. *Draekons and Tia Aurans. The Aven of your future had a Tia Auran in captivity—I saw her when I flew close enough for him to snare me.*

He shared his memory with Alex and she gasped in recognition as she saw Lady Mystique bound by snaking black chords around her body.

That's—That's—

Aes Daega is Tia Auran, Alex, Xiraxus said. *In your future she would have already met you in this past, so when Aven captured her and found a way to force her to do his bidding, I believe she deliberately chose to pull me through so that I would bond with you and bring you back with me, knowing that it had, to her knowledge, already been done.*

As Alex looked over the thinning crowd of draekons still dripping tears into the bowl, she wondered if it was possible to have a brain aneurysm from an overload of impossibilities that ridiculously made sense.

This is madness, Alex said, even her thoughts sounding strained.

The good news is, he didn't succeed, Xiraxus said. *With the kind of power it would have taken for Aes Daega to pull me through, she won't be able to repeat the process anytime soon with another draekon. And, if the Tia Auran of your day is anything like who she is here, I'd hazard a guess that she willingly surrendered herself to ensure your visit to the past. Bound by* traesos *coils or not, I wouldn't be surprised if as soon as you arrive back in your time, Aven finds he is missing his powerful prisoner.*

From what Alex knew of the ancient woman, she didn't doubt Xiraxus's assumption about Lady Mystique's capabilities. And that was a relief, since she wasn't keen on adding yet another name to her 'to rescue' list.

This hasn't changed anything, Xiraxus said, reading her inner turmoil. *Now you're just better informed of Aven's plan.*

And that he's desperate, Alex added, *but I guess I already knew that.*

Looking up over her shoulder again, Alex took in the relaxed, open face of the Aven who would one day become a monster. She just couldn't figure out how things would go so wrong. Even now, passionate though he was with his anti-mortal ideals, there was nothing *evil* about him. All he wanted was separatism from them, not to kill them. What would happen to make him snap and murder them all?

"What do you see when you look out there?" Alex whispered to the prince.

Standing so close, when he tipped his head down to her, they were barely a breath apart. Trapped with her front pressed up against the boulder, she still couldn't put any distance between them, so she quickly swivelled her head to continue watching the ceremony, trying to ignore the heat of him at her back.

"I presume you don't want a literal answer?" he enquired.

She nodded, watching as the final draekons shed their tears into the bowl.

"I see the Giving of Life," Aven said quietly, his exhalation stirring the hairs on the back of her neck. "And I see the receiving of it."

Choosing her next words so very carefully, Alex asked, "Do the draekons receive anything in return for their tears?"

"As humbling as it is to admit, Meya has nothing their great race needs in order to survive, in order to flourish above the clouds," Aven said. "The Draekorans willingly give the *Z'ao* to us as an offering with no expectation of repayment."

Alex watched as the last draekon—Xiraxus—flew down to make his tear sacrifice before returning to the raised outcropping where only Zaronia remained, all the other beasts having disappeared into the darkness of the night. Taking that as their cue, the seven Meyarin councillors stepped forward to stand in a circle around the pool.

Moving as one, the Meyarins reached down, rising up again with their fingers clutching the edges of a flexible kind of glass that Alex hadn't noticed providing a clear, thin barrier above the *traesos* bowl, the *Z'ao* sloshing about within the transparent boundary. Together the Meyarins shuffled away from the pool, moving closer to each other until the *Z'ao* formed the shape of a massive teardrop, its silvery liquid contained fully by the glassy substance.

"We thank you for your sacrifice," one of the Meyarins said, looking up at Zaronia and Xiraxus. Though his head was covered by the glorious robes, Alex recognised the voice as belonging to the king.

"It is ours to freely give," Zaronia returned. "May the blessing of the stars be yours forevermore."

With a bow of his head, Astophe and the rest of his council called forth the *Valispath* and disappeared, the *Z'ao* held carefully between them.

Say what you must, Alex, Xiraxus said to her, having clearly been eavesdropping on her words with Aven. *Do what you can to help your future, but remember that you can't change the past. What will be, will be.*

Alex watched as he and his mother spread their wings and took off into the night before she summoned her courage to turn around and face Aven. Now that they had no one to hide from, there was no need for them to be so close, yet he didn't back away.

"The draekons give their tears freely to Meya," she said, ignoring her discomfort at the lack of personal space, "even knowing they'll receive nothing in return." She braced herself and finished by revisiting their metaphor from weeks ago. "Does that not make you—*us*—like sheep to the wolves?"

Aven's body locked. His eyes flared at her meaningful words, widening in startled wonder before he managed to compose himself. "What you're implying, it's not the same."

"Isn't it?" Alex pressed. "The draekons freely provide Meya with what it needs to continue advancing as a race, to continue flourishing... Just as Meya does for the mortals of Medora."

"We don't want to *become* draekons, though," Aven said, his words oddly strangled.

"The mortals don't want to become immortal, despite what you would believe," Alex whispered. "You said it once yourself, Aven: a sheep can never become a wolf." She reached out and placed a hand against his heart, partly to keep him at arm's length, and partly because she could see his turmoil and wished to provide him a small comfort. "Whatever you think of the humans, they're not stupid. They know they can never ascribe to the glory of an eternal race. It's biologically impossible to change what they are, what they were born to be. They only wish, as you do, to flourish in this world. Would you deny them the help you can provide when it is at such little cost to you?"

He was as still as a statue under the moonlight, but she could see his golden eyes warring with emotion.

Glancing over to the now empty basin, Alex quietly said, "A few tears aren't much to the draekons, but they are everything to Meya." Turning back to look at him meaningfully, she quoted, "'Of those to whom much is given, much is expected.'" Her fingers curled tighter into his chest as she whispered to finish, "You have a responsibility to those dependent on you, Aven. Just as Draekora willingly sacrifices for Meya, so too should Meya follow their lead and support the mortals."

Knowing there was nothing more she could say, Alex waited, watching an inner battle play out across his features. When he eventually released a slow breath, she felt her nervous body relax, but she tensed again when his arms snaked around her, pulling her in for a crushing hug.

"You champion their cause as a mother would fight to protect her child," he whispered into her ear. "But unlike the irrational urges of a guardian parent, your reasoning is… pertinent. Thank you, Aeylia, for sharing your insight. I think I understand better now."

While Alex appreciated his gratitude and hoped that perhaps *something* she'd said had penetrated enough for him to carry it through to the future, she was also alarmed by her current physical predicament—and very much wanting to escape.

Hyper aware of everywhere her body pressed up against his, she found she had no idea what to do with her arms; one hanging awkwardly by her side, the other still on his chest, squashed between them. She decided to use that one to her advantage and increased the pressure against him, thankful when he got the message to step back.

"It's late," he said, saving her from having to come up with a way to fill the gaping silence left in the wake of their worryingly intimate embrace. "You've given me much to think about, but the festival is tomorrow and we both need our rest."

She gave a nod and, before she could put more space between them, he reached out and entwined his fingers with hers, activating the *Valispath* around them and sending them back towards the earth. All the while, she delicately tried to pull free of his grasp, but his fingers only tightened around hers.

Thirty-Three

"Well, aren't you quite the vision?"

Alex whirled around at Niyx's words, her eyes sweeping him from head to toe. He looked like the Meyarin adaptation of a darkly tailored Prince Charming, attired smartly in a black ensemble of collared, vest-like jacket, pants and boots. Even the addition of the sword scabbard at his waist didn't detract from his overall refined air—it just added to how impressive, and slightly dangerous, he looked.

"The same could be said about you," she said with a grin, reaching up to straighten the black filigree mask adhered to his skin, travelling from his left cheek over one eye and coiling diagonally up to finish above his right temple. "You should come with a warning this evening: 'Watch out ladies, I'm on the prowl.'"

Niyx threw back his head and laughed. "If we're to come with warnings, yours would have to say: 'Looks may be deceiving.'"

Alex laughed in return. "Touché."

For the first time since trying to play the part of an immortal, Alex actually felt like she was pulling it off. And that was largely thanks to the outfit the queen and Kyia had chosen for her to wear to the masquerade ball, which was beyond anything Alex had ever seen, let alone worn. When she'd first gazed upon her reflection in the mirror earlier that night, she'd struggled to recognise herself in the dress that looked as if it were made from starlight itself. With a sweetheart neckline, the strapless silvery bodice fit tight to her waist before flowing like waves of molten liquid to the floor. Strands of impossibly thin Myrox were embroidered in swirls across the silky fabric, giving the illusion of radiating light as she moved. Added to that was her shimmering skin from her link with Xiraxus, and Alex felt like she was lit up like the star on the top of a Christmas tree. And yet, she didn't feel gaudy at all, not with the glittery opulence worn by those all around her. She actually fit in with the ethereal race of immortals as if she were one of them, and not merely a human playing dress-up.

"I don't suppose you've seen Aven yet?" Niyx asked, pulling two glassy flutes of bubbling liquid off a passing tray and handing one to Alex.

"Still no sign of him," she responded, taking a sip to keep from nervously chewing on her lip.

The festival was in full swing, as it had been for hours, yet no one had seen Aven at all that day. After an oddly silent trip back to the palace last night, Aven had dropped her off to her room with a soft smile, and neither Alex nor anyone else had seen him since.

That morning she'd been woken as per normal for a dawn sparring session with Niyx, with him reminding her that, summer banquet or not, they only had one day left before she would return to her time and needed to make the most of it. Butterflies had hit her stomach at his words and she'd readily agreed, knowing that while she'd already come so far thanks to his training, there was always more room for improvement.

After finishing their gruelling workout, she'd had breakfast with Niida and played three games of Stix with Astophe, before returning to training *again*. Alex was particularly pleased with herself when, for the first time ever, she managed to win their sparring match—a match in which Niyx hadn't been holding back at all. The approving gleam that entered his eyes had been all the praise she'd needed; it hadn't even mattered that she'd had to lather her numerous wounds with *laendra* to heal any evidence of her mortal blood that had spilled during her conquest. She had fought a Meyarin properly—and *won*.

Thankfully, he called it quits for them on that high note, releasing her to go and enjoy the early afternoon street entertainment that would last until the masquerade.

Skipping through the streets spilling with people, music, food and everything a citywide celebration should be, Alex had been beside herself with glee. She'd felt so alive, surrounded by such vibrant energy. Acrobats and fire twirlers had captivated audiences, and Meyarins had danced without reservation, even drawing Alex in to join them, their merriment contagious.

When the sun had begun to lower on the horizon, Alex had returned to her room where Niida and Kyia had been waiting with unrestrained excitement, both already wearing their own stunning outfits. They'd helped Alex into her magical gown, presenting her with a mask that was equally beautiful, delicately embroidered with thin strands of Myrox that adhered to her skin as if she'd been born wearing it. The three of them had then joined the king and Roka—who Alex had been happy to see, given his absence of late; but she'd been even more pleased to note his open-mouthed reaction upon seeing Kyia in her formalwear—before joining the carousing citizens of Meya, many of whom were packed into the palace ballroom.

Alex had felt a note of pride while taking in the revelling Meyarins and their dazzling attire. Despite having known not the first thing about immortal fashion, she, along with Kyia and Niida, had pulled off a miracle with the outfits. Not a single individual was left lacking in the wardrobe department—males

364 · Lynette Noni

and females alike looked fit to be kings and queens. And she had helped make that happen.

Standing on the sunset balcony of the ballroom with Niyx, Alex came to the sharp realisation that she would miss the Meya of the past. Come tomorrow, she would no longer be considered one of them; she'd no longer be known as Aeylia the Meyarin, she'd be back to being Alex the mortal. She'd once more be targeted by the scathing ire of the future councillors, as well as the hatred of a queen whom she had come to adore. Niyx would detest her, Aven would be back to wanting her dead. And as for Xiraxus, she had no idea what fate would befall him or if she'd ever see him again.

Sure, some things she would be relieved to have back to normal, like Roka and Kyia being together, and Zain not being a wanted criminal. She was also looking forward to not having to worry about hiding her identity, and she couldn't wait to reunite with her friends and family, even if to them no time would have passed. But even so, Alex knew she would forever leave a piece of her heart in the past.

"What troubles you, Aeylia?" Niyx asked, pulling her eyes from the setting sun and back to him.

"It's nothing, Niyx," she answered with a sigh. "I'm just thinking about tomorrow. About the future."

"That sounds like much too weighty a consideration for a party affair," a new voice interrupted.

As one, both Alex and Niyx turned around to find Aven standing directly behind them, his eyes staring at Alex with such unconcealed awe that she struggled not to fidget at his blatant perusal.

"Where have you been all day?" Niyx demanded, his voice filled with irritated concern.

"There was something I had to do," Aven said vaguely, tearing his gaze from Alex to look at Niyx. "A last-minute festival matter of great importance. But I'm here now."

Here he was, indeed; a striking vision of black and gold, wearing the colours of Royal House Dalmarta with pride, just like the rest of his family.

"I actually have a favour to ask of you, Niyx, if you don't mind?" Aven said. "Aeylia, would you excuse us a moment? I promise, I'll be right back."

She nodded, perplexed as to his singular wording that implied he would be returning alone. Alex had to make a quick decision—either she ducked out and later offered an excuse for disappearing, or she accepted that this was one of the last moments she would ever spend on amicable terms with her future enemy. Regardless of how careful she knew she had to be around him, Alex wasn't ready to say goodbye to the Aven of the past just yet. So she stayed put and patiently waited, staring out at the fading sunshine bathing the glorious city and its street-strewn partygoers.

"Sorry about that," Aven said a few minutes later as he approached her again. "It should be a crime to leave someone as beautiful as you alone on an evening like this."

Discomforted by his disturbingly sweet compliment, Alex said, "There's plenty going on around here to keep me entertained."

Aven gave a short laugh, looking down at the revellers celebrating up a storm. "It does appear that everyone is enjoying themselves."

"You've done a fabulous job, Aven," Alex said, her tone genuine. "You should be really proud of yourself."

He waved aside her praise and jokingly said, "No one cares about what I did; they're all just happy to be wearing such fine clothes."

Alex felt her lips curl upwards, knowing that he was just being humble and realising how ridiculous that was. *This* was why she wasn't ready to end her time with him, because come tomorrow, humble Aven would be a thing of the past—literally.

"I have a surprise for you," he said, his eyes bright. "But first, I want to—"

Whatever he wanted, Alex didn't hear, because right then a deafening cheer rose from the ballroom as a troupe of performers began a choreographed aerial display that seemingly defied gravity. Like all the onlookers, Alex was hypnotised by their flowing movements and limbered stunts. It was only when she felt Aven's gentle touch on her bare shoulder that she turned back to him, having forgotten that he'd been in the middle of speaking.

"Do you mind if we go somewhere quiet and talk?" he asked, speaking loudly over the increased music and applause. "It'll only take a minute."

She looked from him to the acrobats and back again, feeling torn. It had been one thing to wait for him on the balcony, but it was another entirely to leave the party with him.

"Please?" he said, seeing her indecision.

It was his vulnerable tone that got to her, prompting her to give a slight nod of agreement against her better judgement.

Smiling widely, Aven stepped closer and activated the *Valispath*. He didn't say anything as they soared away from the palace, nor did he speak as they rose atop the Golden Cliffs and continued into the Silverwood. It was only when they came to a stop at the edge of Raelia that he turned to her, the last rays of sunlight shining through the canopy and catching his golden mask, creating an angelic effect.

"Do you remember this place?" Aven asked.

More than you can know, she thought, looking around the forested crossroads, but all she said was, "I do."

"Do you remember what you told me that night?"

That Alex didn't recall, so she shook her head.

"You said that no one can tell us how we should feel," he recounted. "As a prince of Meya, I've had to live my life by a set of values. I've resented that, never knowing if I believe what I believe because *I* believe it, or because it's what's *expected* of me. My disagreement with my father over the mortals was the first time I felt anything strongly enough to question my family and fight for something I *truly* believed in. It was a powerful, heady feeling to stand for a cause I considered just, to have others stand alongside me."

He paused, took a breath, moved a step closer. "Last night, you made me realise how wrong I was."

Alex's mouth opened in a silent gasp.

"I became so determined to prove that I could have different feelings, that I could have beliefs that were my own, that I became blinded by my passion for what I considered justice. I wouldn't listen to reason—my father's, Roka's, not even yours. Even when I began to wonder if I was being naïve, if it wasn't the big deal I was making it out to be, I was then too afraid to change my stance, fearing my feelings again weren't my own, but rather those that were expected of me. But last night, Aeylia, you helped me see that I was wrong, and that even if I wasn't, none of it matters."

He reached out a hand, pressing it against her bare cheek, the tips of his fingers just touching her mask. Too transfixed by his words, she didn't have the presence of mind to pull away.

"I won't lie to you," he said. "I still don't like the idea of us giving so much to the mortals, since I do consider them inferior, regardless of the parallels you so astutely highlighted with our dependence on the Draekorans. But I realise now that Meyarins far older and wiser than myself have decided in favour of supporting the mortals. Those same Meyarins have listened to my voice and the voices of my Rebels, and now I understand it is time for me to yield to the leadership of our city and have my *Garseth* stand down. The council will decide what is best for our future, and the future of the mortals. I don't have to agree with them—you helped me realise that—but as a citizen of Meya, I do have to respect their decision. And now more than ever I'm okay with that."

Mind reeling, Alex repeated, "Now more than ever?"

A smile touched his lips. "Let's just say that of late I haven't been as... dedicated to my own cause as I should have been. Something much more important has been distracting me."

Oh, crap, Alex thought, noting the meaningful look in his eyes. Suddenly realising just how close they were standing, with his hand still on her cheek, she pulled back, retreating a step.

"Aven," she said, her voice a whisper.

"Aeylia, surely you must know how I feel about you."

She put up a hand between them but he ignored it and moved closer, prompting her to edge backwards again. "Aven, please—"

"Everyone seems to know," he said, appearing both amused and slightly exasperated. "My mother is in raptures. Apparently she picked you for me the moment she first laid eyes on you. She's been thanking the stars ever since your arrival."

Alex resisted the urge to groan. She'd thought Niida was just that nice to everyone. But now she wondered how much of their bonding was because the queen saw her as a potential daughter-in-law.

This is so not good, Alex thought, wondering how she was supposed to find a way out of her current predicament and wishing she'd left the ballroom balcony when she'd had the chance.

"Are you going to say anything?" Aven asked, still heading towards her, with them now moving deeper into the dense trees surrounding the clearing.

Alex pushed away a thin, low-hanging branch that poked into her back, snapping it as she continued scrambling backwards through the forest.

"Aven, I'm not sure——"

"I am, Aeylia," he interrupted, his expression fervent as he reached out in a blur of movement, grabbing her shoulders to stop her retreat. "I've never been more sure of anything in my life."

Alex felt like a caged animal, caught in his grip as she was. She shrugged her arms, trying to dislodge his hands, but he wouldn't release her.

"Take a moment," he offered. "Think about it and you'll realise that I'm right. That *we're* right. Please, Aeylia—you know what I'm saying is true. Don't you feel the same?"

Niyx! Alex cried frantically in her mind, having no idea of the etiquette required to carefully but effectively turn down a prince's unreciprocated advances. *Aven's just told me that he——*

She couldn't finish her line of thought so she shoved the memory of Aven's declaration through their mental link and asked, *What should I do?*

Niyx's response was immediate, a string of curse words in her mind, followed by, *I was hoping he'd wait until the festival mania had passed and then it wouldn't matter since you'd be gone. But there's nothing for it now—you have to tell him the truth.*

Alex's eyes widened. *Are you crazy?*

Not that truth, Aeylia, Niyx said. *The truth of how you feel about him.*

But I don't like him like that, Niyx, Alex said. *You know I don't.*

It's not me you have to tell, Aeylia. Just be gentle—he's in a vulnerable place right now.

Yeah, no kidding, Alex thought, but she didn't project that to Niyx. Instead she focused back on Aven who was still waiting for her response, presuming, most likely, that she was taking his advice to 'think about it'.

Hands shaking, Alex reached out and placed her fingers over his heart. His face brightened at her familiar action, thinking she was agreeing with him, so she quickly forced herself to quietly say, "Aven, I'm so sorry, but I just don't feel that way about you."

Immediately his brightness seeped away, and as if the sun itself was attuned to his emotions, the light faded from the forest as twilight descended. Alex would have considered it poetic if she hadn't felt so awful.

"You're a wonderful friend," she said, not believing she was pulling the 'let's be friends' card, but since her Meyarin dating practices weren't exactly up to speed, she had nothing else to work with. "I would hate to jeopardise that when I know I can't return what you feel."

In a flash, his hands moved off her shoulders and he stepped back, breaking free of her touch. He ran a hand through his honey-coloured hair, unable to meet her eyes.

"At the risk of sounding egotistical, I wasn't expecting that," he said, his voice rough.

Alex stepped towards him. "Aven—"

"No," he said, holding up a hand. "Just—Just no."

And with that, he spun and strode purposefully back through the dense trees, as if his sole mission in life was to get away from her.

Go after him, Alex told herself. *Go after him or you won't get a chance to say goodbye.*

If she let Aven out of her sight, if he had a chance to retreat into his rejection and lick his wounds, she knew she wouldn't see him again that night. He'd soon take off on the *Valispath* and disappear. And tomorrow, she would be gone. She couldn't stand the idea of their last meeting in the past ending with him storming away from her in humiliating defeat.

"Aven, wait!" she cried, picking up her skirt and running after him, ignoring the branches snagging on her gown as the thick forest resisted her hurried movements.

"Aven, please," she said, stepping up behind him just as he shouldered his way past a thin overhanging branch.

Because all nature hated Alex, she wasn't surprised when the branch didn't snap, but instead it flung back to slap her in the face, causing her to cry out in pain, "Ouch!"

Her startled yelp halted Aven's retreat and he spun around, his face showing that he hadn't realised she was so close.

"Stars, Aeylia," he said, his expression instantly apologetic. "I didn't know—"

"It's not your fault," she was quick to tell him, rapidly blinking her eyes as they teared up from the sting. "I know you didn't do it deliberately."

"Still," he said, bending slightly to get a better look at her face in the shadows of the fading light.

"It's okay—it doesn't even hurt anymore," she lied, taking in his now agonised features and wondering how much of that look was because he thought he'd hurt her, and how much of it was because of how *she'd* hurt him. "Truly, I can't feel it at all."

Aven's body was so still. All Alex wanted to do was comfort him; apologise for not returning his feelings; let him know how much she'd enjoyed their time together. But before she could say anything, his eyes caught hers, and she swiftly inhaled at the tormented fire in them.

Then, without another word, he bolted.

One moment he was there, the next he was gone.

Alex blew out a frustrated, sad breath and carefully picked her way back through the remaining forest, realising that the only thing *worse* than her last sight of him being his humiliated defeat, was his *panicked* humiliated defeat.

Miserable with her thoughts, once Alex reached the open crossroads she called up the *Valispath*, but she wasn't ready to return to the palace just yet, so she guided it to take her to her familiar spot on the edge of the Golden Cliffs.

Standing there overlooking the celebrations in full swing, Alex took a moment to steady herself and then called out to Niyx, *You might want to check in on Aven. I'm not sure if my 'gentle' was gentle enough.*

A mental sigh came as his response. *What happened?*

Alex showed him, hating that she had to watch it all again, and *especially* hating the look on his face at the end. Something about it just ripped her to shreds.

Where are you? Niyx asked.

Top of the cliffs, Alex answered, knowing he wouldn't need any more information, since where she was standing was the place where she'd Claimed him.

There's no way Aven will want company right now, but I'm guessing you could use it, Niyx said. *Stay where you are, I'll be there in a minute.*

She was grateful for his support, even if right then she didn't feel as if she deserved it. Not when she'd just brought so much distress to his best friend. *I'm sorry, Niyx. I stuffed everything up.*

Shut up, Aeylia, he said. *Just tell me you at least acted grateful when he told you about his surprise gift?*

That gave Alex pause. *His what?*

His gift—His present for you. When Alex remained silent, Niyx added, *Didn't he tell you about his surprise? Why he was missing all day? The favour he asked me?*

I have no idea what you're talking about, Alex said, though she did recall Aven mentioning before they'd left the ballroom balcony that he had a surprise for her.

Niyx made a frustrated sound, though whether it was aimed towards her or Aven, she wasn't sure. *Then you don't know about the mortals.*

Putting the pieces together, Alex replied, *Actually, I do. He told me he's giving up his Rebel cause.*

Despite knowing that it wouldn't last, it still meant a lot to her that Aven had been willing to see reason because of her encouragement.

No, Aeylia, that's not—I'm not talking about his change of beliefs, though it's good to see you helped him see reason.

His response surprised Alex, since they'd never before discussed the depth of his affiliation with the *Garseth*—she'd deliberately avoided the issue given what she knew of his future.

Someone had to open his eyes to how ridiculous he was being, and light knows he wasn't listening to me, Niyx continued. *I don't know what you said to him, but you did well on that one.*

Alex wasn't sure if it was appropriate to say 'thank you', but before she could figure it out, Niyx spoke again.

But that's not what I meant when I said you don't know about the mortals. I'm talking about the ones who are here in the city tonight.

Alex jerked violently and mentally whispered, *What?*

Aven spent all day searching for them, Niyx continued. *A small group of traders he thought you'd like to see again, or so he told me when he pulled me aside and asked me to keep an eye on them until you returned. Their invitation was his gift to you—a gesture of his intent to end his rebellion against his father's policies. It was his way of showing you that you mean more to him than any plan for what he considers justice.*

Alex felt as if the ground had just been torn out from underneath her. Black dots blurred at the edges of her vision as words screamed across her memory, words spoken to her months ago from the dungeon where D.C. had briefed her on the history of Meya: *'The next time a human trading delegation entered the city, they killed them. All of them.'*

Aeylia? Niyx called, at the same time as Xiraxus, with the draekon having sensed her distress. She didn't answer either of them, so lost in her panic as she was.

"Aeylia?"

This time the words were spoken aloud, Niyx having now arrived on the cliffs beside her.

She turned woodenly to him and opened her mouth, unable to respond, let alone get her thoughts together.

He reached out a hand, touching his fingers to the space just beneath her eye, right near the edge of her mask. "Stars, what happened to your face?"

Lost in her panic, Alex barely heard his question.

"Wait, is this…" Niyx trailed off, frowning in concentration. "In your memories…" His face paled. "Aeylia, is this where the branch hit you?"

Numb with fear, she struggled to draw air into her tight chest. "It's nothing, Niyx," she wheezed. "We have a much bigger problem right now."

It didn't matter if the humans weren't in the city tonight to trade—they were still a trading delegation who had entered the city. D.C.'s history report may have been wrong with its implication, but the horror of the remembered words struck Alex much worse than the sting of any branch to her face. If that version of history was correct, Aven's *Garseth* were going to massacre the humans—tonight.

"But that doesn't make any sense," Alex said out loud, her eyes remaining unfocused even when Niyx whispered her name in a strangled sounding voice.

Ignoring Aven's recent change of beliefs, there had been no evidence as of yet that he exhibited any desire to kill mortals— just to end the trade agreement. There was no way he was going to take off on a murderous rampage tonight that would see D.C.'s words come true. For that to happen, he would need something impossibly drastic to push him over the edge. Something that—

"Aeylia," Niyx whispered again, his horrified tone piercing through the haze of her mind this time. "Please tell me Aven didn't see your face."

Before she could lose her thin grasp on her panic and break her promise by ordering him to forget about her face, he pulled his hand away, holding his thumb up so she could see the reason for his stricken expression.

Blood.

Deep red blood.

She slapped her hand to her cheek, feeling the thin welt just beneath her eye and the trickle of blood on her skin.

"*No*," she gasped, remembering the agonised look on Aven's face, the fiery torment in his gaze. That hadn't been his reaction to her rejection—it was his reaction to seeing her blood. It was his reaction to realising that he'd been lied to by a mortal, betrayed by a mortal... That he'd *fallen* for a mortal.

If there was anything that could send Aven over the edge of reason and turn him into a cold-blooded murderer, Alex knew that could do it.

Another memory came to her then, one that had eluded her when she'd tried to recall it weeks ago upon realising it was a valid warning from the Niyx of the future: *'With the lashing of the branch, the time will be at hand. All will change... Or rather, nothing will.'*

Eyes welling with terror, Alex didn't wait a moment longer. She took a running leap off the cliff and ignored Niyx's startled yell as she summoned the *Valispath* around her, heading straight for the palace.

Thirty-Four

It was the screaming Alex heard first, her Meyarin ears picking up the sound long before her eyes caught sight of the reason for it. Her mind blanked at the frenzied cries, causing her to relinquish control on the *Valispath*, which dumped her unceremoniously a few streets away from the palace.

Feeling as if she was moving through a fuzzy haze, Alex hurried her way through the masses of Meyarins until a space opened up at the base of the palace where a group of armed *Zeltora* were trying to calm those who couldn't get away fast enough. It seemed surreal to think that just minutes before they had all been laughing and dancing. And now they were screaming.

Unlike the stricken Meyarins trying to escape, Alex pushed her way forwards, her eyes trained on the grizzly sight in front of her.

They were all there. All six of them. Bensie Hayes and her fellow humans. Alex couldn't remember the names of the others, but she recognised their faces. Aven had found them and invited them to the festival—as a present for Alex.

A present he and his *Garseth* had slaughtered in an act of blind rage.

Walking on deadened legs, Alex moved close enough to squat down and pick up Bensie's beret, ignoring the splatter of blood on it as she pressed the cap tight to her chest, heedless of the stain it was leaving on her dress.

She heard a whimpering sound and looked around only to realise the noise was coming from her. She pressed her quivering lips together, but the sound continued inside her head, like a high-pitched ringing in her ears.

"Aeylia, what—what happened here?" Niyx whispered, having apparently followed her from the cliffs.

She turned to see his whitened face, his gaping, horror-struck expression as he took in the mindless, violent carnage in front of them.

It was then that she knew.

He'd had nothing to do with it.

She stared as the realisation washed over her. Niyx may have been Aven's best friend, he may have supported Aven, gone to the *Garseth* meetings, been a constant by Aven's side… But he'd had nothing to do with the deaths of the humans. He didn't even believe in the anti-mortal cause, if his earlier words were true.

Niyx was… He was *innocent*.

And yet, in her future, he'd been imprisoned for thousands of years.

"I'm sorry, Niyx," Alex said to him in a whisper. "But I have to break my promise."

He was too stunned by the gruesome scene before them to take notice of her words, to even turn away from the sight of crimson spilling into the *myraes*-lit city street.

All around them the masked Meyarins were still screaming and running, crying and shouting, but Alex ignored them all to focus on what needed to be done.

Given his closeness to Aven, Niyx would eventually end up imprisoned for a crime he didn't commit, but she would do everything in her power to give him a head start before the *Zeltora* began to track down Aven's known accomplices. It was the least she could do after everything he'd done to help her. He was not her enemy—not now, not in the future. She knew that now.

"I'm sorry, Niyx," she whispered again. *Sorry for so, so much.*

"What *happened* here?" he asked again, finally dragging his eyes to hers.

Knowing secrecy didn't matter anymore, Alex answered with one word: "Aven."

Niyx reared back in disbelieving shock. Alex watched his face contort into a painful mixture of emotions: devastation, anger, sadness; both surprised and strangely not surprised at what his friend was capable of when pushed. Then, with the purple of his eyes standing out vividly against the black of his mask, he whispered, "The Meyarin in your future. The enemy of yours—the one who Claimed you, who wants to destroy the world…"

Alex nodded, the truth settling like a vice against her chest. "Yes, it's Aven. That's who you were training me to fight. That's who I need to defeat to keep that vision from coming true."

Niyx looked as if his world had just crashed around him. "How could he—Why would he—*How could he*—"

"I'm sorry, Niyx," Alex said for the third time. "But for what happens next, you shouldn't be anywhere close to here. You should get away, as far and as fast as you can. Trust me on that. It won't—" Her breath hitched, but she caught the sob before it could escape. "It won't make much of a difference, but it might make some."

"Aeylia—"

"Don't follow me, Niyx." Despite her whispered words, her voice was firm as she broke her promise to not give him an order against his will. She felt the tugging between them, and tears welled in her eyes at his anguished, knowing look.

"Aeylia, what—"

Before he could finish his broken question, she reached forward and wrapped her arms around him, pulling him close for a tight, desperate embrace. "I'm so sorry, Niyx," she whispered one last time into his ear—sorry for everything he would go through, sorry for everything she couldn't protect him from. "But this, at least, is one promise I *can* keep."

As he stiffened in her arms, she silently summoned A'enara behind his back, slicing the blade along the scar at her palm. She was so numb that she barely felt the pain as she pulled back and, quick as a flash, reached for Niyx's hand, her blade carving open his flesh. His eyes widened in understanding and he tried to break free, but it was too late. Alex had already joined their bloodied hands together—red and silver.

Trae Gaverran sae, she whispered into his mind, the power of the words flowing between them. With tears of apology, regret and fear in her eyes, she gave her final order to him aloud as well. "I Release you, Niyx."

As if the line tugging between them was suddenly cut, Alex felt the link that had connected them start to uncurl with the Release of her Claim on him.

His expression was ravaged as he looked down at her. "Aeylia—"

She wouldn't let herself wait to hear whatever he was going to say. She knew the words would kill her, just as she knew she needed to get inside the palace to find Roka. History told her that Aven and his *Garseth* took off after their slaughter before onlookers could capture them, but she knew he would soon be found and brought before the king, and when that happened, she had to be prepared.

… Because after he offered a feigned apology for his actions, he would then try to kill his father and brother.

D.C. had said their deaths were only avoided thanks to the arrival of the guards, but looking around at the mayhem in the streets, Alex guessed that might not be an accurate retelling. She was the only one who understood the threat Aven posed to his family. She was the only one who knew to stop him before he could do more harm.

"Don't follow me," she whispered again to Niyx. While he was no longer bound to follow any new commands, that one was given before she'd Released him and would remain in effect, hopefully giving him a fighting chance to stave off his inevitable imprisonment for as long as possible.

With one last look at his tortured face, she spun on her heel and took off into the palace.

Alex sprinted up the spiral towers, passing traumatised Meyarins along the way. She didn't slow, not even when she sailed by Kyia who had her arms around a shell-shocked Niida, both looking up just in time to catch the blur of Alex running by. The queen's sorrowful golden eyes told Alex she knew Aven was responsible—that her worst nightmare had come true. But it was Kyia's emerald gaze that almost caused Alex to stumble in her near-flying steps, because the Meyarin's focus was locked onto the blood of the scratch on Alex's face. Too panicked to care about hiding her mortality anymore, Alex didn't stop, ignoring Kyia when she choked out a sound of shocked alarm.

Alex! Talk to me! What's going on down there?

Running through the palace, Alex realised she had been so lost in her own fear that she'd not heard Xiraxus screaming for her attention ever since she'd left the Golden Cliffs. Now heading up the grand staircases towards the throne room, she called back, *Aven just killed the humans, Xira! They're dead! And it's all my fault!*

A stunned silence reached her before he replied, *I'm almost at the city, Alex. We can't wait for tomorrow—we need to get you back to your time now, before anything happens to you.*

I have to save Roka and Astophe first, she said, nearing the throne room. *I have to—*

She broke off when the sound of a struggle reached her ears, along with the shouted yells, "I'm not with him, you *kregons*! I'm the one who caught him—I *brought* him to you! Prince Roka just told you to let me go—so *let me go*!"

"It doesn't matter that you're not a traitorous *Garseth*; you're still a wanted criminal," came a grunting reply as the struggling sounds continued. "We'll lock you in *Taevarg* and deal with you once this situation with the prince is under control."

As Alex rounded the corner and reached the hallway leading to the throne room, she came to a sliding stop at the sight of Zain fighting not one, not two, but six *Zeltora*, trying to free himself from their hold.

"Aeylia! What—"

Alex spun around at Kyia's voice, the female Meyarin having chased after her. But she didn't have time to deal with Kyia right now, nor did she have time to deal with Zain—and that was because she'd heard his shouted words: *'I'm the one who caught him—I* brought *him to you!'*

Aven was already in with the king. And so was Roka, according to Zain's other exclamation. If Alex didn't hurry...

"Help him!" she screamed at Kyia, pointing to Zain. "I need to get past them!"

She wasn't sure whether it was the shrill sound of her panicked voice or the terrified look she was certain she wore, but for whatever reason, Kyia decided to trust Alex, tearing off down the corridor to defend Zain against the *Zeltora* and clear a path for Alex to break through.

Knowing her two friends could handle themselves, Alex advanced forward until she reached the double doors into the throne room, bursting through them and skidding to a halt.

Her breath came out in gasping pants as she took in the sight before her: Astophe lying face down on the ground, silver liquid leaking from his back and staining his formal clothes;

Roka struggling against Aven, trying to hold his brother back but weakening by the second from the blood gushing out of his femoral artery.

At the sound of Alex's entrance, Aven leapt up from where he was crouched over Roka, the sword he held dripping silver to the floor.

What little breath remained in her lungs fled at the murderous expression on his face.

"You!" he bellowed. "You did this!"

"Aven," Alex wheezed out, hands raised in supplication. "Please."

"They wouldn't listen to me." He slashed his blade violently towards his father and brother. "They wouldn't listen when I told them what you'd done, what you *were*. They were more concerned by what happened to those vermin out there." He hissed his last words, throwing his hand to indicate the bloodied streets beneath them. "They didn't even *care* that a mortal had been lying to us for weeks, betraying us, *for weeks*."

"I didn't betray you," she whispered.

"*I fell for you!*" he screamed, his eyes molten gold. "I actually thought—" He broke off with a strangled sound, raised a knuckle to his mouth as if needing to bite back his words.

"When I came in here," he said, his voice lower, but still simmering with fury, "my own father wouldn't believe me about you, didn't *care* about you, not after what my *Garseth* and I had done to his precious mortals. But Roka—my dear *brother*—" Aven spat the word, mercilessly stamping his boot down on Roka's wound and eliciting a desperate cry of pain from the downed prince. "He already *knew*."

Alex's stomach clenched as she jolted forward, only to freeze again at the look Aven levelled her. All she could do was watch with muted shock as the white-faced Roka tried to rise only to collapse on his blood-spouting leg with another muffled groan.

"He knew the filth you were and he never told me," Aven hissed. "The person I trusted most in this world—he just watched, laughing, as I fell for a disgusting *mortal*."

"Aven—"

"*Shut your mouth, human!*" Aven roared, taking a threatening step forward, only to halt again. He inhaled loudly and rolled his neck as if to compose himself. "The only way to ensure our glorious city remains free of your infestation is if I sit on the throne." He pointed to Astophe and Roka again. "They have to die. For the sake of Meya, I've done what was needed. And having intimately experienced the deceit you disgusting mortals are capable of, I would do it again in a heartbeat, if you hadn't already ripped mine to shreds with your betrayal."

Alex caught a sob in her throat. The Aven in front of her wasn't the one she had come to know in the past, but nor was he the one she knew in the future. The Aven of her time had spent years channeling his rage, sharpening his focus into calculated strategy. But *this* Aven was spitting fire, blinded by an animalistic bloodlust. If he'd only stop for a moment, he would realise that everything he'd said—none of it made sense. The mindless killing of mortals. The murdering of his own *family*. These weren't the actions of someone who had been betrayed or rejected. They were the actions of someone who had stepped over the edge of sanity, someone who was too far gone to come back to reason.

It was only because she realised she was dealing with a very different kind of danger—a very different *Aven* to the menace she knew in the future—that Alex was prepared to react when faced with what he did next.

"The king will be dead in moments," he whispered, a feverish expression on his face, his gaze unfocused. "As will my brother."

And with an upward swing of his arm, his sword slashed down towards the now barely conscious Roka, aiming straight for his heart.

The blade didn't make contact though, and that was because Alex leapt forward, summoning A'enara in a burst of fire to meet his strike mid-air.

Aven's teeth snapped at her, the intensity of his fury sending a tremor down her flaming arms.

"No mortal will deny me of what is rightfully mine," he stated fiercely. "Least of all *you*."

And that's when he turned to her fully, lashing out with his sword.

Reacting on instinct and trusting what she'd learned from Niyx, Alex met Aven thrust for thrust, over and over again, not allowing herself to think beyond the next parry, the next deflection, the next lunge. He was competent, very competent, but his skills hadn't yet been honed by thousands of years like the Aven of the future. And that gave Alex an edge over him— or at least put her on somewhat equal footing. With every attack she managed to defend against and with every offence of her own, his eyes widened more and more at the realisation that she was fighting him not as a mortal, but as a Meyarin.

And when his shock overcame him so much that with one heaving sideways slash she was able to force the sword from his hands to clatter across the room, he stood gaping at her, only to roar, "WHAT *ARE* YOU?"

It was then that Alex did something stupid. Something *so damn stupid*. And it happened because the doors to the throne room were flung open, revealing the fight-rumpled Zain and Kyia—Kyia who, with fear flooding her features, bolted for Roka, just as Zain moved to the king's side, bellowing for the guards they'd likely just sent scrambling. But when those guards surged into the room, they were so stunned by the scene that they froze. They only managed to leap into action when another group of Meyarins stormed into the room—a handful of Rebels who Alex recognised from the midnight meeting at The Scarlet Thief—and it was then that all hell broke loose as swords went flying between *Garseth* and *Zeltora*, with Kyia and Zain jumping up to join the guards.

It was in watching all this that Alex had stupidly, *stupidly* taken her eyes off Aven, giving him the opportunity to make his move against her unguarded self.

Before she knew it, he was upon her, his hands covering hers as they wrestled over A'enara. She struggled against him, watching agony fill his face as the flames seared into his flesh; but pained or not, he didn't loosen his hold.

Exerting a force stronger than anything she could defend against, he shoved their grappling hands in a downwards arc faster than Alex could stop. The momentum was too much for her to stave off, and with a sickening squelching sound, the ice-coloured blade slashed down…

… and drove violently into her stomach.

Alex sucked in a choking gasp, the pain instantly flooding her body as she hunched over in shock.

ALEX! Xiraxus screamed in her mind, followed by the distressed roar of the draekon rumbling outside, echoing across the city like a clap of thunder.

There was no way she could respond to him. Not when she was blinded by shards of lightning tearing through her middle; not when she was drowning for air, barely able to draw hacking, wet breaths into her lungs.

She sank to her knees, and as she did so, Aven lowered himself with her, his hands still over hers at the hilt of the blade lodged in her abdomen.

In the back of her mind, Alex wondered how long it would take before Kyia and Zain helped the guards overcome the

Garseth, how long before anyone realised she was on her knees at Aven's mercy. But since she could still hear the clashing of swords ringing in an eternal echo, she knew no one would reach her in time. She was on her own.

Struck with the realisation that she was going to die, Alex couldn't do anything when Aven released one of his hands and raised it to her face, peeling the mask from her skin and casting it aside. He stared deeply into her eyes for a long moment, his bloodied-red fingers cupping her cheek in a mocking caress, before he leaned forward to whisper in her ear, "I swear by the stars that you and the others slain tonight will be the first of many. Of that you have my word."

And then with a brutal heave he yanked A'enara from her flesh, causing her to double over and collapse at his feet, her body convulsing as her hands weakly pressed against her fatal wound.

"No mortal was ever intended to wield this blade," Aven said, rising to stand and looking pitilessly down at her from above. "You, at least, will never taint it with your filth again."

He then looked away from her, taking in the chaos of the *Zeltora* battling the *Garseth*, a muscle clenching in his jaw at the realisation that he wouldn't be able to finish what he'd started with the king and Roka. He released a furious, frustrated snarl and spun on his heel, sliding A'enara into the empty scabbard at his waist. The weapon was bonded to Alex, so it wasn't his to summon—yet—and she knew that if she had the strength to lift her hand she would be able to call it back into her possession, keeping it from him and the unspeakable things he would go on to do with it. But with her vision fading alarmingly fast and her now numb body suffocating for oxygen, all she could do was watch him sprint away with her weapon in tow. The moment he was outside the throne room's wards she knew he would activate the *Valispath* and flee from the city, from his home, from the place he wouldn't see again for thousands of years, not until Alex herself helped him to return.

With a gagging, heaving, sobbing sound, Alex rolled over, staring unseeingly up at the opulent ceiling of the throne room as she hazily contemplated the vicious cycle of time, the utter irony of the cosmic joke that was her life.

It was just as her ears began to deafen and darkness spread across her vision that the doors flew open once more and in stumbled Niyx, his hands pressed to his bleeding stomach, his eyes wild in search of Alex amid the chaos.

"Niyx, you traitorous *Garseth*!" Zain yelled, fighting three Rebels at once. "You'll pay for what you've done—just like the rest of your friends!"

Niyx ignored him and staggered over to Alex, reaching down to draw her gently up into his arms. "*You*, kitten, are going to be the death of me."

And that was the last thing she heard before her eyes rolled into the back of her head and all turned black.

Thirty-Five

"She's going to be all right."

"I know she's going to be all right. I'm the one who told you that after I shoved enough laendra *down her throat and over her stomach to last her a lifetime's worth of stab wounds."*

"I didn't need you to tell me—I can feel it. It's slow, but she's healing."

"I can feel it too, draekon. More than you, I'd wager, since I doubt you've just experienced the phantom skewering of your small intestine. For the record, it's not as pleasant as it sounds."

"That doesn't sound pleasant at all."

"You're a quick one, Xira."

Alex groaned at the buzzing voices, wanting them to disappear so she could stay asleep, preferably forever.

"Aeylia? Can you hear me? Kitten, I need you to open your eyes."

A gentle hand patted her cheek, lightly tapping against her skin. She wrinkled her nose at it, wanting it to go away and let her rest.

"That's it, time to wake up now," the soft voice said, turning harder to finish, "so I can kick your ass for letting Aven stab you—and therefore, *me*—in the gut."

With a gasp, Alex's eyes opened as recollection of everything that had happened flashed through her mind. She bolted upright, thankful when Niyx's reflexes made him move fast enough to avoid a collision between their heads.

Sucking in heaving gulps of air as if she'd been underwater for too long, Alex couldn't hold her weight and collapsed back to the ground. The hulking face of Xiraxus immediately blocked out the view of the dark sky above her, his concern evident in his eyes.

"You're okay, Alex," the draekon said soothingly. Then he corrected, "Well, actually, you've lost a lot of blood—too much. You're really weak, so try not to get too worked up or you'll faint again."

"And wasn't that a load of fun, carrying you up here on the *Valispath* and trying not to pass out myself from *your* injuries," Niyx added in a mutter.

"How—How—" she panted out, but she didn't have the strength to finish her question verbally, so she called out to Niyx in her mind, stunned and dismayed when she felt the connection between them firmly back in place.

How are you still bonded to me? she asked him. *I Released you! I said the words! I did exactly what the book said to do!*

"You did everything right," Niyx said out loud. "But for a Claiming bond to be truly severed, the recipient of it has to be willing to be Released. When I felt the initial uncurling of the bond after your words, I needed to have said, 'I accept my Release'—but I didn't. It was me who wouldn't let go of the connection between us. That means your Claim on me is still effective."

Well, there definitely hadn't been anything about *that* in the book she'd read.

Alex's face scrunched up in confusion. *But... Niyx, why would you...* She took a shallow breath and tried again. *Didn't you want to be Released?*

He offered her a quirky, one-sided grin. "Turns out you're a riot to be around, kitten. Like a one-stop entertainment shop. Who would willingly give up that kind of fun?"

I don't have the energy for what you consider 'humour' right now, Alex told him. *Please, Niyx. I don't understand.*

His face turned serious and he helped her up into a seated position leaning against Xiraxus's front leg. The move cost her, with pain surging through her middle and her vision dotting at the edges, Niyx wincing along with her. When she was able to focus again, she discovered they were situated at their lookout atop the Golden Cliffs. Hours must have passed since she was last there, since the moon had now well and truly risen in the sky.

"You can't be here," she managed to gasp out, looking at Niyx with wide eyes. "They think you're one of the *Garseth*. You need to get as far away from here as you can before they come looking for you."

"There's nowhere I can go that will be far enough away," Niyx returned quietly. "And since you're so determined that I try to escape, I have to presume that, in your future, I don't."

Alex couldn't hold his gaze, but that in itself was telling.

Niyx released a sigh and nudged her shoulder gently, calling her focus back to him. "You're very weak, Aeylia, but you're not safe here. Aven may have fled, but if I know him—and I *do*—he'll still be nearby, at least until he can no longer find sanctuary in the city. Xiraxus is confident that he now has the strength to return you to your future, so you have to go with him. Tonight."

Alex nodded, knowing it was time. She'd already caused enough damage. For all she knew, a sneeze gone wrong could start the Medoran equivalent of the bubonic plague next, so good was her luck of late.

"Will you answer my question first?" she begged hoarsely, needing to know. "Will you tell me why you wouldn't let me Release you?"

"Aeylia, I'd just learned that my *best friend* had turned into a raging psychopath," Niyx said quietly. "I'm smart enough to realise that merely by association, I'm automatically labelled as a traitor, and no one will believe otherwise since I *did* willingly attend the Rebel meetings he hosted, with plenty of witnesses to testify to that. No one will ever believe I was only there to make sure Aven wasn't planning anything too foolish."

Niyx shook his head, angry with himself. "Along with all that, you'd just told me it's him you have to defeat to avoid the destruction of this world." He raised an eyebrow and finished, "Do you really think I was willing to risk you dying here in the past if it meant *that* was the future we'd be heading towards?"

"How did you know I'd be in any danger?" Alex asked, certain she hadn't given anything away earlier about going to face Aven inside the palace.

Niyx's expression was as dry as his tone when he replied, "Aeylia, you told me not to follow you. For future reference, that's a dead giveaway."

With a furrowed brow, Alex asked, "You're right, I *did* tell you not to follow me. I ordered you, actually. You shouldn't have been able to—"

"I didn't follow you, not technically," Niyx broke in. "I merely decided I wanted to walk around the palace, and I just *happened* to visit every room until I accidentally stumbled upon you. Loopholes, kitten. There are always loopholes."

Alex closed her eyes slowly, feeling so very tired. But a sudden resolve came over her and she opened them again. "Niyx, you have to let me Release you from the Claim."

"I have to do no such thing," he returned. "*Someone* has to make sure you stay alive long enough to save the future. Who better than me, since I can feel everything you feel? Even your draekon here only gets impressions of your emotional health, not your physical. It's win-win for you, between the two of us."

"Niyx, listen to me," Alex said firmly, hating herself for it but doing it anyway. "You *will* accept the Release of my bond on you."

When the familiar tug didn't come with her command, Alex frowned and Niyx let out a self-satisfied laugh.

"Sorry, kitten, but I'm not actually Claimed by you anymore, we're just bonded by blood. Consider it a promotion. All the benefits, none of the puppeteer work."

Alex looked at him in alarmed puzzlement.

"You Released me from the Claim you had over my will," Niyx explained. "But in choosing not to accept that Release, I maintained the connection between us. Since that was my choice, it gave my free will back to me while allowing us to keep all the other bonuses, like me sharing your death and us violating each other's minds."

Alex's lips twitched at his wry words despite her better judgement. But she forced herself to sober and said, "You don't understand, Niyx. If you don't let me Release you properly, I can't tell you what's going to happen when I get back to my time. Your future—"

"Ah, so I *am* in your future?" he cut in. "That's good to have confirmed, at least. But don't tell me anymore. I'm guessing from the way you're looking at me that it's probably best if I don't know what joyous times await me."

Alex pulled a face at his blasé attitude, frustrated that he wasn't taking her seriously.

"Hey," he said in a deliberately soothing tone, reaching out to squeeze her shoulder. "I get it, okay? Or I don't, and that's okay too. But either way, you have to accept that this is my decision, and I'm sticking with it. Let me do the noble thing here. Light knows, this is a rare event for me."

Looking into his clear eyes, Alex knew he wasn't going to yield, so she did the only thing she could in her exhausted state—she nodded.

"Good," he said, squeezing her again then letting go. "Now—"

With an almighty shift, Xiraxus moved out from underneath Alex, causing her to sprawl onto her back with an exclamation of pain as he spread his wings out above them.

"They're coming!" the draekon hissed, his eyes glued to the horizon, seeing something that their Meyarin sight couldn't detect. "We must hurry!"

"Up you get, Aeylia," Niyx said at once, leaning down to carefully pull her up into his arms. She had no idea how he was managing to lift her weight with such ease or overcome the pain of the stab wound that was taking much longer than normal to heal. All he did was wince slightly as he manoeuvred Alex until she sat atop the draekon. Meanwhile, she was struggling to remain conscious and not throw up from the sheer agony of the wound.

"It's because of A'enara," Niyx said, reading Alex's pinched expression at the pain they both felt as he hastily wrapped a strap of coiling black *traesos* around her torso, securing it like a seatbelt in a loop across the front of Xiraxus and back again. "The *laendra* needs more time to combat the effects of the blade. The wound has sealed, but you still need time to heal."

Alex nodded, mostly in an effort to try and keep her eyes from closing, and said, "Same thing happened to me last time I was stabbed by A'enara. Fletcher said I nearly died then, too."

"You survived that, so you can survive this," Niyx said brusquely. "I'm not kidding, kitten. I'll kick your ass if you die and take me with you."

"I don't think it's humanly possible to kick my ass if I'm already dead," Alex mumbled, exhaustion overwhelming her.

"Good thing I'm not human then," came Niyx's light-hearted response. "Now, pay attention," he said, tugging on the *traesos* bindings. "This is so you don't fall off halfway across the *abrassa* when you pass out—and you will, considering your current state of specialness."

"Be nice," Alex slurred out.

"When you get to your end, summon A'enara to cut through the *traesos* and—"

Alex shook her head and interrupted, "Can't do that. Aven stole it from me. I can barely lift my hand right now, and I definitely don't have the energy to call it back."

"Aven stole it from you *here*, Aeylia," Niyx said, an urgency to his tone as he looked uneasily out over the cliffs. "Right now he can claim ownership of the blade, and given time, he'll be able to manipulate it in small ways, like changing the length and summoning it short distances. But you're bonded to it, and since you arrived here with it in your possession, when you return to your time, it's *your* weapon, not his."

That was true, since Alex had technically already taken it from him in her time. The Aven of the future definitely didn't have A'enara in his ownership anymore.

"So, I cut through my bindings…" Alex prompted, aware in the back of her sluggish mind that they were pressed for time.

"With A'enara," Niyx continued, his voice hurried now. "The Bringer of Light can pierce through anything, even the purest of darkness. I would have strapped you in with Moxyreel, but since *traesos* is a substance pulled directly from the *abrassa*, I think it'll secure you better for when you faint again."

"Stop making me sound like such a wuss."

He flashed a grin. "No offence, kitten, but as amazing as my training skills are, all this"—he gestured towards himself—"can't be taught. You'll have to stick with your wussy status until you can prove me wrong."

Alex opened her mouth to respond, but Xiraxus interrupted, "They're almost upon us—we *must* go! Now!"

His words shook some sense back into Alex and she looked down at Niyx with growing dread. "Go, Niyx. You have to get away from here."

Niyx ignored her. "Get her out of here, Xira. I'll hold them off."

"What?" Alex gasped out. "Niyx, no! You have to go!"

But her words were drowned out by the flapping of Xiraxus's enormous wings stirring the trees around them and sending loose rocks scattering over the side of the cliff. With a heaving push, he launched off the edge and into the sky just as Alex witnessed a dozen *Zeltora* arrive and engage Niyx in combat.

Niyx! Get out of there! she screamed as Xiraxus pushed upwards, flying faster and faster, the force of the wind shooting pain through her tender body.

I'll never forget you, kitten, Niyx replied, and she watched the sheer number of his attackers overcome and drag him onto the *Valispath*, which Alex knew would offer a one-way ticket to the prison, *Taevarg.*

Niyx... she whispered, unable to finish as her mind was clogged with emotion.

I'll see you soon, my mortal friend, he whispered back to her, unknowingly repeating the words he'd said to her once before— long into the future. *But not as soon as you'll see me.*

That was the last Alex heard from him before a familiar inky darkness surged into existence in front of her, blacker than the night sky, blacker than any black she'd ever seen.

Hold on, Alex! Xiraxus called. *This is going to be rough!*

Alex. Alex, wake up.

"Alex! You have to wake up!"

WAKE UP, ALEX!

With a shudder, Alex came to, her eyelids fluttering open to find she was slumped over Xiraxus, held in place on his back thanks to the *traesos* bindings.

She looked around in confusion, seeing that they were perched on top of the Golden Cliffs again, but without Niyx or any *Zeltora* in sight. Summer was now replaced with a thick snow blanketing the ground and dusting the city in the distance. It was also the middle of the day, rather than the moonlit night from which she'd fled. One thing remained the same, though—her thin, silky formalwear, leaving Alex frozen to her very core.

"Xira?" Alex slurred out through chattering teeth.

"Alex, you have to hurry," he said, his voice sounding anxious. "It was harder to wake you than I anticipated."

"'s okay, Xira," Alex mumbled. "'m just tired." *And ridiculously sore*, she thought, her shivering frame aggravating the throbbing in her stomach. That said, the agony had lessened considerably, the previously excruciating pain now replaced with what felt like a whopper of a bruise across her midsection as opposed to a blade still twisting through her insides.

"I'm glad you're okay, Alex, really I am. But I've been here too long—the *abrassa* is closing. I don't have much time to return home. Aven is still nearby and will have seen our return through the Void. And in your state, you're in no position to face him. We both need to get out of here, and quickly."

A bolt of adrenaline shot through Alex and she pushed herself upright, ignoring the pain in her stomach and the biting cold. She didn't hesitate to summon A'enara, overwhelmingly relieved when the weapon materialised in a blaze of flames.

Wasting no time, Alex sliced through her bonds. The mere touch of A'enara burnt up the *traesos* coils entirely, disintegrating them before they could even reach the ground.

She quickly slid down to the snow, wincing as the move jarred her wound. She then looked up at Xiraxus, realising with sudden grief that this was likely the last time she would ever see him.

"Don't be upset," he said quietly, sensing her heavy heart. He lowered his large head to her face, his fiery blue eyes as soft as ever. "Do you remember the oath I swore to create the link between us?"

Alex shook her head, trying to control the urge to give into her sadness.

"It translated to, 'Heart I give you, soul to share, strength and mind, both here and there. Forever and always, *vaeliana.*'"

Alex did remember that from seeing his memories, uttered in the lilting, musical language that she now knew belonged to the Tia Aurans.

"Forever and always, Alex," Xiraxus repeated, nudging her gently. "Both here and there."

Gritting her teeth against her welling tears, she wrapped her arms around his snout, barely managing to circle him halfway but still feeling comforted by their embrace. "I'm going to miss you so much, Xira."

"And I you," he said. "But we are bonded, now and forever. No time or distance can change that."

Heedless of her pain, she squeezed him hard, throwing all of her love into the hug before letting him go, conscious that time was of the essence.

"I hope to see you again, my friend," he said meaningfully to her. And then with one final rub of his head, he crouched down on his haunches and leapt off the snowy cliff and into the sky, opening the inky *abrassa* and disappearing from sight.

Thirty-Six

Drawing a broken breath, Alex knew she had to move before
Aven caught up to her. He was likely furious, having lost his
only chance at securing a draekon—unless, of course, he knew
another Tia Auran willing to be captured in order to make sure
Alex's journey to the past led to the events of their current time.
As annoyed as she was at Lady Mystique for giving no warning
of the catastrophic outcomes she would be responsible for, Alex
still hoped the ancient woman could escape from Aven's wrath
unharmed. All she could do was believe in Xiraxus's faith that
'Aes Daega' was capable of handling herself.

A crashing in the bushes reached Alex's heightened hearing,
the sound still far away but loud enough to remind her that she
shouldn't tarry. She summoned the *Valispath*, only to find that
she *couldn't* summon the *Valispath*. Thinking that she perhaps
wasn't concentrating hard enough, she tried again, but to no
avail. When her third attempt failed, she realised with a jolt of
horror that now, thanks to Aven's disinheritance, his blood was
invalidated—the blood in her veins—and now neither of them
could access the invisible rollercoaster.

Thinking a very nasty word that would horrify her mother,
Alex paced along the edge of the cliff, wondering if she had
it in her to make the gruelling climb down the icy rock face.
She knew from experience that it was hard enough doing it in
summer, but now, having been stabbed with a flaming sword, it

would be even more challenging—impossibly so. That left her with only one option if she wanted to make it back to the city on her own.

Grasping the hem of her bloodied dress that had definitely seen better days, Alex forced herself into a sprint, panting against the glacial air burning her lungs and the jolting of her still healing wound.

She slid to a halt atop the nearest waterfall, knowing that jumping over the edge would be the swiftest and safest plunge into the valley. But she was also aware that entering the frosty water with her already weakened, blood-deprived body would quite possibly send her into a near catatonic state of hypothermia.

Pacing restlessly, she came to a quick decision and took off into the forest, yanking up a fistful of *laendra* as she heard the sound of Aven's footsteps closing in on her.

Sawing A'enara into one of the flowers, Alex swallowed a mouthful of the sticky nectar, relieved to find that even with how much was already working in her bloodstream, the healing plant still gave her an instant kick and warmed her from the inside out. Balling her fingers around the remaining stems, she spun on her heel, sprinted back to the edge of the cliffs, and before she could talk herself out of it, leapt off the waterfall.

Sailing down with the icy water, Alex was aware in a distant part of her mind just how impossibly cold she was. But thanks to the *laendra* firing through her nerve endings, the temperature wasn't as debilitating as she knew it should be. And when she finally crashed painfully—oh, so painfully—into the surface of the river, Alex was able to swim to the shore and drag her quickly numbing body up onto the ice.

Hands shaking so hard she struggled to summon A'enara again, Alex had to swallow one of the flowers in great chewing hunks before she was able to still her fingers enough to slice another one open and guzzle the liquid inside. It took three entire buds before Alex was able to stumble up to her pins-and-needles feet, shaking her head against her double vision and wondering in some kind of shock-induced haze how she'd managed to keep her dainty Meyarin heels on her feet in spite of everything she'd been through in the past few hours.

Moving step by step into an increasingly powerful run that sent blood circulating around her near frozen limbs, Alex made her way through the snowy streets of the city, sprinting past shocked-looking Meyarins as they took in her state of disarray. She knew she must look a fright, dripping wet in a stunning dress with a gaping tear in the middle that was stained by mortal blood. And then there was the golden shine of her *vaeliana* skin. Given all that, she wasn't much surprised when they cried out in alarm and gave her a wide berth.

Panting from the exertion of running with only the help of the *laendra* fuelling her, Alex powered onwards, ignoring the pain, ignoring the cold, ignoring the growing deterioration of her energy levels. Stride after stride she flew through the city until she reached a building she had visited only once before in the dead of the night. Bursting into the dark foyer entrance, Alex skidded to a halt, searching for signs of anyone who might stop her. But there was no one. No guards, nothing; just like when she'd last been there with Roka. Apparently *Taevarg* was impenetrable enough with its *traesos* foundation to not need security on hand. A fact for which Alex was grateful.

Heart thudding in her chest, she took off down the staircase and along the labyrinthine corridors until she stopped in front of the impossibly thick cell door she remembered as belonging to Niyx. Standing before it, Alex didn't know what to think or how to feel. She had no idea what she was about to find inside, no idea which Meyarin would be behind the door— the cocky but caring Niyx she'd left in the past, or the Niyx who'd had millennia to bitterly rot in prison. He'd scared her, the Niyx of the future... but that was back when she hadn't known him.

Shaking her head, Alex deliberately shoved away her fears. For all his flaws, Niyx was one of the strongest Meyarins she knew. And even if he *was* mad from his time spent isolated in *Taevarg*, the fact remained that he'd been imprisoned for a crime he'd never committed. It was high time he was liberated.

Knowing she was doing the right thing, Alex stepped forward, hoping beyond hope that part of the Niyx she knew remained in him.

Squinting at the lock where Roka had inserted his engraved-Myrox key to open the cell, Alex recalled that the only thing powerful enough to destroy *traesos* was pure light energy from beyond the stars. A'enara, Alex knew, could pierce even the purest of darkness, and it was also wrought by the Tia Aurans— *the race beyond the stars.*

With a self-satisfied smile—and the knowledge of what she'd already seen the blade do to the bonds that secured her to Xiraxus through the Void—Alex summoned her weapon, certain for once that something was about to go right for her. Plunging the flaming point of the blade into the lock, she wasn't at all surprised when blue fire engulfed the entire door, dissolving it until only melted shards of black crystal remained bordering the edges.

Sending A'enara away, Alex hesitantly stepped through the still-smouldering ruins of the door until she came to a stop inside the cell.

There he was, standing by the far wall, looking the same but also so, so different. Gone was his healthy tan, his proud bearing, his confident, easy grin. He looked older, too. Not much, but enough to be noticeable. But it was his amethyst eyes that caused her to inhale sharply with unease, staring as he was at her with no discernable emotion. His face, his expression, everything about him was perfectly, scarily blank.

"You look different," she managed to choke out.

The silence between them seemed to last a lifetime as he stared at her bloodstained, tattered self.

"Funny," he finally said, trailing his gaze along her exposed skin and clearly noting the shimmer of her bond with Xiraxus that she certainly hadn't sported the last time she'd visited his cell. "I was about to say you look exactly like I remember. Time has been good to you, *Aeylia*."

Alex felt something in her relax at Niyx's words, even more so when a hint of a smile touched his lips. When it did, she hitched out a shuddering breath and flew forward, launching herself into his arms.

He made a pained grunting sound as he caught her on the fly, saying, "Easy, kitten. I feel like I've been stabbed in the stomach all over again, thanks to you. It wasn't fun the first time around; I could have done without the repeat."

A laugh bubbled out of Alex as she pulled away from him, swiping under her watery eyes as she eased her grip and stepped back. "I'm sorry. It's just so good to see you being so... you."

He raised an eyebrow. "Who else would I be?"

She sent him a 'seriously?' look and said, "How about the jerk who implied I was one of Aven's *Garseth* the first time I visited Meya?"

He waved a hand. "I was lonely. I figured if I had a cellmate, things would have been much more interesting around here. Especially if I could torture you with all the things I knew about you before you'd met me."

Alex narrowed her eyes. "And how about the super creep from a few weeks ago who I thought was going to crush my windpipe?"

He appeared puzzled for a moment before his expression cleared. "That was only a few days ago for me, Aeylia. And that 'super creep' as you call him was a product of impatiently having to wait for any news of your appearance, disappearance, or reappearance in either time stream. For thousands of years, all I've done is wait. When you came with Roka that night, it may have stretched the limits of my patience." Strangely, his mouth curled up at the edges. "But you know now that I never would have hurt you—not unless I wanted to hurt me, too."

"So it's still in place?" Alex asked, knowing what he was referring to but needing confirmation even though he'd already mentioned his sore stomach. "The bond?"

Since I feel like I have frostbite creeping up my extremities, I'm going to say yes, Niyx said dryly into her mind.

Alex couldn't believe it. She couldn't believe any of it. Suddenly overwhelmed by a wave of emotion, she looked up at him and whispered, "Niyx, it's all my fault."

His response was instant. "I know."

"Everything that happened—Aven murdering those humans—he did that because he was mad at me. He was banished because of me. He hates mortals *because of me*. Who he is today—it's *all my fault*." She ran her fingers through her hair, tugging hard. "No one will remember, Niyx. They'll think it was just some—just some random, faceless, nameless mortal. None of them have any idea I'm to blame for the single greatest threat to this city. To this *world*."

"And you can't tell them."

Alex looked up sharply.

"What do you think will happen to you if they find out, Aeylia?" he asked, reading her look. "What do you think will happen if *Aven* finds out? What will happen if he realises the mortal he blames for him losing everything is alive, thousands of years after she was dealt a killing blow at his hands?"

"It wouldn't be good," Alex mumbled, looking at the ground.

Niyx laughed bitterly. "No, it wouldn't. It would only make an already bad situation worse. And believe me, the situation is *already* much worse than you could possibly imagine." He reached for her, tilting her head back up to meet his. "Do you know what nightmare has haunted me all these years?" At her quick shake, he said, "The vision of the future I saw through your eyes. That terrifies me, kitten, because I know—I *know*—we're so close to seeing that future come to pass. Everything rests on you."

Alex hated hearing his words, hated the pressure of them.

"I didn't understand it years ago," Niyx said. "Even after you left, I didn't understand why you, one mortal amongst so many, claimed to be the only person with a chance of defeating him. It didn't make sense to me, not even with your *vaeliana* and your connection to A'enara. Why not Roka? Zain? Kyia? Stars, even me? I mean no offence, but despite the blood running in your veins, you're not a Meyarin, Aeylia. All the training in the world won't change that. So why would *you* have to bear the burden of conquering Aven?"

Alex opened her mouth to respond with her wholehearted agreement, but he continued before she could get a word out.

"But I understand now. I may have been trapped in here over the years, but I know more than you could possibly imagine." He broke eye contact, glancing unfocused over her shoulder. "Aven is powerful beyond measure, even beyond what Roka might believe. I won't lie to you, kitten. I wish I didn't have to say this, but I'm not sure… I'm not sure you can overcome him."

Alex gulped back her fear, hating the knowledge that he wouldn't have said something like that if he didn't mean it.

"But I also know that if you can't, then no one can," Niyx continued softly, meeting her eyes again. "What Aven has done over the years, the number of beings he's Claimed—it's turned him into something else. Something that no man or woman, mortal or immortal, should ever become." His gaze unfocused again as he added, "I've heard rumours… Horrible, unspeakable rumours of what he's capable of now. If they're true, there's no one in this world who can possibly stand against him—no one but you."

"But why, Niyx?" Alex whispered. "Why only me?"

"Because of your gift, *Alexandra Jennings*," he said, using her real name for the first time and showing he really did know a lot more than he should, given his imprisonment. "The strength of your will is what you can count on to protect you from him; hopefully, to protect us *all* from him. Human, Meyarin, Draekoran; the life forces flowing within you make up a volatile cocktail, Aeylia. Even as a mortal, you managed to break free of his Claim from sheer willpower. Imagine how much stronger that gift of yours is now, supplemented by not one, but two immortal bonds. On its own, no matter the circumstances, your will reigns supreme over his."

Before he could say more—or she could respond—a soft beeping noise echoed from an object nestled in the raggedy blanket on Niyx's pallet. His eyes travelled to it as he listened, and when the beeps ended his jaw was clenched, the rest of his body stiff with the hard lines of tension.

He turned back to Alex and his features softened.

"I said I'm not sure if you can defeat him, Aeylia," Niyx whispered. "But by the stars, I'm going to do everything I can to help you try."

She frowned at the look of apology on his face, not understanding, but then as quick as a flash he reached forward and pinched his fingers into her neck, causing her to cry out in startled pain as a nerve zinged from the top of her head to the bottom of her feet. Without any say in the matter, she collapsed into his arms as if paralysed.

"Believe it or not, I'm doing this to protect you," he murmured, carrying her over until she rested across his pallet where he then proceeded to begin mummifying her by wrapping her almost obsessively tightly within his blanket.

What the hell, Niyx? Alex screamed at him when she couldn't force the words past her stiffened lips.

"The effects aren't permanent," he said, ignoring her question. "And since you're not technically wounded and your nerves are just… having a time-out, thankfully this is one of those other loopholes where I'm not stuck feeling the effects with you."

NIYX!

"That beeping noise you heard?" he said, pulling a small, circular disc out from near her head. "It was a message. Like everyone else in this city, Aven's followers have always believed me to be loyal to the cause of the *Garseth*, and this"—he flicked the disc with a finger—"is how they've remained in contact with me over the years. What I just heard is something I need to respond to at once, and since you've so very kindly decided to liberate me, I'm so very kindly going to make sure you stay safe and warm while I do what must be done."

What did the message say, Niyx? Alex demanded. *What must be done?*

"You know, I'm still very sore, which means you must be feeling much worse," Niyx said contemplatively. "I think it's best if you rest until the paralysis wears off."

Realising instantly what he meant, Alex's eyes widened and she yelled, *No! Don't you dare*—

But before she could finish screaming her thought, he reached out to touch her neck again, and with another shooting blaze of nerves, Alex's eyes rolled to the back of her head and in an instant she was asleep.

Thirty-Seven

When Alex woke again, the first thing she realised was that she was no longer in *Taevarg*. The second was that she had no idea *where* she was. What she did know was that she wasn't alone.

Sitting beside her makeshift bed inside what looked to be a Myrox-canvassed tent was Zain. His shoulders were slumped, his head was cradled in his hands—everything about his posture caused Alex's pulse to throb in her ears as she pushed herself into a seated position, absently noting that her stomach was no longer tender at all.

The moment she moved, his head jerked up, the relief on his otherwise strained features clear as day.

"It's good to see you awake, little human," he said quietly, his tone rough. "When you didn't stir for so long, we feared it might be the same as…"

His voice trailed off, becoming so hoarse with emotion that Alex knew something must be very, *very* wrong.

"Zain, where am I?" she asked, looking around the sparse tent and then down at her body, finding her ruined dress had been replaced with what appeared to be an exact replica of the winter clothing she'd been wearing when she'd left through the *abrassa* the first time. "What happened? How did I get here?"

"You were out on the *varrungard*," he answered, looking down at his hands. "We were taking turns checking in on you to make sure you were travelling well when a roar sounded out over the forest. Aven"—he spat the name, his expression fierce— "discovered a way to pull an ancient draekon long departed from this world through a Void in space; a draekon who Aes Daega—a wise woman known to us—says you saved from entrapment, an action that resulted in the two of you bonding before it left this world once more."

Zain looked at the glow of the *vaeliana*, seemingly entranced by how it made her skin shimmer.

As far as he was aware, she was still sketchy with her ability to use her Meyarin senses, so without being able to explain how it was now her natural setting, all she could say in response was, "What are you looking at, Zain?"

He gave her a small, comforting smile, but even that seemed to take great effort. "No one has bonded with a draekon in my lifetime—it's strange to see the physical mark I've only ever heard tales about."

Feeling a sharp pain in her chest at the undeniable proof of his memories being gone, she played along and asked, "Physical mark?"

"A golden lustre to your flesh," he said. At her fake wide-eyed look, he said, "Don't worry, little human. It's not noticeable to anyone but a Meyarin—or you, when you eventually learn to control your senses."

Alex squinted at her hand as if she were trying to see it. "I'll have to take your word on that. But ignoring this new bond of mine, what else has happened? Is there a reason we're... wherever we are?"

His face tensed again as he moved back to his explanation. "The draekon, it turns out, was both a desire and a distraction."

Apprehension flooded Alex and she waited for him to explain.

"For whatever reason," Zain said, "Aven wanted to get his hands on one of the ancient beasts. But while he was closing in on his downed prey, he had another plan in effect as well. To assassinate his father and brother."

Alex's heart stopped. "What?"

Zain's face showed a storm of emotions. Fury, pain, fear, sadness. It hurt Alex's eyes just to look at him, and when he didn't respond, she dreaded the worst.

"Zain, please tell me," she rasped out.

He swallowed and said, "King Astophe is dead."

No. Not Astophe. Alex closed her eyes as images of him flew across her mind, from the first time she met him and felt the comfort of his presence, to all the times they shared together in the past—the dinners, the breakfasts, the moments in between. A sharp pain punctured her chest when she remembered how he'd patiently taught her how to play Stix, acting like a proud parent every time she'd won a match. Hours and hours they had played together—but never again.

"What happened?" she somehow managed to ask.

Zain's jaw was clenched so tight that Alex feared he'd break it. "The king was slain by the sword of the traitor Niyx."

Alex felt the room spin around her. *"What?"*

"His fellow *Garseth* found a way to free him from *Taevarg* and he went straight for the palace," Zain said in a hollow voice. "It was the surprise of it all, I think, that gave him the advantage. From what I hear, when he burst into the throne room, the full council was in attendance, but they were all too stunned by his appearance to stop him from throwing himself at the king, spearing a blade right through Astophe's heart. He died instantly. And in the chaos, the murderous traitor managed to disappear."

No. It couldn't be true. It *couldn't* be.

NIYX! she screamed in her mind. *Niyx, answer me, damn it!*

But there was no response, no matter how loud she yelled for him.

With watery eyes, she focused back on Zain and, remembering his earlier words, forced herself to ask, "Roka?"

Zain's eyes closed in one slow, defeated motion, and Alex felt a sob well in her throat.

"He's still alive."

She slumped forward with relief. "Oh, Zain. For a moment there, I thought—"

"He's also... not."

Her breath hitched. "What—What do you mean?"

Zain stood despairingly to his feet. "Come. I'll show you."

On leaden legs, Alex rose and followed him out of the tent and into the crisp, winter air. She had to shield her eyes from the late afternoon sun, blinking to clear her vision, but when she was able to properly see where she was standing, she felt her body lock with recognition. It looked so different to when she'd last been there, covered now in snow as it was. The crescent of mountains still looked the same, with their white-capped peaks, but they reached down to touch a dead meadow reminiscent of a desolate icy tundra, the bioluminescent flowers now a lifeless, sickly grey.

Turning away from the miserable wasteland until her eyes stretched over the open horizon, Alex had to bite her cheek to keep from releasing a sound of anguish at the sight before her. The once vibrant Draekora was now reduced to a bunch of crumpling, ruinous islands. The thriving forests were dead. The lakes had dried up. Even the volcanoes no longer spurted with fiery life. It was as if when the draekons disappeared, they'd taken the heart of Draekora with them.

"Where—" Alex cleared her throat against the raspy sound of her voice and asked the question expected of her. "Where are we, Zain?"

"On one of the floating islands of Draekora, far above the city of Meya, a land abandoned long ago," Zain said, gesturing for her to follow as he moved through what looked like a makeshift settlement filled with Myrox tents and huts of all shapes and sizes. "We had to find a safe place to set up a resistance now that Aven has taken over leadership of Meya. Or as safe a place as possible."

Alex's steps stuttered. "Aven's taken Meya?"

Zain gave a terse nod. "With Astophe dead and Roka... indisposed... Aven had free claim to the throne."

"But... What about Niida?"

Hands clenching into fists at his side, Zain said, "The queen was inconsolable with the death of her king and the state of her eldest son. She welcomed Aven back with open arms, surrendering herself and all those unable to escape in time. This"—he indicated towards the scant number of Meyarins wandering shell-shocked throughout the camp—"is all who managed to get away. A handful of *Zeltora* and a small number of council members, court officials and citizens. There are maybe fifty of us who were able to escape before..."

"Before what, Zain?"

"Before he had his telekinetic humans immobilise our race so he could begin to Claim them all, one after the other," Zain answered, his eyes pained with the devastation of what Aven had done. "By now, every Meyarin not here with us will be at his mercy, bound to him forevermore."

The enormity of what he'd just said almost brought Alex to her knees. She wrapped her arms around herself, her body shaking uncontrollably at the nightmare they now faced. If Aven had unlimited, unrestricted control over the immortal beings, what chance did the rest of the world have? How could she possibly stop the apocalyptic vision of the future from coming true when he had so much power at his disposal?

"The only reason any of us managed to get out in time is because, after what happened to Roka, we knew we had to get

412 · Lynette Noni

him away, get him somewhere secure, so we were already on
the move when they struck. With Aven's disinherited blood still
invalidated as long as Roka remains alive, he can't access the
Valispath to reach us here. While he could command one of his
Claimed Meyarins to deliver him—since their own blood still
enables them to use the Eternal Path—he won't risk not having
his own means of escape at hand. Because of that, Draekora
is the safest, most isolated place for us to rally ourselves and
consider what must next be done."

Alex could tell from his tone that he had no clue what they
would do. What they *could* do.

Niyx, please—I need you to answer me, she called in her mind,
desperate to hear from him, but there was still no response.

Rendered silent by the shock of everything Zain had told
her—everything that, for him, had happened in the few hours
she'd been unconscious—Alex followed mutely as he led her
into a circular tent much larger than the one she'd awoken
in. There were three people inside, but she barely spared a
glance at Kyia and, strangely, Lady Mystique. She only looked
at Roka, whose prone body lay so still that he was seemingly
lifeless.

Ungluing her legs, Alex walked shakily over to his bedside,
staring down in dismay. She couldn't reconcile this unmoving
image of Roka with what she knew of him. He was so full of life,
so full of energy... But now... Now something was very wrong
with him.

Unable to ask the question, Alex found comfort in watching
the steady rise and fall of his chest.

She felt a soft flutter against her hand as trembling fingers
entwined with hers, and she forced her eyes up from Roka to
look at Kyia standing vigil beside her, her body visibly shaking.
The female Meyarin's clothes were ripped and her normally
immaculate hair was like a haystack around her head, but it

was the dried tear tracks on her cheeks that revealed the depths of her grief as she looked down upon her beloved.

Alex's gaze travelled across to Zain and Lady Mystique who stood on Roka's other side, both of them staring solemnly at the fallen prince.

Pulling herself together, Alex finally managed to whisper, "What happened to him?"

Kyia's hand twitched in hers but the Meyarin didn't loosen her grip.

"When the draekon was somehow pulled through the Void," Zain said, and Alex's eyes flicked instantly to Lady Mystique, who responded with a slight shake of her head to indicate that no one knew the Tia Auran had been the one to open the *abrassa* for Aven, "Roka took off to find you, Alex. He was certain his brother was involved, so Kyia and I followed him. But unbeknownst to us, the draekon had already flown you to safety."

Zain closed his eyes and continued. "We ran into some of Aven's gifted humans in the forest, ones his *Garseth* brought through to Meya on the *Valispath*. It was sheer luck that none of the humans we crossed paths with had gifts able to incapacitate us, and we dispatched them with ease. But during the process, we were separated. Kyia and I ended up in one place, Roka in another. And he…" Zain trailed off, unable to say more.

Lady Mystique continued for him. "Roka ran into Aven—and me, though I was struggling to work my way out of chains at the time."

She held out her hands, showing Alex the painful-looking black welts seared into her flesh. The *traesos* coils hadn't done that to Alex—but then again, she wasn't Tia Auran. Who knew what effects the dark matter had on other beings?

"With us were a handful of Meyarin Rebels but also another human," Lady Mystique continued. "One with a gift the likes of which I've never seen nor heard of before."

Alex knew that was saying a lot, coming from her, and none of it was good.

"Aven was furious over losing the draekon," the old woman said, "but with his ultimate goal being to take the throne, Roka's appearance was an unanticipated boon. He already had someone in place to take out the king"—Zain was quick to snarl Niyx's name, but Lady Mystique ignored him with deliberation and continued—"but he hadn't dreamed he'd be able to get rid of them both at once." Her tone suggested she struggled to believe it herself. "Roka was always the more capable of the two when it came to a fair fight. So when they engaged in battle, Aven soon turned to cheating."

Alex's eyes flicked down to Roka then back up to Lady Mystique again. "What did he do?"

"The human who was with him, a man named Grimm Helkin, he… did something to Roka," Lady Mystique said, her eyes filled with sorrow. "One minute Roka had nearly overcome Aven, the next Aven ordered Grimm to incapacitate his brother. I may not have been able to break free in time to prevent it, but I *did* manage to escape just in time to save Roka from the killing strike of Aven's blade."

Kyia's hand twitched in Alex's again, and Alex tightened her grip, sending as much strength towards her friend as she could muster.

"I delivered him to Kyia and Zain, telling them to get as many people out of the city as possible, certain that Aven would head straight there," Lady Mystique said. "In return, I promised I would find you and bring you safely to Draekora."

Sudden understanding washed over Alex at the meaningful look in the old woman's eyes. The reason she was magically back in the winter clothes she'd worn on her *varrungard*, the reason no one had questioned why she'd been found wrapped in a blanket in the cell of an escaped prisoner—an escaped *murderer*—was because Lady Mystique had covered for her.

Overwhelmed by the lengths to which the Tia Auran had gone to protect her—or so she presumed, though really, Alex had no way to be sure of the woman's true motives—all Alex could do was send her a small smile, which was returned, if sadly.

"I only had a chance to examine Roka properly after we all arrived here," Lady Mystique continued, her voice quiet. Careful. "From what I gather, the diagnosis is… not good."

"But he's alive, right?" Alex asked. "I can see him breathing—that means he's alive."

"Yes, child, he's alive," the woman confirmed softly.

"So, what? He's just unconscious?" Alex looked at the downcast faces around her. "I don't get it—he's a Meyarin. If he's not dead, then surely whatever this is can be fixed. Why don't you just force some *laendra* down his throat and… encourage him to wake up?"

Lady Mystique shook her head regretfully. "He's not injured, Alexandra. There are no wounds to heal."

Alex read into the words she wasn't saying—if there was nothing wrong with him, then not even a blood-bonding ritual could be used to wake him.

"Then what's *wrong* with him?" she demanded.

"He's in a coma, Alex," Zain answered quietly. "The gifted human Grimm Helkin did something to shut down his mind and send him into a deep sleep."

Kyia's grip on Alex turned painful, but Alex didn't try and loosen her fingers, relieved to have them as an anchor.

"How do we help him?" she whispered out. "How do we wake him?"

"We kill Aven," Zain said in a hard, unrelenting voice. "Then those he has Claimed will be free, as will the effects of their gifts."

"No!" Alex blurted out, her tone shrill. "You can't do that!" When Zain's eyes narrowed into slits, she quickly explained, "If you kill Aven, you won't be freeing those he's Claimed—you'll be *killing* them."

It was Kyia who spoke then, a broken whisper of sound. "What?"

Alex turned to her. "The link between them—if you hurt Aven in any way, that will funnel out to everyone he's connected to. Ignoring the unspeakable fact that most of your race is now Claimed and would be wiped out in one go, consider the idea that if the bonded humans die, we don't know what that would mean for their gifts. It could swing either way—with Roka awakening, or with him remaining like this forever."

Kyia's already pale face turned so white that Alex worried she'd collapse to the floor. Zain too looked stricken. Lady Mystique merely held Alex's eyes in support.

"If we can't kill Aven, then does that mean all hope is lost?" Kyia whispered.

"All hope is never lost," Alex said firmly, unsure where her confidence was coming from but knowing *someone* had to offer it to them. "We just have to find a way to free everyone from his bond before we defeat him."

Said like that, Alex realised how ridiculous it sounded, especially since it was unlikely he would willingly Release any of his captives, which meant they had to hope like crazy that they would find one of Niyx's revered loopholes before too much damage was done.

"Look," she said, reading the disbelieving faces around her. "It's obviously a work in progress. For now, what we have to do is focus on keeping Aven contained long enough for us to figure out how to save them all. He's going to start going after the mortals soon, as we always knew he would"—the vision of burning cities and screaming people of all races filled her head again and she shook away a shiver—"so we need to do what we can to prepare them for what might be coming."

Alex's eyes returned to look down at Roka as a rough plan came to mind. "The humans of Medora have an active military force, and while I know they won't stand much of a chance against the power of Meya"—and she *did* know that, mostly because she'd seen it—"there are other races on this planet too, right? Shadow Walkers, Flips, Jarnocks... Plenty of other beings who we can rally to our side."

Zain was shaking his head. "They won't aid us. Aven presents no threat to them."

"But he does," Alex said, knowing from her vision that it was true. "He despises humans most, but his hatred is so strong that his vendetta is against all mortals, spilling out to the other races."

And all because of me, Alex's mind whispered, but she swatted her thoughts away, unable to deal with that right now—perhaps never.

"What are you suggesting we do, Alex?" Zain asked, crossing his arms. "Create an army of mortals to defend against him until we can find the means to free those under his command and thus strip him of his power?"

Alex ignored his derisive tone and simply said, "That's exactly what we're going to do." She then looked around the tent that was definitely a far cry from the Meyarin palace and amended, "Or, that's what I'm going to do. You have to make sure Roka stays safe up here from Aven. Because even if you don't think he'll have someone use the *Valispath* to bring him here, that's not a risk we can afford to take."

Zain and Kyia stared at her like she was mad. Lady Mystique, however, wore a small, satisfied smile.

"Since we now have a plan," the old woman said, "I think it's time for Alexandra to return to the academy." With her eyes on Alex, she finished, "If my timing is correct, your classmates will soon be arriving back from holidays in preparation for your classes to begin again tomorrow."

Incredulous, Alex just responded with, "You're joking, right? I can't go back to Akarnae—not now!"

The woman's gaze was firm on hers when she said, "I can't stress the importance of this enough, Alexandra. Right now, there is no place safer for you than at the academy and within close proximity to the Library. Not to mention, you'll need easy access to the doorways so you can visit the other races inhabiting Meya. All the while, naturally, keeping on top of your studies."

With her last words, Zain lost his morose composure and snorted. Kyia also managed a slight curl of her lips. Alex, while pleased to see them lighten even if just a little, still couldn't believe Lady Mystique thought that after everything that had happened, she should go back to her classes. Yes, she desperately longed for the comfort Akarnae provided and she couldn't wait to see her friends and family again, but with what lay ahead...

"Have no fear, child, for all shall work out just as it should."

Alex's gaze shot back to Lady Mystique when she reverted to the melodic language of her people, repeating words she'd said just weeks ago—but really millennia ago.

The old woman gave a knowing wink to Alex before she nodded at Kyia and Zain, placed a gentle hand to Roka's cheek, and, with a flash of light, promptly disappeared from sight.

Not even blinking at what Alex still considered a seriously weird but increasingly common happenstance, Zain sighed and looked over at her.

"It would take a stronger Meyarin than I to go against the wishes of the great Aes Daega," he said, moving away from Roka's side and gesturing for Alex to follow. "Come, little human. Let's do as she said and get you back to Akarnae."

With a nod of resigned agreement, Alex leaned down and pressed a kiss to Roka's cheek, whispering a promise into his ear that she would find a way to wake him. She then turned and hugged Kyia tightly, the Meyarin trembling only slightly now, and Alex offered her the same whispered promise, feeling Kyia's arms wrap even tighter in response. When they broke apart, Alex wiped away a single tear and followed Zain outside, stepping close as he activated the *Valispath* to leave Draekora behind.

Regardless of his intent, Alex didn't allow him to take her back to Akarnae. Not because she wasn't planning on going there—she knew enough about the 'great Aes Daega' to realise she would be wise to follow Lady Mystique's guidance—but because she didn't want Roka to be left without Zain's protection during their travel. The *Valispath* was impossibly swift, but given how lost the Draekoran Meyarins currently were, she wasn't willing to take the chance that Aven might capitalise on that in the time Zain was gone.

Thankfully, although he offered a weak argument, he quickly gave in to her demand that he drop her off at the much closer Raelia where she would open a doorway and be back within seconds.

When they reached the snow-covered clearing, Alex didn't waste any time before calling forth the door, and it appeared in an instant before her.

"First order of business for you is to find if there's a way you can step straight through to Draekora," Zain said, reaching into his cloak and pulling out the belongings he'd kept safe for her during her *varrungard*—her ComTCD, Shadow Ring and Myrox necklace. While handing them over, he cast alert eyes around the clearing, searching for any sign of a threat.

"I'll get right on that," Alex agreed, pocketing her items, amazed and grateful that he'd managed to keep hold of them even in the chaos that had developed. "I'm sure the Library will show me a door."

When Zain moved to step away from her, she reached out to touch his arm. "Can I ask you something? Just quickly?" At his nod, she said, "How did you end up in the *Zeltora*? Was it something you always wanted, to protect the people of Meya? Or..." She trailed off, not letting on how much she knew, but still burning with curiosity after having left him in the past as a criminal—albeit, one who had been fighting against the *Garseth* upon her last sight of him.

"No, little human, it was quite the opposite. I wasn't much interested in helping our people at all," Zain answered.

"What changed?" she asked, trying for an openly inquisitive expression.

"Mostly it was because Roka wouldn't stop badgering me about it," Zain said ruefully, and Alex had to cough to hide her laugh, knowing the prince had followed through on his promise to her. "But also because there came a time when I realised I wanted to fight for a purpose beyond my own. That there was more meaning in serving others than serving myself."

Alex's eyes were soft on him when she said, "That's very honourable of you, Zain. I, for one, am pleased you came to that decision. As I'm sure is Roka." Her curiosity sated, she clapped a hand to his chest. "Speaking of badgering princes, you better get back to him. But don't worry—I'll see you again soon and update you on Operation Mortal Army."

The look he shot her said more than his words could when he instantly replied, "We are absolutely not calling it that."

"Bye, Zain." Alex hid her smile and gave him a shove. "Go keep our prince safe."

With a telling eye roll, he took off on the *Valispath*, and she stepped forward into the doorway. She only had one foot through when she heard her name called across the clearing, and she spun around, nearly falling to the ground at what she saw.

It was Niyx. And he wasn't alone.

Because in his arms was the unconscious form of Jordan.

Thirty-Eight

"Niyx," Alex gasped, lost for any other words.

"I don't have long, Aeylia," he said, striding towards her. "I have to get back to the palace before Aven notices my absence."

His words jolted Alex back into her right mind enough that she began a swift retreat, prompting Niyx to pause mid-step and cock his head to the side. He sighed, carefully lowering Jordan to the snow-covered ground at his feet.

"Aeylia—"

"You killed him," she breathed out. "They're saying you killed the king."

There was a loaded silence. "No," he returned, his voice filled with grief, "I didn't. But they have to think I did—*Aven* has to think I did."

Alex didn't understand. "But—You—"

"Just watch, kitten."

An image entered Alex's mind and she witnessed Niyx's memory play out with vivid detail as he used the *Valispath* to travel from *Taevarg* to the palace throne room. He burst through the doors, startling the council members as he raced towards the king standing at the head of the room.

What happened next was nearly impossible to comprehend, since a fraction of a second before Niyx crashed into Astophe, the king opened his mouth in a surprised gasp. The king sank to the ground, Niyx lowering with him and pulling back enough for Alex—and the council members—to see the blood soaking Astophe's chest.

So caught up in how quickly the attack had been carried out, no one else saw what Alex did: Niyx held no weapon, nor was there any visible blade protruding from what she knew was the king's fatal stab wound.

Lasa Riza let out a bloodcurdling scream, prompting the others from their disbelieving stupors to surge forward and apprehend Niyx, but it was too late, for he'd already vanished into thin air.

Horrific comprehension washed over Alex as the memory faded from her mind. Even if she hadn't seen Niyx's lack of weapon or the king's too early gasp, the *Valispath* couldn't be accessed inside the throne room—and yet Niyx had disappeared instantly.

Her dread-filled eyes came to rest on her best friend lying unconscious on the snow—her best friend whose gift meant he could disappear with a single thought and share his ability with others.

"It wasn't you—it was Jordan," she whispered to Niyx. "You were trying to save Astophe, weren't you? The message you received was about the attack—it told you Jordan was on his way to murder the king."

"No one can know but us," Niyx returned firmly. "I managed to knock Jordan out before he could inform Aven his task was done, and I've since explained to Aven that your friend sustained a head injury leading to capture prior to the assassination."

"But—that means—"

"I told Aven it was me who killed the king," Niyx said, following her train of thought. "And there are six council members—three of whom remain in the city—who can attest to seeing exactly that."

424 · Lynette Noni

"*Why*, Niyx?" Alex cried. "Haven't you already been blamed long enough for the crimes of others? Everyone hates you! Why would you make it worse?"

"Because you need someone on the inside, Aeylia," he returned without hesitation. "Someone who Aven trusts implicitly. Someone he thinks has been rotting away in prison for millennia because of their loyalty to him." He paused. "Someone who was willing to kill the king of Meya for him, without first being Claimed and ordered to do so."

At his words, Alex inhaled quickly, remembering that with Aven's ruling over the city, everyone in it was now Claimed, including—

"Niyx, did he bond with you?"

Niyx made a face. "Do me a favour and never say something like that again."

Alex remained silent, waiting in trepidation for his answer.

Seeing the fear on her face, he moved closer, and this time she didn't retreat, not even when he held his hand out, palm facing forward, to show her the second scar across his flesh. The first she'd caused when she'd attempted to Release him. The second was new. But before she could do anything—like knock him out, grab him and Jordan, and run far, far away—he spoke.

"Don't look so scared, kitten." He offered her a half smile. "Turns out that even though I'm not under your thumb anymore, the Claim of our connection—of *your* willpower—is still flowing strongly in me. Too strong for Aven to override, since your will is stronger."

He glanced pointedly from her to Jordan, and Alex's body jolted as the potential implication of his words sunk in. Thoughts whirling, she hardly dared to hope in the theoretical plan coming to her mind. Would she—*Could* she—Was it even possible…?

"As far as Aven's concerned, he thinks I'm Claimed," Niyx

continued, interrupting her reeling thoughts and calling her attention back to him. "If he tells me to jump, I make sure I jump. The only hiccup is that we obviously have no mental connection since his Claim failed, but I managed to follow enough of his spoken commands for him to believe there must be a glitch in my mind that prevents me from hearing his non-verbal orders."

The shadow that crossed Niyx's face told Alex that those spoken commands he'd followed to prove his loyalty were the likes of which she didn't want to know—nor would he tell her.

"Niyx," she whispered, placing a hand on his chest to comfort him.

He shrugged, trying to act like it didn't bother him when she could see that it did. "For the greater good, right, kitten? And when I help you kick his ass, it'll just make the victory all that much sweeter."

When he saw that she remained unconvinced, he lowered his voice and said, "I've had thousands of years to come to this decision, Aeylia. I know what I'm doing. Just as I know that, for a time, life isn't going to be much fun for me as I cater to my ex-best friend and new king's beck and call. But newsflash, sweetheart, life hasn't been much fun for a while. A little longer won't do me much more harm."

She hated, absolutely *hated* the position he was in; the position he was deliberately placing himself in. And that must have read all over her face because he quietly said, "I once asked you to let me do the noble thing—I'm now asking it again." His lips twitched as he finished, "Though, no matter what you say, it's not like your wussy mortal self can stop me."

She huffed out a laugh, knowing his words were said in a deliberate attempt to cheer her up.

"I have to get back to the palace," Niyx said. He pointed at Jordan. "I'm guessing you know why I brought him here?"

426 · Lynette Noni

Alex hesitantly nodded, struggling to believe that she might be able to do the impossible and actually free Jordan. "I think so. But—"

"No buts about it, kitten," Niyx interrupted. "You've got this. Believe me when I say you're stronger than you realise."

She had to blink back tears when his words prompted a memory of Roka saying the same thing to her not so long ago: '... *never forget that you are stronger than you realise and more capable than you could ever imagine.*'

Alex looked up and found Niyx's clear eyes soft on her. He reached forward and pulled her to him, wrapping his arms around her and holding her tight. Then, just as swiftly, he released her and stepped back.

"Save your friend," he said. "But before you Release him, you must order him to forget what happened with the king. No one can know about that but you and me, do you understand?"

Alex despised the idea of commanding anyone to do anything ever again, least of all Jordan—if it was even possible for her to do so—but she nodded her agreement, knowing Niyx wouldn't ask if it wasn't important.

"I'll be in contact when I can," Niyx promised, "but don't worry if that's not as often as you'd like. I need to be careful with my thoughts because while your willpower kept me safe from Aven's Claim, I have no way of knowing if I'll be protected from the strong mind readers now wandering around the palace, as well as a few other mortals with annoying mental tricks up their sleeves."

She nodded her agreement again, knowing caution was needed if he was to survive his role as a spy.

"In the meantime, I'd greatly appreciate it if you would do your best not to get yourself—and by extension, me—killed."

Her mouth opened in indignation. "Hey! I don't plan these things. They just... happen."

"Which leads me to my last point," he said, stepping backwards from her and calling the *Valispath* up around him. "If you think our training is over, kitten, you're wrong. We've barely begun to scratch the surface of what you need to learn if you want to defeat Aven. As soon as I can figure out how to sneak away, that's when our *real* training will begin."

And with a wicked grin, Niyx took off, swiftly disappearing from sight.

Not letting her mind linger on the horrific imaginings of what he likely had in store for her, Alex turned her focus to Jordan. Her stomach clenched with nerves at the idea that she might be able to free him from Aven, right here, right now— presuming that what Niyx had said about her willpower was true. It seemed impossible. And yet... if there was one thing Alex had learned from her time in Medora, it was that nothing was truly impossible.

Calling forth all the hopeful determination she could muster, she strode over to her best friend on shaky legs, knelt in the snow at his feet and whispered, "Please, *please* let this work."

At her silent command, A'enara blazed into her hand and Alex swiftly sliced the blade across her trembling palm with a grimace, adding to the collection of silvery scars she was building there. Hesitantly, so hesitantly, she rolled Jordan onto his back, pulling his hand to her and slicing his palm as well.

After a deep breath, followed by two more, Alex slowly joined their bloodied wounds together, linking her fingers with his as she dredged up the courage to mentally call out to him.

Trae Menada sae, Jordan!

Just like with Niyx, it took a moment before anything happened, but *unlike* with Niyx, when the initial linking occurred with Jordan, her subconscious mind violently slammed into his. Niyx had been nearly dead when she'd completed his ritual, his mental fortitude weak from the severity of the Hyroa blood poisoning his system. Jordan, on the other hand, was perfectly healthy. She wasn't bonding with him in order to heal him from a fatal wound or illness, but rather to Claim his will as her own. The resistance she felt in attempting to do so was like a knife stabbing into her brain, accompanied by the sound of screaming so loud that it was like shards of glass piercing her eardrums.

And then suddenly the pain stopped, the screaming silenced and Alex's mind tumbled out into… a rose garden?

Whirling around, recognition—and understanding—hit Alex as she looked upon the sprawling marble mansion of Jordan's childhood home, Chateau Shondelle, the place where Aven had Claimed him.

"You should not be here."

At the hostile voice, Alex turned again, only to find an avatar of Aven standing further back amongst the roses. But it was what was positioned beside him that captured Alex's attention, because in a thick cage, there stood Jordan, his hands straining against the bars as he let out a silent scream.

Alex felt chills travel down her spine at the memory of Aven's grip on her own mind, the feeling of screaming but with no one able to hear. It had been five weeks in real time since Jordan had left the academy to visit his parents, five weeks of his being under Aven's control. Alex had only suffered a few minutes as his puppet. She couldn't imagine the mental anguish of what Jordan had been forced to endure. She absolutely refused to allow it to go on any longer.

"You're done, Aven," Alex said, locking eyes with him. "You have no more power here."

Seeing his fiery glare made her feel like he was stabbing her all over again. Completely gone was any of the light of his younger self. This Aven didn't remember her at all, and given how they'd ended things in the past, that was probably a good thing.

"I don't know how you made it in here, Alexandra," he said. "But it's *you* who has no power. Jordan is mine. I've Claimed him. And there is nothing anyone—least of all an insignificant mortal like *you*—can do about it."

"That's where you're wrong."

Her tone was firm, unwavering, and, above all else, knowing. It was the last that caused Aven's eyes to flicker with uncertainty, that caused him to reach for his sword, that caused him to lunge towards her. But Alex was ready for him.

It seemed that even in the mindscape of Jordan's subconscious, Alex was still able to summon A'enara, and the weapon appeared in a blinding blaze of glory stronger than ever before.

Aven faltered in his steps, but he then rallied himself and continued eating up the distance between them while bellowing out an enraged, "You may have stolen my weapon and bonded with the draekon intended for me, but I refuse to allow you to have the boy! He is *mine*!"

"You're wrong, Aven," Alex said again, her voice calm as a sure confidence ran through her veins. She lowered A'enara loosely to her side, suddenly understanding that this wasn't a battle of swords, but of wills.

'On its own, no matter the circumstances, your will reigns supreme over his.'

Niyx's words flooded her mind, giving her the assurance she needed to hold her ground when Aven reached her and, with a roaring cry, swung his sword towards her neck.

Watching as if in slow motion, Alex didn't move, didn't even flinch. All she did was wait until the blade was less than an inch away from her skin, and that's when she gave *her* command.

"*Stop.*"

Instantly, the weapon came to a freezing halt, as did Aven, who stood motionless before her.

430 · Lynette Noni

"You have a choice now, Aven," Alex said, her voice quiet even as his eyes scorched with liquid fire. "You can keep your Claim on Jordan and remain here with us where, as you can see, my will reigns over yours. *Or...*"—she paused for dramatic effect, mostly because she found it almost sadistically pleasing to torment him—"... you can give up your Claim and willingly Release him to me." She reached forward and patted him mockingly on the cheek. "Take as long as you want to think about it. I have all the time in the world."

In their past skirmishes Aven had always recognised when it was time to retreat, and the same was no less true now. With a single spoken command, Alex had out-willed him and seized control over Jordan. Unless he wanted to remain trapped with them—and obedient to Alex—he really only had one choice.

With an expression that promised a world of retribution, Aven barked out the words of the Release and vanished from the space. Almost instantly, the cage holding Jordan disappeared from sight in a genie-like puff of smoke—and so too did Chateau Shondelle and its surrounds.

With Alex's overriding connection to him now complete, her consciousness fell swiftly back into her own body. Her eyes shot open in time to see her friend surge up to his feet only to collapse onto his hands and knees in the snow, gasping as if he hadn't been able to draw air into his lungs for weeks.

"A-A-Alex," he tried to hack out between gasps. "H-H-How—"

"Shh," Alex hushed, reaching out with a comforting hand. "Just catch your breath."

She felt the tug of the Claim between them as her unintentional order took effect. With a wince and a mental *'oopsie'* to herself, she didn't retract the command, knowing that he was close to suffocating and needed all the help he could get.

Aware that he wasn't capable of answering right now but still wanting to make her point, Alex rubbed soothing circles on his back and said, "Do you remember when you and Bear once told me that there's no such thing as magic?" She paused as she reflected over everything that had happened since then—including her stint in Jordan's flipping *mind*—and finished, "You're both so full of it."

He let out a startled laugh, his only concession, but it was enough to tell Alex that he agreed with her statement wholeheartedly.

As soon as his desperate panting began to ease, she helped him sit back up, waiting anxiously to see what he would do next. She had, after all, technically stolen his will from him, just as Aven had done. But she was hoping—

"You have no idea how good it is to see you," he whispered, his voice a rasping, choking sound, his bright blue eyes swimming with emotion. "No idea."

And without any hesitation, he threw his arms around her, pulling her to him so tight it was almost painful.

Alex returned his desperate hug, scarcely believing it was really happening. Fearing she would soon wake up and realise it was all a dream, she held on all the more tightly, afraid to let go.

When they eventually drew apart, it was with wet eyes and wobbly smiles, but as much as Alex wanted to remain in the beauty of the moment, she knew their jubilation couldn't last forever.

"Jordan, I need to tell you something," Alex said quietly.

"I already know about Luka, Alex," he said, his voice just as quiet.

His words surprised her because, with everything that had happened over the last few weeks, she'd forgotten all about his brother—and what the confirmation of his death would mean to Jordan.

432 · Lynette Noni

"I know it was all a lie, that he's not really alive," Jordan continued. "When I told you all that, even though Aven gave the verbal commands that I could speak freely, he mentally negated those orders, forcing me to say what I said. He knew that if you thought I'd willingly chosen to have him Claim me, then you'd be more devastated than you already were."

"He was right," Alex whispered, replaying the awful scene in her mind, the visual being easy to summon considering they were currently in the same location the traumatic moment had taken place.

"None of it was real, Alex. Nothing from after I returned to the academy from visiting my parents—until now."

Sorrow washed over her at the depth of her friend's entrapped misery, and she straightened her spine with renewed determination. "I'm going to Release you so you're back to being you, *just* you," she said. "But before I do that, I'm so sorry, Jordan, but I have to give you an order."

His eyes instantly shadowed. "What order?"

Tentatively, Alex asked, "Do you remember what happened with King Astophe? Did you, um, see?"

Jordan looked confused at first, like he didn't know what she was asking about, but then realisation hit him. His face paled and his eyes widened in horror.

"I killed him—I killed the king of Meya!"

Seeing that he was about to lose it, Alex reached out and grasped his shoulder. "It wasn't you. Listen to me—*it wasn't you!*"

Jordan just shook his head, denial spreading across his tortured features.

"Jordan, I have to make you forget that you did that," Alex said, powering onwards. "I can't tell you why, just that it's important. That's the order I have to give you before I Release you. But now I want to ask you something."

He was in shock, she could tell, but she needed him to snap out of it, so she sighed and carefully commanded, "Please calm down."

At once, he calmed. Then he shot her an annoyed look, to which she held up her hands in apology.

With rueful reluctance, he questioned, "What do you need to ask?"

She bit her lip but decided she at least owed him this, since it was within her power to give. "When I make you forget that... *event*... do you want me to order you to forget the rest as well? Everything that happened while you were under Aven's control?"

Alex was grateful when Jordan gave it proper consideration and didn't cry out an immediate response, showing she'd done the right thing by offering. She had no idea what he would choose—she had no idea what *she* would choose, if given the option. But she also wasn't surprised with how he eventually answered.

"As much as I want to forget," he said softly, "I think a part of me needs to remember what was done to me so that I know what I'm fighting for." He shot her a quick look. "We *are* going to fight him, right?"

"Absolutely."

Jordan nodded. "It means a lot that you gave me the choice, Alex. But my answer is no. Just take the memory you need, but leave the rest."

Offering a slight, somewhat proud smile at his decision, Alex hurried to get the rest over with. "Jordan, I order you to forget that you killed King Astophe. If anyone asks, you were discovered and knocked unconscious before you could complete Aven's command."

Instantly the tug seared between them, and Jordan's eyes stared into nothing for a moment before refocusing again.

"What were you saying, Alex? I'm sorry, I didn't hear you."

Alex smiled inwardly and stood to her feet, wiping snow from her backside as he rose beside her. "I was just making sure you know that when I say the words to Release my Claim on you, you have to accept them, otherwise we'll still be linked." She'd learned *that* the hard way, though in hindsight, she was grateful for Niyx's 'noble' decision. "Aven's Claim transferred directly over to me so you didn't need to do anything when he let go of your mind, but you will this time if you want to be truly free."

"Got it," Jordan said. "Accept the Release." Then his features turned puzzled. "Uh, how do I do that, exactly?"

Alex laughed at his refreshingly Jordan-like bafflement, surprised by her ability to feel humour despite everything she'd witnessed that day. "After I say the words to Release you—which will be voiced mentally, by the way—you need to say, 'I accept my Release' in Meyarin. So you'll need to say, *'Trae morras rae Gaverran'*."

She made him repeat the phrase a few times until she was confident he would get it right.

"Ready?"

With an arched eyebrow, he responded, "To no longer be under someone else's control?" He nodded the obvious. "Definitely."

So Alex summoned A'enara back and, ignoring Jordan's startled oath at the sight of the flames dancing around her skin, she quickly sliced first her palm and then his, joining them once more. She then touched on their mental connection and called out the words of the Release, *Trae Gaverran sae!*

Just as instantly, she felt the severing of the connection between them, with it starting to uncurl as it had when she'd attempted to Release Niyx. But unlike then, when Jordan's mental voice responded with his rehearsed phrase, the uncurling ceased and there was a definite snap, like the breaking of a branch, and Alex could feel no trace of the link anymore.

Jordan? she called out hesitantly. *Can you hear me?* And when no response came, she let out a deep sigh, overcome with relief.

"It really worked," Jordan exclaimed in tearful wonder. "You did it, Alex. You saved me. Just like you promised."

Blinking back her own tears, Alex offered him a trembling smile, which quickly turned into an incredulous huff of amazed laughter. He reached out for her until they were both hugging again, crying and laughing from the weight of their relief.

When they finally pried themselves apart, Alex wiped a hand across her wet face and linked her arm in his, leading him towards the open doorway.

"I know a few people who are going to be very happy to see you," she said, grinning softly up at him. "Let's get you back to Akarnae."

Alex was overcome with happiness when she saw the disbelieving hope on his face, knowing he surely doubted this moment would ever come.

Her smile was more tremulous this time as she nudged him and whispered a meaningful, "Come on, Jordan. Let's go home."

Stepping through the doorway with him, Alex had no idea what lay ahead. The future was a terrifying thing; something that, no matter how strong her will, she had no control over. But she did have a choice. A choice not to fear what was yet to come. Because fear would keep her from doing what she knew she had to do.

She had an army to rally.

She had a gift to refine.

She had a prince to awaken.

But most of all, she had a Meyarin to defeat…

… and a world to save.

ACKNOWLEDGEMENTS

Only three books in and I already feel like a broken record when it comes to thanking people, but this book never would have become what it is without the help of some real champions cheering me on.

As always, unending thanks go to God, my family and my friends, all of whom continue to stick by me through my authorly neurosis and understand when I'm in my writing hobbit hole for days (often weeks) on end. You guys make it worth it every time I resurface for air... especially when you come bearing chocolate.

To everyone at Pantera Press, thank you for being more than just 'my publishers', but rather, my publishing *family*. I am speechless by how wonderful you all are—I honestly think there must be something in your water. Special thanks go to Ali for considering a round of mini golf as 'professional development' and for the brilliant TV show recs (your self-professed bad taste has zero grounding in reality!), as well as to Susan for all the publicity magic that has led to an unforgettable journey so far.

To my editorial team, especially James Read and Desanka Vukelich—*thank you*. This book has been precious to me from the very beginning and I'm so grateful for how much you helped make it shine. Thanks also to the talented designers at XOU Creative, to whom all I can say is: *Omigosh, I loooooove this cover!!!*

To my incredible agent, Victoria Wells Arms, and her amazing assistant, Brigette Torrise, for all the invaluable advice, encouragement and support throughout my great big adventures in the publishing world.

To my small team of 'critters' (aka critiquers), Emily Davison, Dana Summer, Frannie Panglossa and Jenna Harper—thanks heaps for your treasured feedback and hilarious fangirling (and, um, sorry for the tears, girls).

To all the wonderful bookstagramers, booktubers, book bloggers, book-*everything*ers out there who passionately post their love for this series all over social media, you guys are the BEST. There are way too many of you for me name, but I adore you all and I'm so, SO thankful for your support! Special mention to Kaysia from @bookskay who won 'The Chosen One' competition and revealed *Draekora*'s cover with more contagious excitement than I could have ever dreamed possible!

Lastly, I'm forever (and ever and EVER) grateful to every single person reading this series. I'm truly humbled by how much love you have for Alex and her friends, and how willing you are to share that love with the world—and with me! I'm seriously an emotional mess every time you contact me to say how much you've enjoyed each book, so THANK YOU!!! You all absolutely rock and I can't wait for you to experience what comes next!!!

Until then, as Xira would say, '*Forever and always*'—to all of you. *Big hugs*

Australian author Lynette Noni studied journalism, academic writing, and human behaviour at university before venturing into the world of fiction. She is now a full-time writer and the #1 bestselling and award-winning author of *The Medoran Chronicles*, the *Whisper* duology, and *The Prison Healer* series.

www.LynetteNoni.com
Facebook.com/Lynette.Noni
Twitter.com/LynetteNoni
Instagram.com/LynetteNoni